Death of Television

THE COVID MURDERS MYSTERY: BOOK TWO OF TWO

CONAL O'BRIEN

Conal O'Brien

The COVID Murders Mystery: Book Two of Two

Soft-Cover ISBN: 978-1-66786-271-2
eBook ISBN: 978-1-66786-272-9

Go to *conalobrien.com* to learn more about this book and other Bookbinder Mysteries *for Gwen*

Contents

Prelude

Wednesday, July 14th, 2021

It was just before ten and Paula DeVong was wrapping up her nightly hour-long network news show. In the back row of the darkened control room, Executive Producer Jock Willinger was leaning back in his command chair not paying much attention to Paula's face on the monitor. Jock was absorbed in his own world of problems. So far, the COVID pandemic had given him a long reprieve. The Network had not exactly stood by him, but had adopted a wait-and-see posture. Then last week, a lawsuit was filed in the Supreme Court of New York spelling out his history of sexual harassment at TVNews.

Something Paula was saying on-air caught his attention:

"And be sure to tune in tomorrow night. I'll have an exclusive story that you will love. Or hate." She was grinning and her eyes were shining with her trademark ruthlessness.

"Oh, fuck me," Jock mumbled in the darkness. He wondered if Paula's next big story was going to be about him and his legal troubles. How the Network would surely let him go. About how Paula herself would become executive producer.

God, I hate being played by that smug primping bitch.

1

Jock ran his lean fingers roughly through his thinning gray hair. He had always been gaunt, but now he looked old and faded. He still dressed the same every day: a black suit, white button-down shirt, and a very thin tie. He still chain-smoked, though only in his office. He wished he could find cigarettes that were still made in the UK, but those factories had moved out of England years ago. Like him. But he was beginning to think it might be the perfect time to move back home to Liverpool.

The end credits were finished and a commercial for a prescription drug came on.

"Good show, guys," Jock said as he stood up. There were some murmured thanks. One of the writers turned around to watch him go. Jock had started to hate her. She was young and pretty in an athletic kind of way and good at her job. But Deni Diaz was one of the women who had brought the lawsuit against him.

"Deni," he said, "tell Paula I want to see her upstairs. Right away."

"Yes, Jock," she answered measuredly.

"There's a good girl," he said patronizingly and left the room.

Deni clenched her teeth.

Her good friend Greg Schaefer leaned close to her and said, "Don't let him get to you. He's a *shite*, and you are not."

She looked at Greg's kind open face and smiled at his attempt to sound British.

"How is that man still here?" Deni muttered.

"The fifth ring of hell was all booked up. The governor got there first and took his room," Greg said sotto voce. Deni laughed in spite of herself. Greg was her closest friend, and she loved how he could always make her feel better. He was cute and handsome and so together. He always dressed perfectly, looking casual but enough fashion-forward to earn the respect of the executives upstairs. He was the type of guy she would love to be with. But Greg was gay and proud of it.

"Don't worry," Greg said softly, "he'll be gone by Monday."

"You think so?" she asked hopefully.

"There's no doubt," Greg answered. "I've been told."

"Wonderful show tonight, Paula!" Anna Canneli said too loudly as she followed Paula across the open newsroom floor. The staff was still there, gathered in relaxed groups letting go after the long day's work. Paula ignored her assistant, strode up the few steps into her glass-enclosed corner office, pulled a tissue from her desk drawer, and blew her nose fiercely.

"You're not sick, are you?" Anna whispered, horrified as she closed the door behind her.

"Of course not," Paula snapped back. "My nose was just raped by a Q-tip. Again! Fuck this place!" She added as she sat with a huff. She was annoyed that the network had insisted that because of the Delta variant every-one in the studio would again have to be tested once a week. No exceptions. Paula had been able to duck it before the show. But it was Wednesday, orders were orders, and she was waylaid by the studio nurse as she came off the set.

"I know what you mean," Anna said soothingly.

Paula looked at her. Anna was frumpy, chubby, and disliked by the rest of the newsroom staff. But Paula didn't care. Anna had always been completely loyal to her and that trait made her irreplaceable.

"Are they fresh?" Paula asked.

"Yes." Anna smiled proudly. "I bought them this afternoon."

Paula opened a lower drawer and pulled out a small box. She tipped open the lid and studied the four milk chocolates inside. A puzzled look crossed Anna's face but vanished after a moment as she watched Paula choose a caramel, take a bite, and grunt in happy approval. Anna beamed.

There was a light tap on the door and Paula said, "Come in."

Deni Diaz opened the door and remained standing in the doorway.

"It's Jock," she said. "He wants you to come up and see him right away."

"Thanks, Deni," Paula said graciously. "And Deni, you did great tonight. I hardly knew Roxie was gone."

"Thanks," Deni said and she smiled widely. "Though I don't need this kind of pressure in my life. I'm glad it was just for a night. Have you talked to Roxie?"

"No, but she texted," Paula answered cryptically. "They're driving back from his place in the Hamptons."

"At least somebody's gettin' some." Deni grinned wickedly as she left.

Anna fidgeted for a second before she timidly asked, "Who is Roxie getting some... from?"

"Never mind that," Paula said as she picked up her laptop. "You come with me."

"Me? To Jock's office? Why?" Anna asked, looking completely lost.

"I think it might be good to have a witness. Come on," Paula commanded and walked out. Anna followed at her heels like a faithful pet.

*   *   *

It was past eleven thirty when work was done and everyone was gone. It was rare for Paula to be the last to leave, but tonight she had a very important dinner to attend at midnight. In her private bathroom, she checked her makeup and adjusted her open-neck blouse so that her impressive rose quartz gemstone could be seen better. She loved the way it dangled on its silver chain so enticingly above her breasts. She remembered who had given it to her. And why. And she grew sad to think of what was about to happen to him. To Paul Marin. He was once so important in her life. But that was all done now.

Oh, well. Live and learn.

She straightened her shoulders, grabbed her purse, and walked out through the large quiet newsroom. Past the glass wall to the lobby, she got into an elevator and headed down to the street level. The desk attendant wished her a good night. She gave him a friendly wave and pulled on her cotton face mask. She hated wearing these things and wasn't sure they did any good against COVID. But she did appreciate that it kept her hidden from the world. She used to love the way fans stopped her on the street, asked for her autograph, or posed with her for a selfie. But since the pandemic, all that contact just frightened her. So now, with her mask in place, she could move about unnoticed. Especially at night.

Out on the sidewalk, she turned south and started walking slowly. She had lots of time to get there. And this was a night she wanted to savor, to remember for as long as she lived. Tonight, papers would be signed making it official. Paula would be the new executive producer of the show, and her stories would no longer need the consent of the *Slimy Limey* Jock Willinger. Paula smiled.

And what a story I have!

It was still hot and humid. Paula slowed down. It wouldn't do to show up all sweaty. And she was having a little trouble catching her breath. She stopped under a building scaffold to collect herself. She pulled her mask down and took a deep breath. She felt somebody watching her. In the shadows of the scaffold, maybe eight feet away, was a grizzled-looking man in dirty clothes and an aggressive stance. He started to come closer but stumbled and fell to his knees. She walked away quickly, her mask dangling from one ear. She felt that there were too many people everywhere. Some of them seemed to recognize her, but she ignored them and kept walking.

She opened a button on her blouse trying to cool off, and somewhere in the growing confusion of her mind, she registered annoyance that she was messing up her perfect look. She shook her head trying to clear her thoughts but that only made her feel dizzier. Suddenly, a couple of tourists with sticky ice cream cones stepped too close, a handsome man in a tuxedo gave her a nasty look, and an old woman sitting on a box with a hand-printed sign that said *Psychic Readings: $2.00* looked up at her and laughed as she stumbled past.

Paula struggled to comprehend what was happening. It felt like she was taking up too much space. The sidewalk was hard to manage. She walked slower. An older balding man, all sweaty and hurried, had to break his stride as he tried to get past her.

"Darling, pick a lane!" he jeered as he pushed by.

She felt outrage at being bumped. Especially now. And by an asshole who wasn't even wearing a fucking mask. She felt angry at herself that she must be getting sick. And of all times for that to happen.

Did anyone just get sick anymore?

She leaned against a darkened shop door and breathed. It seemed to help. She knew that she'd be all right. She knew that Calvin would help her. They could forget dinner and go right up to his place. He could be so sweet and protective when he wanted to be.

Paula reached up and pulled the dangling mask from her ear and used it to dab her forehead. Calvin may love her right now, but it wouldn't do to show up a mess. She looked up, trying to get her bearings. The yellow glare of the streetlight made her eyes water, but she could see that she was at Broadway and 62nd Street. She hadn't come as far as she thought. It didn't matter. The restaurant was only a few more blocks south. She looked down at her hands and saw they were trembling.

I need some water.

With an effort, she pushed herself away from the storefront and started off again slowly. By the time she'd walked a couple of steps, she could hardly see. She tried to breathe but she couldn't seem to expand her lungs enough. It was like she needed to yawn but it hurt to try. She swayed on her feet. People streaming past were giving her funny looks—most seemed annoyed at her for breaking the flow of the busy sidewalk. She tried to walk on but her balance faltered and she stumbled forward falling to the concrete.

And nobody stopped.

Paula DeVong lay on the sidewalk for a half hour before somebody called 911. Her fall to the pavement and the way people kept walking past her was captured on an overhead security camera.

Chapter One

Thursday, July 15th, 2021

Fat Nicky sat in back of his yellow Maserati sedan. His close-set dark eyes checked the time on his cell. It was half past midnight. He sighed impatiently.

"I'm gonna get some air," he told his driver. "You stay here."

Nicky opened the door, gripped the top handle with one hand and the doorframe with the other. Though he was only thirty-four years old, it took an effort for him to lift his obese body out of the car. He closed the door, smoothed his slicked-back hair into place, and started walking across the sandy parking lot toward a shuttered lobster shack. This little place on the Connecticut shore had once been his favorite for a quick lunch, but it had closed during the pandemic. Nicky leaned against a corner of the weathered building and looked down a wide grassy slope to the beach and the dark water of the Block Island Sound beyond. His cell rang.

"Yeah," he grunted.

"The EMTs got here a few minutes ago," a tough-looking man said as he watched the scene across the street.

"Where?" Fat Nicky asked.

"On Broadway and," the man looked up for the street sign, "62nd." And more cops are just arriving." Across the street, a paramedic pulled a stretcher out of an ambulance as a patrol car stopped. A couple of cops got out and started waving off a handful of curious tourists taking pictures with their phones.

"Paula DeVong is on her way to the ER," the man said.

"Got it." Fat Nicky hung up. He found a number on his cell but hesitated before he pushed it. The world as he knew it was about to change, and he wanted to remember this moment. He had come a long way since his childhood on the streets of New York. And he had the scars to prove it. He chuckled darkly and hit the number with his chubby thumb.

Paul Marin was leaning on the glass door of his Fifth Avenue penthouse looking out past the terrace at the lit-up buildings across Central Park. His cell rang and he grabbed it.

"Tell me," he commanded.

Fat Nicky's jaw tightened in anger, but he held himself in check. "Paula DeVong is on her way to the hospital."

"Okay," Paul said. "Then you're good to go. Send your guys in."

"Consider it done," Fat Nicky answered obediently and hung up. "That was fucking pointless," he murmured as he dialed a number.

"Cut the power," Nicky ordered.

* * *

The 1:00 a.m. rebroadcast of Paula's earlier TV News program was just coming on. The concierge of her apartment building on 82nd Street, just off Broadway, turned his laptop to see Paula's face more clearly. Even though she could be a little snooty, he liked having a celebrity in the building. And he liked the way she stuck it out, staying in the city when so many of the residents had left when the pandemic came. He looked around the nicely refurbished marble lobby of the elegant 1920's building. He wondered when it would all be over and they could go back to normal.

On-air was an upward-trending graph as Paula's voice reported that the rise in cases was entirely due to the Delta variant, that several universities had announced that vaccines would be required for students returning in the fall, and that Los Angeles was reinstating its mask mandate.

The concierge sighed. And then the lights went out.

"Ah shit," he muttered. "It's always something."

After a few seconds, the bright glare and buzz of the emergency lights mounted on the ceiling came on. The concierge got up and walked outside the lobby to the sidewalk. He looked up and could see that not only was his twelve-story building blacked out but so were all the buildings on the block. He looked toward Broadway and could see the flashing yellow lights of a ConEd utility truck parked by an open manhole. He debated whether he should leave the building unprotected, but there was no one around. He walked away toward Broadway.

From the back of a dark green van parked a few doors down and across the street, two young men quietly got out. They were wearing ConEd uniforms with toolbelts, blue helmets, work gloves, and COVID face masks. Keeping an eye on the departing concierge, they entered the building, crossed the lobby to the fire escape door, switched on their flashlights, and jogged purposefully up to the sixth floor. They entered the dark hallway and went quickly to the fourth and last apartment door. One of the men fitted the edge of a prybar against the wooden frame and forced the lock. They moved inside the apartment and silently closed the door. Without a word, the two men each began a methodical search.

In the bedroom, one of the men opened a white lacquered closet door. His flashlight flitted across three rows of high-heeled shoes on racks, open shelves of cotton sweaters and folded shirts, and above a dozen designer purses. He lifted each of these to feel their weight. One bag had something in it. He looked inside and found a small digital camera. He flipped open the screen, searched the menu, and pushed play. A thin, attractive face of a young woman with blue eyes and long brown hair filled the screen. Someone off camera asked her to begin. She took a breath and said:

My name is Lucille, and I'm wanted for a crime I never committed. I'm here to set the record straight.

The man turned off the camera and put it in his toolbelt. He put the purse back exactly where it had been, closed the closet door, and rejoined his partner who was searching a cabinet in the living room.

"Got it," he said.

They went to the front door, listened, stepped out, and closed the door behind them. They quickly retraced their steps through the hall, down the six flights of stairs, and out the fire door into the lobby.

"Ah, there you are," the concierge said impatiently as he came back in. "What the hell happened? Ya cut the wrong line?"

One of the men laughed a little and said, "We're working on it." They walked past him and out of the building.

"Fuckin' assholes," the concierge mumbled as he went back to his desk to call the managing agent of the building.

Down the block, the two men got back into their van and pulled off their masks. As one man started the engine and carefully pulled out, the other got out his cell phone and hit a number.

"We got it."

"Good man," Fat Nicky answered, hung up, and smiled. He opened his arms, spread his chunky legs, and leaned back on the wide wooden bench, his great girth sagging the boards. In front of him, the waxing crescent moon was low on the southern horizon illuminating a bright path across the ocean water. It reminded him of when he was a little boy in Sicily sitting on a beach in the moonlight with his father.

Ah, fuck it. Only the strong will survive.

Nicolas Abruzzo had been in America since he was four, some thirty years ago. After his father was killed, he was secreted out of Sicily and sent to live with relatives in the Bronx. Nicolas was a fighter from the first, and by the time he was in his teens, he was established as someone to be feared. When he was in his early twenties, he acquired the nickname Fat Nicky because of his size. But lately his men had taken to calling him just Nicky. Or Boss.

Nicky looked at his cell phone and found a number.

Paul Marin was sitting with his feet up on his designer sofa sipping a drink. His phone rang.

"Did they find it?" Though Paul was trying to remain calm, the worry was plain to hear in his voice.

"Of course," Nicky assured him. "My guys know what they're doing."

"And Lucille?" Paul asked.

"It's covered. They're heading there now." As often happened with Nicky, his Bronx inflections became more pronounced when he got angry. And Paul knew this.

"What is it, Fat Nicky? What's going on?" Paul asked.

"I will call you as soon as I hear," Nicky said quickly and hung up.

Paul got up, went to the bar, and refilled his drink. He wondered about this new rebellious tone coming from Fat Nicky. He opened the balcony doors and stepped out. The glowing light of the city below highlighted the strong Greek features of his handsome almost feminine face and powerful eyes. He leaned on the metal railing and sighed. The world below seemed so ordered and perfect from this height. The traffic on Fifth Avenue could hardly be heard, and the lights of the tall buildings across Central Park sparkled mysteriously. He used to feel like he owned New York. But in the last year, everything had changed.

He didn't know why he'd let Lucille live this long. Maybe he was getting soft. Or maybe he was just tired of taking orders from his mother. But one way or another, he'd be able to put that chapter behind him tonight. He took out his cell and dialed a number.

"I need to see you," he said and listened. He smiled. "I'll be there as soon as I can."

∗ ∗ ∗

By one forty, the night air had cooled a little in the Lower East Side of Manhattan. Lucille walked south on Avenue C. She was relieved that there was no one around. Dressed in jeans, a dark blue shirt, her long hair hidden under a cap, and wearing a blue face mask over her nose and mouth, she blended easily into the shadows. It was a skill she'd been perfecting for the last sixteen months, because it served her purpose. She had made it her mission to follow and learn everything about the people who were once in Paul Marin's secret school. Six people had gathered every Sunday night at midnight to listen to the teachings of Paul and his *Voices*. At least that's what Paul had called them. They were some kind of spirit guide. She had been in class only twice before she recognized who Paul truly was. Then the classes were finished, Paul betrayed her, and now she spent her days hiding. But in the darkness of night, she felt safe enough to venture out. And her work had paid off. Now she knew enough. It was the moment when justice would come for Paul Marin.

Or it should have been.

She turned the corner at 3rd Street and moved quickly down the sidewalk. She stopped in front of an old seven-story building. She looked around carefully as she reached for her keys. She undid the lock and went in. Inside she ignored the elevator, as she always did, and went through the fire door and up the steps. She was more fit than she had ever been, though thinner. At the top floor, she came to a small landing with only one door. This studio apartment belonged to Paula DeVong, a woman who recently she'd come to trust. She unlocked the door, went in, and switched on the light. She jumped to see someone standing by the closed window curtains.

"Where the fuck have you been?" Ida Orsina kept herself from shouting, but only just, as she marched across the room.

"I... didn't know you were coming tonight," Lucille answered.

"I told you to stop going out," Ida said emphatically.

Lucille looked at her sister and knew that she could not tell her where she had been. She loved Ida and was grateful to her for protecting her. But Ida, ever strong force-of-nature Ida, was also a lifelong friend of Paul Marin's.

"It was important," Lucille said simply.

"Fine. Whatever." Ida grabbed Lucille's bag from the floor and shoved it at her. "You're leaving here."

"What? Now?"

"Yes," Ida spoke harshly, "this fucking second. Move."

Lucille saw the strain and worry in Ida's eyes, nodded once, and gathered up her few things. From a paper bag under the bed, Lucille pulled out a small notebook, a half dozen off-the-shelf burner phones still in their packaging, and shoved them in her bag.

"Making lots of calls, are you?" Ida sounded suspicious.

"They're for emergencies, and they're untraceable," Lucille answered as she joined her by the door. Ida turned out the lights, and without another word, they left.

As they came out of the lobby, Ida looked quickly up and down at the parked cars that lined the quiet street. A loose strand of her henna-red hair fell across her eyes, and she impatiently swiped it off her face. Her pageboy hairdo was less perfect than usual and her face was shiny with a mist of sweat. Ida was a strong, good-looking, unique woman who wore designer clothes mixed with trendy thrift store finds. In contrast, her sister Lucille looked pretty, elongated, and elite.

Lucille hid her long hair under her cap and put her mask on. Ida pulled up her mask, slung her green leather bag across her shoulder, seized Lucille by the arm, and moved her quickly down the street toward the avenue. At the corner, she hailed a cab and gave an address a dozen blocks north.

At 14th Street, Ida paid the driver, pulled Lucille out, banged the door closed, and the cab drove away. They walked west two blocks and then Ida hailed another passing cab. She told the driver an address on the Upper West Side.

A dark green van slowly turned onto 3rd Street off Avenue D and double-parked halfway down the block in front of the building Lucille and Ida had just come from. Two men dressed in ConEd uniforms and COVID masks got out. Once again, they used a prybar to break open the lock on the inner lobby door. They quickly went up the fire escape stairs and came to the sole apartment on the top floor. One of the men reached into his toolbelt and pulled out a semiautomatic pistol with a suppressor on the barrel. He looked to his partner who quickly pried opened the door, and they pushed in. They put on the lights, looked under the bed, opened the curtains, and looked out the window. The man with the gun climbed out onto the rooftop. He walked around the entire square structure of the studio. He came back inside and shook his head.

The other man hit a button on his cell. "The girl is gone. All her stuff too."

"Why am I not surprised. It's like she knew exactly when to run," Nicky said menacingly. "Goddamn Paul Marin. We'll attend to this later. Things are in motion here. Head back."

"Yes, Boss," the man answered and hung up.

Nicky put his phone away and took a long deep breath. The warm air off the water cleared his head. With a grunt, he got up and started walking up the hill toward his Maserati.

* * *

It was just past two in the morning when Ida and Lucille got out of the cab at Broadway and 73rd Street. Ida handed some cash to the driver through his open window and told him to keep the change. He murmured a sleepy thanks and took off. Ida scanned the area. A homeless man was sleeping on a bench in Verdi Park, and though it was late, the subway station still had a few people coming and going. Ida grabbed Lucille by the arm and ushered her away.

They stopped at a tall mid-century apartment building half a block west of Broadway. There was no doorman. As Ida opened the street door, Lucille looked up at the strip of sky between the rows of buildings. She could see the moon but no stars. The lights of the city always hid those.

Ida pulled her into the small foyer, took out a key, and unlocked the inner door to the lobby. It was clean but dull and forgotten. And it was quiet. Apartment buildings had been much quieter since COVID began. So many people had moved away. The elevator door opened and the two women got in. Lucille reached up to remove her mask, but Ida stopped her and indicated the small security camera in the upper corner of the cab. Even the old buildings had security these days. They got out at the top floor—the eighteenth. There were six apartment doors on this level. Even though Lucille had never been here before, she was almost certain where they'd be going next. As expected, Ida led her through the landing door and up a flight of steps. At the top was a small hallway with one door. Ida unlocked it and let them in.

"Finally," Lucille said as she pulled off her face mask and looked around the place. It was a small square room with a weathered oak floor, a bed made with white sheets, a small kitchen area with a stone counter and two stools. Lucille went to look out the windows.

"What is it with you and top-floor apartments?" Lucille asked.

"I thought you'd like it," Ida said as she stayed by the door and watched her sister silhouetted across the dark room.

Looking out, Lucille could see that this studio was added onto the existing building sometime in the past, something that happened often in Manhattan where real estate was so precious. There were windows in three directions. To the west she could see across several lower rooftops before the view was blocked by taller buildings. But she could see a bit of the Hudson River past them just a few blocks away. To the east she could see across lower buildings and along the street to where they had just come from: Broadway near the subway station. And to the north there was a wonderfully open view of the city.

Lucille looked down and across the street where there was a strange and massive block-long building. The top of it was a story lower than where she stood, and she could see a rooftop deck, some gardens, and at the four corners, large ornate domes. Even in the darkness, the city lights revealed the terra-cotta gargoyles that decorated the outside walls just under the roofline.

She opened the large window. The hot night air was still and gave no relief.

"Is there air-conditioning?" she asked, keeping her back to her sister.

"No. Sorry."

Lucille let out a shaky sigh. "Why am I here? Why did I have to leave Paula's place?"

"You were in danger there."

Lucille turned and whispered fiercely, "Why? Why now?"

Ida didn't answer.

Lucille walked over to her. "Tell me the truth," she demanded. "Is Paula DeVong dead?"

There was something about Lucille's eyes that worried Ida. There was a wildness there again, like there used to be. For more than a year, Ida had kept her hidden and kept her safe. And in that time, she had seen Lucille get better. Stronger, and calmer. But tonight, something had changed.

"I don't know," Ida said. "Maybe." She took Lucille's hand. "What have you heard?"

Lucille looked at Ida for a second before she laughed. It was a desperate choked sound. She pulled her hand away.

"I don't know anything, remember," she answered defiantly. "Except what you tell me. But even I know something's wrong when you show up in the middle of the night and drag me here."

Ida said nothing.

"And who owns this place?" Lucille gestured disdainfully.

"I do."

Lucille took a breath. "And I'll be safe here, you think?"

"Yes. As long as you're careful," Ida said in the same even tone. "And this place has a special perk. Something you're going to like."

"What are you talking about?"

"You'll see tomorrow," Ida said cryptically.

"Fuck COVID!" They heard a shout from the street some nineteen floors below. Lucille went to the window and saw a small group of teenage boys noisily trotting down the sidewalk toward Broadway.

"Fuck COVID!" they shouted again and laughed. The pandemic had changed everything in the city. But entitled kids from the suburbs still couldn't be kept away. Lucille saw them disappear around the corner and smiled a little in remembrance of who she once was. And of how far she had come.

Maybe Paula isn't dead.

Lucille pulled off her cap and ran her fingers through her long hair.

"There's enough food here for a few days," Ida was saying as she opened the small fridge. "And I've put some frozen stuff in the freezer. The sheets are clean. And you know the drill. Stay inside. Protect yourself. Okay?"

Ida arrived at the window. Lucille turned to look at her. The lights of the city were shining in enough, so she could see the pendant necklace and blue gemstone hanging around Ida's neck.

"Why do you still wear that?" Lucille asked quietly.

"Reminds me of better days, I guess."

"Blue. Like mine was," Lucille said resentfully. "Yours is blue tourmaline. Does he still call you that?"

"No. Not since the class ended."

The memory of handsome Paul Marin drinking out of a chalice, a famous piece of stolen art, flooded across Lucille's mind. She had caused his classes to end. And she remembered Paul's revenge. Making Lucille the main suspect in a murder.

"So, does Paul know where I am?"

"No," Ida said earnestly. "And never will if I can help it."

"Must make it hard seeing him all the time," Lucille said sarcastically.

"I will handle Paul Marin. I always have." Ida forcefully stopped the conversation.

Lucille weighed her options. Then she asked, "So, what do you mean this place has a special perk?"

"You just need to keep an eye on one of the apartments across the street." Ida pointed to a row of dark windows on the top floor of the building below them. "That one. And report to me what you see."

"Why?" Lucille asked.

"Just do it for me."

Lucille noticed for the first time how tired her sister looked. Worry lines had crept into Ida's powerful face, and a certain weariness informed the way she held her shoulders.

"It's late. Go home," Lucille said and hugged her tightly. "And thank you for everything you do for me."

Ida kissed her cheek quickly and marched to the door. She turned back to say something.

"I know"—Lucille cut her off—"lock the door after you go."

"Right." Ida nodded and left.

Lucille walked over, locked the door, and turned back to the room. She slowly sank to the floor and hugged her knees to her chest.

"Oh, Paula." She sighed, tears coming to her eyes.

Please don't be dead.

* * *

For safety, they had moved the pill mill regularly. The market for fentanyl was still exploding, and all an enterprising group like theirs needed was an out-of-the-way place to create the product. This one was a room under a large brick building which in the late 1800s had been a lace factory. During the Second World War, it had been used to manufacture first aid supplies for the army. Various ventures came and went after that until it was left a derelict monument to Connecticut's expanding economic plight. Located under the raised supports of Highway I-95 and close to the shipping docks, the building was nicely located for their purpose. Around three sides of the property, a chain-link fence topped with razor wire provided protection. The loading area of the old factory was on the back side, hidden from view by tall overgrown shrubs and weeds. A locked gate had been installed to keep people away from this entrance, but it had been easily defeated.

Nicky pushed the gate and went in. He walked past two armed guards and down a curved driveway to the open doors of a loading bay. A large van was being packed with boxes by a man with powerful shoulders and strange mismatched eyes. His left eye was noticeably larger than the right. Ladimir Karlovic caught sight of Fat Nicky sauntering in.

"Nice of you to show up when all the work is done," Ladimir called out, his Slavic accent unmistakable. "Got a smoke?"

"Someday you will surprise me," Nicky said as he reached into his pocket and pulled out a pack of cigarettes, "and you will have your own."

"What else are friends for?" Ladimir smiled as he lit up.

"How soon do we go?" Nicky asked.

"Ten minutes. They're just finishing downstairs."

Nicky turned and walked out of the loading dock.

"Where are you going now?"

"Get some coffees for the road. It's a long drive to Vermont. Tell the boys to hurry up. I won't be long," Nicky called as he walked back down the driveway toward the gate.

"Lazy bastard." Ladimir smirked and went back to work.

At the gate, Nicky gave the two guards a look, and they followed him out. They walked a block on the empty street and turned into a deserted parking lot bordered by freight train tracks that led down to the Cross Sound Ferry docks. In the darkness, they could see a dozen vehicles parked.

"Get the car," Nicky instructed his men, and they walked away toward the water. Nicky took out a cigarette and a lighter. He placed the cigarette in his mouth and lit it. Headlights turned on, and all the vehicles but one headed past him and around the corner to the factory. The one car stopped next to Nicky, and two men in FBI field jackets got out and stood watching him. Nicky took a drag on his cigarette and slowly exhaled the blue smoke.

Near the docks, another set of headlights came to life and started slowly toward them. As it moved closer, they could see it was a yellow Maserati sedan. It parked behind the FBI car, the engine shut off, and Nicky's two men got out and stood leaning against the doors.

One of the FBI agent's phones pinged. He read the text and showed it to the other agent. He looked at Nicky and said dismissively, "You guys have a good night."

"Thank you," Nicky said. He walked over to the Maserati and eased his large body into the back seat. His two men got in the front, and they drove away.

Nicky checked the time on his watch. Sicily was six hours ahead. It was nine forty-five in the morning there. It was a perfect time to call her. He took a long steadying breath, hit a button on his cell, and waited.

"Pronto," a man's voice said.

"It's Nicolas."

"Memento," the dutiful voice said, and the line went quiet as he was put on hold.

A very old woman in a long black dress sat looking out a terra-cotta arched window at her courtyard below where thick vines grew across the tall walls, their roots reaching deeply into the mortar of the ancient blocks of stone. Two men with automatic rifles slung over their shoulders patrolled the yard near the massive closed gates. She sighed. This villa had belonged to her family for five generations. Now there was only one person left who could take over when she was gone. But she worried about him. People feared him, which was good. But would her grandson be smart enough to lead?

There was a soft knock on the open door and her man came in.

"Nicolas," he said as he lifted the handset of a phone and handed it to her. She gripped the armrest of her tall elm-wood chair and pulled her body forward. She straightened her back and took the phone. She turned her weathered crow-like face, and her small dark eyes commanded the man to leave. He bowed respectfully and closed the door as he left.

"Yes?" she said in English, her voice surprisingly strong and clear.

"I have news," Nicky reported. "Ladimir Karlovic has been arrested."

The old woman's fingernails dug into the wood of her chair, but she kept her voice calm. "Tell me what has happened Nicolas."

"Paul and Ladimir have gotten so careless," Nicky said sounding sad. "The Connecticut factory was raided."

"And Paul?" she asked with true concern.

"He wasn't there," Nicky answered scornfully. "He was in New York, not paying attention, as usual."

"But you are safe?" she asked.

"Yes." Nicky assured her. "I always know how to take care of myself."

"And what about business? How soon before you can get started again?"

"Soon. I will take care of everything here, I promise," Nicky said confidently.

The old woman looked out over the walls at the rolling acres of her vast vineyards. The morning was hot and the air still. She knew that this news changed everything and she would have to make a call. And she knew that her grandson was waiting for her reaction.

"Your news has surprised me, Nicolas," she said carefully. "I will call you tomorrow. You must take care of yourself."

"Grazie, Nonna," Nicky said and hung up. He chuckled, pleased with himself. His Maserati was just entering the highway, heading south, and picking up speed. He looked out the window to his left and watched the headlights of the endless stream of cars across the concrete divider heading north into the darkness behind him.

He hit a number on his phone.

The curtains in Greg Schaefer's bedroom were open, and the street-lights below created a gentle glow on the high ceiling. On top of the white linen sheets, two perfectly matched naked bodies lay tangled together catching their breath. On one bedside table was a silver chain pendant with a single green gemstone. On the other, a cell phone lit up and buzzed noisily. Paul rolled over and grabbed it.

"About time," he said. "Tell me."

"Tell you what?" Nicky sounded surprised. "How could you know, it only just happened."

"What are you talking about?" Paul controlled his impatience. Greg sat up next to him and looked intrigued. Paul hit the speaker button so he could hear. "Tell me that you have Lucille Orsina by now."

"No, we don't," Nicky said aggressively. "And do you wanna know why? Because somebody told her we were coming, I'm thinking. Any idea who could have done that?"

Paul clenched his jaw in anger.

"But that's not why I'm calling. I have news." Nicky fought to keep the triumph out of his voice. "The Connecticut factory was just raided."

"Shit," Paul said dangerously. "By who?"

"Fucking everybody. The feds, local cops, a SWAT team from the state. Like an army. They got everything. And Ladimir too." He sounded sad.

"I see. But not you, Fat Nicky," Paul said quietly.

"No, I was lucky tonight. I was out getting some coffees for the drive. I got back and they were everywhere."

"Where was our protection?" Paul asked.

"That's a good question." Nicky leaned back in his leather seat and smiled. "You know what, Paul? For something like this to happen, it doesn't make your leadership look too good. You know?"

Paul swung out of bed, went to the windows, and looked down at the streets of the West Village. "What have you done, Fat Nicky?"

"You know, it's funny that you don't know this about me. I really hate being called Fat Nicky. When I was a boy and first got to America, some of the kids in the neighborhood liked to call me *Pimpi*. Do you know what that means, Paul?"

"No. I don't."

"Piglet," Nicky said bitterly. "Cute, no? I found that beating those kids was better than explaining to them about the problem with my glands. They learned. And then, when I'm older, I meet you and Ladimir. And you guys call me Fat Nicky. Like we were friends."

"Like we were friends," Paul repeated as his eyes grew dark. "For the sake of those who got us here. For the *Trias*."

"Everything changes, Paulie. The old ways die out. Then it's time for the new." Nicky hung up and turned off his phone. He closed his eyes and settled back in his seat.

"Good for you, little *Pimpi*," he said to himself.

Greg's perceptive blue eyes were fixed on Paul's naked body across the room. Greg reached for his pendant necklace, carefully fastened it around his neck, and arranged the light green gem on his muscular chest. It was called hiddenite. A name that made him smile, because it was a gift from Paul that no one else knew about.

Greg brushed his fingers through his short brown hair, got out of bed, and went to stand behind Paul. He wrapped his arms around Paul's chest and pressed his naked body into his back. He could feel Paul's heartbeat.

"You ever think it might be time to change all this?" Greg whispered close to his ear. "There are other places besides New York. I would come with you. If you asked me."

"Ah, Greg," Paul said sadly. "I can't leave. This is who I am. This is what I do."

"You do... whatever your mother says," Greg said without challenge. "No matter how much it costs you."

"You don't understand. There is nowhere on planet Earth where we could be safe." Paul turned around and held Greg's face in his hands. "But thank you for the offer." He kissed Greg's lips and held him close.

* * *

By 8:00 a.m. the day was already hot, windless, and humid. At the TVNews studio, senior staff and network brass were assembling for a special meeting.

In her glass-enclosed corner office on the eighth floor, Roxie Lee was sitting at her desk crying. Someone knocked on the door and she pulled a few tissues from a drawer and wiped away her tears.

"Come in," she called, her voice breaking.

"Sorry," Moira Weyland said as she came in and closed the door, "but they're all here. We should go in."

"Right." Roxie stood and looked out the window at the masses of people below walking on the hot sidewalks of Columbus Avenue. Even from this height, she could see that only a small percentage were wearing masks. Lincoln Center across the street was closed but somehow New York, even during this global sickness, still attracted the curious. Her mind tried to find a pattern in their movements, some reason for the way those jostling bodies didn't collide. They seemed unreal and relentless. She looked up and saw her reflection in the window. Roxie was beautiful. Her powerful eyes, very dark black skin, and sensual figure had always gotten her noticed. And had helped her rise in the food chain of television news. But this morning, she wondered what it was all for.

"I go away for one night and all the world goes to fucking hell," she said softly.

"I know." Moira was trying to say something helpful. But there was nothing to say. Paula DeVong had been Roxie's friend.

Roxie cleared her throat. "All right." She turned, and Moira was struck by how even now Roxie was so in charge of herself.

"Are you ready for this, Moira?" she asked.

Moira was an attractive, ambitious, up-and-coming reporter. Roxie had been giving her more on-air time lately, and the audience seemed to like her. But would the ratings stay solid if she were to host the show?

Moira saw the way Roxie was studying her and understood. She brushed a strand of curly red hair away from her eyes and said a little too quickly, "Yes, Roxie, I'm ready. I'll make you proud of me."

"That's what I want to hear," Roxie said as she led her out of her office.

The news had brought people into work early, and as Roxie and Moira made their way through the large newsroom, everyone grew quiet. At the door to the conference room, Roxie turned back and addressed them. "We still have a job to do. The show will still be on tonight at nine o'clock. You are here because you are the best in the business. So, let's get to work."

The group almost audibly sighed in relief, and Roxie and Moira went in.

One flight up on the executive level, Calvin Prons was happy for the first time in as long as he could remember. He poured a shot of whiskey into his coffee and sat at his massive metal desk. He turned his leather chair and put his feet up on the sill of the floor-to-ceiling windows and looked out at the rows of buildings baking in the sun. He took a deep air-conditioned breath and smiled.

Dead on the pavement and nobody stopped.

"Like some goddamn angel came down from heaven to save my ass," he said out loud and laughed. He checked his watch, took a large gulp of coffee, got up, and went into his private bathroom. He examined his face in the gold-rimmed mirror. At forty-seven, he was still a good-looking man with broad shoulders, a square jaw, and authoritative eyes. But he could see his thinning blond hair, sagging chin, and ever-growing belly that even a well-cut suit couldn't hide.

Fuck it. I'm still the power.

He adjusted his tie and headed for the door.

As he stepped out into the large wood-paneled reception area, an attractive, young secretary saw him and stood up.

"I was just about to call you, Mr. Prons," she said. "They are ready for you downstairs."

"Thank you, Barb," he answered, pleased with himself that he remembered her name. She had been here only a few days. The one before her had gotten too interested in Jock's goddamn lawsuit.

He walked past her and down the open-tread glass staircase to the eighth floor. The staff in the newsroom looked up, but Calvin ignored them. Through the glass wall of the conference room, the group saw him coming and sat down. Calvin sat at the head of the long white table between Roxie and Jock Willinger, who seemed especially tired and pale.

Next to Jock were two older men in dark suits who Calvin introduced as the network lawyers. Next to Roxie sat Moira, Greg, and Deni. Calvin cleared his throat to begin, but something caught his eye. In the back corner of the room sat frumpy Anna Canneli, a notepad on her lap. She was a mess: her eyes red from crying, her shoulders slumped, and her drab clothes even more disheveled than usual. Roxie got up and went over to Anna.

"You don't need to be at this meeting," Roxie said not unkindly.

Anna was startled to be the center of attention, but she looked relieved and stood up to go. Then she looked worried.

"But please don't leave the studio," Roxie said as she took her gently by the arm and walked her to the door. "The police will be here soon and will want to talk with everybody. And nobody is to go into Paula's office until they clear it. Okay?"

Anna looked confused. "I'll be in my office," she mumbled as she passed Roxie and left.

"Thank you, Roxie," Calvin said as she sat back down. He folded his hands and began in a low, serious tone. "The police have confirmed that Paula DeVong was found lying dead just a few blocks from here last night."

Roxie wrapped her arms around her chest. Deni leaned into Greg, and he put his arm around her shoulders. Jock's face twitched.

"An autopsy is being conducted," Calvin continued. "But they think she may have died of a stroke, a complication from COVID. She tested positive."

Roxie looked to Calvin, and he indicated that she should carry on.

"It has been decided," Roxie said reassuringly, "that our show will proceed without interruption. Tonight's entire hour will be a tribute to Paula, about her career and what we thought of her as a person."

"Moira Weyland will be hosting tonight," Calvin said as he turned to her and smiled.

Moira smiled back and a little nervously said, "Thank you for your faith in me."

"So, we have some work to do," Roxie said. "Deni, we'll need..."

"Got it," Deni said before she could ask. She turned her laptop around so Roxie could see. It was a picture of Paula looking young and eager, and printed across the bottom: *Paula DeVong 1983–2021.*

"Well done, as always, Deni," Roxie said.

"Had that all ready to go, didn't you?" Jock sneered at Deni suspiciously.

Deni forced herself to be civil. "We've all known for hours. It's my job to be prepared."

"You're right." Roxie stepped in quickly. "What else do you have, Deni?"

Deni began speaking about the various approaches they could take. Roxie's cell pinged. And as Moira joined in with some ideas she'd had, Roxie privately read the text:

Need to see u!

It was from Paul Marin.

* * *

At noon it was still humid and close to ninety degrees. A sedan pulled up outside an impressive building on 73rd Street just off Broadway. The street-side back door of the car opened, and a man wearing a face mask and FBI identification got out and scanned the area. He came around the car and tapped on the curbside back door. The door opened, and Artemis Bookbinder carefully looked out. He had made so much progress in the last year, but it still took a moment before he found the courage to step out into the germ-filled air. It was a blessing that the sidewalk was empty. He took a short breath through his face mask and got out. Artemis was very thin and tall with a full head of neatly trimmed brown hair. His handsome face was dominated by intense dark blue eyes. He wore a spotless white button-down shirt, black jeans, and blue nitrile gloves. He looked up at the eighteen floors of the building's ornate facade. It had been a long time since he'd been here.

"Are you okay?" Agent Makani Kim asked kindly.

"Yes." Artemis turned to his friend. "Thanks, Mak."

Artemis set his shoulders and pushed through the large revolving door. Mak signaled to the driver and followed Artemis in.

The vaulted lobby was a city block-long celebration in black-and-white marble, with grand chandeliers and mirrored panels.

"Wow," Mak murmured appreciatively. "So, this is the famous Ansonia."

Built in 1903, the Ansonia Hotel was the wonder of its time. Located just steps away from the new subway station on Broadway and filled with every luxury, it immediately became home to wealthy families and celebrities from theater, opera, and sports.

Artemis led the way to the center of the unique space. Sitting at a high desk near the elevators was a uniformed older man wearing a face mask. "Welcome back, Professor Bookbinder," he said happily. "It's been a long time."

Artemis winced, as he always did, when somebody addressed him by his old job title. But he managed a friendly tone and said, "Hello, John, been well?"

"Very well. But we've all had enough of this COVID thing."

"Yes. Me too," Artemis said candidly. "And this is my friend Makani Kim."

"Nice to meet you, sir," the older man said as his eyes scanned Mak's FBI badge. He turned back to Artemis. "So, your movers are all gone. They finished maybe an hour ago. You guys moving in today?"

"No, tomorrow," Artemis said. "We're just here to see how they did."

"Well, welcome home, Professor," the concierge said as he reached under the desk and pushed a button that opened one of the six elevators behind him.

"Thanks, John. See you later," Artemis said as he and Mak walked into the black-and-silver cab and pushed the button for the top floor.

The doors opened on the eighteenth floor to an impressive marble lobby with a vintage wood table and a bowl of fresh-cut flowers. To one side was a set of doors that opened to a wide hallway. But Artemis led Mak to the other side. Here a grand staircase with well-worn white marble steps and a dark wood banister led down floor after floor in a graceful repeating soft-edged rectangle. Above the stairs was a large iron and glass dome.

"It was painted over during World War II," Artemis explained, his voice low and distant. "When we lived here, there was talk about having it restored. I'll have to see what happened with that."

Mak watched his friend and waited. It was only sixteen months ago when Artemis had collapsed. The death of his wife and the worldwide onset of COVID had made it impossible for him to leave the room he was staying in.

After a moment, Artemis turned and said, "Come, see the rest."

Across the lobby, they went through the doors into the wide hallway. Artemis explained:

"The more recent renovations are nice, but they aren't correct to the period. But considering her history, it's a miracle that the Ansonia is still here at all."

In 1903 the building was a marvel, but as often happens in New York, it was soon eclipsed. The extravagant beaux arts decorations fell out of favor, and by the 1930s, hotel tenants were moving out. By mid-century, the building's owners were dividing the massive suites into smaller units in a desperate attempt to survive. By the 1970s, the Ansonia was operating as an apartment building but had become a dangerous place where drug deals were made in the dark neglected hallways. The owners gave up and sold the building to a firm that planned to demolish it. But thanks to the outcry from people of the neighborhood, the building was saved. After much effort, the Ansonia was declared a landmark. New owners bought the building, and a series of renovations began. The process of renewal was bumpy and slow. But in time, the Ansonia was brought back and regained its reputation as a quintessential place to live in New York.

Around a corner and at the end of a hallway, Artemis unlocked the door to apartment 18-18.

"So, when we bought this place, it had been divided long ago into four small apartments. We renovated it back to the original 1903 suite configuration," Artemis said and opened the door.

They stepped into a long elegant hallway with a black-and-white marble floor edged with a border of slate. Above were three evenly spaced pendant lamps, and along the glossy white walls were several doors and a large window. At the far end was an alcove with a tall gold-framed antique mirror.

"It's hot. Let me get the air going," Artemis said and walked down the hallway. At the mirror, he turned left and went into the large open living room. Here windows looked out in two directions, and the sun was gleaming across the newly refinished herringbone oak floors. Artemis hit a button, and the quiet whir of the cooling system came on. He turned to look at the room. The white walls reached up twelve feet in graceful curves that followed the articulation of the structure of the grand copper domes on the rooftop above. All around were boxes and furniture that had been placed where the movers had been told to leave them. All the things that he and Emily had so carefully chosen together. So many things.

I have the right to breathe.

It was a mantra that his therapist and old friend Leah Carras had taught him.

He steeled himself and slowly pulled off his face mask. He let the air come into his lungs.

"This place is amazing," Mak said warmly as he came in. But he stopped when he saw the strained expression on Artemis's face. Mak backed off a few steps to give him room.

"Take off your mask, if you want," Artemis said, pulling himself together.

"You sure?" Mak asked.

Artemis nodded, and Mak pulled off his mask. He turned and walked into the open kitchen.

"Love the stainless steel and glass," he offered.

"It's a little too deco, I suppose," Artemis said, "but Emily wanted it, so..." He trailed off and Mak turned to look at him.

"Right," Artemis said with resolve. "Let me show you around."

He led him back along the hallway to the first room nearest the front door. It was a nice-sized bright room with curved bay windows and a cushioned seat. There was a bed, an old chest of drawers, and several boxes still taped shut. The walls were painted with wide yellow vertical stripes, and the windows were bordered with heavy purple curtains.

"I know." Artemis smiled for the first time. "But this is Delia's room and she wanted it this way."

"Well, it's..." Mak was trying to find the right word. "Lively," he said with a smile.

"Each bedroom has its own bath," Artemis said as he led the way down the hall. "This is Silas's room." They walked into a smaller room with off-white walls and built-in bookcases. One large window looked out across an ornate exterior wall at a wide-open city view.

"Was this his room when you lived here before?" Mak asked.

"Yeah."

"How long has it been?"

"Oh, about eight years, I guess."

Artemis's office was further along the hall. It was painted in a deep forest-green and lined with oak bookcases. Like Delia's bedroom, it had curved bay windows with a cushioned seat, a private bath, and a large closet. His wood desk was in place, and as everywhere, unopened cardboard boxes filled the space.

Artemis led Mak back down the hall to the antique mirror and turned right into the master suite. The large room had views in two directions separated by a wall, with a small fireplace and a decorative mantel.

"Does it work?" Mak asked.

"Yes. It took some doing, but we had it converted to gas. A local artist did the tile work." Artemis pulled off his nitrile gloves and gently touched the inlaid design that surrounded the fireplace.

"Emily wanted it to look like an Etruscan mosaic," he said very quietly. "I thought that was wrong. But she was right." Artemis walked to the curved bay windows. From here, past the buildings that lined the street, he could see a slice of the Hudson River glistening a few blocks away. A tall white sailboat was just sliding out of view.

I don't know how to be here without you.

And all around he could feel Emily. He turned and saw Mak watching him from across the room.

"It's hard being back," Artemis said. "But we should have been out of Drew's house a long time ago."

"She wouldn't say that," Mak said.

"No, she never would." Artemis smiled.

Mak turned and looked out the window. Here the open view was to the south.

"Is that the Freedom Tower?" Mak asked surprised. "That must be what, five miles away?"

"Yes," Artemis answered as he came over. "It's just chance. All these lower buildings haven't grown up yet into this." He indicated a mid-century building across the street and to the right. It stood a full story taller than the Ansonia.

*   *   *

Lucille lay naked on the white sheets in her new prison. Because no matter what her sister called it, this place was still a prison.

She'd been awake all night. The apartment was too hot, and the open windows didn't help. And there was still no news. And in her mind, all she could see was Paula DeVong lying motionless on a sidewalk.

She delicately wiped the sweat from her face with her fingers. She got up and wandered over to the window. She leaned against the curtains and looked out north across the buildings and saw the hazy air radiating up in waves from the hundreds of rooftops. She looked at the gardens on the roof of the large building across the street. They were wilted in the heat. She let her eyes drift lower to the row of windows in the top-floor apartment that her sister had pointed out. And there she saw something. Two men were standing by a window talking. One man answered his cell phone and walked away. The other turned to look out the window. A visceral shock ran through Lucille's body as she recognized him.

Artemis. What are you doing there?

Lucille slowly rolled her naked body along the wall past the curtains so he wouldn't see her.

But why should I hide?

She pressed her hands into her breasts, her nipples were hard. Her fingertips lightly traced down her body, across her hips, and between her legs. And she was almost overwhelmed with an impulse to stand naked in the window and call out his name. She wanted him to see her. She wanted to be revealed to him. To shout that she never killed his wife, never could have harmed her. That all she wanted now was to help him. To protect him.

She felt how wet she was. Her breathing started coming faster. She stepped back into the open window and looked down.

And he wasn't there.

She gasped for air. Suddenly she wasn't sure that he'd been there at all. She fought to clear the confusion in her mind. It was so unbearably hot. She sank to the floor below the window, leaned against the wall, and tried to focus.

"I am the Angel of Death and I will be feared," she whispered the mantra that had empowered her. But now the words felt hollow and gave no comfort.

*   *   *

"Good afternoon, Ms. Lee," the uniformed desk attendant said to Roxie as she entered the glass-fronted lobby.

"Hey, Jimmy," she said as she walked past his marble-topped station.

"I saw Doctor Marin go up," he added discreetly.

Roxie nodded to him as she got into the sleek elevator and pushed the button for the thirtieth floor. Roxie checked the time. It was just past two. It had taken forever to get out of the studio. The elevator door opened. Roxie got her keys out and walked to the end of the elegantly decorated hall. She opened her apartment door, went in, dropped her keys on a table in the foyer, and locked the door behind her. The air-conditioning was on high, and she stood still listening as she cooled off. She could hear the shower running in the master bathroom. She walked into the living room where large corner windows looked out across the hazy-hot Hudson River, past the cliffs and buildings of New Jersey to the distant blue hills.

Roxie went to the fully-stocked built-in glass bar and poured herself a drink. It was early and she had a show to produce that night, but strange times called for strange measures. She looked up at the large painting hanging on the wall above the bar. It was a surrealistic piece created by Max Ernst in 1925. It was a picture of contrast: in the top half was an image of the golden sun and below a modern take on a world destroyed. Ernst called it *Earthquake, Or the Drowning of the Sun.*

Roxie loved everything about it. Because it was a gift from Paul. Because it had been chosen for her by a dear old man, the art dealer Raphael Sharder. And because ever since she was little, she wanted to own a true piece of art. She took a sip of her drink and walked to the windows across the room.

Roxie came from Georgia and some family money but never enough to afford a painting like this. But she had learned early on how to make friends. Especially powerful friends. People who had helped her climb the ladder in television news, like Calvin Prons, head of her network. And people who had believed in her, like Raphael Sharder. She missed that old man so much.

And Paul. He had always believed in her. And they had always helped each other, in business and in bed. But now she was worried. More than a year ago, a stolen piece of art was found in Paul's *sacred* schoolroom. So far, the authorities didn't know about Paul. But Roxie had to do serious damage control with the members of his class, *explaining* that Paul didn't know the piece was stolen and cutting some deals to assure their loyalty. And then. Paula DeVong wanted more.

Paula, why were you so greedy?

Roxie set her drink down and pulled open the large sliding window. The double-pane glass was six-foot square but easily slid on a track that ran outside the adjacent window. There had been a safety limiter on the frame, but she had removed it so it could be opened the full six-foot width. Roxie had no fear of heights, and she sat comfortably on the edge of the wide wood sill that ran the length of the windows. She felt the warm air against her body. She gazed to the north where a bit of the distant George Washington Bridge could be seen. To the south she could see some of the piers where holiday ocean liners docked. A year ago, that industry had been shut down completely. But in the past few months, there had been a resurgence of passengers determined to ignore the lingering pandemic for the sake of a vacation cruise.

Roxie looked west at the wide Hudson River. Running the length of the near bank was the West Side Highway: four lanes of never-ending traffic on massive raised trestles. Even with the window closed, there was always a persistent hum of cars thirty stories down. But with the window open, the sound came up in a surprising constant roar. Roxie smiled sadly. She had gotten used to it all. She had loved it here. Loved what she'd achieved, who she'd become. Until now. She looked across the room at the Ernst painting.

She heard the bathroom door open, and Paul came in wrapped only in a towel from the waist down. She looked at his muscular wet body, handsome and unique lavender eyes. She walked slowly to him. "I need to know," she said distinctly, "how could this have happened?"

"I don't know," he answered calmly, turned away, and poured himself a drink at the bar. "Did you get the box?"

"No," she answered, "it wasn't there. I searched everywhere."

Paul's eyes flashed with anger. Then he recovered himself and turned back to her. "Would she take it with her?"

"I don't think so."

"Well, maybe she threw it out," he said reasonably. "The trash was empty?"

"Yes."

Paul took a sip of his drink and shrugged. "Then it's gone."

"Let's hope so," Roxie said uncertainly.

Paul put his glass down and moved close to her. "Know what we need right now?" He ran his hands slowly across her hips, unbuckled her belt and unzipped her pants. "I've been missing you so much," he said huskily.

"When in doubt"—she smiled and unbuttoned her shirt—"there's nothing like a good fuck." Paul laughed. She pulled off her clothes and revealed her perfectly proportioned body. She unsnapped her bra, dropped it, and stood naked before him, except for her ruby pendant necklace.

He pulled at his towel and let it fall to the floor.

"I see you really have been missing me," she said admiringly.

Paul reached up, and carefully wrapped his fingers around the red gem hanging on her chest. "Thank you for everything you do for me," he said. He knelt down, held her hips with his hands, and started gently kissing her. As his tongue slowly penetrated her, Roxie let her head fall back and let out a deep moan.

*　*　*

Taki Fukuda was starting to like this place. The sun was warm, and his big wood chair on the shaded porch was comfortable. He heard a cry of a seagull and scanned the lawns that sloped down to the little boat dock and the wide ocean waters beyond. There was something he seemed to be forgetting. Something about the seagulls. He turned his head and forced himself to focus on the IV bag hanging on the pole next to his left arm. The bag was almost empty.

Ah... I remember. That's to keep me from remembering.

He giggled at his own joke. The seagull called again, and Taki tipped his face up to search for it.

There was a time when Taki cared about his appearance. But now, if he could see himself, he wouldn't know who he was. Once he had been pleasantly plump, carefully coiffed, and always dressed in a dandified gentlemanly fashion suitable for a high-end shopkeeper. But now he looked older than his sixty-five years, his face thinner and sallow; his blond hairweave was still attached to his head, but it was matted and off-center. He couldn't remember what had happened to his favorite madras plaid sports jacket. Or his powder blue pants. Now he was always in the same plaid pajamas and a white cotton waffle-weave bathrobe. On the chest pocket of the robe was a logo and a name: *St. Anthony's Hospital, Gilmore Island, CT.*

"What's black and white and brings me an IV?" Taki muttered to himself as he saw the old nun coming out of the terrace doors. Wearing a long old-fashioned habit, she was walking slowly toward him using a wood cane for support. Taki was trying to see her clearly, but the effect of his medicine was making him so sleepy.

"Sister Mary Horrendous," he joked carefully as she got nearer.

"And how are you today, Mr. Fukuda?" She looked down at him. The fierceness of her dark eyes and hawklike nose made him wince.

"Taki," he said mildly for the millionth time. "Everyone calls me Taki."

The old nun looked up and saw a very fat man in his mid-thirties coming across the lawns toward them. As he got nearer, she could see his shirt was wet with sweat and sticking to his body.

"Nice to see you again, Nicolas. No one told me I'd be having a visitor today," she said guardedly.

"The world is full of surprises," Nicky said as he sat down in the large Adirondack chair next to Taki.

"It's too hot. And it's been a long night," he wheezed.

The old nun sat down on the other side of Taki and saw that he had fallen asleep, his chin resting on his chest. She raised her small dark eyes up and said, "Anything in particular I can do for you?"

"For me? No," Nicky said and turned to look at the wide lawn set with chairs and the ocean beyond. "It's so peaceful here. You can ignore all the troubles in the world beyond."

"It suits me," the old woman said.

Nicky looked at Taki. He poked at the nearly empty IV bag that fed his arm. "So, how long do you think you can keep feeding this shit to sleeping fairy here?"

"A while yet," she answered evenly.

"Until when?"

"Until the world revolves again and things grow calm."

"That might take a long time." Nicky laughed.

"Why?" she asked sharply. "What's happened?"

Nicky wiped the sweat from the back of his neck with his fleshy hand and smiled at her. "The world has revolved, I guess."

The old nun sat quietly sizing him up. "And how is your grand-mother, Nicolas?"

"Still as scary as ever."

"I always liked her," she said.

"And she likes you." He smiled. "But no one lives forever."

The old woman just watched him.

"You know," Nicky said disparagingly, "I never got why you ran away and became this." He waved a hand at her nun's habit. "Are you even religious?"

"In my way, I suppose," she answered. "Why? Do you need me to pray for you?"

Nicky felt the danger behind her gentle words. "I always thought that you should have been the one in charge of your family. You would have been the best of them." With an effort, he pushed himself up out of his chair.

"Nice to see you again, Nicolas," she said.

"And you, *Khloe*," he answered. "I'll tell my grandmother you said hello. She'll be glad to know that you are still safe and sound after all these years."

Nicky walked away down the porch steps and across the lawn.

The old woman leaned back in her chair. It had been many years since anyone had called her by her real name, Khloe. And she understood what it meant. She looked over at Taki who was snoring. She had wondered when this moment would come. And now that it was here, she felt utterly too old and unprepared for it.

*   *   *

It was two minutes past nine and the live program was just underway. The TVNews studio looked much the same as it had the night before. Only this night, Moira Weyland was sitting in the white leather chair behind the sleek curved desk.

"We here at TVNews find it hard to accept that Paula DeVong is dead. The shock we feel is still overwhelming. We all miss our friend so much."

A graphic of Paula's face filled the on-air monitors. Greg and Deni stood together watching from the back of the studio.

Greg leaned close and whispered, "Good old Paula, we miss her so much." He rolled his eyes.

"If she could see Moira sitting in her chair, taking over her show…" Deni whispered back. "Maybe a lightning bolt will come down and kill her on-air. Now, that would be newsworthy."

"It would certainly help the ratings." Greg chuckled.

In his office on the ninth floor, Calvin Prons was lounging on a sofa watching the broadcast. As Moira's young earnest face filled the screen and she started to list the many achievements of her fallen comrade, he picked up a phone and hit a button.

In the darkened control room, a small red light on the phone in front of Roxie flashed noiselessly. She lifted it up and spoke softly so as to not distract the staff working the show.

"Yes Calvin?"

"The kid is good," Calvin pronounced. "Tell her I said so."

"I will. She'll be very grateful."

"Good. I like grateful," Calvin said. "Let's keep her that way, okay. We don't need another pain-in-the-ass prima donna like Paula."

Roxie was surprised by his tone. Roxie knew, because Paula had told her, that she and Calvin had been secretly dating each other for months. But as always, Roxie kept her voice obsequious.

"Right, Calvin, I understand. I think we can go a long way with Moira. I'll keep her in hand."

"Good. Thanks, Roxie," he said.

Roxie hung up the phone. The producer's station was a row behind and above where the director sat with her staff in front of a wall of monitors. The show was just coming back on-air after a commercial break. Roxie looked to her left where Jock was reclining in his high-back command chair, his feet up on the console, his arms folded across his chest, and a glazed look in his eyes.

"Calvin is pleased with Moira," she said.

"Whoop-de-do," he murmured sarcastically, his eyes still fixed on the wall of monitors.

Roxie ignored him. She knew that Jock would soon be gone. And she knew who would replace him. She smiled.

One flight above, the newsroom was empty. Most of the staff was gathered in the conference room watching the show or down in the studio working. Anna peeked out of her office cubicle. She held a small box hidden behind her back. Satisfied that no one would notice her, she went over to the glass wall of Paula's office and tried to look in, but the interior blinds were closed. She went to the door and tried to open it, but it was locked. The police had been in there for most of the day, and she was worried. Anna bit her lower lip and retreated quickly into her office and soundlessly closed the door.

*　*　*

Artemis sat decompressing from his earlier excursion out in the real world. He had always loved this room—the little study on the first floor in the front of Drew's brownstone. He was twelve when he first moved here to Brooklyn. Back then the shelves were full of books: adventure stories that his older cousin Drew loved, histories and biographies that his uncle Mathew poked through, and art books and museum magazines that were his aunt Muriel's favorites. Since her death some fifteen years ago, the old house had changed very little. Except in this room. These days Drew read mostly police reports on her tablet, and Mathew had moved the books down to his place in Florida. The shelves now had lots of framed photos of Drew and her parents and the places they had visited years ago.

Artemis smiled at his uncle Mathew sitting in his old leather chair, starting to fall asleep with a newspaper on his lap. Mathew, a retired NYPD captain, had come back to Brooklyn to help protect them. Artemis sipped his single malt and looked out the window. It was dark, but under the street-lights, he could see two cops sitting in a parked patrol car. He wondered if they would still be on the job if Drew wasn't so highly regarded on the force.

Two sedans pulled up in front of the house. FBI agent Steve Filipowski, known to his friends as Flip, got out of the lead car and scanned the area. He looked toward the second car, and a tall woman wearing a COVID mask got out of the street-side back door. Drew Sweeney had a powerful build and an aggressively handsome face which was balanced by her kind, intelligent eyes. She was dressed, as usual, in dark pants and a crisp white dress shirt, which fit the military precision of her movements as she came around the car and opened the curbside back door.

Silas Bookbinder put away his cell, stepped out, pulled off his mask, and pushed his glasses back into place on his nose. He saw his father looking at him through the window and smiled. In the year and a half since his mother died, Silas had grown a foot taller, but he was still very thin. His pale face had grown more handsome and his brown eyes keener. His understanding of himself and time had changed. His fourteenth birthday was a couple of days ago. Aunt Delia had made a cake. Silas looked up at the four-story brownstone. He would miss living here. Drew escorted Silas up the front steps.

"See you guys tomorrow," Flip called as he got back into his car.

They waved and went into the house. Drew pulled off her mask and followed Silas into the study.

"Artemis, I just saw something on my cell," Silas said as he picked up the remote, turned on the television, and flipped the channels. "It's important."

"You guys are home late," Mathew said as he woke up in his chair.

"It's only nine thirty," Drew said to her father as she sat down on the sofa. She looked to Artemis. "How'd you do today?"

"Not too bad," he answered.

Silas found TVNews and turned up the volume. The image was from an overhead camera at night: a woman lying on a sidewalk and people walking past her. Moira Weyland's clear voice said:

"Paula DeVong collapsed and died on a Manhattan sidewalk late last night a few blocks from this studio. She was only thirty-eight years old. She lay on that sidewalk unaided for a little more than a half hour before a good Samaritan finally called for help." The image on the screen dissolved to Moira's sympathetic face. "It is believed that Paula died of a stroke, a complication from COVID."

Moira paused, pushed her scripted pages away, and looked directly into the camera. "When something like this happens, we can only wonder about how much time there is for any one of us. We shouldn't waste a second of the life we have."

"It's about time you two showed up," Delia said loudly to Drew as she came in, wiping her hands on a dishtowel. She turned to see what they were watching. "What's up?"

"Paula DeVong, the newscaster, was found dead on a street last night," Silas explained as a commercial came on for one of the vaccine companies. He hit the mute button.

"What did she die of?" Delia asked Silas.

"COVID. A stroke," he answered factually.

Delia was still a strong force of a woman in her sixties. Since they moved to Brooklyn, she had gained a little more weight, her hair was more gray than brown, and her wide forehead showed more wrinkles.

"Poor woman," Delia said as she sat on the sofa near Drew.

When Delia Twist Kouris's husband died some five years ago, she had come to live with the Bookbinders in New Jersey. There she did most of the housekeeping, cleaning, and cooking and the family had come to love and depend on her. But it was her support and stability in the past year that Artemis was most grateful for.

"There it is again," Artemis mused and took a sip of his drink. "There's something about TVNews...," he trailed off. It had been a long time since Artemis had been able to think about what had happened and not shut down. For so many months, he had been on a strange path lost in a fog of fear and guilt.

"You know those people, right?" Mathew asked, his benevolent eyes watching Artemis carefully. Like Drew, Mathew remembered how Artemis had struggled and recovered from a collapse when he was a boy.

"I know Moira a little. She covered the Gardner pieces we've found. She's okay." Artemis's eyes grew distant. "But I never met Paula DeVong. Strange way to die." He looked to Silas and asked, "Have you heard of anyone dying from a stroke relating to COVID?"

"No," Silas said. "But I'll check it out."

"Thanks." As usual these days, Artemis felt like he was conferring with a colleague when he spoke with his son.

"I doubt there's been enough time for an autopsy yet," Drew said. "This Delta thing is keeping us all busy."

"Can't you put somebody on it?" Mathew asked his daughter, speaking with a knowing from his many years on the force.

"Yeah." She smiled. "I'll ask Clayton to see what he can do."

The program resumed and a picture of Paula wearing her trademark pendant necklace filled the screen. Artemis's eyes focused on the large, clear pink gemstone.

"Well, that's enough news of the day for me," Delia said as she took the remote from Silas and turned off the television. "You both did have dinner, right?" she asked Drew.

"Yep." She smiled. "NYPD's finest donuts." Silas laughed a little.

"Oh no…," Delia started to protest, but Drew stopped her.

"Of course, we did. We had some burgers at that little place on Third."

"*Eat Good Here.*" Silas shrugged. "Weird name."

"But good food." The wrinkles on Mathew's face deepened as he smiled in remembrance. "We used to love going to that place. Nice to know it's still there."

"Well, okay," Delia said as she stood up. "I'll make us all some herbal tea." She looked to Silas. "No coffee tonight. We have a big day tomorrow and you'll need a good night's sleep."

"Yes, Auntie," Silas answered. She was actually his mother's aunt, but to Silas it was all the same.

"I've got us all packed and ready," she stated. "And Drew's people will be here at 10:00 a.m. prompt to escort us to Manhattan." She was smiling, but it sounded like an order.

"Absolutely," Drew confirmed.

"Thank you, Delia," Artemis said sincerely, "for doing everything. As always."

"Love is doing," she said with her customary jovial force and turned to go.

Artemis wasn't sure if this was one of her AA slogans, it was sometimes hard to tell. But he smiled and said, "So, you're saying that you love us?"

Delia stopped at the door, barked out a short laugh, and pronounced, "Silas, I love. You, I love putting up with." With that, she left.

Artemis grinned. It was as close as he was going to get. And he was grateful.

Silas's phone pinged with a text.

"It's from Ray," he reported.

"He's up kinda early," Mathew said looking at the clock on the mantel. "What time would it be in Italy right now?"

"Quarter to four in the morning," Silas answered as he read the message.

"Where is he now?" Mathew asked.

"Still in Livorno," Silas said as he looked to Artemis.

"Anything?" Artemis asked distantly. He and Ray Gaines hadn't spoken to each other in over a year. Once, the senior FBI agent had been one of Artemis's closest friends. They had worked together on the Gardner Museum robbery since Artemis was a boy. A year and a half ago, they had recovered two of the stolen thirteen pieces. Then everything went wrong. And Artemis still blamed Ray Gaines.

"No," Silas answered. "Nothing yet."

"He'll never find him," Artemis muttered.

"Why not?" Drew asked.

"Just a feeling," Artemis said and drained his glass.

Chapter Two

Friday, July 16th, 2021

It was almost five in the morning in Livorno and still dark out. Ray put his cell phone aside and picked up a newspaper from the bedside table. The Italian papers were optimistic that COVID was weakening. Summer tourism had come back, and the economy was doing better. But there were worrying reports about the Delta variant numbers growing in several regions.

He sighed and tossed the paper on the floor. Ray rubbed his weathered face with his hands. He was tired but couldn't sleep. The room in the little pensione was comfortable enough. It was the sort of place that Ray had always liked when he traveled: clean, simple, and quiet. The night air had cooled enough for him to open the window, and from his bed, he could see across the low walls and buildings of the old medieval town and beyond the glimmer of freight ships being unloaded at the commercial docks.

Ray was frustrated. Because of the pandemic, it had taken a year before he was granted permission to come to Italy to look for Bert Rocca, and by the time he arrived in mid-June, the trail was very cold.

They had been able to confirm that Rocca boarded a large container ship that left Port Newark, New Jersey, the night of Emily Bookbinder's murder, March 5th, 2020. Three weeks later, that ship docked and was unloaded in Livorno. The ship's records showed no passengers. The crew denied that Rocca was ever on board. But Ray had spent days walking the vast docks showing Rocca's photo to longshoremen. Several people said they saw a man matching his description getting off the ship. With the help of Interpol and local authorities, Ray had been given access to security camera footage of the docks for the time in question, but nothing concrete emerged.

Ray leaned back against the headboard. He had trusted Bert Rocca, a man he had worked with for over forty years. But now he realized how little he had known him. He didn't know why Bert had come to Italy. He had no traceable family here. Ray didn't know what his connection was to the cargo ship he'd escaped on. Interpol had traced the owners of the ship to a corporation headquartered in Croatia and filed an official protest. Ray knew how pointless that was. And that his time was running out.

He had twice been able to defer his retirement because he was the lead investigator on the Gardner Museum robbery. But in the fall, he would turn sixty-five and his FBI career would most certainly be over.

He closed his eyes. He felt old and his body was tired. When he got in last night, the elderly woman who ran the pensione had smiled at him with pity. That bothered him. He started to drift off to sleep.

A sound of scuffing paper somewhere woke him up. He turned on the light and saw that an envelope had been slipped under the wood door of his room. He got out of bed with a soft groan, got the envelope, unlocked the door, and looked down the hallway. No one was there. Ray closed and locked the door and went to the open window. He looked down four stories to the entrance of the pensione. A young man in dark clothing came out and jogged away down the deserted stone street and disappeared through an opening in a wall built by the Medici five hundred years ago.

Ray sat on the edge of the bed near the light, opened the envelope, and pulled out a typed letter. Across the top of the page was a company letterhead: *Karlovic Worldwide*. It was the corporation that owned the cargo ship Bert Rocca had escaped on sixteen months ago. Embossed above the name was a curious symbol of a three-headed serpent. Ray registered the image before he read the letter. It was a request for a meeting in Croatia, with travel details and a hotel reservation. Ray pulled out of the envelope an airline voucher for a charter flight from Pisa.

The letter then set out specific terms. There were conditions that had to be agreed to, and in return, information would be given in regard to the location of FBI agent Bert Rocca. The letter was signed by Andre Karlovic.

Ray reread the letter. He got his cell phone, found a number, and pushed it.

"Sorry to call you so late, Sir," Ray said. "But something's come up and I'll need your approval."

Three hours later, Ray sat in a private jet looking out the window as they headed out over the eastern coast of Italy. The morning was clear, and far below he could see the ferry boat leaving Ancona heading out on the wide calm blue waters of the Adriatic. He smiled to think that it was a nine-hour passage by boat to Croatia but he would be landing in Dubrovnik in fifty minutes.

He wondered about this meeting and why Andre Karlovic was suddenly so eager to be helpful. And Ray wondered if, after all this time, Bert Rocca was still alive.

*   *   *

In New York, the morning news had reports about the governor's sexual harassment inquiry, wildfires on the West Coast, and warnings that the numbers of virus cases across the country were again on the rise.

It was another hot, muggy morning in Manhattan. Delia took out her new keys and opened the door to apartment 18-18 of the Ansonia.

"God bless all who live here," she said ceremoniously as she pulled off her COVID mask and entered. Silas and Agent Filipowski followed her in and pulled off their masks.

"This is really beautiful," Flip said appreciatively.

"Check out my room," Silas said as he led the way to a door halfway down the hall.

"I'm going to start in the kitchen," Delia announced to Artemis and Drew as they came in. She marched off with purpose. Artemis walked in a few steps across the black-and-white marble floor. He carefully reached up a nitrile-gloved hand and pulled off his mask. He slowly let the cool filtered air into his lungs. Drew watched him as she closed and locked the front door. She took off her mask.

"How's it going over there, Artie?" she asked quietly.

"I hate it," Artemis said, "when you call me that, Mary Drew."

"Say that again," she taunted back, "and I'm gonna have to sneeze on you, germ-boy." For a second, Drew thought she'd gone too far. Artemis's jaw tightened and he looked worried. Then he laughed at himself.

"Germs from you would probably only make me stronger," he said.

"They might." Drew smiled.

"Will you give me a hand unpacking?"

"You bet," she said and followed him down the gleaming white hallway.

"Nice finish on the walls. I don't remember that."

"The painter did a white marble effect by brush," Artemis explained as he led her into his office. "And then finished it with a few coats of clear wax. Makes it look like Venetian plaster."

"I like it," Drew said as she looked around at the piles of sealed boxes. She took out her Swiss army knife and flipped it open. "I'll cut 'em and you unpack. God knows by now, I've learned not to touch your stuff, especially the books."

"Thanks," Artemis said, and they got to work.

"That's nice." Flip was looking out the large six-over-six wood windows in Silas's room. Framed by the ornate exterior walls was an impressive open city view looking south. "How long has it been since you guys lived here?"

"About seven, maybe eight years," Silas said as he took some boxes off his desk.

"Good to be back?"

"I guess." Silas sat at his desk, pushed his glasses back into place, and started setting up his laptop. There was something familiar about sitting here, how the light came through the windows and the vague sounds of traffic so far below. And then, like a whisper in his ear, Silas remembered a voice. His mother was calling his name. She was off in the kitchen maybe, just down the hall. Then as suddenly as it came, it went away and he felt so alone.

Flip sat on the edge of the bed.

"Are you okay?" he asked.

"Yes," Silas answered.

"Maybe we could go out for a run. There's a track in the park near here."

"I remember that." Silas smiled a little. "But it's too hot out. Maybe later, when it cools down. Besides, Delia will want us to help her with the unpacking."

"Flip!" Delia called loudly in a tone of friendly command. "I could use your help in the kitchen."

"It's like she heard you." Flip smiled and headed for the door. "On my way," he called back.

Silas sat looking up through the windows at the blue sky above. When he was little, he and his mother used to play a game naming the animals they saw in the shapes of passing clouds. He'd forgotten that until just now. But the sky above was blue and clear without a cloud in sight.

In his office, Artemis pulled a thick pile of folders from a box. He cleared some space on his oak desk and began sorting them by date.

"Your father's files?" Drew asked as she cut open some boxes piled on the curved window seat.

"Yes." Artemis sat at his desk and looked at the stacks of records and notes, all of which were about a still unsolved case: the 1990 robbery of the Gardner Museum in Boston. His father's last case had become an obsession for Artemis. He pulled off his nitrile gloves and carefully rested his hands on the paperwork.

So much history. So much pain.

In the kitchen, the house phone rang.

"If you could put those cups up there," Delia said as she pointed to the top green-glass shelf, "that would be a great help."

"No problem," Flip answered amiably and started to unpack a box sitting on the stainless-steel countertop. This definitely wasn't part of Agent Filipowski's job description. He was there to protect Silas. But he didn't mind helping out where he could.

"Hello?" Delia answered and listened. "Yes, send her up. Thank you." She hung up and went out to Artemis's office. She leaned in the doorway. "Leah's coming up."

"Thanks," Artemis said.

"You both look like you're working hard," she said surveying the mess of packing paper and opened boxes on the floor between Drew and Artemis. "How about a cup of tea?"

"Sure, thanks," Drew answered for both of them, and Delia went down the hall to the front door. She unlocked it and looked out. An older woman with white hair rounded the corner. She was wearing a mask and heavy glasses, but her smile was obvious by the deep wrinkles around her keen eyes.

"Hello, Delia. My, what a place this is," Leah Carras said warmly as she stepped into the apartment and Delia closed and locked the door. Leah had helped Artemis when he was twelve years old and couldn't face the world. She had come out of retirement to help him again.

"Thanks for coming," Artemis said as he came down the hall, stopping some six feet away.

"My pleasure," Leah said.

"Please." Artemis gestured. "Take off your mask."

She pulled the mask off her ears and breathed in. "Such nice cool air in here. Do you know what's so wrong about everything out there?" She waved vaguely at the world beyond the walls. "We've been told to be afraid to breathe. And that can't be right."

"I'm glad you're here," Artemis said simply.

"Me too," Leah answered.

"I'm making a pot of tea. Care for some?" Delia asked her.

"No, thanks. I'm too hot for tea. But maybe a glass of water, if you don't mind."

"Coming right up," Delia said with her usual verve, and she marched off down the hall.

"Hey, Leah." Silas was smiling as he came out of his room. He had never been told about how she'd helped his father when he was a boy. Silas only met her last year after everything had gone wrong. At first, he wasn't too sure about her. But Artemis was getting better and he knew it was largely because of Leah's support. "So, what do you think of this place?"

"It's amazing," she answered. "How are you liking being back in your old home?"

Silas looked up at his father and answered, "It's fine. It'll be good for us."

"I agree," Artemis said.

"Silas, would you mind showing me around?" Leah smiled. "I want to see everything."

"I'll get back to work, then," Artemis said gratefully and walked back to his office.

"This is Delia's room." Silas led Leah into the yellow-and-purple decor.

"Very... enthusiastic," Leah said gently. "And I love the curved bay windows and seat."

"All the rooms on this side have that," Silas explained as he stepped back out into the hall.

"This is my room," he said as they walked in.

"I like where your desk is. You get a nice look at the city when you sit here." Leah wandered over to the bed where several large cardboard boxes had been opened but not yet unpacked. "What's all this?" she asked curiously as she lifted up an old photo album.

"Things that belonged to my mother," Silas explained as he came over. He lightly ran his fingers across an old green shoebox tied with a string. "She kept some stuff from when she was a child."

"That's nice." The old woman smiled. "Have you looked at these things much?"

"No," Silas admitted, "I haven't. I wanted to, but..."

"That's okay," Leah said kindly. "But someday you might."

Delia came in with a tall glass of water. "There's no ice yet, but it's filtered."

"Thank you, Delia," Leah said as she took the glass. "I think you all will be very happy here."

"Come, see the rest of the place," Delia said proudly as she took over the tour.

Drew looked out the window in Artemis's office. The view to the west was blocked by a taller building. "If you have to look out at a building, this one's kinda beautiful," she said.

"The Level Club," Artemis explained as he organized his books and put them up on the built-in shelves. "Neo-Romanesque. Built in 1927 by the Freemasons as a men's club and residence. Like this place, it's gone through a lot. It's a condo now."

Drew studied the elegant terraces on the floors below and was satisfied that they were not a security threat. She looked to the left and could see a bit of the sidewalk and street eighteen floors down. She smiled as she saw Mak Kim get out of an official-looking car and greet one of the uniformed cops on patrol.

Artemis's cell phone rang. He picked it up off the desk and checked the caller ID.

"Hello, this is Artemis."

"Hi. This is Moira Weyland. I know it's been a long time, but I hope you remember me."

"Of course I do, Moira. How are you?" Artemis sat down in his desk chair and looked to Drew. She stopped working and sat on the window seat interested. Artemis put the phone on speaker so she could hear.

"I'm well enough." Moira walked out of the TVNews building and quickly crossed Columbus Avenue.

"We saw your show last night," Artemis said. "You were great."

"Thanks." She spoke a little louder as she turned north on Broadway where the midmorning traffic was heavier and the sidewalk full of fast-walking New Yorkers ever eager to get somewhere. "So, Artemis, I wondered if you might have a minute to talk with me about something."

"Sorry, I'm not doing any interviews anymore," Artemis said as he grinned at Drew. "But I can hook you up with someone if you like. I think Detective Drew Sweeney would love to talk with you."

Drew gave him a one-finger salute.

"No, Artemis. I want to talk with you off the record. I have something to give you." Moira stopped outside a coffeeshop at 69th Street. She looked around to make sure no one was overhearing.

"Okay," Artemis said. "What's on your mind?"

"Not over the phone," she answered.

"Well." Artemis felt panic in his chest, but he pushed it away and said, "I suppose I could meet you at TVNews."

"No," Moira said loudly as an ambulance's siren got closer. "But could I come see you in Brooklyn?"

"No, we're not living there anymore. We've moved back to Manhattan. In fact, we're just unpacking right now."

"Where in Manhattan?" she asked as the ambulance sped by heading uptown.

"The Ansonia." Artemis heard the siren through his phone. And he heard the same siren somewhere outside getting closer. "Moira, where are you?"

"I have always loved that building," Moira said as she turned and looked. The ambulance was just passing the block-long beaux arts facade of the Ansonia. "I'm on Broadway a few blocks south of you. I could come see you right now, if it's all right."

Artemis could hear the urgency in her voice. But his mind was overloading with worry about the pandemic. "No. Not here. I'd... rather be outside. What about the park?"

"Sure," Moira answered. "Central or Riverside?"

"Riverside," Artemis said. "You know the running track near 73rd Street?"

"Yes," she said. "When?"

"I can be there in ten minutes."

"Thank you, Artemis. I'll see you there soon," she said and hung up.

Drew saw the strain in Artemis's eyes. "Mak is downstairs with my guys. You'll have protection."

"I'm not worried about that," Artemis said truthfully. "I just don't know if I want to do this anymore."

"You don't know what she's got. Maybe it's not related to anything," Drew said.

"That's true." Artemis sighed and stood up to go.

"Wait," Drew said as she came over to him. "Where's your gun?" A year ago, with Drew's help, Artemis had become a licensed private investigator so he could legally carry a weapon again.

"It's right here." Artemis pulled out his keys, unlocked a lower drawer in his desk, and opened it. It was empty. "Oh, right." He reached down, got his briefcase off the floor, and pulled out a pistol.

"It's gonna come in handy in your briefcase," Drew said as she took the gun and examined it with military precision. "Where's the clip?" she asked.

"Here," Artemis said as he reached into the briefcase and pulled it out. Drew took it from him and started to load the pistol, but Artemis stopped her.

"Don't. I'm not taking that thing."

"Why not?" she asked. "How is carrying this any different from when you were a cop?"

"Exactly," Artemis answered. "I'm not a cop anymore and haven't wanted to be for a long time."

Drew considered. She handed the unloaded gun and clip back to him. He put them in the lower drawer and locked it.

"I'll take you downstairs," Drew said supportively.

"I can't get over how far you can see." Leah was smiling as she and Delia stood in the living room bank of windows looking south across the open city view.

"So, will you still be coming to work with Artemis? He seems so much better," Delia asked quietly.

"Yes, for a while," Leah said.

"At least your commute got easier. Did you really walk here today?" Delia sounded impressed.

"Yes, it's not far. I'm just six blocks up on Columbus. Though, it was a little hotter out than I expected."

"You've been there a long time?"

"Oh, yes," Leah said. "The apartment belonged to my father, and I inherited it. So, you do the math." She laughed a little. "I've been there forever."

Delia leaned closer and whispered, "And you're near the place where Artemis's parents were killed."

"Yes, God bless them," Leah said. "And that's a reason, too, why I'll keep coming to see Artemis for a while."

A movement in a window of the top floor of the taller building across the street and to the right caught Delia's eye. But when she looked, no one was there.

"I'm going out for a while," Artemis said as he and Drew came in.

Leah turned and met his eyes. "Good. It's a nice day for a walk," she said approvingly.

Artemis smiled a little and started for the door.

"I'll be right back," Drew said to Agent Filipowski as she followed Artemis out.

Drew and Artemis put on their masks and left the apartment, locking the door behind them. As they walked down the wide public hallway, Drew texted an alert to Mak and her team outside, and Artemis pulled on a fresh pair of blue nitrile gloves. Drew thought this was serious overkill, but she loved Artemis and anything he needed to do to help himself face the world again was all right by her.

They took the elevator down to the lobby and headed for the 73rd exit. Drew went first through the revolving door and looked around. She saw her officers and Mak nearby. Satisfied, she turned back to Artemis, and he pushed his way outside. He was surprised how dense and hot the air was. And how breathing through a mask took so much more effort.

"I hear we're taking a walk?" Mak said agreeably as he neared, his voice a bit muffled under his mask.

"Yes," Artemis confirmed.

"Call me if you need anything," Drew said.

"I will." Artemis turned west toward the park. He looked down the sidewalk. It was hot, and there was no one to be seen between the row of parked cars and the fronts of the buildings.

I have the right to breathe.

With a determined effort, he willed himself forward. Mak walked with him, giving him as much room as he could on the sidewalk. With a nod from Drew, one of the uniformed cops followed them at a distance. Drew watched them go for a while, then she returned back inside the Ansonia.

Mak walked with Artemis in silence until they got to West End Avenue. As they waited for the light to change, he said, "Ask you something?"

"Sure."

Mak was reassured to hear the calm in his voice. "Why haven't you been vaccinated?" He spoke without challenge. "Wouldn't it make it a lot easier to go outside if you knew that your body had some defense against this thing?"

The light changed, and they walked on. "It might"—Artemis sounded faraway—"if I accepted that. Silas has done a great deal of research and we have... concerns."

"Then he's been talking to Ray for sure," Mak said laughing a little. "He doesn't trust the vaccines either."

"But he must have gotten a shot by now," Artemis said. "Doesn't the agency require it?"

"Not yet," Mak said. "But they will soon. In the meantime, it's been recommended, let's say very strongly, that we get with the program. And I'm certain that Ray's been vaccinated or they never would've let him travel to Italy."

As they crossed Riverside Drive and turned south heading for the park entrance, Artemis asked with curiosity, "Have you been vaccinated?"

"Yes," Mak answered. "But I kind of wish I hadn't. I don't really know what they injected in me. I wish there'd been more time for testing."

"I understand that," Artemis said. "I'm the guy who once got a flu shot and got so sick that I couldn't stand up for a week."

They entered the park at 72nd Street and walked past a bronze statue of Eleanor Roosevelt set in a round raised bed of ivy. Artemis pointed and laughed a little. Someone had put a COVID mask on the statue's face.

"She was a free thinker," Artemis said. "I wonder what she would have said about mandating vaccines."

"Might have supported it," Mak offered. "She believed that government had a responsibility to help the people."

They walked past a fenced dog run, where a few people had brought their pets to let them run free. But it was so hot, the dogs were just lying together under the shade of a bench while the owners stood chatting.

With the cop still following them at a distance, Mak and Artemis walked through an arched tunnel that ran under the West Side Highway.

Then they descended a long flight of stone steps that still looked much as it had when the park was built in 1874. A little way along, they came to an oval running track with a few rows of stone benches set into a hill on one side. On the other side was a fence that protected the track from the paved path running beside the wide waters of the Hudson River.

Artemis sat on the top stone bench and Mak sat to his left six feet away. The cop who had followed them found a place to stand in the shade of some trees at one end of the track. Though the path by the river was crowded with bikers, runners, and tourists taking pictures, the track area was deserted, as Artemis had hoped it would be.

"I used to come here to run when I was a kid," Artemis said. "They used to keep it in better shape."

"You lived near here?" Mak asked.

"Yes, just a few blocks away." Artemis looked out at the river and to the Jersey cliffs beyond. "Would you mind," he said, "if we took our masks off? We'll be able to breathe better."

Mak pulled off his mask and smiled easily at his friend. "It's a great idea."

Artemis took off his mask and pulled off his gloves. His hands were red and wet. "That's better," he said and took a cautious breath. He rubbed his hands together to dry them. "Thanks for talking about the vaccine. And for not making me feel like the enemy."

"Not a problem," Mak said genuinely. "There's too much argument going on everywhere."

Artemis saw Moira approaching from the path by the river. She walked past the cop, and Artemis waved to let him know that she was all right. Moira saw him and smiled. She was dressed for the heat in white cotton, her curly red hair kept back with a headband, and she wore no face mask.

"Nice to see your faces," she said as she neared. "Personally, I don't think wearing a mask does anything to stop the germs."

"Just the same," Artemis said quickly, "social distancing is still a good idea."

Moira noticed the urgency in his eyes. "Absolutely." She sat on a bench a comfortable distance away.

"Though you may be right about masks," Artemis said. "We wear them but I can still tell if someone's had garlic last night, what perfume they're wearing, or"— he turned to Mak—"if they've just had a cigarette."

"Damn." Mak shook his head and smiled. "Busted."

"Nice to see you again, Agent Kim," Moira said. "I didn't know you'd be here."

"I asked Mak to come along," Artemis said. "He watches out for me."

Moira understood. "I was so very sorry to hear of your loss, Professor," she said sympathetically.

Artemis nodded once.

"I can give you guys some space if you like," Mak said as he started to get up.

"No." Moira stopped him. "You're going to want to know about this too." Mak looked interested. "But you both have to promise that this is off the record."

"Yes," Artemis agreed.

"Okay," Mak said.

"Thank you." Moira dropped her head and breathed out. "Where to begin?"

"Is this about Paula DeVong's death?" Artemis asked.

"Yes," Moira said as she looked up. "And about your wife's death too."

For the first time in a long while, Artemis's eyes came alive with a cool fire.

She dug into her bag and pulled out a flash drive. "I'd lose my job if they found out I gave you this." She held the drive out to Artemis. He examined it uncertainly. Then Mak reached over and took it from her.

"What's on it?" Mak asked.

"It's a copy of footage we got from the overhead security camera showing Paula lying dead on the street."

"Yes," Artemis said, "I saw it on your show last night."

"You only saw a piece of it," Moira continued. "Paula lay dead or dying on the sidewalk before anyone tried to help her. This is the footage of the only person who did. I might be wrong, but I think it's Lucille Orsina, the woman you're looking for in connection with your wife's death."

Artemis sat still taking this in.

"Why didn't you show that part?" Mak asked.

"I wanted to," Moira said emphatically. "But I was told that I was probably wrong and not to cause trouble for an innocent bystander."

"That sounds proper." Mak shrugged.

"Wait." Artemis looked up sharply. "Who said you couldn't show it?"

Moira smiled a little nervously. "That's the point. Calvin Prons wouldn't allow it."

"Lucille's ex-husband." Artemis considered. "Did he recognize her?"

"Yes, he did," Moira said. "We were all in his office yesterday looking at the footage. There was Paula on the ground and people just walking by. Maybe they thought she was drunk or maybe they thought she had the virus. Whatever. But I looked at Calvin, and it seemed like he was smiling. It was so weird. So, as the footage played, I kept an eye on him. And when Lucille appeared about a half hour after Paula fell, there's a moment when she looks up and I am certain he saw what I did. It was her. And I only know that face from the pictures you guys released to us. But Calvin was married to her. If I had any doubt, his reaction confirmed it."

"What time was this meeting?" Mak asked.

"Um, late morning," she answered. "Around eleven, I guess."

"And who else was there?" Artemis picked it up.

"Roxie Lee and Deni Diaz."

"And not Jock Willinger?" Artemis said as he recalled the name. "He's the executive producer, right?"

"Well, for the next ten seconds." She smiled a little.

"He's quitting? Or was fired?" Artemis asked.

"That's something I can't talk about. Let's just say that he's not too happy about it."

"Okay." Artemis took this in. "So, who will become the executive producer when Jock leaves?"

"Ah." Moira shifted uneasily. "That's the thing. It was common knowledge in the studio that Paula DeVong was about to be named EP of her own show."

"And now she's dead," Mak said quietly.

"Right. And there's something else. After the show on Thursday night, Paula had a meeting in Jock's office. Just Jock, Paula, and Anna Canneli, her assistant. No one knows what the meeting was about. But a little more than an hour after that meeting finished, Paula was dead."

"So," Artemis asked, "who gets the job now?"

"It's not official, but I know that it will be Roxie Lee," Moira said.

Artemis looked up at the trees at the edge of the running track. Not a leaf was moving, the air was so still.

"Think she'll do a good job, Roxie Lee?" he asked.

"In fact, I do." Moira sounded relieved. "It's been a stressful time with Jock in charge. Roxie has been a good boss and fair to me."

"But she didn't go to bat for you about showing the footage of Lucille," Mak said.

"No. She didn't."

"Thank you, Moira," Artemis said sincerely. "Is there anything else?"

"I would appreciate it"—she smiled at Artemis—"if you would let me know what you find out."

"I will. But it might not be on the record."

"Fair enough." She got up and stuck out her hand to shake his. Then realizing what she'd done, she quickly pulled her hand back and laughed loudly at herself. "Am I ready for this thing to be over, or what? Sorry about that."

"No worries," Artemis said as he and Mak got up. "It's been really nice seeing you again, Moira."

"You too." She smiled and walked off back the way she'd come.

Mak looked at Artemis. "You up for a little meeting? We all have some work to do if she's right about this."

Artemis's jaw clenched and unclenched. "Yes," he said, his voice tight and controlled. "Let's do that."

*   *   *

Roxie picked up the gold pen and uncapped it. She looked across the desk at Calvin leaning back in his chair. Sunlight through the floor-to-ceiling windows of his office highlighted his thinning blond hair, strong jaw, and cruel eyes. He smiled at her. Roxie leaned over the front of the desk and signed the document. Calvin's eyes were drawn to her low cleavage where her ruby pendant dangled so promisingly close to her beautiful breasts.

Roxie stood up and handed the papers to Calvin. He gave them a quick glance. "Congratulations, Roxie. I couldn't be more pleased," he said. "It won't be official until Jock is gone. I'll be taking care of that after the show tonight."

"Decent of you to let him finish the week," Roxie said.

"He won't see it that way." Calvin chuckled. "Anyway, I couldn't be happier the way this has worked out. I have complete faith in you, Roxie."

"Thank you, Calvin." She smiled.

"Okay, get back to work," he said easily. "I'll see you later."

Roxie turned to go and Calvin leered at her sensual body as she walked out and closed the door.

Like an angel delivered me from hell.

He laughed a little to himself.

*   *   *

It was midafternoon and a soft breeze was coming in from the ocean, and the smell of salt water woke Taki from his nap. He was sitting in a large wood chair on the gently sloping lawns about halfway between the building and the old wood dock. Taki heard a screen door slam, and he craned his neck around to look at the porch. The old nun was coming out past a couple of patients sleeping in deck chairs. She was carrying a small tray in one hand and leaned heavily on the wood handrail as she came down the steps and started toward Taki.

Something's different.

Taki looked at his arms and wondered. They were bruised and sore but there was no needle, no tube, and no IV bag. His body felt tired and weak, but his mind was definitely clearer. The old nun arrived, set the tray down on the wide arm of his Adirondack chair, and sat down with a grunt next to him. Taki looked at the tray and saw some toasted English muffins with butter and jam, a cup of coffee, and a small glass of orange juice. He cautiously picked up a muffin and bit into it. He smiled widely, smearing the red jam across his teeth.

"That's wonderful," he mumbled as he chewed. He couldn't remember the last time he had tasted anything so delicious. "This isn't my usual dose," he managed to say after he swallowed.

"No," the old nun said as she watched him.

"All we need now are some seagulls," he said as he took another bite. "You'd think they'd be around by the water or on that dock." Taki took a sip of coffee. It was warm and bitter but felt so nice running down his throat and his mind seemed to clear even more. He looked at the old woman curiously. "Where am I?" he asked.

"St. Anthony's Hospital, Gilmore Island, Connecticut," she answered evenly.

"Yes." Taki pointed to the logo on the breast pocket of his white bathrobe. "It says that here, but"—he looked up at her—"where am I?"

"A long-term care facility for people who have terminal diseases," she said.

"And do I have a terminal disease?" Taki's eyebrows raised up in worry.

"No," she said. "So, how are you feeling now, Mr. Fukuda?"

"Taki." He smiled a little. "Everyone calls me Taki."

"All right, Taki. How do you feel?"

Something was certainly different. She had never called him that before. "I had a strange dream about a very fat man coming to see me. You were there. He seemed"—Taki searched for the word—"dangerous. And, I think maybe that it wasn't a dream after all."

"No." She looked pensively out to the ocean. "I have liked living here. When it's hot like this, it reminds me of where I grew up."

"That must have been a very long time ago." Taki smiled mischievously. But when the old woman's eyes flashed at him, he stopped smiling. Then she laughed. It was a throaty, strange dark sound. Taki's eyes grew wider.

"You're right," she said. "It was forever ago." Then she reached up her thin veiny hand and laid it on his neck. Taki was afraid to breathe.

"Your temperature feels good," she said professionally. "We will be traveling tonight." She took her hand away. "Will you be up for that?"

Taki's newly cleared mind suddenly fogged over again. "Up for it?" he repeated. "We...?"

"Yes."

"Where are we going?" he asked.

"You'll see," she said and pushed herself up out of the chair. "Finish your food," she instructed and turned to go.

"Wait." Taki's voice was weak but urgent. "I don't understand. Why should I trust you?"

"Because"—the old woman stared down at him—"I am the person who has kept you alive."

Taki heard her words, but they made no sense. "Why... did you do that?"

"Because I had a brother. And he loved you," she said.

"A brother...?" Taki looked up at her face, her eyes. "You do remind me of someone..."

"My brother was known in this country as Raphael Sharder."

"Raphael!" Taki exclaimed. He took a deep breath and tried to clear his head. "In my dream. The fat man. He called you by a name...?"

"I am Khloe," she said. "But you can call me Mr. Fukuda."

Taki gaped at her. "You just made... a joke."

She kept staring at him.

"Sister Mary Horrendous made a joke," he whispered in wonder.

"Rest up, Taki. You'll need your strength tonight," she commanded.

"Um..." He reached up and touched his matted weave. "Do you think I could have a hair brush? I must look a mess."

She studied him. Then she nodded once and walked away back toward the residents building.

Taki leaned back in his chair and closed his eyes. He tried to remember. Raphael had said something once. Dearest Raphael. He said... that he had a younger sister. But that she had died a long time ago. He had named his yacht after her as a remembrance. Khloe. Because he had loved her. A long time ago.

*　*　*

Paul Marin walked quickly down Fifth Avenue. He scowled at the ever-present busloads of tourists across the street posing for selfies on the steps of the Metropolitan Museum. He turned the corner at 83rd Street and went through a glass door into a small marble lobby. He pressed a button on the intercom box.

"Yes?" an efficient voice asked.

"It's Paul," he said impatiently. A buzzer sounded, and he pushed through the stainless-steel inner door into a tasteful waiting area with cream-colored leather furniture and hanging glass panels of black-and-white photos.

"Flora," he greeted his receptionist as he headed past her toward his office.

"I didn't expect you so early," she said agreeably. "You don't have anyone booked for two hours yet." Flora had been working for Paul for years. She was a woman in her sixties with short slate-gray hair, intelligent eyes, and a matronly manner.

"I know," Paul said. "And no calls," he added curtly as he went in and closed the large mahogany door.

"Yes, Doctor," Flora said.

Paul's office was a study in duality. The sleek furniture and modern wood desk were contrasted by heavy brocade window curtains and restored wood-paneled walls. He walked into his private bathroom and splashed cold water on his face. He grabbed a monogrammed towel and dried himself. He went back and sat in the leather desk chair. He pulled out his cell phone and found a number in his contacts. He sighed loudly, leaned back in the chair, and put his feet up on the desk. He rolled his head toward the window, pushed the curtains aside with his hand, and looked out at the museum across the street. It was an impressive building with steep steps and tall colonnades. He wondered why he never noticed that anymore. He only saw the droves of tourists like so many bugs spreading everywhere.

What's happened to me?

He slowly ran his fingers through his hair and massaged the back of his neck.

"Fuck it," he muttered sadly. He hit the number on his phone.

"Yeah?" Fat Nicky said impatiently as he waved his empty espresso cup at one of his men, who went off to get him another.

"Where are you?" Paul sounded annoyed.

Nicky looked around at the closed restaurant. Sunlight filtered through the blinds and played across a half dozen cafe tables topped with upside-down chairs, an empty wood bar, and racks of glasses covered with sheets. Nicky loved this little place because it was owned by friends who always knew how to take care of their own. But a year and a half of COVID had forced them to close the place. At least for now. Still, Nicky was always welcome.

"The Upper West Side," Nicky said.

"That's vague."

"What do you want?" Nicky grunted as his espresso arrived.

"Where's the camera? I want that footage," Paul demanded.

Nicky picked up the small camera from the table and pushed a button. Lucille's face appeared on the flip out screen. He turned up the volume:

My name is Lucille, and I'm wanted for a crime I never committed.

He turned it off.

"Little Lucille gave a very interesting interview," Nicky said pleasantly. "She's very pretty. Very believable. And she has so much to say about you. And the stolen thing you kept from that museum. And how you sent her to take the fall for a killing. So much shit she said." He snickered.

Paul's eyes glinted with anger, but he controlled his voice. "Nicky, what do you want?"

"Thank you, Paul, for calling me Nicky"—he smiled—"that means something to me. So, let me ask you a question. Have you found Lucille yet?"

"No," Paul admitted.

Nicky sucked his teeth loudly. "That is a problem, Paul. Because she could always make another of these interviews. And you will always be at risk. To yourself. And to all your friends."

Paul said nothing.

"I don't suppose your mother has had any ideas on how to handle this. Or have you forgotten to tell her about it?"

"She thinks"—Paul chose his words carefully—"that you and I should work this out between ourselves."

Nicky laughed. "That's good. Like when a kid gets all beat up at school and his mama tells him to get back there and stand up for himself. Really makes a man of you."

"Something like that," Paul said.

"Okay, Paul, here's what we're gonna do," Nicky shifted his weight and his cafe chair groaned perilously underneath him. "My guys are out looking for Ida, so I can ask her where she's hidden her sister. Now, you probably already asked her, 'cause she's like your best friend and all. But Ida doesn't seem too eager to help you. Me... I don't have that problem. People always help me. Always."

"Leave Ida alone. I will find Lucille." Paul assured him.

"And you sound so sincere, it's like I should trust you." Nicky shook his head. "But I so fucking don't. So, it works like this. Whoever finds Lucille first, wins. Got that?"

Paul heard the line go dead. He got up, went to the bar, poured himself a drink. He slowly walked back to the front of his desk. He knocked back the drink, got his phone, and hit a button.

"Where are you?" Paul asked.

"I'll be right back," Ida said to the woman lying on a treatment table with a mud mask on her face and slices of cucumbers over her eyes. "At work," she said into the phone as she left the room.

"You're in danger," Paul said urgently. "Get out of there now."

Ida stepped into her office and closed the door. "What's going on?"

"The Connecticut factory was raided, and Ladimir was arrested," Paul explained quickly.

"Oh, fuck," Ida said as she sat at her desk. "How did that happen?"

"Fat Nicky betrayed us," Paul said angrily. "And he's looking for you."

"Why?"

"To get to Lucille."

"Paul, I told you, I don't know where she is..."

"He's going to kill her," he said, cutting her off. "And then you."

Ida had wondered if this day might come. But it was still a shock.

"Thank you, Paul," she said.

"Call me when you can." He hung up.

Ida took a sharp breath, grabbed her bag from the patinaed desk, and left. She went down the hall past the treatment rooms and into the trendy reception area. Hanging on the brushed stainless-steel walls were Ida's collection of vintage Navajo rugs. Because of COVID protocols, the room was empty, except for the receptionist who sat behind a Murano-glass desk.

"Ronnie," she said to the young, efficient-looking man. "I just got an emergency call. Cancel the rest of my day."

"But Ida," he said in alarm, "what about Mrs. Palmer?"

"You'll need to clean her up and get her out," Ida instructed as she walked away to the large street-level window that looked out on Madison Avenue. "No charge for the day and tell her the next one's on the house."

Ida wondered if she would ever be back here again. She carefully pushed the sheer curtains aside and looked out. The late-afternoon traffic was heavy, and the sidewalks were busy. She caught her breath as she recognized one of Fat Nicky's guys standing across the street, smoking a cigarette. Ida roughly brushed her fingers through her short red hair and formulated a plan.

"Bye, Ronnie," she called as she went out the door into a small lobby. She turned away from the main entrance on Madison and walked back toward the elevators. She turned a corner and followed the elegant hallway to a glass door of a shop.

"Hey, Helen," she said cheerfully to the middle-aged assistant sitting near a jewelry case, reading a magazine.

"Ida, how nice to see you," Helen said as she stood up. "You have to see what just came in. They're Peruvian!" She held up a chuky gold bracelet.

"Not today, dear," Ida said as she made for the street door. "I just wanted to say hello."

"Oh, okay," Helen said disappointedly.

The shop's entrance was on 65th Street. Ida walked out, quickly looked around, and headed east away from Madison. At Park Avenue, she crossed to the northbound side and hailed a cab.

"The Mark Hotel," she told the driver. She knew that she couldn't go back home. They would be waiting.

She got out at 77th Street and Madison. She checked the sidewalk and went into the hotel. Off the lobby was a lounge that she had been to many times. At first, it had been a comfortable, classy place to bring new clients. But she had come to love it because it was roughly halfway between her office and her apartment and was a discreet place where she could be alone and think. And right now, Ida had a lot to think about. She settled into a chair near the front windows that looked out to the street. Daylight was fading, and everything seemed normal enough. An elderly couple stood admiring the ever-present flower cart in front of the hotel. A waitress came over, and Ida ordered a gin martini.

*   *   *

It was just past 9:00 p.m., and Lucille silently slipped back into her dark top-floor apartment. She had left the windows open hoping to cool the place off. But the humid night air had brought no relief. She pulled off her mask and cap and tossed them angrily across the room.

"Fucking prison." She gasped as she went to the north-facing window. She looked at the Bookbinder apartment across the street and recognized two people sitting on the window bench with their backs to her. She quickly knelt down, leaned her elbows on the sill, and observed them. Artemis and his son Silas were talking together like old friends. She liked that. A couple of people came over to them. Lucille ducked and sat on the floor because she knew who they were too. The tall, strong woman was Drew Sweeney, a cop. The handsome Asian American man was an FBI agent. Lucille had spent many nights in Brooklyn during the last year watching them all from the shadows.

She wiped the sweat out of her eyes, turned back, and peered over the sill. The four people moved away from the window and out of sight. Lucille rested her chin on her hands and wondered if she would ever be herself again. Not a fugitive. Not a prisoner. Just be Lucille.

"All right, let's start," Drew said as she sat at one end of the dining room table. Silas sat next to her and opened his laptop. Mak handed him a flash drive.

"This is a copy of what we got from Moira Weyland today," he explained as he sat.

Drew looked up at Artemis. He was standing behind his chair at the far end of the table.

"I'm going to stand for a while," Artemis said trying to keep the anxiety out of his voice.

"Fresh coffee," Delia said as she went around the table and filled up their mugs. "Though I think it is far too late for this." She poured a half cup for Silas. "Especially for a growing boy," she said tolerantly and went back into the kitchen.

"This is time-stamped 11:34 Wednesday night," Silas said as he turned his laptop so they could all see the overhead image of the sidewalk in front of a dark storefront. A woman staggered into view. She leaned against the building and looked up. It was plain to see it was Paula DeVong. Her hand touched her face and her eyes closed. Almost gracefully she dropped to her knees and fell to the ground. She was lying on her side motionless, and a young couple walked past without looking at her.

"Fucking New Yorkers," Drew said disgustedly. "In a crisis, we're terrific. But look at this."

"Lots of people walked past her," Mak said.

"Maybe they thought she was drunk," Silas offered.

"Go to 12:06 a.m.," Mak said as he checked his notes. Silas adjusted his glasses, rolled the footage up to the time, and let it play. After a couple of seconds, a thin woman in a cap and a dark face mask carefully approached Paula's body. She looked around, knelt, and touched Paula's face. Then she pulled out a phone and hit three numbers.

"We've found the call in the 911 database. It's from a burner phone, which is what she's used before," Mak reported.

"Can we hear it?" Silas asked.

"My guys are working on it," Mak answered. "Should have it soon."

They watched as the woman on the phone looked up toward the streetlight.

Silas hit a key and stopped on the image. "I think she's trying to figure out what block she's on."

Artemis walked closer, and they all studied her upturned face.

"It's her," Silas said softly. "Lucille."

"I agree." Artemis sounded faraway.

"Fuck me," Drew muttered. "Sixteen months later and she's still here in New York."

Silas pushed a key, and Lucille finished the call and hung up. She looked around, opened Paula's purse, and searched through it.

"What's she looking for?" Artemis murmured.

"Cash?" Silas asked.

"Don't think so," Drew answered. "Paula's wallet was found in her purse with a little more than a hundred and all her cards intact."

Lucille's search grew more frantic. Then she gave up, put the purse back next to the body, got up, and left.

"Go to 12:14 a.m.," Mak said. "This is footage from a different overhead camera a few blocks south near Columbus Circle."

The footage showed a wide shot of a busy sidewalk and stairs descending to the subway station.

"Stop there," Mak said and Silas hit a key.

"We believe that's the same woman," Mak explained as he pointed to the back of a figure on the screen. "Watch this."

Silas keyed the image back into motion, and the woman threw something into a trash can and quickly trotted down the subway steps.

"Assuming that was her burner phone," Mak said, "it's gone."

"Do we have her on any other cameras?" Drew asked.

"No," Mak answered. "Which is strange because the station has lots of lenses."

"Maybe not so strange," Artemis said. "She's gotten good at hiding." He looked to Drew and asked, "What about her sister, the dermatologist?"

"Ida Orsina." Drew nodded. "She told us that she and Lucille weren't close, and we never found anything current to link them."

"Might be time to talk with her again," Artemis said respectfully.

"Yep," she concurred.

"And Lucille's ex-husband, Calvin Prons?" Silas asked Drew.

"We'll be at TVNews tomorrow morning," she answered. "But I did talk with him today by phone. He just repeated what he's said all along, that Lucille is crazy and he hasn't heard from her."

"And he hates her." Artemis remembered.

"Yes," Drew confirmed.

"Okay," Mak said as he leaned back in his chair and lifted his mug of coffee. "So, what about the break-in at Paula DeVong's apartment the night she died."

"It happened just past one thirty in the morning," Drew reviewed the facts. "The building lost power, and the desk guy went out to talk to an emergency crew down the block. When he gets back, he sees two guys dressed like ConEd workers leaving the building."

"And he can't ID them because they are wearing face masks and helmets, right?" Artemis asked quietly.

"Right," Drew answered, noticing the faraway look in his eyes. "Where are you, cousin?" she asked gently.

"In the past," Artemis said. "One thirty in the morning. Two guys in false uniforms. Reminds me of the night they robbed the Gardner."

Drew said nothing. Mak sipped his coffee. Silas looked up at his father.

"Everything reminds you of that." He smiled a little.

"That's true enough," Artemis said as he came back from his inner journey. "Was anything missing at Paula's place?"

"Not as far as we can tell," Drew said. "There was cash there, jewelry, her passport."

Artemis walked to his chair and sat down. He took a sip of coffee.

"Is it hot enough?" Delia asked as she came in carrying a carafe.

"Yes, thanks," Artemis answered. She smiled at him and started around the table topping off their mugs.

"There's something else," Mak said to Artemis. "I don't know if you're up for it, but Sammi Lau is finally back in town."

"The barber." Artemis closed his eyes. "I was wondering about her."

Sammi Lau worked and lived on the edge of Chinatown across from the abandoned building where the classes were held. In that schoolroom, following a tip from Lucille, they had recovered a stolen Gardner Museum object—an ancient Chinese chalice.

"Where's she been?" Artemis asked as he opened his eyes.

"Hong Kong," Mak explained. "She was there when COVID closed the borders and by the time they opened again, her grandfather had died."

"Of COVID?" Delia asked sympathetically.

"Yes, that's what she says," Mak answered. He turned back to Artemis.

"I'm meeting her tomorrow morning. Wanna be there?"

Artemis looked down at the coffee cup in his hand. He swallowed hard. It had been impossible to think about the case. About the facts and the consequences. He could see Emily's lips and her green eyes, and he felt pressure gripping his chest, compressing his lungs.

"Breathe," Delia said kindly as she topped off his cup.

Artemis looked up at her face. He could see the concern in her eyes. He took a breath. He looked to Mak, who was watching him without judgement. He looked to Drew. As always, she radiated a quiet support for him. He looked to Silas, and behind his glasses, his eyes were calm and patient. Just like his mother's eyes.

I have the right to breathe.

Artemis looked to Mak and said, "Yes. I'd like to be there."

"Are you sure?" Delia asked.

"It's time," Artemis answered simply. Delia threw a worried look to Drew and went back into the kitchen. Drew picked up her cup and followed her out.

"Are you okay?" Drew asked as she poured her coffee in the sink and rinsed off the cup.

Delia was staring out the large kitchen window at the lights of hundreds of buildings shining for miles in the clear hot night.

"I just worry it's too soon," she said. "I don't want to watch him fall apart again."

"I know," Drew said as she put the mug in the dishwasher. "But maybe he needs to get back in the fight."

Delia dropped her head. "Promise me you'll keep an eye on him."

"I always have." Drew smiled easily. "And I always will." She walked over to Delia and looked out at New York. "How are you liking living here? Or is it too soon to tell?"

"Oh, I think we'll all do fine," Delia said as she looked up, her usual positive tone returning. "The apartment is beautiful; we're close to the shops, and there's an AA meeting in a church basement just a couple of blocks away. I'm planning on getting there tomorrow afternoon."

"What time?" Drew asked.

"Five."

"Good," Drew said approvingly. "I'll come by and walk you there."

Delia smiled widely at her. "Thank you, Drew. I don't know what we would have done without you and your father. You must be relieved to finally have us out."

"No, we're gonna miss you being around, and"—Drew smiled back at her—"now we'll have to do all the housekeeping ourselves. How much does that suck?"

Delia's phone on the counter rang, and she went to answer it. She looked at the caller ID. "Speaking of AA," she said apologetically. "It's someone I'm sponsoring in Brooklyn. She's a little freaked out that we've moved."

Drew gave her an understanding nod and went back into the dining room.

"Hello," Delia said. "How are you tonight?"

* * *

At 10:00 p.m., the end credits rolled on Moira Weyland's second show anchoring TVNews. The overhead lights in the darkened control room were switched on.

"Good show, everyone," Jock said officiously. "And another week of making television magic comes to an end." His whiny nasal voice made the ironic statement sound nasty. The staff stopped gathering their things and turned to look at him.

"What?" he said bitterly, his Liverpool inflection getting more pronounced. "Waiting for me to make an announcement?"

After an uncomfortable moment, the staff resumed their work. The phone on Jock's console blinked and he picked it up.

"Hello," he said and listened. "I didn't know you were still here. I'll be right up." He hung up and left the room.

In the front row by the wall of monitors, Greg and Deni looked at each other and smiled.

"Has the *shite* finally hit the fan?" Deni whispered happily.

"Roxie asked me to put empty boxes in Jock's office just before the show," Greg whispered back. They put their heads together and let out a sigh of relief.

Jock walked up the open glass stairs to the executive level. He looked to the woman sitting at the large curved wood desk in the middle of the reception area.

"He's expecting you," she said politely.

Jock went over to the door and took a breath before he turned the knob and went in. Calvin was standing by the well-appointed bar pouring himself a drink.

"Want one?" he asked without looking up.

"Sure, thanks," Jock said as he closed the door behind him.

"Hey, sit," Calvin said as he poured a second drink. "Fucking crazy week, huh? Just glad it's over."

Jock sat down on a leather chair in front of the desk. Calvin came over and handed him his drink.

"Happy days," Calvin said as he clinked his glass against Jock's. "I think Moira did all right tonight." He sat down and put his feet up on his metal desk with a thump.

"Yes," Jock murmured. "She'll do for now. But we should get someone with more experience."

Calvin's eyes narrowed. "See... like that. You don't like that girl. And she doesn't like you."

"That fucking lawsuit," Jock said acridly.

"I know, but it's become the writing on the wall," Calvin said sympathetically. "They've set a court date. You'll have to appear."

Jock took a gulp of his drink and set the glass down on the desk. "Look, Cal, you and I go back a long way..."

"Nah." Calvin cut him off. "This is television. And you're only as good as your last rating."

"Well, the overnights were fair," Jock said, his voice growing higher and more desperate. "We can't tell yet if the audience will like the new girl."

"That's the point, Jock. I like the new girl," Calvin said clearly. "So, you're finished here. Clean out your office and get out."

Jock said wearily, "Now?"

"Yes," Calvin answered as he lifted his desk phone and hit a button. "Send them in."

The door opened and two uniformed studio guards walked in.

"Gentlemen," he addressed the guards. "Please stay with Jock as he packs up his office and make sure that anything that belongs to TVNews stays here. Collect his ID and let me know when he's out of the building."

Jock shook his head disgustedly and got up to go. "You know, Cal," he said as he turned back by the door, "you're no saint either. They'll be coming for you next."

Calvin smiled. "No, they won't. Goodbye, Jock."

Jock started to say something but changed his mind. He turned and walked out, the guards close behind. Calvin took a long sip of his drink and smiled. He picked up his desk phone.

"Come in, please," he said.

His eyes hungrily took in the pretty young secretary as she walked across the office and stopped in front of his desk.

"I really appreciate you staying so late tonight, Barb," he said warmly. "Maybe I could buy you a drink to say thanks?"

"I would love that." She smiled.

"Great," he said and smiled back. "I've just got one more thing to wrap up, and the week is done. Ask Roxie and Deni to come up, would you?"

"Yes, Cal," she answered promptly, left the office, and closed the door.

In the corner office a floor below, Moira gently set her laptop on the desk. The police had finally finished going over everything and had released the room. Yesterday this had been Paula DeVong's office. Her immense framed photo was still hanging on the wall.

Moira sat down in the big leather chair and swiveled to look out the floor-to-ceiling windows. Buildings, as far as she could see, were sparkling with light, and Columbus Avenue eight stories below was still jammed with late-night traffic.

"Do you need any help setting up?" The plaintive voice of Anna Canneli broke the silence. Moira turned to see the frumpy woman standing defensively in the doorway.

"No, thanks," Moira said. "It's late. You should head out."

"Okay," Anna said and started to go, but stopped as she saw Moira opening the drawers of the desk. Anna's face twitched.

"Everything all right?" Moira asked.

"What?" Anna stuttered. "Yes. It's just that..."

"It's just that," Moira cut her off not unkindly, "this was Paula's desk. I know. And this is a rough transition for me too. I'd be thankful for any help you can give me."

Anna's eyes froze, but she managed a small smile.

"Good night, then," Moira said. Anna nodded and left. Moira watched her through the glass wall as she went into her adjoining office, came out with her bag, and walked across the large open newsroom toward the elevators. The doors opened, and Anna stepped in.

And Moira wondered about the after-show meeting in Jock's office the night Paula died. Only three people were there: Paula, Jock, and Anna. And she felt sure that Anna would never tell her what was said.

Moira let out an exasperated groan and resumed looking through the desk drawers. The police had taken most of Paula's things, and the studio staff had cleared out the rest. But still she hoped that there was some note or memo left behind, anything that might give her a clue about what happened at that meeting.

Upstairs Roxie and Deni arrived in the reception area.

"He's expecting you," Barb said as she looked up from her magazine. "Please go in."

"You're working late," Roxie said knowingly as she and Deni headed past her. Roxie knocked once and opened the door.

"Come in," Calvin said as he took his feet off the desk and sat up. "Please shut that."

Roxie closed the door as she and Deni came in and sat in front of his desk.

"Drinks?" Calvin asked as he got up, went to the bar, and topped off his glass.

"Love one. Whatever you're having," Deni said a little too enthusiastically.

"Me too," Roxie said as she smiled and raised her eyebrows at her.

"It's just been a wild couple of days," Deni explained.

"Here you go," Calvin said as he handed them glasses. He retrieved his own and sat back down at his desk. "As you might have guessed, Jock Willinger is no longer working here at TVNews."

"Good," Deni said and sipped her drink.

"I agree," Calvin said. "Roxie Lee is the new executive producer of the show effective immediately."

"Thank you, Calvin," Roxie said graciously as Deni grinned.

"I see Deni's pleased with the news." Calvin chuckled as he looked to Roxie. "So, here's your first command question: do you think little Deni here is ready to step into your shoes?"

Deni felt a wave of hot anger spread across the back of her neck, but she managed to keep her face calm and her eyes attentive.

"Or should I bring in someone with more experience?" Calvin asked.

Roxie smiled and said, "Deni is more than up to it. She'll do a great job for us."

"Thank you, Roxie," Deni said gratefully. Though she had known this was about to happen, it was still a thrill to hear the words.

"I wonder though," Calvin said cautiously. "How the network will feel if that damned lawsuit keeps going on."

Deni's eyes focused on him. She sipped her drink.

"It's not that you and the others don't have a case against the *Slimy Limey*," Calvin said with a smile. Deni laughed to hear him say the name that Jock was secretly called by the rank and file of the studio.

"But the network feels"—Calvin continued almost apologetically—"it would be helpful to get all that bad publicity behind us. After all, Jock has been fired. He's out, disgraced and without benefits. That seems like justice to me. But how are you seeing this, Deni?"

"Thank you for firing that bastard," Deni said as she considered. "And I guess that'll have to be enough for me."

"Good—" Calvin started, but she cut him off.

"But that is the last fucking time you call me little Deni. Okay?"

Calvin eyed her for a moment. Then he laughed. "Fair enough. That's a deal, Ms. Diaz. Congratulations, you are the new supervising producer."

The two women leaned forward to clink their glasses against his.

"And I hope you guys don't mind working tomorrow," he added as his eyes lingered on their cleavages. Both women were wearing gem pendant necklaces that sparkled enticingly. "You'll need the day to sort out your new offices."

"We don't mind that at all," Roxie said happily.

Jock stepped out of his office carrying a cardboard box containing his personal things. Across the reception area, the door to the only other office was closed. But he could hear Calvin laughing with a couple of women and he could guess who they were. Jock looked at Barb who was at her desk, looking in a mirror, touching up her very red lipstick.

It's so unfair.

Jock smirked and started off with the two studio guards close behind him.

"Good night, Mr. Willinger," Barb called out cheerfully.

"Bite me," he called back in a nasty wheeze as they headed down the steps to the newsroom. There he stopped for a last look. Across the vast empty room, he could see someone in Paula's glass-walled office. It was Moira Weyland. Arranging her things. And Jock's eyes burned with hate.

Moira felt something, looked up, and saw Jock and the two guards. She saw him clutching his box of belongings and knew what it meant. She looked down embarrassed for him.

Jock's face flushed red. He turned away and walked toward the elevators beyond the glass wall. There he handed his studio ID to one of the guards and got into the elevator. To his surprise, both guards got in with him and pushed the button for the lobby.

"Really making sure I'm gone, huh?" He sneered.

"Yes, sir. We are."

* * *

It was just before midnight when two people quietly stepped out onto the long back porch of St. Anthony's.

"I don't think I'm correctly dressed for this," Taki whispered weakly. He was still in his pajamas and bathrobe. The old nun shifted her cane and handed him her cloth shoulder bag.

"It's so heavy. I thought nuns took a vow of poverty." He joked softly as he offered the old woman his arm to lean on. She gave him an odd look before she took his arm. Moving as silently as they could, they made their way down the steps and across the dark lawn toward the beach. The night air was cool, and fog was coming in across the smooth waters of the sound. As they neared the dock, they could see a small motorboat tied up at the far end, bobbing a little in the wake.

The nun's cane tapped a steady rhythm as they started walking across the wood planks. A compact old man with a beaver-like full head of white hair heard them, climbed out of the boat, and up onto the dock.

"Right on time," the man said, his Liverpool accent clear.

"Thank you for coming, Toby," she greeted the man, kissing his cheek. "I am in your debt."

He shrugged. "Not a bit, Khloe. It's good to see you again."

Khloe smiled a little and turned to see how Taki was doing. He was a little breathless from their walk, but his eyes were bright and his cheeks were flushed with healthy color.

"Taki Fukuda, this is my old friend Captain Toby Brown," she said. "He's here to help us."

Taki looked at the tough little man and then at the small open boat tied to the dock. "Captain of that?" he asked nervously.

"Don't panic," Toby said as he rolled his eyes. "That's my boat out there." He pointed to a large white yacht moored a quarter mile out, her lights twinkling through the growing fog. "The Lady Sheila," he added proudly as he took the bag from Taki.

"After your granddaughter. Very good," Khloe said approvingly.

"We better get a move on." Toby led them to the end of the dock and hopped into the boat. He reached up and took hold of the old woman's hips. She handed her cane to Taki, and Toby lifted her into the boat and helped her sit in the back by the outboard motor.

"Okay, Mr. Fukuda, you're next," Toby ordered as he grabbed the cane out of his hands and returned it to Khloe.

"Everyone calls me Taki," he muttered as he shuffled closer. He felt sure that he had met Toby Brown before, but his still befuddled mind couldn't remember where. "Maybe I could sit on the edge first?"

Across the lawn, a light came on at the back of the building. Taki turned to look at it in alarm. Then he felt two strong arms wrap around his belly, lift him off the dock and into the swaying craft. As he was pushed to sit on a cooler, Taki looked up at the little man amazed at his strength.

Toby untied the boat, sat next to Khloe, pulled the cord on the motor, and it growled to life. He pushed them away from the dock and turned the runabout toward the open water. As they gained speed, Taki clutched the sides of the boat with both hands. He looked at the old people.

"This doesn't bother you?" he called to them over the noise of the motor.

Toby barked out a cruel laugh, but the old nun looked at Taki with pity.

"I've always been a good sailor," she said.

"Of course," Toby said loudly. "It's in your blood!"

"You've gained weight, Toby," she said, notably changing the subject. "Not that it doesn't look good on you."

Toby laughed a little and turned to look at Taki. "That's a nice color for you, green."

"I'm not," Taki said as his head began to swim, "wearing any green."

"No. But your face is," Toby scoffed as he moved a plastic bucket closer to him. "So, cross your legs and brace your nuts. We're almost there."

The old nun laughed, and the dark mischievous sound brought Taki back to himself a little. He tightened the belt of his bathrobe, took a long breath, and focused on her.

"Assuming we make it to the big boat, where are we going?" he asked urgently.

But neither Khloe nor Captain Brown answered him.

Chapter Three

Saturday, July 17th, 2021

It was six thirty in the morning in Southampton, and a lean healthy woman ran along the ocean's edge, her gray-blonde ponytail bouncing in rhythm with her long even strides. Barbara Borsa had always loved this stretch of beach, and she sprinted the last hundred yards to the gap in the dunes where she turned for home. The fog was lifting, and the day was already warm and humid. Barbara wiped the sweat from her neck, slowed to an easy jog, and made her way along the quiet back streets of town. In a couple of blocks, she came to the house that she and her sister had lived in since they were children.

Barbara opened the front gate and stopped when she saw a young woman sitting on the brick steps of the front porch.

"Waiting for me?" Barbara said curiously as she approached.

"If you're Barbara Borsa, the attorney?" the young woman asked as she stood up.

"I am."

"I know it's very early. But your sister said I could wait for you out here. My name is Sheila Brown. I run the marina on the other side of the bridge."

"Nice to meet you," Barbara said in a careful professional tone. "What can I do for you?"

Sheila held out a manila envelope. "I was asked to give you this."

Barbara took the envelope, opened it, and pulled out some papers. She read a bit and looked up surprised. "Do you know what this says?" she asked.

"Yes, I've been told."

"Let's go to my office," Barbara said as she unlocked the second entrance on the front of the house. "Maybe you'd like some coffee?" she added as she led the way.

* * *

By eight thirty, the morning was a humid ninety degrees and clouds were gathering in the skies above Manhattan. Paul Marin got out of a cab at the edge of Chinatown and walked quickly along Mosco Street. He was dressed in jeans and a tight white tee shirt, a look he liked because it showed off his muscular chest. At the corner of Mott Street, he stopped and looked around to make sure no one was following him. He scowled at the rows of graffiti-covered booths that had been set up along both sides of the narrow street where cars once parked. They were haphazard-looking structures of corrugated metal, canvas, and semitransparent vinyl. Because of COVID, restaurant owners had been allowed to construct these alfresco shelters. It was too early for customers, but staff from one of the Cantonese places were busy cleaning up the mess left by the homeless during the night. Paul crossed the street and walked south. He stopped halfway down the block in front of an old eight-story building completely covered with netted construction scaffolding. He took out a set of keys and unlocked a black metal door. He slipped inside, closed the door, and locked it. He took a flashlight out of his back pocket and flicked it on.

The place had once been a souvenir shop but had closed many years ago. Now there was nothing left but dirt, tarnished tin ceiling tiles, and the smell of mold.

Paul made his way past a wall of broken wood shelves and through a door in the back. At the end of a hall, he came to a large built-in bookcase.

Paul shined his light on a small rusted panel on the wall. He got his fingertips under an edge and opened it. He reached inside, tightened his hand around a metal lever, and gave it a gentle pull. He heard the snap of a lock opening. He took hold of a corner of the bookcase, pulled, and it swung open revealing a well-worn flight of stone steps descending down a dark brick tunnel. The air inside was stale and dry. Paul took hold of the iron handrail and started down. Along the way were stubs of candles in tallow-stained niches, but Paul ignored these. At the bottom of the steps, he came to a small square room. On the wall in front of him was a metal door with a large brass knob, green with age. He turned the knob, and the door opened with a loud creak. Paul stepped into another small chamber and closed the door behind him. Like the passage upstairs, on this side the closed door was perfectly disguised as a weathered built-in bookcase.

The passage from the shop on Mott Street down to this neighboring building was created in the 1920s when it had been a speakeasy. Paul had come to love this place and all the secrets kept here. He shined his light across the room on a tall wood door. He opened it and went through into a much larger stone chamber. He was standing on a small square stage in front of a semicircle of six gold folding chairs. Paul smiled.

Here I can be myself.

He shined the light around and was relieved to see that the six large standing candelabras were still there. He looked up at the wide vaulted ceiling and saw where years of burning candles had darkened the stone. He looked around the stage and realized that his big iron and leather chair was gone. He wondered why the cops had taken that and nothing else.

He fished a lighter out of his pocket, stepped off the stage, and went to one of the Gothic dark-bronze candelabras. He slowly lit each candle. Six lights in a circle below. And a higher one in the center.

They all believed that was me.

Paul turned off his flashlight, walked back to the stage, and sat on the edge facing the gold chairs. He looked up and to the right.

"If you ever were really there," he said softly. "Now would be a good time to let me know. I'm in a world of shit and I don't know what to do. Please help me."

He sat waiting for a minute. Then he dropped his head. "Well then, fuck me."

He picked up his flashlight, got up, and walked to a door across the room. He opened it, shined the light up another flight of uneven stone steps, and started up. At the top, he pushed open a metal door and stepped around a corner into a shadowy crumbling space. This had once been the Necropolis Bar, and Paul could remember many nights here partying and doing business. But it had been closed for more than twelve years now, after the police raided the place and drugs were found. Paul wasn't there that night. He had been warned.

Paul shined his flashlight on a tangled pile of yellow police tape lying on the dusty floor. That was from last year when the cops had found his school and an ancient chalice stolen from the Gardner Museum. He looked around at the cracked walls, the rotting-wood bar, and the fractured mirrors. He walked carefully through the debris to where the front entrance was. On the wall by the door was a large fresco painting.

Paul knew that coming back here might be a risk. But he needed to see this picture again. He wanted to get more light on the image, so he unlocked the heavy front door and carefully pulled it open. The hinges cracked loudly. The outside metal security gate was pulled down, and tiny shafts of daylight came through the cracks. Paul moved to the gate and carefully peered through one of the small openings. He could see a two-story building across Doyers Street. There was a ground floor barbershop and through the window, he could see someone sweeping up in the back. Other than that, there was no one around. He turned to look at the picture on the wall.

It was a mythical depiction of a three-headed sea serpent, each of the faces fierce and proud. Paul knew that it was a copy of an Etruscan fresco found in an ancient tomb in Italy. The serpent, guardian of the underworld, had been the inspiration for the Necropolis Bar.

Paul reached out his hand and touched one of the fierce faces.

Abruzzo.

He touched the head in the middle.

Karlovic.

Then he slid his fingers to the third head. The eyes of the beast were wild and cunning.

Mother.

He pulled his hand away and stared at the image.

"And you want me to become you," he murmured sadly. "Or die."

He heard the sound of voices outside and carefully turned to look through a space in the security gate. His mind flooded in panic as he saw three people across the street. Though they were wearing COVID masks, he knew who two of them were: Artemis Bookbinder and Mak Kim, an FBI agent. They were talking to a feisty-looking young Chinese woman in front of the barbershop. She wore no mask and was smoking a cigarette. When he realized that they didn't know he was there, Paul's heart rate slowed and he took a deep breath. He watched as the woman tossed her cigarette into the street and they followed her into the shop.

I'm so out of time.

Paul noiselessly closed the heavy inner door. Using his flashlight, he made his way back through the bar and down the stone steps. In the vaulted basement, he went over to the burning candelabra. He blew out each of the six lower candles and looked up at the taller center flame.

"Blow out your candle, Mother," he said ruefully, adapting a line from a play he once loved. "And so... good night," he whispered and blew it out.

"COVID has made a fucking mess in Chinatown," Sammi Lau said disgustedly as she sat in one of the three barber chairs and threw her legs over the padded arm, her knees poking through strategically placed holes in her faded black jeans. Sammi was a hard-looking woman in her mid-twenties. Her short black hair had streaks of fuchsia that gave her a retro-pop-goth feel, but her eyes were friendly. "Souvenir shops are boarded up and the restaurants are dying. My uncle has kept this place going. But only just. I was probably better off staying in Hong Kong. But what the hell. You guys wanna sit?"

"I'm good," Artemis said, his words a little muffled through his mask.

"How are things in Hong Kong?" Mak asked as he sat in the chair next to her and pulled off his mask.

"Well, it's been a rough time there," she answered. "My grandfather died of this thing. But I think you know that, right."

"Yes," Mak said kindly. "Your uncle told us. Sorry."

"Thanks." She nodded. "So, you guys found a stolen chalice across the street. It was Chinese, and I'm Chinese. So, I must have all the answers." She was smiling. "What can I do for you?"

"You live here? In this building?" Artemis said trying to keep the strain out of his voice.

"Yep, right there." She pointed up at the ceiling. "Top floor front of a two-story building across the street from that place." She indicated the building across the street with the closed metal security gate. "I get it. You want to know if I saw anything."

"That's it," Mak said easily.

"Nope. Sorry you guys wasted your time," she said with finality. "So, if you don't mind, I really have to get back to work cleaning this place. I got a customer coming this morning."

"Look." Artemis stepped back a little and pulled off his mask. "We really need some help here."

There was something in the way he spoke, a sadness that caught Sammi's attention.

"I like your blue eyes," she said to him.

Artemis smiled a little. "Thanks."

"Surviving on this street means," Mak said to her, "that you're either a very tough person or you've developed a convenient blindness."

"Yeah, like that," she confirmed. "I don't need any enemies here. I take care of myself and stay out of trouble."

"Sammi," Artemis said quietly as he turned away and walked to the front window. "My wife is dead. There's a connection between the people who went to some sort of a class over there and her killer." He turned to Sammi. "Please. There must be something you can tell us."

Sammi pulled out a pack of cigarettes from the pocket of her shirt, put one between her lips, and lit it. "Want one?" she asked them. Artemis shook his head, and after a moment, so did Mak.

"I'm trying to give it up," Mak said.

"My uncle hates it if I light up in here," Sammi said as she waved the smoke away from Mak. "But what the fuck." She looked at Artemis. "I'm sorry to hear about your wife. But what's to see out there. Some kids buying drugs or a homeless guy peeing." She stretched out her hand, opened a drawer, and pulled out a green-glass ashtray.

Artemis said nothing but stood watching her as she rolled the ash of her cigarette against the edge of the glass.

"Okay. Okay." She sighed a little. "I always made sure my apartment lights were out well before midnight on Sunday nights." She took a long drag on her cigarette before she continued. "I didn't want them to know I was watching. You never know who you're gonna piss off around here. A little before midnight they'd come: five women and one guy."

"Always the same people?" Artemis asked.

"Yeah, I think so," she answered. "There's a streetlight just in front of the shop and I could see them pretty well. Then at exactly five minutes to twelve, the metal gate was rolled up from the inside by a big scary-looking guy with funny eyes. The six outside people go in, and the guy with the eyes stays out. He pulls down the security gate and locks it. Then he stays there, hot or cold or wet or whatever, guarding the place. Sometimes, when the weather was okay, another guy would come along and hang out with him."

"Would you recognize them if you saw them again?" Mak asked, sounding official.

Sammi took a hit of her cigarette. "I don't even want to hear you ask that," she said clearly. "I'm talking to you right now. But that's it."

"Understood." Artemis agreed and then asked, "What was it about his eyes?"

"Um—" She considered. "They didn't match too well, like they were lopsided or something. He was maybe in his thirties, and his face was all right. The other guy was probably about the same age, but it's hard to say 'cause he was really big." She opened her arms to show them. "I mean like huge."

"What else about that guy?" Mak asked.

"He looked like a hood. Slicked-back hair and little eyes. Something nasty about him."

"Okay," Artemis said assembling the information in his mind. "And what about the people who went in? What did they look like?"

"All fairly young and good-looking." She closed her eyes to remember. "There was one Black woman, really beautiful. She seemed to be more in charge than the others. But it was hard to tell. Nobody said anything."

"Anyone wearing jewelry, like a necklace?" Artemis asked.

Sammi opened her eyes surprised. "Yes," she said. "When it was hot out, like now, I could sometimes see these single-stone necklaces on the women. Lots of different colors, kinda glittery in the streetlight. The Black woman had a really big red gemstone."

"And the man who went in with them? Did he have one?" Artemis asked.

"I don't think so," she said slowly. "But I'm not sure."

Artemis smiled at Sammi. "That's really helpful. Thank you."

She smiled back at him.

"And how long was this going on?" Mak asked.

"I don't know when it started." She shrugged. "But they met every week. I'm pretty sure."

Mak looked at her questioningly.

"Well, I do have a life, you know. But if I was home on a Sunday night, I'd turn out the lights and watch. It was going on for as long as I've lived here."

"And how long is that?" Mak asked.

"A little more than five years."

"So, what happened when they came out?" Artemis turned to look at the building across the street again. "You said the guy with the strange eyes pulled down and locked the metal gate after they all went in."

"That's right. I did." She sounded pleased that Artemis was paying attention. "And that's the weird thing right there."

Artemis turned and looked at her. "What?"

"They never came back out. Ever." She stubbed out her cigarette and sat up in the chair. "After a couple of hours, the guy with the eyes would get a text on his cell and he'd go."

"That's very interesting," Artemis murmured. "We should get out of your way and let you get on with things. But thank you, Sammi. Thank you very much."

"You're welcome," she said as she watched Artemis leave. Mak stood up and gave her his card.

"Please call me if you think of anything else," he told her and left.

Mak found Artemis outside on the sidewalk deep in thought, looking at the building across the street.

"Are you okay?" Mak asked.

"Yeah," Artemis answered slowly. "It feels like I've been living in a dream for a long time. It's good to be waking up."

"I'm truly glad," Mak said as he pulled out his cigarettes.

"You just said"—Artemis smiled at him—"that you're giving them up. Again."

"Yeah, I know," Mak said as he lit up. "But it helps me think. And we just got a lot to think about, right?"

"Absolutely," Artemis said. "What time was Drew going to be at TVNews this morning?"

Mak smiled. "Soon. We can get a cab on Bowery." He took a quick drag, tossed his cigarette, and they started walking south on Doyers Street. Artemis pulled out his cell phone and hit a number.

"Silas," he said. "We got something. Can you find a building record for us?"

*   *   *

With the six-hour time difference, it was three thirty in the afternoon in Dubrovnik, Croatia, and Ray Gaines was pacing by the large windows in his hotel room. He had thought that after yesterday's instructions and rush to leave Italy, the meeting with Andre Karlovic would have happened last night. But when he checked in, he was handed a note directing him to wait. Until now.

He had slept badly. The room was comfortable enough: a well-restored second-floor studio with exposed wood beams across the ceiling and arti-san-sculpted walls. But the city was crowded with college-aged tourists, and it had been a noisy night below. Ray checked his watch and leaned out the large casement window, the bright sunlight making him squint. The wide plaza below was bordered by beautiful sixteenth-century buildings with ornate carvings and columns. It was full of people shopping at covered stalls selling fruits and vegetables.

There was a knock. Ray picked up his cell phone, room key and opened the door. A nice-looking young man wearing dark pants and a white polo shirt greeted him courteously.

"Good afternoon, Agent Gaines. My name is Feliks. If you will please come with me, I will take you to Mr. Karlovic." Ray noticed the three-headed serpent logo embossed on his shirt pocket. He nodded to the man. They walked down a well-used marble staircase, past alcoves with Christian religious pictures, through a wood-paneled lobby, and out into the heat of the day. Inside the fortress walls of the old city, cars were not allowed and the limestone streets had a polished luster acquired from centuries of visitors. They walked past rows of red umbrellas and cafe tables full of people. Ray noted that no one was wearing a mask.

"Your COVID numbers," Ray asked as he walked alongside the man. "How are they here?"

Feliks smiled widely. "Here there is sun and all is well," he said indifferently as they turned a corner and headed under a tall archway in the thick fortress walls.

"Where are we going?" Ray asked easily.

"To the docks," he answered. "Mr. Karlovic will meet you on his yacht."

They came out of the short tunnel-like passage at a place crowded with tourists taking pictures and checking their cell phones.

"They are waiting for the ferry to Lokrum Island," Feliks explained as they made their way past the group. "It's a wonderful place, just out there." He pointed across the sparkling blue-green waters of the bay. "Have you been?"

"No," Ray answered as he looked around. Here, outside the medieval eighty-two-foot-high walls of Dubrovnik was a peaceful marina full of smaller boats. "Where's the yacht?"

"Moored just out there, off Lokrum," Feliks answered as they arrived at the far end of the wide dock. "This will take us there in a few minutes."

Down some steps cut into the stone pier was a classic twenty-foot launch with a covered seating area. On board, a young crewman, dressed in the same dark pants and white polo shirt, stood up as they carefully came down the steps. He reached out a hand to Ray to assist him. Ray accepted the help, stepped into the gently rocking boat, and sat near the back on a white leather deck chair. Feliks untied the lines, hopped in, and sat near Ray.

"Would you care for something to drink?" he asked. "Perhaps some champagne. Or a glass of cold water?"

"No, thank you," Ray answered. The engines fired up and the launch turned toward the open water. The speed increased, but the trim cut of the hull kept the ride smooth. A spray of sea salt misted across Ray's face.

"There she is," Feliks said proudly and Ray turned to see a magnificent white yacht moored in the calm waters off the island.

"It's beautiful," Ray said appreciatively. "One hundred and eighty, I'm guessing."

Feliks smiled, impressed. "Yes, she's fifty-five meters."

"And it's a classic line. Vintage, like me." Ray smiled at the young man.

"Good, again, sir," Feliks said. "She was built in 1938 as a private yacht for a British movie star and has had quite a colorful past. She was used during the Second World War to help rescue troops at Dunkirk. She has, of course, been completely refitted."

Ray could hear the obvious pride in his voice. "What's she called?"

"Trinitas."

Ray registered the name. The launch slowed as they came alongside the yacht, and Feliks got up and grabbed hold of the wood and metal stairs rigged amidships. He stepped over and held the boat close. The crewman again assisted Ray as he transferred his weight onto the stairs and followed Feliks up to the deck.

"This way please, sir," Feliks said formally and led the way aft. Ray followed taking in the fine details of the ship: the polished teak outer walls, the perfectly joined deck flooring, and the gleaming silver railings. They came to a large open-air salon with a fixed canopy of thick white muslin. The furniture was cream-colored leather with white accent pillows. Sitting in the shade was a very thin, elegant old man. He had high cheekbones, a full head of short gray hair, and trimmed mustache and beard. His shrewd brown eyes studied Ray.

"Special Agent Gaines, thank you for coming all this way to see me," the old man said with a gentle Slavic accent. He stood up with an easy dexterity and held out his hand. "I am Andre Karlovic."

Ray walked over to him and shook his hand. "It's good to meet you."

Andre smiled, the wrinkles around his eyes and across his forehead deepening. Ray had learned much about this man in the last twenty-four hours. He knew that he was eighty-nine years old and the head of a multinational banking corporation that he'd taken over from his father in the 1960's.

"Thank you, Feliks," Andre said agreeably to the young man, who tipped his head respectfully and left them alone. "Please sit, Agent Gaines. I think you'll find it very comfortable here in the shade."

Ray sat in a large deck chair under the awning. He looked out across the wide bay and took a long breath of the clean sea air.

"It is truly beautiful here," Ray said. "You grew up here?"

"Oh yes," Andre answered with quiet pride.

"But you went to school in America," Ray added. "You got your master's in business at Harvard."

Andre smiled. "Very good. You have been reading up. May I offer you something to drink? Perhaps, if it is not too early, some white wine?"

"Thank you," Ray said. Andre went to a glass-and-teak bar and poured two glasses of pale yellow wine. "This is from Istria," he said as he handed it to Ray.

Ray sipped it and smiled. "It's very good."

"I'm glad you think so," Andre said as he set a bowl of dried figs and nuts on the table in front of Ray. "It is the perfect thing to drink on a hot day like this," Andre added as he sat down in the large chair next to Ray. Andre sipped his wine.

"So," he said as he put his glass down. "You have read my proposal. I hope we will be able to help each other."

"I have been given the authority to do what you've asked," Ray said evenly. "If I am convinced that your information is genuine."

Andre looked at his eyes. "I want my grandson moved to a safe location. I want this to happen today."

Ray met his gaze and waited. Andre reached into a briefcase on the deck beside his chair, pulled out a large manila envelope, and handed it to him. Ray took out a half dozen pages of an official-looking coroner's report in Italian. He read each page carefully.

"This says that the body is unidentified," Ray said. "Seems to be just another COVID death. What makes you think it's him?"

In response, Andre pulled a smaller envelope from the briefcase and gave it to Ray. Inside was a cell phone in a clear plastic bag.

"This belonged to your agent, Bert Rocca. It was found near the body," Andre said.

"Where did you get this?" Ray asked.

Andre smiled. "That I am not at liberty to say. But getting it here is why this meeting was delayed for a day. I do apologize for making you wait."

"It will take some time for us to tell if this is really his phone," Ray said.

"It is Bert Rocca's phone," Andre said. "I give you my word. And you will go see for yourself. To Avola, in Sicily, to prove that the dead man is the one you've been looking for. The plane that brought you here to Dubrovnik is at your disposal."

Ray considered for a moment. "Okay."

"My grandson," Andre said, "is in extreme danger in your prison system. I want your word that he will be taken to a safe and comfortable place immediately."

"I promise it," Ray agreed. "I will make the call."

"Thank you," Andre said sincerely. "Do you have any children, Agent Gaines?"

"No, I have the kind of job that could put a family at risk," Ray answered candidly. "And I never wanted to chance that."

"Ah." The old man ran his lean fingers through his gray hair. "I understand. My only son was killed, many years ago now. But I still wonder what he would have become." He sipped his wine and looked across the blue water to the popular beaches of Lokrum Island not far away. "All these young people. Playing on the sand, rowing kayaks around the island. I hardly even go into Dubrovnik anymore. It's too crowded. They have made many films here and television shows, up on the walls and through the town, and so they come. Did you know"—he waved his hand at Lokrum—"that a king's throne from one of those shows is still there on the island? They left it so all these children can go there and take selfies pretending to be king."

Ray sipped his wine and listened.

"For me," the old man said, "it is a question of time and of what happens when it runs out." He turned to look at Ray. "I want Ladimir to be sent home. Here to Croatia. To me."

"I don't have that authority," Ray said truthfully.

"Not yet, perhaps," Andre said slowly. "But I think you could make this happen if I provide you with information regarding another case that you have been working on. For a very long time."

Ray wondered how much this man knew about him. "Which case?"

"*The* case," Andre answered. "You are the FBI's lead investigator of the Gardner Museum robbery, Boston, 1990."

Ray waited.

"You have found two pieces of stolen art. My congratulations," the old man said. "But you have no idea where the other eleven pieces are. Perhaps I could assist you with that. Would that make a difference in helping Ladimir find his way home?"

"It might," Ray said carefully. "If—"

"—If you believe that you can trust me. Because such information would only be given *after* my grandson is home. That must be the way of it."

"I will give it some thought," Ray said and sipped his wine.

"Good." The old man smiled a little. "Because when you get to Sicily and see the body of Agent Rocca, you will know that I am a man who can be trusted. And then we will be able to speak further about these important things." Andre pulled a business card from his shirt pocket. There was a handwritten number on the back. "I will await your call."

He handed the card to Ray and stood up. Ray got up, and Andre walked him back the way he'd come in. Ray felt the heat of the sun as he stepped out from under the awning. He stopped at the rail and looked out at the sparkling Adriatic beyond the island. Andre stood next to him.

"Feliks will see you safely back to your hotel and will wait to take you to the airport and assist with the officials," Andre said.

"Mr. Karlovic," Ray said. "May I ask you something?"

"Of course."

"Maybe twenty years ago, a fresco of a three-headed sea serpent was discovered decorating an ancient Etruscan tomb in Italy," Ray said.

Andre rested his thin fingers on the railing and chuckled. "The FBI really is so... knowledgeable. So, yes?"

"I saw a copy of that same picture in New York, on the wall of a bar where we recovered one of the stolen Gardner pieces."

"You said," Andre answered serenely, "it was a copy. Anyone can make a copy."

"That's true," Ray continued. "But that same three-headed serpent is the logo of your company. It's on your letterhead. It's on the shirts of your crewmen."

Andre looked at him and said nothing.

"Your boat is called the Trinitas. I'm getting a theme here," Ray said and smiled a little.

Andre smiled back and said, "I do like you, Agent Gaines. You ask a proper question. But I will not give you a direct answer. However. Keep that question in your mind in Sicily. Three heads. One body."

Ray nodded taking this in.

"I look forward to hearing from you," Andre said and offered his hand.

"You will," Ray answered, shook his hand, and walked away forward along the outside deck. He found Feliks waiting at the top of the steps. Feliks followed Ray down the stairs, and as before, the crewman on the launch assisted him on board. Once he and Feliks were seated, the boat was untied and they started off toward the old city. Ray looked back to the yacht and saw Andre still standing at the railing watching them. There was something about the old man, his gray hair glowing in the sunlight, standing like a statue on his vintage boat that gave Ray a chill.

"A flight plan has been filed for your trip, and your plane will be ready to depart in an hour," Feliks said efficiently. "If that is acceptable to you."

"Yes," Ray said loudly over the sound of the engines. "That's perfect."

Andre Karlovic watched the launch in the distance as it slowed down and turned in a wide curve approaching the stone docks. He walked back into the salon, sat in his chair, and picked up his cell phone. He called up a number and pushed it.

"Pronto," a man answered.

"It is Andre," he said.

"One moment, sir," the man said courteously, and Andre heard the line go quiet as he was put on hold.

An old crow-like woman sat in a large wood chair under the shade of several tall palm trees. Looking out over the neat rows of vines and rolling hills, she could see the town of Avola in the distance and beyond, the vast Ionian Sea blue and calm in the afternoon light. Her name was Marta Abruzzo, and when she was a girl, such a long time ago now, she had loved to go into Avola where she could swim at the town's beach, explore ancient ruins, or wander the paths between the strange raised crypts in the cemetery. She sighed.

Her claw-like fingers wrapped around an earthenware cup and lifted it to her wrinkled lips. She took a sip and sweet pulpy orange juice rolled across her tongue and cooled her throat as she swallowed.

The loggia door opened at the back of the palazzo, and her man came out carrying a phone. He made his way past an armed guard, down the redstone steps to the grassy plateau where she sat.

"Trias," he said respectfully as he handed her the phone.

Marta turned her beak-like face, looked at him with her small dark eyes, and asked, "Which one?"

"Mr. Karlovic," he answered and walked away back toward the palazzo.

She pushed a button on the phone and said, "Hello, Andre. Is he coming?"

"Good afternoon," he said cordially. "And yes. Agent Gaines should be arriving in Avola early this evening. He will, I'm sure, be contacting his friends in Interpol and the Italian authorities. But I expect him to be at the morgue first thing tomorrow."

The old woman took a breath. "Very well. Thank you for calling me. I will take care of everything. I assure you."

"It is always a pleasure, Marta," Andre said and hung up. And he hoped, after all their years of friendship, she could still be trusted.

He lifted his glass and sipped the light Istrian wine. The yacht rolled gently in the wake of a passing boat and the bright sun, now low on the horizon, flashed under the awning and into his eyes.

* * *

By 11:00 a.m. in Manhattan, it was still ninety degrees, a steady rain was falling, and although it was Saturday, some of the TVNews staff had been called in to work to help with the transition of offices.

Roxie Lee stood looking out the windows in her eighth-floor corner office, listening to her cell phone, waiting for the beep.

"Paul, it's me," she said controlling the worry in her voice. "I just need to talk. Call me when you can." She hung up, turned back to her desk, and finished packing her personal items into a couple of boxes. She looked at the space around her and smiled a little. The staff had called this office the Watchtower because from here the supervising producer could keep an eye on the block-long newsroom. Through the glass office walls, she could see Deni at her workstation. Like Roxie, she was gathering her things.

Across the room, Greg arrived carrying a closed wet umbrella. He left it in the stand by the reception desk, pulled off his COVID mask, and made his way over to Deni. They picked up her boxes and headed for the Watchtower.

"Good morning," Greg said as they paused at the open door.

"Good morning"—Roxie smiled—"or should I say good afternoon."

"Sorry, it's the rain. The subway's a mess."

"No worries," Roxie said. "Come in."

They walked in and put the boxes down. Roxie came around the desk and hugged Deni.

"Welcome to your new office. You so deserve this." Roxie held her at arm's length. She looked at Deni's pendant necklace and the gem hanging on her chest. She undid one button on Deni's shirt so the stone could be seen more clearly.

"*Pink Sapphire,*" Roxie said her secret name.

Deni whispered, "I miss the classes."

"Me too." Greg added.

"I'm so proud of you both," Roxie said. "The way you've carried on. And your loyalty."

"Thank you," Deni said. "I could never have gotten here without your help."

"Of course you could have." Roxie smiled at her and turned to Greg. "Could you give me a hand getting my stuff upstairs?"

"Glad to." Greg lifted the heavier box off the desk. "And by the way, should I be looking for a new job now that Jock is gone?"

Roxie laughed. "You are still the assistant to the executive producer. Me."

"Thanks, Roxie," Greg said warmly. "I was just checking."

"Everything is going to be all right," Roxie reassured them. "I promise."

Deni and Greg took that in.

"Let's head upstairs so she can settle in," Roxie said as she picked up a box. "And Deni, could you do me a favor? Come up and interrupt me in fifteen minutes. I'll be in a meeting that I'll need to get out of."

"Not a problem," Deni said.

"Thanks." Roxie walked out and Greg followed to the door. There he turned back and smiled.

"I'm so happy for you," he said genuinely and left.

Deni walked around the large glass desk and sat in the tall leather chair. She leaned back and smiled. "I'm pretty damn happy for me too."

Roxie and Greg walked up the open-tread glass stairs to the executive level where a frumpy woman was sitting slumped on a sofa in the reception area. She heard them coming and looked up with worry. Her eyes were red from crying.

Barb the receptionist saw Roxie, put down her hairbrush, and said apologetically, "Ms. Canneli has been waiting for you."

"I see." Roxie came over to Anna. "I have a few minutes before an appointment. Why don't you come in and we can talk," she said kindly.

Anna nodded, and Roxie led the way into her new office. Greg rolled his eyes to Barb, who smiled knowingly in response. Then he followed into the office and closed the door.

"Please sit down," Roxie said graciously to Anna as she stepped behind the large desk and put down her box. Anna cautiously sat in one of the two chairs in front of the desk. Greg put his box down by the built-in bar.

"There's fresh coffee made," he said to Roxie.

"No, thanks," she answered as she sat in the large black leather desk chair. "Damn. Jock really had no taste. This place so needs a makeover."

"Perhaps you could do something a little less... reptilian," Greg offered and Roxie laughed. She turned to Anna who was sitting with her shoulders rounded forward and her arms wrapped around her chest. "Would you like some coffee, Anna?"

"No, thank you. I just want to know..." She trailed off.

"You want to know." Roxie looked at her with pity. "If you still have a job here at TVNews."

"Yes," Anna said almost to herself.

"You do," Roxie said plainly.

Anna looked up surprised. "But... what will I do?"

Behind her Greg sarcastically shrugged his shoulders, but Roxie ignored him.

"What you have always done," Roxie answered. "Be the assistant to the star of the show."

"You want me to be"—Anna seemed confused and alarmed—"Moira Weyland's assistant?"

"I do," Roxie said firmly. "And you better learn how to say her name so it doesn't sound like a disease."

"I..." Anna opened and shut her mouth a few times trying to get her mind around the idea. "Isn't there anything else I can do?"

"You could stay at home, collect unemployment, and look for something else," Roxie answered. "But I hope you'll stay."

Anna stood up and smoothed her wrinkled brown dress with her pudgy fingers. "Yes. I would very much like to stay. Thank you, Roxie."

"You're welcome," Roxie said. "So go downstairs, find Moira, and tell her the good news."

Anna's mouth twisted into a forced smile as she turned and left.

"You're too nice for your own good," Greg said as he closed the door behind her.

"No, I'm not." Roxie started to unpack her things. "We'll need her to be our eyes and ears."

The phone on her desk rang; she lifted the receiver and listened.

"Thank you, Barb. Please send them in."

The door opened, and Drew Sweeney came in, her NYPD badge displayed on her belt.

"Nice to see you again, Detective," Roxie said.

"And you, Ms. Lee. I think you know these men," she said as Mak and Artemis came in. All three were wearing masks.

"Of course, Agent Kim and Doctor Bookbinder," Roxie said with a smile. "I'd know those faces anywhere. Please sit down."

It had been well over a year since she'd seen these people. Then, they had been investigating the death of an old art dealer, her friend Raphael Sharder. Drew and Mak sat in the chairs in front of her desk. Artemis sat away from them on a sofa along the wall.

"Would anyone care for coffee or tea?" Greg asked politely.

"No, thank you," Drew answered, and Mak did the same. Artemis seemed to not hear the question for a second, but then he shook his head no. Drew looked at him with concern. Artemis met her eyes to let her know he was okay.

"Thank you, Greg," Roxie said. "I'll give a call if I need you."

Greg went into his adjoining office and closed the door behind him.

"If you guys want"—Roxie gestured—"I don't mind if you take those off."

"Thanks," Mak said as he and Drew pulled off their masks with relief. Artemis's hand reached up but then he changed his mind and left it on.

"So," Drew said as she looked around the large office. "Congratulations on your promotion."

"Thank you."

"Did it come as a surprise?" Drew asked. "We heard that Paula DeVong was supposed to be getting this job."

"Yes, she was," she answered smoothly. "And I was the next obvious choice after her."

"Jock Willinger was fired because of the pending harassment case, right?" Mak asked.

Roxie wondered who they'd been talking to. "Sorry. I'm not allowed to speak about that."

"And Moira"—Artemis joined in, his words slightly muffled behind his mask—"is the new star of the show?"

Roxie turned to him. "Yes. It's a tryout, but I think Moira will do fine." She looked at his intense blue eyes and saw how much sadder they were since they last met. "Are you sure you wouldn't be more comfortable without that thing?" she asked.

Artemis sighed. "No. Probably not." Then, despite his misgivings, he pulled off his mask. "But you will be."

His face was thinner but still handsome. Roxie said sympathetically, "I was so sorry to hear of your loss, Artemis. How are you doing?"

The question caught him off guard, but he managed. "Not too bad. Thank you. It's been a long year."

"Has there been any progress on finding out who killed Raphael?" she asked.

"No," Artemis answered. "Nothing to report yet."

"You know what?" she said easily, "you never got to see my Ernst painting. I'd love to show it to you sometime."

Artemis smiled and said, "I would really like that. Are you free later today?"

Roxie looked surprised and laughed a little. "No, I'm afraid not today."

"Ah, okay." Artemis was still smiling, but she could see his disappointment.

"But I could do tomorrow night. Say around seven?" she offered.

"Perfect," he answered.

"I'll send my details." Roxie got her cell and started typing. "What's your number?"

Artemis gave her his number, and she sent the text. He pulled out his phone and checked the information.

"My place is just over there, a few blocks away." She pointed out the large windows. "By the river."

"Great, thanks."

Roxie turned back to Drew. "Yesterday I told the NYPD all I could about Paula and I know you have that. But today you've brought along the FBI and an art historian. So, how can I help you?"

Mak took the lead. "We'd like to ask you about your necklace."

Roxie's left hand went up, and her fingers wrapped around the large clear ruby hanging on her chest. "That's"—she paused searching for the right word—"unexpected. What do you want to know?"

"Who gave it to you?" Mak asked.

"A friend," Roxie said, having recovered herself. "We talked about that the last time you were here."

"Sixteen months ago," Mak confirmed. "And you said then that your friend valued his privacy."

"Good memory," she said. "And he does."

"Can you tell us anything about a class that met every Sunday night at midnight downtown on Doyers Street?"

"Doyers?" Roxie recalled. "Yes. That's where you guys found the second Gardner piece. The Chinese chalice. We covered it. Moira Weyland was the reporter on the scene."

"Gu," Artemis said quietly.

She looked puzzled.

"The chalice," he explained. "It's called Gu."

She chuckled. "That's right."

There was a knock on the door, and Deni came in.

"Oh, sorry to interrupt," she said. Artemis made a mental note of Deni's silver necklace and the light pink gem hanging on her chest.

"It's all right," Roxie replied. "What's up?"

"They need you down in the studio," Deni said apologetically. "Some crisis about what to do with Jock's old chair."

"Really?" Roxie scoffed. "Burn it."

Deni laughed. "Sorry, but I think you better come handle it."

"Okay. I'll be there," Roxie said good-naturedly. "Go keep the peace."

"Thanks Roxie," Deni said and left.

"Sorry, duty calls," Roxie said. "Was there anything else?"

"Would it be all right," Drew asked, "if we spend some time in the studio and talked to some of your people?"

"Of course," Roxie answered without hesitation. She picked up her desk phone, hit three numbers, and said, "Please come in."

A moment later, Greg entered from his office. "How can I help?" he asked.

"Detective Sweeney, Agent Kim, and Doctor Bookbinder will be here for a while. I'm sure they'll want to speak with the staff. Please assist them in whatever they need."

"My pleasure," Greg said as he went and stood by the door.

"Thank you for seeing us, Ms. Lee," Drew said as she got up.

Roxie stood. "Please let me know if there's anything else I can do."

"Thank you," Drew said and she and Mak headed out.

"And I"—Artemis stood—"will see you tomorrow night, if that's still okay?"

Roxie smiled. "Yes. It is definitely okay."

"See you then," he said, pulled on his face mask, and left the office. Greg looked at Roxie with concern before he left and closed the door.

"Where would you like to start?" Greg asked Drew. She looked at the pretty receptionist who was busy checking her eyeliner in a small mirror.

"Downstairs in the newsroom," Drew answered, and Greg led the way down the stairs.

"Have you heard anything from your sister, Beth?" Artemis asked as he followed behind the others a few steps.

"No," Greg answered worriedly. "There's been nothing in all this time. And I've contacted everyone who might know. Nothing."

As they stepped off the stairs, they saw Anna talking with Moira at the coffee station. Moira said something dismissive to Anna, who then walked away to her little office and slammed the door. Greg led the others over to Moira who was fumbling with a stack of paper cups trying to free one.

"Fuck," she muttered.

"Can I help?" Greg asked. Moira turned sharply to say something to him but stopped when she saw the others.

"Yes," she said, straining to be civil. "You can tell me why Paula's door-mat has been assigned to me. Don't I even get a say in who's my assistant?"

"No," Greg said happily. "You've had your own show now for what, two days? Roxie told Anna that she's your assistant. And you will just have to suck it up."

Moira looked like she might implode. Then she took a long dramatic breath. "Fine!" she said emphatically. "Fine! I couldn't be happier." She turned away, marched off to her office, and slammed the door.

"The transition's going well," Greg said satirically. "It's a little rough on the doors, but other than that..."

Drew grunted a short laugh. "Let's start with that one," she said and nodded to Anna's closed door.

"Well, why not"—Greg quipped as he led them across the newsroom—"you've got a gun, after all."

Greg knocked on the door and announced loudly, "The police are here for you, Anna." Several people in the newsroom looked up with interest.

The door opened ferociously, and Anna glared at Greg.

"Ah, there you are," he said sweetly. "This is Detective Sweeney, Agent Kim and..."

"Artemis Bookbinder, I know," she cut him off nastily. "We've met."

"We'd like to speak with you, Ms. Canneli," Drew said.

Anna scowled at them but relented. "Okay. Come in." She stepped back into her little office and sat behind the metal desk. Drew and Mak followed her in and stood in front of the desk.

"You going in?" Greg asked Artemis.

Artemis could see the small space, crowded with shelves of binders and files. He felt panic in his chest. He swallowed hard and got hold of himself. "Yes," he answered and started in slowly.

"I'll be out here if you need me," Greg said as he sat on a nearby desk.

"I loved Paula and she loved me." Anna's voice was muted and strained. "Did she really die from COVID?"

Artemis stood in the open doorway trying to keep as much room as he could from the others.

"We're looking into it," Drew said as she noted Anna's nervous fingers fiddling the pens on her desk. "Did she have any enemies here in the studio?"

"Yes," Anna answered readily and then realized she may have said too much.

"It's okay," Drew said as she sat her powerful body on a corner of the desk. "We need to know that sort of thing. It doesn't mean you're accusing anyone. We just want to get the feel of things."

Anna looked up at her. "Jock Willinger hated her so much. He knew that she was going to get his job."

"Thanks," Drew said. "Anyone else?"

"Calvin was sleeping with her," she said. "Though no one was supposed to know. But Paula kept no secrets from me."

"Ah." Drew smiled a little. "And?"

"Deni Diaz and Greg Schaefer, always so funny, mocking everybody behind their backs. And have you noticed who's gotten a promotion?" Anna raised up her hand and pointed a finger at the wall behind Drew. "Her. Moira." Her voice was raspy with anger. "She's in there now, busy setting up all her little things. That was Paula's office. And they just gave it to her."

"Can I ask you," Artemis said, "what are these pictures with numbers for?" Three photos were thumbtacked to the wall next to where she was sitting. They were of Deni, Greg, and Jock Willinger. Each of them had small numbers handwritten in the corners and across their faces. Greg's photo had many more numbers than the others.

"Oh, that." Anna smiled maliciously. She looked at Artemis's eyes accessing whether she could trust him. Then she said, "It's a thing I learned from my grandfather. When people are mean, you can do something about it."

"What?" Mak asked. "You put a curse on them?"

Anna looked at him with distrust. "Where are you from anyway? Japan?"

Mak shook off the insulting tone in her voice and answered patiently. "Hawaii. Before that my people came from Korea."

Anna just stared at him.

Artemis brought her back. "Your grandfather was Sicilian?"

Anna seemed impressed. "Yes."

"And is he still alive?"

"No," she said sadly. "He's been gone a long time now."

"We heard that on Wednesday night, the night Paula died," Drew picked it up. "That she had a meeting with Jock after the show. And that you were there."

"Yes. And Jock wasn't too happy she brought me along. But Paula said that she wanted me to be there as a witness."

"Could you tell us what that meeting was about?" Drew asked.

"There was some story that Paula wanted to do. It seemed like she and Jock had talked about it before. He told her that she couldn't do it, and when she started to argue, he just waved her off and rolled his eyes."

"What did Paula say?" Drew asked.

"Well." Anna squinted her eyes as she remembered. "She laughed. And Jock looked like he was going to shout. He got red around his neck. And she said that it didn't matter because he'd be out soon enough. And by Monday, she wouldn't need his approval for anything. Then Jock just got quiet and we left. And I was really glad to get out of there."

"How was Paula after that meeting?"

"Fine." She smiled. "No, she was great. She was in a good mood and sent me home early."

Drew asked Anna for her home address and phone number. Anna looked worried, but she got a piece of paper, wrote down the information, and impatiently handed it to Drew.

"Thank you, Anna. You've been a help," Drew said as she stood up to go.

Anna nodded, and they left her office. She grabbed a fine-point marker and frowned at the photos on the wall. She added two numbers on Greg Schaefer's forehead with dark determination.

"Where to?" Greg inquired as they walked back through the newsroom.

"Is Calvin Prons here today?" Drew asked.

"On a Saturday?" Greg grinned. "Not a chance. But Barb upstairs can schedule an appointment with him if you want."

"I'll do that later," Drew said as they stopped near the stairs. "Can we go down to the studio?"

"Sure," Greg answered. "But there isn't much crew in today. We don't shoot again until Monday."

"That's okay," Mak said. "We'll talk with whoever's there."

"Right this way," Greg said, and they started down the steps.

"And we're going to need Jock Willinger's home address and number," Drew added.

"Not a problem," Greg said cheerfully.

Across the newsroom, Moira watched through the glass wall of her office as they disappeared down the stairs. Like the Watchtower at the opposite corner, she had a commanding view of everything that happened on the floor. She rolled the blinds closed and went back to the desk. Her laptop was there and her bag next to it. But everything still felt like Paula's office.

Television is temporary.

Someone had told her that once. She couldn't remember who. She walked over to the large windows looking out toward Lincoln Center across the busy streets. The rain was still falling but more gently now. She leaned her head on the glass and closed her eyes.

* * *

"Thank you, Doctor. I owe you." Detective Jerome Clayton Collins hung up his desk phone at the 19th Precinct and opened the file on his laptop that the pathologist had just sent. He took a gulp of coffee as he read the report.

Clayton was an ambitious, young Black man with a strong build and clear sharp eyes, who had recently gained notice as an innovative CIS researcher.

He whistled to himself, picked up his cell phone, and hit a number.

"Hey," Drew said as she stepped away from the others in the studio control room. "You get it?"

"Yeah," Clayton answered. "It just came in. Paula DeVong died of a stroke which is presumed to be related to COVID. She tested positive."

"Right," Drew said.

"But there's more." Clayton scrolled the report. "The OCME is going to hold the body for a while because Paula DeVong also had an overdose of phentermine in her system." Clayton started typing on his laptop.

Drew stepped outside the control room and onto the wide studio floor. She walked away from the staff near the news desk and cameras. "What's phentermine? Weight loss?" she asked.

"Yeah, weight loss. It's been in use since 1959," Clayton read as he found the information. "Phentermine is in at least three prescription drugs. It's supposed to be used short-term. And symptoms for an overdose are confusion, irregular heartbeat, or seizure. Normal dose is up to... 30 mg per day. And she had"—Clayton flipped back to the coroner's report and his eyes moved quickly across the information—"about three times that amount in her system."

Drew sat on the steps in the back of the studio. "Does that rule out her just forgetting and taking an extra pill or two?"

"No, it doesn't," Clayton answered.

"Well, assuming she had a prescription, we need to find her doctor."

"I'm on it." Clayton agreed. "I'll call you when I get something."

"Thanks," Drew said and hung up.

Clayton took another sip of coffee and started working on his computer. His cell phone rang and he answered, "Detective Collins."

"Clayton...?" a woman's voice asked uncertainly.

He stopped working. "Yes. Who's this?"

There was a long silence before she said, "Beth Schaefer. You gave me your card. Do you remember me?"

Clayton's eyes widened in surprise. He had met her only once, sixteen months ago. She was the manager at Raphael Sharder's Manhattan gallery and she had disappeared the day after he was murdered. "Yes, I surely do. We have been looking for you everywhere. Are you okay?"

"Yes," she answered carefully. "I really need to talk with you."

"Good," Clayton said encouragingly. "Where are you? In Canada?"

"No, I'm..." Beth pulled the phone away from her mouth and ran her fingers through her short dark-blonde hair. She was a young, good-looking woman in her early thirties. She was dressed in jeans and a tee shirt with a knapsack on her shoulders. She walked down a grassy trail to a small sandy beach. There she sat on a large stone looking out at the smooth waters of a wide tree-lined lake. The day was hot, and the air was clean. She took a deep breath. "I'm in the United States. In Maine. At a place called Moosehead Lake." She looked down at his card clutched tightly in her hand. "But I'd like to come back to New York."

"Okay—" Clayton started, but she cut him off.

"But I don't want to be arrested when I get there."

"Beth," he assured her, "we just want to talk with you."

She gazed at the far shore where a pair of Canadian geese gracefully circled down and landed in the shallow water. "I saw the news about Paula DeVong and... I'm worried. Would it be possible to just talk with you?" she asked hopefully.

"No, Beth. There's a lot of people who want to see you. It will be pretty official," he said reasonably. "But I'll be there. And it'll be all right."

"I'll call you tomorrow," she said and hung up.

Clayton leaned back in his chair and closed his eyes, processing what had just happened.

In the TVNews control room, Greg stood in the back row watching Artemis, Mak, and Drew talking with one of the staff. His cell phone rang; he checked the ID and stepped out of the room to take the call.

"Where have you been?" he said urgently as he walked away from the door. "I've been so worried."

"I've been busy getting out of Canada without a passport," Beth walked back up the hill and entered a trail running through the woods. "I'm coming home."

*　*　*

"I brought you lunch," Delia said as she came through the open door to Silas's room. He was absorbed with his research on two laptops on his desk and didn't hear her. She put down a plate with a sandwich and a tall glass of cold milk. She moved behind him and placed her hands on his shoulders. He looked up surprised.

"Sorry to disturb you," she said. "But I want you to eat something."

"I will, Auntie, thanks," he said and started working again.

"Now," she demanded, and he looked around at her. She was smiling but seemed tired and worried.

"How are you doing?" he asked kindly.

She laughed. "Trust you to say the right thing. I'm good. I've gotten everything unpacked and where it should be and for the most part, clean and ready for use. But maybe I could do with a nap."

Silas had never heard of Delia taking a nap before, and his curiosity showed in his large brown eyes.

"It's just that," she explained, "there's an AA meeting at five and it's a new group for me. Drew's coming by to walk me there. God bless her."

Silas smiled at her, understanding. He picked up the sandwich and took a large bite. "It's very good," he mumbled with his mouth full. Satisfied, Delia nodded to him. Silas put down the sandwich, took a sip of milk, pushed his ever-sliding glasses back into place on his nose, and returned to his search.

"What are you working on?" she asked as she sat on the edge of his bed.

"Something that Artemis asked for," he answered as he worked. "You know that schoolroom on Doyers Street? Under that abandoned bar, the Necropolis?"

"Yes, I remember."

"It seems"— Silas's voice grew soft as he focused on his task—"that the school has a secret entrance somewhere, and I'm looking at owners and renters of the neighborhood buildings."

She watched him so focused, so dedicated to what he was doing. She wondered if he would ever have a more normal life. A life beyond the pandemic where he could be out with kids his own age. She missed the boy he was before. But she was proud of the man he was becoming.

"A year ago, we learned," he explained, "that the building was owned by this guy." He pointed to one of a dozen note-filled Post-its on the wall beside him. "Aldo Mancini. But we haven't been able to find him. His listed address is a building in Queens that burned down five years ago. Clayton sent me this NYC link, and I've been looking to see if Aldo Mancini owns any other building around there. But the records are kind of a mess." He took a quick sip of milk and frowned. "Do we have any coffee made?"

"No," Delia said firmly.

"Okay," Silas said agreeably as he started to get up. "I can make some."

"I'll do it," Delia said with a resigned chuckle, got up, and headed off to the kitchen.

On his second computer, Silas called up a map of the streets at the edge of Chinatown. Zooming in, he saw that the buildings directly behind the Doyers Street school all faced Mott Street.

*   *   *

In Southampton, it was eighty-seven degrees. But unlike Manhattan, some ninety miles to the west, the skies had cleared and a fresh breeze was blowing in off the ocean. Patty Figgins, a durable woman in her late sixties in a brown maid's uniform, walked briskly along the sidewalk on Main Street pulling a large roller-board suitcase behind her. As she went, she turned her round face from side to side, and her little eyes darted warily along the parked cars and shop fronts. She came to the entrance of the Primrose Restaurant, a favorite place among the locals. With an effort, she managed to push the large glass door open and pull the heavy suitcase inside.

"Hey, Maddy Griff," she said too loudly, her Irish descendancy clear in her words.

Behind the long wooden bar, Madeline Griffin, a thin pleasant-looking woman in jeans and a button-down shirt looked up at her exasperated. She pushed a loose strand of silver-blonde hair off her forehead and quickly came over.

"Patty, pipe down." Maddy Griff chided her. "You're not performing at the Grand Ole Opry, all right. Did you get everything?"

"I think so," Patty whispered apologetically.

Maddy Griff turned and called to a waitress pouring coffee for the only customer, "I'm going to be off the floor for a bit. Hold the fort." It was the quiet time between lunch and dinner. Business had been disastrous during the first year of COVID but had recovered a good deal when the warm weather came this season. Maddy Griff, like all the merchants in town, watched the news everyday wondering when the Delta variant would disrupt everything again.

She led Patty Figgins past the bar, through a green wood door to a small clean hallway decorated with black-and-white nautical prints. They passed the restrooms, and at the end of the hall, Maddy Griff unlocked another door.

"Here, let me handle that," she said as she easily lifted the suitcase and started up a narrow flight of stairs. "Make sure that's closed behind you," she added as Patty followed her.

At the top, they came to a landing with floral-papered walls. Maddy Griff went to a closed door and knocked loudly.

"Come in," an old woman's voice answered.

Maddy Griff opened the door. Inside was a small bedroom with sage-colored wainscoting and a bright open view of the backyard garden below. Sitting in two rocking chairs by the window was a truly odd couple. One was an old nun dressed head to toe in an old-fashioned habit sipping a mug of coffee. And the other was a disheveled-looking older man of Japanese descent, with a badly matted hairweave, wearing pajamas and a white waffle-weave bathrobe.

"Did you get in all right?" Taki asked eagerly as he saw the suitcase and Patty's flushed face.

"Oh yes," she said trying to sound nonchalant. "Nothing to it. There was nobody there. It was easy-peasy."

With an effort, Taki pushed himself out of the rocking chair and went over to Patty. He kissed both of her cheeks and said warmly, "Thank you."

"You're welcome, I'm sure." She smiled pleased with herself.

Taki looked to Maddy Griff and said sincerely, "And thank you for taking us in."

"Not the slightest problem," she said as she lifted the suitcase, put it on the bed, and opened it.

"Ahh," Taki exclaimed as he lifted up two of his favorite shirts: one a festive Hawaiian design with large blue orchids and the other a pink button-down dress shirt. "Hello, boys, I've missed you so much!"

Behind him, the old nun chuckled darkly.

"You know," Taki said as he turned to her, "it's really creepy when you do that."

"I know," she said as her eyes flashed mischievously. "It runs in my family."

Taki looked bewildered. "I don't ever remember Raphael sounding like that."

"No, he wouldn't. He was always the artist," she said fondly. "I meant like our father. That was a man."

Taki nodded vaguely and turned back to explore the contents of the suitcase.

"Raphael's lawyer should have been contacted by now," the old woman said to Maddy Griff. "Have you heard from her?"

"Yes, Sister..." she began but was cut off.

"Khloe is my name. I prefer to be called that."

"Right," Maddy Griff said slowly. "She needs some time to verify the documents that were delivered to her. At least until tomorrow."

The old nun eyed her suspiciously. "What's her name again?"

"Her name is Barbara Borsa." Maddy Griff smiled reassuringly. "And she's a friend."

* * *

The Correctional Center in Hartford, Connecticut was ten acres of bleak, short brown-brick buildings surrounded by high chain-link fences and coils of razor wire. A metal door swung open, and four FBI agents escorted Ladimir Karlovic out to a private parking area. He was dressed in an orange jumpsuit and his ankles and hands were cuffed. Ladimir's odd eyes glanced around fearfully as two agents steered him into the back seat of an unmarked silver van. The doors were closed, and the engine started. Ladimir peered out the front windshield and saw two dark sedans leading them out past the security gate, onto a busy street, past a bail bonds office and a used-car lot. Almost immediately, they turned onto the entrance ramp for Highway I-95 southbound.

"Where are you taking me?" Ladimir asked, trying to sound unconcerned. The agents didn't answer. "Should I be afraid, or do I say thank you?"

The agent sitting to his right said, "It's a two-hour drive. Just relax."

Ladimir sat back in his seat.

Outside the detention center, a young FBI agent watched the silver van as it traveled out of sight on the highway. He pulled out his cell, scrolled for a number, and punched it.

Nicky looked out the front window at the over-hot sweaty New Yorkers hurrying by. He was glad the place had air-conditioning. With his great girth, it had been a long time since he was comfortable outside in the heat. But he was beginning to feel like a caged animal inside the closed bar. His cell rang. He checked the ID and answered. "Yes?"

"Something's up and I thought you should know," the FBI agent said.

"Thank you. That's appreciated," Nicky said politely.

"The FBI just moved your boy Karlovic out of Hartford."

Nicky sucked a quick angry breath through his teeth. "Where are they taking him?"

"I don't know," the agent said. "But it wasn't our Connecticut guys. They were from New Jersey. The order came directly from Washington. That's all I know."

"Thank you, my friend," Nicky said calmly. "I will not forget this." He hung up and started to pace very slowly along the length of the wood bar, unsure what it all meant. He came to a decision and hit a number on his cell.

Paul was sitting on the floor in his penthouse leaning against the sofa staring out the large glass balcony doors at the dark clouds above. His phone rang.

"Did you find Ida?" Paul asked.

"No," Nicky answered impatiently. "And that's not why I'm calling. Ladimir was just moved to an unknown location by the feds. And I want to know... did your mother do this?"

Paul's eyes looked worried, but he controlled the tone of his voice. "No. But maybe you should ask your grandma. Or old man Karlovic."

"Fucking old people," Nicky growled scornfully.

"Do you really think the Trias aren't aware of what you're doing?" Paul laughed, and Nicky felt a cold sweat break out on the back of his wide neck.

"My grandmother needs me. There is no one else," he said defiantly.

"And Andre Karlovic has only Ladimir. And you've fucked with that when you got him arrested."

"But I never did..." Nicky started but Paul cut him off sharply.

"You're a moron. Hope you've enjoyed the ride 'cause it's time to get off, *Fat Nicky*." Paul hung up.

Nicky wiped the back of his neck with his hand and let out a shaky breath. He got up and went behind the bar, pulled out a bottle of vodka, and poured himself a shot.

* * *

With the time difference, it was nine thirty at night in Croatia, and Andre's yacht was cruising up the Dalmatian coast at a comfortable eight knots. He leaned back in his deck chair as he listened on his cell phone. He looked out at the bright moon shining above the wide dark water.

"Thank you very much. I am pleased." Andre said with courteous formality and hung up. He lifted a glass of champagne and took a slow sip. "It is done," he said to his assistant Feliks who was sitting in a deck chair next to him. Andre handed him his phone. "Would you please get Marta Abruzzo on the line?"

Feliks took the cell and dialed her number from memory. He identified who was calling and listened. "You are on hold," Feliks said as he handed the phone back to Andre. "I think they maybe had to wake her."

Andre chuckled. "None of us are getting any younger. I will call if I need you."

"Thank you, sir," Feliks said, got up, and walked out of the open-air salon.

"Hello, Andre," Marta's voice sounded unusually tired. "Is there news?"

"Yes," he said. "Ladimir has been moved. Agent Gaines has kept his word to me."

"Very good," Marta said as she gently waved away the middle-aged woman adjusting her blankets. Rosa, her niece, nodded and left the bedroom, closing the door behind her.

"Then tomorrow morning I will deal with the FBI agent as we have agreed," the old woman said.

"And what about your grandson?" Andre asked.

Marta sighed. "He grew up without a father. Like Ladimir. Only that boy had you to look up to. To teach and correct him. I have failed Nicolas. And I will take care of what has to be done. I give you my word."

Andre's old eyes grew sad. "Thank you, Marta. And will you call me tomorrow after your meeting with the agent?"

"Of course," she said. "Good night, Andre."

Marta hung up and leaned back into her pillows. But unlike Andre, her eyes were not sad. They were dark and calculating. If Nicolas didn't inherit, then who was left? There was only Rosa, her niece. A dependable woman who deserved to be rewarded for her loyalty. But what of all the things that Marta and her family before her had built? They would surely fall apart with Rosa in charge. It was a problem with no solution. Marta squinted her beady eyes at the cell phone to see better as she found a number and dialed it.

In the closed bar, Nicky jumped at the sound of his phone ringing. He saw the caller ID, collected himself, and answered.

"Nicolas. It is me," Marta said with quiet power. "I need to talk with you."

"Yes, Nonna," he said.

"You were wrong to betray your friends and get Ladimir arrested," she said plainly.

"But, Nonna," he said quickly. "I was only doing what I thought you'd like. Trying to show you that I can be in charge here. Make you proud of me."

"The Karlovics are important to us," she answered fiercely.

"But you aren't here," he pleaded. "I saw a chance for us. Paul is a mess. All the heat on us because of his stolen chalice-thing. He's grown careless. And bored. And Ladimir does whatever Paul says. They are both a problem. And last week, you said that the Voskos family was in disarray and that it was time for Paul and his mother to... *retire*."

"I did say that last week," she pronounced like a death sentence. "And I am taking care of the Voskos problem, with Andre Karlovic's blessing and help. And what do you do? You get his grandson arrested. He is unhappy with me. I am unhappy with you."

"I... I am sorry to have disappointed you," he said sheepishly.

"You are a foolish child," she said wearily. "What am I to do with you now?"

Nicolas heard the threat in her words. "I am so sorry," he said again.

"A leader never apologizes." It was a mantra that she had followed all her life. "They just fix what has gone wrong."

"Thank you, Nonna," Nicky said obediently. "I will do that."

"Good." Marta looked to her bedside table where a photograph of Andre Karlovic stood in a vintage silver frame.

Only the strong will survive.

She cleared her throat. "Stay in touch with me, Nicolas. I want to know everything."

"Yes, Nonna, I will," he answered dutifully and hung up.

He grabbed the bottle of vodka and refilled his glass. "Fucking old crow"—he grunted angrily—"why can't you just die already." He knocked back his drink and poured another.

* * *

Ida reached up and directed the powerful stream of hot water onto her neck in the hope of releasing some of the tension. She groaned loudly. She turned off the water and stepped out of the glass-enclosed shower into a large bathroom with white marble walls and light teal-colored cabinets. She dried herself and pulled on a thick white robe. She inspected herself in the mirror and quickly arranged her short pageboy hair with her fingers.

She went into the bedroom, over to a room service cart and the remnants of her lunch. She ate the last french fry and poured a cup of coffee from a silver carafe. She took a sip and looked around the hotel room. The Mark was built in 1927 and had always been an elegant place. The room had comfortable modern-deco furnishings, warm yellow walls, and plush brown carpeting.

Ida went to the large window, pushed aside the gold curtain, pulled up the sheer shade, and carefully looked out. It was around four in the afternoon; the rain was falling again and Madison Avenue five stories down was clogged with slow-moving traffic. The sidewalks were busy with people hurrying and dodging each other's open umbrellas. As far as she could tell, none of Fat Nicky's guys were down there.

The question that had kept her awake last night replayed in her mind.

Did Marta Abruzzo know what Fat Nicky was doing?

She got her cell, went to the unmade bed, and sat leaning her back against the headboard. She hit a number.

"Doctor Marin's office. May I help you?" the older woman receptionist said.

"Hi, Flora. It's Ida. Is he there?" she asked keeping the worry out of her voice.

"Oh, hello, Ida. Hang on. I'll check." Flora put her on hold.

The desk phone rang in Paul's office. He finished pouring a drink at the bar, set the bottle down with an annoyed thump, went to the desk, and picked up the phone.

"I told you no calls," he said impatiently.

"Yes, Doctor," Flora answered professionally. "Unless it was Ida. And it is."

"Right. Thanks, Flora. Put her through." Paul sat on the edge of his large desk. "Where are you?"

"I'm... safe," Ida answered evasively.

"Good. I'm glad." Paul took a quick sip of his drink. "Ida, I need to know. Where have you hidden Lucille?"

"Why should I tell you?" she asked sharply. "So you can have her killed like Paula DeVong?"

Paul flinched, but he controlled himself. "You know that was an accident."

"Do I?"

"Yes, you do." He got up and went around the desk to the large window. He pushed aside the heavy brocade curtain and looked out at the museum across the street. Even in the rain it was still crowded with wet-looking tourists.

"What happened to you, Paul?" Ida asked sadly. "What happened to the man who heard sacred voices and did so much good for us? And for me."

"I... don't know," he admitted softly. He sat in his desk chair and looked around his well-appointed office. He focused on his framed diplomas hanging on the wall. "Why did you call me?"

"I need to know something," Ida said urgently. "Do you think that Fat Nicky's grandmother told him to get Ladimir arrested?"

"No. Never," he answered without hesitation. "She and Andre go back too far together. I think Nicky's doing this on his own, because he's a greedy, stupid, ungrateful fuck."

"I agree." Ida took a breath. "Paulie, I need something."

"What?" he asked gently.

"I want to call Marta Abruzzo. I need her number."

"Why?"

"She may be the one person who can help me. I know she's always liked me."

"You've only seen her a few times—"

"I know"—she cut him off—"but if Nicky is doing this without her blessing, maybe I can convince her to help me get away from him."

"You would always owe her," Paul warned her. "Forever."

"I can deal with that. Will you give me her number?"

Paul sipped his drink. "If you promise me that you'll take Lucille with you. And she will never make another interview about me and what she knows."

Ida looked out the window at the wet facades of the buildings across the street. "Yes, Paul. I promise." She said the words, but she wondered how much influence she really had with Lucille anymore.

Paul considered for a long moment. "All right, get a pen. I'm not sending it as a text. And it's too late in Sicily to call now. The Crow likes to get to bed early."

"The Crow?" Ida said as she grabbed a pad and pen from the nightstand.

"Don't ever let her hear you call her that," Paul cautioned.

*　*　*

Silas was sitting on the wide sill in his room. The rain had stopped and the late-afternoon sun was beginning to break through and shine across the repeating rows of rooftops stretching to the south. He heard a ping on his laptop, went to his desk, and saw that Ray Gaines had accepted his invitation to a video chat. After a few seconds, Ray's tired face appeared on the screen. He was dressed in his shirtsleeves and the image was shaky as he set his cell phone on the desk in his hotel room.

"Hi, son," Ray said. "You're looking well."

"Thanks, Ray. Good to see you too. Where are you?"

"Avola, in Sicily. Just got here a little while ago."

"So, it's what, ten forty there?"

"Yeah," Ray confirmed. "And it's been a long day. I started in Croatia and there's lots to tell. It would be good if I could update you and Artemis. Is he around?"

Silas saw the seriousness in the senior agent's eyes. "I'm not sure he'll come. But hang on a sec. I'll ask." Silas got up and left his room, went down the white-walled hallway to Artemis's office, and knocked on the door.

"Come in," Artemis called out, and Silas opened the door. Artemis was seated at his large oak desk sorting folders and papers in neat piles. Silas knew that they were documents of the history of the Gardner Museum robbery.

"Ray's online. He says he has information that we should both hear," Silas said.

"You can tell me what he says later."

"I think you should come now. It would be better if you and Ray could see each other."

Artemis saw the concern in his son's eyes and got up. "Okay."

Silas led the way back to his room and sat at his computer.

Ray watched on his cell as Artemis closed the door, pulled up a chair, and sat behind his son's shoulder. He noted how thin and pale Artemis looked, but his eyes were clear and attentive as always.

"Hello, Artemis," Ray said quietly. "It's good to see your face. If only this way."

"Hi, Ray. You look beat," Artemis answered.

"Hell, I'm just getting too old, that's all." Ray shrugged. "I have some news."

"Ray's in Avola, Sicily," Silas said. "That's the east coast, right?"

"Good on you." Ray smiled. "The town is right on the beach looking out across the Mediterranean. Historic. With lots of crumbling buildings." He laughed a little. "Like this hotel."

"Why are you there?" Artemis asked interested.

"I have it from a good source that Bert Rocca died here two days ago," Ray said evenly. "I'm going to verify the body tomorrow morning."

Silas and Artemis sat still taking in the information. Then Silas asked, "How did Rocca get there?"

"Don't know yet," Ray answered. "I'll send you a secure file that'll explain what's happened. And there's a man in FBI custody that Mak Kim is going to be talking to. Artemis, you might want to get in on that. There may be a link to the Gardner case."

Artemis leaned forward and rested his arm across the back of Silas's chair. "What's his name?"

"Ladimir Karlovic," Ray said, pleased to see that Artemis was still interested. "He's the grandson of Andre Karlovic..."

"Head of Karlovic Worldwide"— Artemis picked it up—"global banking with ties to shipping and munitions."

"Yes," Ray said surprised. "I had to ask the guys in Washington for information on him. How did you know that?"

"Something in my father's notes from the early 1990s. He'd heard a rumor that the stolen art was shipped out of America and sent to somewhere along the Dalmatian coast. He made some preliminary notes about Andre Karlovic and his business associates, along with sixty or seventy other possibilities."

"Interesting," Ray said as he rubbed the back of his neck. "Because 1990, the year that the Gardner is robbed, also is the year that war breaks out in Croatia. That might relate to what I've been told. Let's talk after you read the file I'm sending."

"Okay," Artemis said as he noticed the weariness in Ray's shoulders and how much deeper the lines were around his eyes. "How are you, Ray?" he asked.

Ray smiled. "Pretty fair, thanks for asking. And you? Silas tells me that you're out and about again."

"Yes. A bit." Artemis said. "Still finding my way, I guess. Will you contact us tomorrow after you've seen the body?"

"I will."

"Thank you, Ray," Artemis said.

"Good night," Silas added. "Get some sleep."

Ray smiled and reached for his cell. His image jiggled and turned off.

There was a firm knock at the door, and Delia came in a couple of steps, with Drew standing in the hall behind her.

"Just want to let you boys know that Drew is here and I'm heading out to my meeting," she announced. "I'll be back by seven, seven thirty."

"See you then." Artemis nodded.

"And be careful," Silas said.

"I will be," Delia promised him and walked out.

"Not to worry, I'll watch out for her," Drew said protectively and headed for the front door where Delia was waiting. They left, locking the door behind them.

Artemis stood up, went over to the large window, and looked out across the city.

"Are you surprised that Bert Rocca is dead?" Silas asked.

"No," he answered without turning. "You?"

Silas thought about it. "No. I was just wondering when it would happen."

"That's getting me too. Ray said that Rocca died two days ago in Sicily. Where has he been for the past sixteen months?"

"And who has been helping him stay hidden?" Silas added.

Artemis looked at his fourteen-year-old son and smiled. "Exactly. Let's see what Ray finds out in the morning." Artemis sat on the edge of the bed. "So, how you coming on finding that back door to the building down on Doyers Street?"

"It's so frustrating." Silas lifted a mug of cold coffee from his desk and took a gulp. "The NYC building records are a mess and impossible to follow. And I can't tell if that's because they've been screwed with or it's just the way things were done. I asked Clayton for some help because he's got access to lots more than I have."

"Good," Artemis said. Silas's computer pinged, and he opened an email.

"It's the secure file from Ray," he reported. "He sent it to both of us."

"I'll download it on my laptop, and we'll talk after we've read it."
Artemis got up and went back across the hall to his office.

* * *

Drew pushed through the revolving glass door and looked to the two uniformed cops standing on each side of 73rd Street. It was a little before five,
and the air was still hot and muggy. She turned back to the doors and Delia
came out. Drew scanned the area as she and Delia started walking west along
the sidewalk. One of the cops followed them some thirty feet behind.

Across the street, a few doors down, Lucille stood behind the glass door
in the shadows of the small foyer watching them. She made sure her long hair
was tucked up under her cap and her cloth mask in place before she opened
the door, checked the cop by the Ansonia, and headed out. She saw Drew,
Delia, and the escort cop turn north at the corner. Lucille carefully crossed
West End Avenue, and using the row of parked cars as cover, she followed
them. At 75th Street, they stopped at a small weathered church. Drew and
Delia went in and the cop stayed outside on the sidewalk. Lucille sat on the
steps of a brownstone and waited.

Inside, the church still showed many of the original Neo-Moorish
details that were popular when it was built in the late 1800s. At one end of the
vestibule, Drew and Delia saw a sign directing them down a flight of stone
steps where the walls were covered with Christian pictures. They came to a
small meeting hall, with a coffered ceiling, yellow stone columns, and a well-
worn reddish tile floor, where folding chairs had been set up in a wide-spaced
circle. Ten or so people, wearing masks, were just sitting down.

Delia turned to Drew. "Thank you. I appreciate you doing this for me."

Drew smiled. "It's a pleasure. I'll be outside when you leave."

As Drew turned and started back up the stairs, she could hear the
man leading the group welcoming Delia and asking her if she'd like to intro-
duce herself.

"My name is Delia." Her voice rang loudly. "And I'm an alcoholic..."

As Drew got back to the vestibule, the sounds from below faded away. She pushed open the heavy wood door and stepped back outside.

From her perch on the steps, Lucille watched as Drew said something to the cop and he laughed. And she wondered about Drew, how she always seemed to be so sure of herself.

Lucille knew she was tempting fate sitting there so long with two cops just across the street. So, when it was safe, she got up and casually walked away, heading south along the sidewalk.

*   *   *

Delia had left a whole chicken with some vegetables, rosemary, and lemons in a slow cooker so when she and Drew got back from her meeting, the meal was almost ready to be served. After dinner, she insisted that Artemis let her clean things up, and he and Drew went to his study to discuss the events of the day. Silas went back to work on his laptop in his room. Somewhere past eleven, Drew left for her home in Brooklyn. Delia shut off the lights in the kitchen and went to look in on Artemis. She found him at his desk studying something on his laptop.

"Whatever did we do without computers," she said as she pulled the cream-colored curtains across the elongated bay windows. She turned and saw that his glass of single malt was empty. "Can I get you a refill?" She went to the bar tray on the bookcase shelf, got the bottle, and poured.

"Dee, you know you don't have to do that. It must be hard for you, coming in from a meeting and all."

As she recorked the bottle and put it back, she said forcefully, "It's no problem. What doesn't kill you makes you stronger."

"Is that an AA slogan?" he asked uncertainly.

"No." She laughed. "It's Nietzsche. I'm off to bed. See you tomorrow."

"Good night, Delia," Artemis said, and she left. He took a sip of scotch and looked back to Ray's report on his laptop. After a few minutes, he leaned back in his chair and closed his eyes. There was a knock on his door, and he opened his eyes to see Silas come in and sit in front of his desk.

"So, you'll go see this Ladimir Karlovic?" Silas asked.

"Yes"—Artemis was impressed that Silas seemed, as usual, to be sharing a brain cell with him—"I'll talk with Mak about it tomorrow."

"Think his grandfather really knows anything about the stolen Gardner pieces?"

"Very hard to say," Artemis mused as he indicated the report on his screen. "But the logo for Andre Karlovic's company is a three-headed sea serpent. And Ray seems to think that the man actually knows something."

"Enough to get his grandson extradited back to Croatia?" Silas sounded skeptical.

"I wonder." Artemis looked at his son. "We've tracked down so many of these leads. And they've never gotten us anywhere."

"Still, Andre Karlovic is old. Like Raphael Sharder was when he wanted to give back the stolen Rembrandt."

"You mean, he's running out of time?" Artemis asked.

"Yes, something like that," Silas answered.

Chapter Four

Sunday, July 18th, 2021

At eight thirty in the morning, Ray walked into the main entrance of Unico Hospital in Noto, Sicily. The lobby was busy with mask-wearing people waiting for COVID testing. He had been met outside his hotel, in nearby Avola, by a local official from Syracuse and the same woman Interpol agent who had helped him in Livorno. Wearing masks and their identifications, they were met by a representative of the hospital, who led them down a nondescript private corridor to an elevator and down two floors. Outside the basement morgue, they were greeted by a weary-looking woman pathologist. After quick introductions, she took them into the cold locker. She went to a wall of square stainless-steel doors, turned a handle, and pulled out a covered body lying on a slab. She moved the cloth to reveal the face and upper torso.

"Is this him?" the Interpol agent asked.

"Yes," Ray said quietly. "It's him. Bert Rocca. But I have a question." He looked at the pathologist.

"Si?" she said.

"Our information says that he died of COVID. But it seems to me that three knife wounds in his chest might have been something worth mentioning."

"Agent Gaines," the woman said patiently, "it's getting bad here again. The staff is overworked and exhausted. An unknown man was found on the beach in Avola. He tested positive and that is enough. We have no time for investigations."

"And," Ray said knowingly, "hospitals get government payments when the death is caused by COVID. Right?"

She looked away.

Ray sighed and turned to the Interpol agent. "I'll need his dental records and prints sent to Washington immediately."

"Of course," she answered. "His cell phone is already en route there."

"Good," he said. "And can you take care of sending the body there too?"
"Yes. And I will make that happen today if I can. I'm worried the Delta variant may cause another lockdown here."

"Thank you." Ray looked down at Bert Rocca's face. They had known each other since college. He had been his friend. But Ray felt neither anger nor loss. He just felt old and tired.

"I have to send some texts," he said. "I'll be outside the main entrance." He left the room. As he waited for the elevator, he sent off a quick report to Washington. As he walked through the crowded reception area, he wrote another to Artemis and Silas. The automatic glass doors slid open, and he stepped out into the humid morning. He hit the send button.

A young athletic-looking man got out of a dark sedan parked at the curb and headed for Ray. He was dressed in a light-colored suit and tie. He wore no mask.

"Agent Gaines, good morning," he said politely in English.

"Yes?" Ray said cautiously.

"I apologize for meeting you unannounced, but I have been sent to take you to a meeting."

"A meeting," Ray said carefully as he gauged the man's eyes. "With who?"

"Marta Abruzzo," he answered respectfully.

"I don't know who that is," Ray said as he noticed two other men sitting in the car watching them. "So, why should I go with you?"

"I am instructed to say," the man answered as he leaned closer and lowered his voice. "That you should remember the serpent has three heads and one body."

Ray looked at his young face and nodded. "All right. But where are we going?"

"It is not far." The man smiled. "We will go about halfway back along the road to Avola. Perhaps ten minutes."

As Ray walked to the car, the back door was opened from inside. He got in and the man in the suit closed the door and sat in the front passenger seat. Without a word, the driver started the engine and carefully pulled out.

*   *   *

Marta sat in the shade of the palm trees on the terrace, looking out at the hazy morning light across her vineyards. As she listened on her cell phone, her old dark eyes grew sharp and curious. She waved a hand and dismissed her niece, Rosa, who was sitting nearby reading a book. Rosa dutifully got up and walked away across the lawn toward the loggia of the palazzo. As she went up the steps, she passed two men with automatic rifles slung across their backs.

"You say that Nicolas and his boys are looking for you?" the old woman asked into her phone.

"Yes," Ida answered carefully as she paced the length of her hotel room at the Mark. With the time difference, it was 3:00 a.m. in New York.

Marta chuckled. "You must be very clever if they haven't found you. Or lucky."

"Maybe both," Ida acknowledged. She took a quick gulp of cold coffee and waited.

"You interest me," Marta said shrewdly. "And *maybe* I can help you with what you ask. But."

Ida realized she was holding her breath. She sat on the edge of the bed and consciously breathed out. "Yes, Marta?"

"My dear," the old woman said kindly. "Nicolas is my family. If I help you, he will not like it. Still. I heard everything you have said. And I will consider it."

"Thank you," Ida said gratefully. "When do you think...?" She started to ask, but Marta cut her off as she saw Ray Gaines being escorted around the side of her palazzo.

"Ida, I have to go. There is something I must attend to. Call me at noon, your time, and you will have an answer."

"Thank you, Marta. I will call you." Ida heard the line go dead. She took her phone to the small desk, plugged it in, and began to pace again.

The man in the suit led Ray across the lawn toward Marta. As they neared, she turned her crow-like face up to Ray and said quietly, "I am Marta Abruzzo. I thank you for coming, Agent Gaines. I know that you are a busy man. Would you care to sit?" She gestured to the wood chair beside her.

"Thank you," Ray said and sat down.

"And would you care for something to drink? Perhaps some coffee?"

"Nothing, thank you."

Marta dismissed the man with a look. He bowed and walked away.

"It's very beautiful here," Ray said as he looked around.

"I have always loved this place." Marta smiled a little.

"Why did you want to see me?"

In response, the old woman lifted a large cloth bag from the mosaic-topped table beside her. She pulled out a clear plastic bag containing a US passport, driver's license, FBI identification, and a worn leather wallet. She handed it to Ray.

"These belonged to your man," she explained. "His credit cards are still in the wallet as well as some cash, both euros and dollars."

Ray reached into the bag, pulled out the passport, and examined it. "How do you come to have Bert Rocca's things?" he asked.

"He was living here," Marta said readily. "As my guest."

"Why? Who was he to you?"

"Nobody." She smiled. "A friend asked me to let him stay here."

Ray wondered who that friend might be. "How long was Bert Rocca here?"

"A year. He arrived last July." She leaned back in her chair and spoke freely. "I liked him. Nice man to talk to. He liked to shoot at targets with my men. They liked him too."

"How did he die?" Ray asked, choosing his questions carefully.

"So sad." She shrugged. "Even in a little town like Avola, terrible things can happen. He went out for drinks two nights ago. I understand that he wanted to walk by himself in the ruins by the beach. We didn't hear the news of his death until yesterday. These things"—she pointed a thin finger at the bag in Ray's hands—"were left behind in his room. And now I return them to you as an act of friendship."

"It's funny," Ray said, "that he didn't take his wallet when he went out for drinks."

"Yes," she agreed. "But he was a guest here. I think he'd gotten used to my people taking care of things."

"At the hospital, your man said something that Andre Karlovic told me yesterday. Three heads, one body. Like the serpent on his company logo. So, I'm wondering if you were doing a favor for Mr. Karlovic when you let Bert Rocca stay here?"

"No," she said plainly.

"Then was it a favor for the third head of the serpent?" He looked at her expressionless face. "I don't suppose you could tell me who that is?"

"If I gave you that name," she said meaningfully, "I would expect something from you in return."

"I'm listening."

"Are you sure you wouldn't like something to drink?" she said agreeably. "The day grows hot, and the orange juice is especially good."

Ray smiled. "Thanks. I would love some."

Marta raised her hand, and Rosa came out of the doors of the loggia and headed down the slope toward them.

"Rosa," Marta said as she arrived. "Would you bring us some orange juice?"

"Yes, Zia, right away." Rosa smiled and hurried off.

"So, Ms. Abruzzo, what is it you want me to do?" Ray asked.

"Travel to a particular island in Greece," she said clearly, her small eyes alive and cunning. "There is a woman there who can answer all your questions."

"About who is the third head of the serpent?"

"Yes. And other information that you will find"—she paused to select the right word—"important."

"Why can't you simply tell me?" Ray asked reasonably.

"Because you will require proof. She can give you that. I cannot."

"Cannot?" Ray asked. "Or will not?" The old woman said nothing.

"Assuming I travel to Greece and find this mysterious person, why would she speak to me?"

"Because you will give her this." Marta reached into her bag and pulled out a small white envelope sealed with red wax and embossed with a coat of arms.

Ray ran his fingers across his temples and through his short gray hair. "I have to ask. What's happened that you would give up this kind of information? And does it involve the arrest of Andre Karlovic's grandson?"

"Ah." Marta looked out over her vast vineyards. "It's a bad time to be old in the world."

Ray smiled a little. "I've said that myself. Lots of times."

She nodded. "At my age, I have little time left to waste. One of the serpent's heads has begun to rot. It is time to cut it off before it kills the body."

"And Andre Karlovic agrees with you," Ray said shrewdly.

She smiled at him. "Andre said you were smart. I like that."

"So, where in Greece am I going?"

"Andre's plane is at your disposal," she answered indirectly. "My people will help you with the arrangements. The government can sometimes be a problem when it's time to travel."

"Okay," Ray said.

"You kept your word to Andre and got his grandson moved from prison." She studied him. "Before I give you information, I will need your word that something will be done."

Ray took a long breath. He saw Rosa returning down the steps carrying a tray with a pitcher and two glasses. "Tell me what you need."

He expected that the old woman would stop speaking as Rosa arrived, but she continued easily. "I have a grandson in America. In New York, who is a very foolish man."

Rosa poured two glasses of orange juice, set down the pitcher, and turned to go. But Marta stopped her. "No, Rosa. Please stay."

She meekly tipped her head and sat on a weathered bench.

"His name is Nicolas Abruzzo," Marta stated without emotion. "He is called Fat Nicky sometimes. But I know that he does not like that. I will provide you with proof that he has been involved with many serious crimes.

I want him arrested and sent to prison for a long time. And." She lifted her glass of juice and sipped it. "I want your word that Nicolas will never know that I was the one who did this."

Ray lifted his glass and took a small sip. The sweetness of the juice surprised him.

"It is good, no?" she said as she saw his reaction.

"Very," he answered and set down his glass. "I can promise that. No one will know."

"Good," she held out the sealed envelope, and Ray took it from her. Marta sighed and leaned back in her chair. "So now, Agent Gaines, I will tell you a story. There was once a time in the world when three great families bonded together for business, protection, and influence. There is a quiet place in Greece where a man named Philip Voskos was born. He was a powerful man and the best of us. Philip built ships and made his fortune during the war. But then, there was a power struggle and he and many of his family were killed."

She breathed out sadly and closed her eyes.

"When was this?" Ray asked gently.

"Oh, forever ago now," she murmured. "Late in the 1980s."

"And there were relatives who survived," Ray said what he was thinking out loud. "And one of those has become the rotting head that you want severed."

"Yes." The old woman opened her eyes and focused on him. "I will now tell you about your destination in Greece and the person you will meet there."

*   *   *

By 9:00 a.m., the overnight fog had cleared in New Jersey. Artemis sat in the back seat of a moving sedan staring at the text Ray had sent during the night.

Rocca's death is confirmed. I'll call later.

Artemis looked out the window at the ever-moving patterns of dappled sunlight filtering through the tall leafy trees that bordered the Palisades Parkway. It had been a long time since he had made this trip.

Drew was driving, and Leah was sitting next to her in the front. Like Artemis, they were wearing their masks.

"So, Drew," Leah said as she turned to her. "You're a young, handsome figure of a woman. Are you seeing anyone?"

Drew laughed. "Are you offering?"

The old woman laughed with her. "No, really. It would be nice if you had someone to share things with."

"My dad's there. We get along," Drew said evasively.

"He'll be going back to Florida in the fall, and that's an awfully big house to live in all by yourself."

"I can handle it." Drew smirked. "And I've got a gun."

"Mary Drew, you know what I mean." Leah admonished, and behind her, Artemis laughed a little.

"Watch it." Drew warned him over her shoulder. "And that goes for you too," she said lightly to Leah. "And yes, if you really want to know, there is someone that I'm kinda seeing."

"That sounds kinda interesting," Leah said. "What's her name?"

"Anne Riley. She's a trainer at my gym and we swim laps together."

"She must be pretty fit if she keeps up with you," Artemis said from the back seat.

"She was a national champ, so she does okay." Drew reached up and adjusted the rearview mirror so she could see him. "How are you doing back there, Artie?" she said pleasantly.

"You make me feel like I'm six and we're going to the beach," Artemis said. "Are we there yet?"

Leah laughed and turned to look at Artemis. "I bet you were a handful when you were six," she said as her eyes twinkled.

"I guess so," he answered. "I was a lot like Silas." Artemis grew quiet as they turned off the highway at exit two and followed the suburban streets through the hilly town of Alpine.

The morning was already hot, but a few people were out mowing their lawns, watering flower beds, and walking dogs. As they reached the edge of Halesburgh, Artemis felt his chest tightening, and the view of the street ahead through the windshield seemed to narrow like he was traveling through an inverted telescope. Drew turned the car into a driveway and pulled up on the edge of an overgrown lawn. She turned off the engine and got out. She carefully scanned the area as she walked around the back of the car to the other side and opened both doors. Leah got out first, closed her door, and she and Drew moved a few steps away to give Artemis some space.

He looked through the windows at the two-story house with its solid-looking lower stone walls and blue clapboards above. The gardens in front of the porch were dry and needed weeding.

Artemis got out and took a breath. Even through his mask, he could smell the grass and trees. He made a decision and pulled off his mask. He smiled a little at Leah and Drew, and they took theirs off as well.

"That is so much better," Leah said as she breathed in. "And it's lovely here. Do you still feel okay about going inside?"

"Yes," Artemis said firmly. "Would you please come with me?"

"Happy to," Leah said.

"I'll stay out here," Drew offered. "And keep an eye on things."

Artemis pulled out his keys and started across the lawn. Leah followed about eight feet behind. He went up the wood steps of the porch and unlocked the front door. He saw his reflection in the glass door and Leah standing patiently behind him.

"Harder than I thought it would be," he said softly.

"I know," she answered.

A car went by on the road past the front hedges. "It all seems pretty much the same. But it's not."

"No, it's not," she said.

Artemis set his shoulders, opened the door, and stepped into the foyer of the old house. It smelled stale, and the sound of his shoes on the stone floor echoed strangely. All the furniture and their things had been removed a long time ago. The curtains in the living room to his left were closed, and the room was dim. He walked down the front hall, past the wood staircase that went up to the second floor, and at the end he stopped. Through the door to his left was the kitchen. The place where she was killed. He turned to the right and headed into the dining room. Leah closed the front door and followed him, keeping her distance.

Artemis walked slowly to the back pantry where a door led out to the parking area. Outside this door, an anonymous note had been left. A death threat. He turned around and faced the back entrance to the kitchen.

"How are you doing?" He heard Leah's calm voice, and she sounded very far away.

"All right. Thanks," he murmured. He stepped into the kitchen. The room was bright, because the large picture windows in the far corner looked out over the sunny backyard. They had always liked the view too much to put curtains there. He stood in the work area, and his mind registered the cooktop, oven, and fridge. He saw the counter that divided the room with the steel sink and dishwasher. Beyond it was an empty area where they once had a breakfast table and chairs. He slowly walked around the counter and looked down at the floor. All evidence of what happened there had been cleaned away, scrubbed, and disinfected by professionals hired to make it all disappear.

But Artemis could still see Emily's body lying there, her red blood on the white tile floor. He stepped back sharply and bumped into the counter.

He stood frozen, his mind overloading and his breath coming in short raspy gasps.

Across the room, Leah observed him and waited.

Through an act of will, Artemis slowed his breathing. He swallowed hard and whispered, "I'm going to take a look upstairs."

He left the kitchen, and as he went up the old steps, he wondered what exactly had happened that day. Emily got a call and came back home. Delia was in the house, cleaning the bathroom at the top of the stairs. He came to the second floor and stood in the open doorway of the bathroom. Directly in front of him was a white porcelain pedestal sink with a large framed mirror above it. He moved to the sink. This is where Delia stood when she was hit from behind. Her attacker had used the butt-end of the 9mm pistol. The same gun that killed Emily. The same gun that killed Raphael Sharder.

I'm missing something.

Artemis inspected the tile floor by the bathtub. They had found Delia lying there unconscious, her head bleeding and her ribs badly bruised. A movement caught his eye, and he looked up into the mirror and saw Leah just arriving at the top step behind him. He turned around and studied her old face.

She saw the intensity in his eyes. "What is it?" she asked.

After a moment, he shook his head. "Nothing." He walked a few steps down the hall and went into Silas's old bedroom. It seemed somehow smaller with all the furniture gone.

Artemis went further down the hall to the room that had been Delia's bedroom. Even empty, it was an appealing room with corner windows that looked out to the backyard. As he walked back down the hall toward the front of the house, Leah moved aside to give him more space.

Artemis stepped into the large master bedroom. He walked over to the windows, pushed the curtains aside, and felt the morning sunlight on his face.

He looked down and saw Drew leaning on the car. She nodded supportively. He breathed in and turned to look around the empty room.

Emily, please help me.

He turned to the doorway where Leah stood faithfully watching. "I'm going to call the broker. I think it's time to let go of this place."

"Good," Leah said. "Good for you."

*   *   *

All the windows were open, but the morning heat was oppressive in Lucille's rooftop studio. She sat on the floor leaning on the sill looking out at the Ansonia across the street. A movement on the rooftop caught her eye, and she saw an older couple dressed in light clothes slowly walking toward a seating area that was surrounded by raised beds full of dry-looking plants. They sat together on a wood bench. But the day was already too hot, and after a couple of minutes, they gave up and retreated back inside the building.

Lucille wiped the sweat off her face with her hands. She stood up and leaned out the window desperate to find some cooler air. Across the street nineteen stories down, she saw the revolving door of the Ansonia turning, and Delia came out. A young uniformed cop greeted her, and they started walking together west along 73rd Street. Lucille wondered if Delia was going back to that church around the corner. It was Sunday, after all.

Something caught her eye in the top-floor apartment across the street. She quickly dropped down to the floor and peered out over the sill. It was Artemis's son, Silas. He was carrying a green shoebox. He sat on the window seat, opened the box, and looked through it.

"Old photos?" Agent Filipowski asked as he looked up from his laptop. He was sitting at the dining table with a mug of coffee.

"Yes," Silas answered as he opened a yellowed envelope and pulled out some snapshots. "Of my mother when she was young."

Flip closed his laptop, came across the room, and sat next to Silas.

"Look at this one," Silas said curiously. "Maybe she's four or five here." It was a picture of a pretty girl with her left arm held high proudly displaying a bracelet that was much too big for her wrist. It was made of blue glass eyeballs.

"It's called a matiasma, and Delia gave it to her," Silas explained as he poked through the contents at the bottom of the box. "Here it is," he said as he lifted out the bracelet and showed it to Flip. "The eyes are supposed to ward off evil. I guess it didn't work too well." Silas put the bracelet back in the box.

Flip's cell phone pinged, and he checked the text. "It's Mak. I gotta call him and check in." He got up, punched a number, and walked away into the kitchen.

Silas pulled a light blue stone the size of an egg from the box. His mother had kept this on her desk in her office at school. He knew it was from a trip to the southwest that she and Artemis took when they were first married. Silas inspected the piece of turquoise in his hand.

Hydrated copper aluminum phosphate.

He smiled at himself and his need to define everything. He put the stone in his pocket, pushed his glasses back in place, and flipped through the rest of the photos until he came back to the one with the bracelet.

She looks so happy.

He put the photos away. He got up, carried the box back to his bedroom, and put it on the top shelf of his closet. He put the piece of turquoise on his desk. Sunlight coming through the window seemed to wake up the gentle blue color of the stone.

It looks at home in the sun.

Then a new thought crossed his mind. A troubling thought. His eyes were still looking at the blue stone, but his mind was traveling elsewhere.

His laptop pinged, and he saw an invite from Detective Jerome Clayton Collins. Silas sat, hit a button, and Clayton appeared on the screen.

"Where are you?" Silas asked as he watched the jumbled moving image from Clayton's handheld phone.

"Mott Street," Clayton said excitedly. "And we found it. The back door to the schoolroom. Our guys were looking in the wrong place. They assumed the passage would lead to one of the buildings on either side, on Doyers. But it connects to the building behind it. On Mott Street." The image of Clayton settled as he stood still on the sidewalk. Silas could see that he was under a construction scaffold and there was a Chinese restaurant behind him.

"It's amazing," Clayton said. "Real speakeasy stuff. Hidden levers and sliding bookcases. So, let's see." He looked around for the number of the building. Under the scaffold, the front of the eight-story structure was covered with permits, posters, graffiti, and grime. He examined the black metal door he'd come through and could see the outline of a number above the door that had been painted over. "Eighteen," he said triumphantly. "Eighteen Mott Street. See what you can find, all right?"

"On it," Silas said.

*   *   *

It was seventy-nine degrees in Southampton, and the sun was coming and going through clouds pushed by a gentle onshore breeze. Barbara Borsa slung her canvas briefcase over her shoulder, closed the front garden gate, and started walking. In a few blocks, she came to the first stores on Main Street where the sidewalk was full of tourists window-shopping. She came to the large glass door of the Primrose and went in. The restaurant was quiet, as usual, in the lull between breakfast and lunch. Maddy Griff was wiping down the long wood bar, saw her and came over.

"Hi, Barbara," she said. "This way."

Maddy Griff led her through the back hallway, past the restrooms, and unlocked the door at the end. They went up the flight of steps to the door in the center of the small landing. She knocked, opened the door, and they went in.

"This is Khloe Voskos," Maddy Griff said, and she gestured to the old nun sitting in the rocking chair by the windows. "And this is Barbara Borsa."

"How do you do?" Barbara said formally, and the old woman nodded. "And you!" Barbara said happily as she turned to Taki who was sitting on the edge of the bed. He was looking more like his old self, cleaned and dressed in bright colors. "I am so happy to see you again."

Taki smiled widely, got up, made a courteous half bow, and then hugged her. "Nice to see you too, Barbara."

"I have to get back downstairs," Maddy Griff said. "They'll be coming in for lunch soon." She left and closed the door behind her. Barbara set her briefcase down on the small writing desk, took out some papers, turned the chair to face them, and sat.

"So, what can I do for you?" she asked Khloe.

The old woman's eyes narrowed. "You were Raphael's lawyer."

Though it was a statement, Barbara felt compelled to answer. "Yes. Estate lawyer. I did his will."

"Good," Khloe said. Taki sat back down on the edge of the bed, lifted his mug of coffee from the night table, and sipped it slowly.

"I received this." Barbara lifted the papers. "But until yesterday morning, I presumed that Raphael's sister was dead. So, first I have to ask you, is this your birth certificate and are you Khloe Voskos?"

"Yes," the old nun answered. "Raphael decided a long time ago that I would be safer if everyone believed I was dead."

"Why?" Taki asked, and Khloe stared at him for a long moment.

"Why else is Barbara here?" Taki asked gently. "If you don't want to tell her?"

"I know why she is here," Khloe answered. "But I'm wondering why you should be here."

"Because," Taki said simply. "I loved Raphael, and you are his sister. I would like to help you, if I could."

The old woman's eyes grew softer. "After all you've been through, you want to help me?"

"If I can," Taki smiled a little.

"All right then." Khloe pushed down on the arms of her chair, stood up with a grunt, and stepped to the window. She looked down at the back garden where blue hydrangeas and purple salvias were growing along the wood fence. "It's peaceful here," she said quietly.

"I've always loved Southampton," Taki agreed.

"Greece. October. 1988," Khloe said as she turned to look at them. "My father, Philip Voskos, was killed. He was a great man, ran a shipping empire. And when he died, everything fell apart. People wanted Raphael to take over. They trusted him, but he refused." She looked at Taki. "Raphael was an artist. He loved to paint. He knew that he wasn't suited. So, he decided he would be safer in America. That's when he changed his last name to Sharder."

"And enrolled in the Art Students League of New York," Taki interrupted wistfully. "That's where we met."

"I know," Khloe said as she leaned on the back of the chair.

"Who killed your father?" Barbara asked, sounding like a lawyer.

"People who have been dealt with." Khloe's eyes flashed a warning. "That is all I will say about that."

"Okay," Barbara said. "So, what happened to you?"

"Raphael had records changed, and everyone thought I had died with my father. He smuggled me on board one of our ships, and we left. Forever. I was destroyed by what had happened to my family. I became this." She opened her arms displaying her nun's habit. "And I lived."

"Raphael left money to a charity, and no one has been able to figure out why," Barbara said. "Oak Bluffs, in Connecticut. Does that have anything to do with you?"

"Did he?" Khloe seemed surprised. She smiled a little. "Yes, that would be so like him. Raphael never forgot. Oak Bluffs is a place for recovering addicts. They have done some good. They also own the institution where I have been working and living for many years, St. Anthony's. When I first got there, it was owned by the church. But some years ago, the money ran out and it was sold, intact, to Oak Bluffs, under the agreement that they kept the name and the staff." She turned and looked sadly at Taki. "I am sorry that your time there was so... unpleasant. But people wanted you gone, and I was trying to protect you."

"I know that now," Taki said. "Nothing in the world is ever all good or all bad. And don't worry, I don't remember too much about it anyway."

The old woman gauged him for a moment, then chuckled darkly.

"You really have to stop doing that," Taki said. "It's kind of creepy."

"I think I liked you better," the old woman said as she suppressed a smile, "when you were drugged all the time."

Taki was unsure how to take this. He smiled uncertainly.

"I have to ask," Barbara said. "What was your brother Raphael's involvement in the 1990 robbery of the Gardner Museum?"

Khloe studied Barbara. "We'll come to that."

"Well, if I can prove your identity," Barbara said, "you may have certain claims on his estate."

"No," Khloe said plainly. "I don't need money, and it's better for me if the world still thinks that Khloe Voskos is dead."

"Okay," Barbara said. She turned to Taki. "The estate is still tied up in probate. It may be a long time, if ever, before you see any settlement."

"How much did Raphael leave him?" Khloe asked curiously.

"Twelve million and ownership of the gallery here in Southampton," Barbara stated.

Khloe looked at Taki. "My, my. He must have *really* loved you."

Taki shrugged. "He was always so kind to everyone. Always."

"So," Barbara said to Khloe. "If you have no interest in his estate, what can I do for you?"

"I am in danger. And Mr. Fukuda is too." She gestured to him but kept looking at the lawyer. "There is a fight for power going on. Like when my father was killed. I need you to tell the authorities what I know. Will you do this for me?"

"Yes," Barbara said with formality.

"Good," Khloe took a breath. "I will need protection for the rest of my life. They must agree to this before you give them my information."

"I understand," Barbara confirmed. "May I take some notes?"

"Of course." Khloe waited as Barbara got a legal pad and pen from her briefcase. Then she began:

"My brother had no part in the actual robbery in Boston. He agreed to do one thing only. The stolen pieces were hidden on his yacht, and he sailed with them to Europe."

"To where exactly?" Barbara asked carefully.

"Somewhere on the Dalmatian coast. That's all he ever told me," Khloe answered.

"And what about the Rembrandt hidden in his mansion? Was that your brother's payment?"

"No. That was a gift. From his niece."

"And who is that?" Barbara asked.

"No," Khloe said apprehensively. "She is too dangerous to be named."

Barbara tapped her pen against the pad. Then she asked, "Did she kill your brother?"

Khloe's eyes grew murky. "I'm not sure, but I think perhaps, yes."

Barbara made a note. She looked up at Taki. "Is there anything you want to tell me about all this? It might help if you can corroborate."

"I probably shouldn't say too much," Taki answered politely.

"But Raphael must have shown you the stolen Rembrandt," she said reasonably. "At least once in all those years. And told the story of how he got it?"

Taki smiled a little. "Raphael always wanted to protect me from his past. I mean, he told us that his sister Khloe was dead. Look how that worked out."

The old woman chuckled.

"And that gorgeous Rembrandt painting," Taki said nostalgically. "I can see it in my mind, but it's like something from a dream long ago. A dream of better times when Raphael was still here."

* * *

It was cloudy in Manhattan, and the temperature was a comfortable eighty-two degrees. Delia had the window open in the laundry room where she was shifting wet clothes from the washer to the dryer. She heard the front door open and went out to the hall.

"Where's Leah?" she asked as Drew and Artemis came in and locked the door.

"We dropped her off at her place," Drew answered.

"I see." Delia put her hands on her hips. "Well, all the more for you two. I made some lunch. Come on." She turned and marched off to the kitchen.

"How was church?" Artemis asked as he and Drew came in.

"Helpful," Delia answered enthusiastically. "The sermon was good. You should come along some time." She scooped chicken salad onto plates.

Artemis smiled at Drew as they sat at the kitchen table. Delia set the plates down in front of them. "Silas and I have already eaten," she said as she poured them tall glasses of iced tea. "So, I'm going to get back to the housework. Still so much to get organized."

"Thank you." Artemis smiled at her.

"You're welcome," she said cheerfully and started out, but stopped near the doorway as Silas came in and stood by her.

"How was it, Artemis?" he asked.

"Okay," Artemis answered. "I called the broker. She's going to list the house."

"I think that's the right thing to do," Silas said.

"Me too." Delia approved and walked out.

Silas came over and sat at the table.

"You okay?" Drew asked as she gauged the serious look on his face.

Silas considered and decided on a new topic. "Have you heard from Clayton yet?" he asked Drew.

"No," she said.

"He found the secret passage out of the Doyers Street schoolroom. It leads to a building on Mott Street."

"That's great," Drew said. "Do we know who owns the building?"

"Well, that's what's so frustrating," Silas answered. "We found the name of a company, Iridescent Holdings, Ltd., but we can't find any information on them anywhere."

Silas's phone pinged, and he checked the text.

"It's Clayton," he said as he got up. "He's back in the precinct." Silas headed toward his room and Artemis and Drew followed. Silas sat at his laptop and opened a video chat with Clayton.

"Hey, guys," Clayton said as he saw Artemis and Drew pulling up chairs behind Silas.

"Nice work finding that secret passage," Artemis said.

"Thanks." Clayton smiled.

"And what about the company that owns the building on Mott Street?" Drew asked.

"Iridescent Holdings." Clayton nodded. "We've been looking in NYC records for any connection between that name and the owner of the building on Doyers."

"Aldo Mancini." Silas pointed to the name posted on the wall by his desk.

"And there's nothing so far," Clayton said.

"Which is impossible," Silas added.

"That's true," Artemis murmured to himself. Silas turned to look at his father.

"What's up?" Clayton said after a moment. "Artemis, you got something?"

"Maybe." Artemis focused on the intelligent face on the screen. "That's a generic name, Iridescent Holdings. Could be centered anywhere. Can you do a search in another country?"

"Absolutely." Clayton looked interested. "Which one?"

"Italy," Artemis answered. "Check around 2003, plus or minus a year, in a town called Sarteano."

Clayton wrote down the information and said, "Okay. What's there?"

"A serpent," Silas answered, understanding. "In 2003, *The Tomb of the Infernal Chariot* was discovered in Sarteano. It's full of fourth-century BCE wall paintings, including a three-headed sea serpent."

"The guardian of the underworld," Artemis emphasized.

"And an exact replica," Silas continued, "is on the wall of the Necropolis Bar on Doyers Street."

"And that bar opened in 2003 or 2004," Artemis concluded.

"I'm on it," Clayton said hurriedly and began a search on his computer.

"Good work," Drew said.

"Thanks," Silas answered distractedly and turned to his father.

"What is it?" Artemis asked quietly.

After a moment, Silas changed his mind and said, "It'll wait." He turned back to his computer and started working.

*   *   *

At noon, as directed, Ida had made her second call to Italy. Marta Abruzzo had agreed to help her. And she had advised Ida to leave the Mark Hotel as soon as possible. It seemed that Fat Nicky had friends that could help him trace a credit card if he asked.

Carrying only her shoulder bag and dressed in the same clothes she wore the day before, Ida cautiously came out of the hotel lobby, walked to a black town car parked at the curb, tipped the doorman, and got into the back. The door closed, and the driver, an older man in a black suit wearing a neatly tied white turban, looked at her in his rearview mirror.

"Where are we going today?" he asked happily in a thick Indian accent. She gave him an address and he smiled. "That is close enough to walk, but I am very willing to drive you there."

She sighed. All she needed now was a chatty driver. He checked his side mirror and pulled out. 77th Street ran one-way to Fifth, and that ran one-way south. Though she was only going a few blocks north, traffic was heavy and the ride slow. They turned east on 76th Street, north on Park and finally turned onto 84th Street. Ida could see one of Fat Nicky's men standing under the metal awning in front of her apartment building, talking to the doorman. She instructed her driver to take them into the parking garage. She leaned down in her seat, as if she'd dropped something, as they went past the entrance, turned into the garage, and drove down the dark ramp.

"I'll be back in a few minutes," she informed the driver and hurried out of the car. She punched in a code and opened a heavy metal door and started up the steps. Ida's apartment was on the tenth floor, but she couldn't risk taking the elevator. She forced herself to climb in a quick steady rhythm until she reached the tenth floor. She caught her breath and carefully opened the tall wooden door to the hallway. She looked both ways and was relieved that no one was there. She hurried down the hall to a door at the end, keyed open the lock, and slipped inside as noiselessly as she could.

She took a quick breath and headed to her bedroom. Inside the master closet, she grabbed two large shoulder bags off a shelf. She pushed her hanging clothes aside and knelt on the floor in front of a built-in metal safe. She hit a six-digit code, opened the door, pulled out dozens of thick stacks of banded cash, and loaded them into one of the bags. She closed the safe and went to a large copper desk cluttered with piles of fashion magazines, scraps of papers with notes, southwestern pottery, and cups of colored markers. From a drawer, she retrieved her passport and wallet and shoved them into the bag. From the dresser, she selected a half dozen pieces of clothing, some jewelry, packed them, and walked out. At the front door, she turned back. She knew that she would never see this place again. She took a couple of short breaths, like a runner preparing for a race. She stepped into the hall, closed, and locked the door behind her and hurried off to the same door she had come through before.

She kept her pace as she jogged back down the ten stories and out through the basement door. She got into the town car, startling the driver who had fallen asleep.

"Oh." He smiled, embarrassed. "There you are. Where shall I take you now?"

"Get to 96th and Fifth and drive south. I'll tell you when we get there."

"Very good." He accepted this cheerfully as he turned the car around and drove up the ramp. Ida bent low and peered out the window as they turned toward Park Avenue, making sure that Fat Nicky's man hadn't caught sight of her.

*   *   *

"Got something," Clayton said as he pushed a key and looked up into the camera on his laptop. "I just sent a file."

"Yep," Silas acknowledged as his fingers worked rapidly. His eyes darted through the information and he smiled. "Hang on. Artemis and Drew need to see this."

He got up from his desk, went across the hall and into the study where Artemis was working on his computer and Drew was pacing by the bay windows as she listened on her cell.

"Clayton's online. He's got something," Silas reported and headed back to his room.

"I'll get back to you." Drew ended her call as she and Artemis followed.

"What is it?" Drew asked as they sat in front of Silas's laptop.

"You were right, Artemis," Clayton said. "I found a record of Iridescent Holdings, Ltd. The company was licensed in Milan in 2002 and had an address in Sarteano. It seems they moved in 2004. And so far, I can't find that address."

"But what about this?" Silas smiled as he pointed to a name in the file that Clayton had sent. "Look who's listed as president of the company."

Artemis and Drew leaned closer as Silas read, "Anna Canneli. The woman at TVNews who was Paula DeVong's assistant."

"Wow." Clayton tipped his head. "I mean, what are the odds?"

"Astronomical," Artemis answered as his eyes came alive.

"I think," Drew said to him, "we need to go talk with Anna Canneli. She lives nearby. On 76th Street between Columbus and CPW."

The address startled Artemis. "That's weird," he said.

"It is," Drew agreed. "I'll call her and set it up."

"Good," Artemis said as he got up. "And we should walk there. Gives us some time to..." He trailed off. Drew saw the worried expression on his face, and she knew exactly what was going on. That particular block was where Artemis had lived as a boy. And on that block, his parents were shot and killed.

"What are the odds?" Drew said, echoing Clayton.

Artemis repeated, "Astronomical."

Silas turned to him. "I'd like to come with you."

"No," Artemis said a little louder than he'd intended. "I would appreciate it"—he managed more softly—"if you and Clayton keep after this thing. I'm pretty sure that someone related to Anna Canneli changed his name to Mancini. It could have been done in Italy. But I think it was probably something that happened in New York in that same time period, 2003, give or take."

Silas saw the strain on his father's face. "Okay."

*　　*　　*

As Ida's town car passed 88th Street on Fifth Avenue, she slid down in the back seat and pulled her cap over her henna-red hair. Outside of Paul's apartment building, she saw two of Fat Nicky's men sitting on their parked motorcycles laughing with the doorman.

"Would you like to stop at the museum?" her driver asked. "It is only a few blocks away."

"No. Just drive around."

He glanced at her in the rearview mirror. "Anywhere?"

"Yeah. You choose," she said sadly. She took off her cap and shook her short hair free. She undid a button on her blouse and looked down at the clear blue gem hanging on her silver pendant necklace.

Blue tourmaline.

She pulled out her cell phone and made a call.

"Where are you?" she asked.

"I'm home," Paul said as he stepped out onto the balcony of his penthouse and looked across the park to the tall buildings of the Upper West Side.

"Two of Fat Nicky's guys are hanging out in front of your building."

"Still?" He leaned over the railing and looked down twenty-one stories. "Yep, I see them. Assholes."

Ida's car turned right onto the 79th Street transverse through the park. "I called to say goodbye, Paul."

He walked back into his apartment, went to the bar, and poured a drink. "So, the Crow is helping you get away?"

"Yes, she is."

"Did she say anything about Fat Nicky getting Ladimir arrested?"

"A little. Nicky acted on his own, and she's not happy about it. Just like you thought."

"Well, that's something anyway." Paul walked back out to the balcony and sat in a lounge chair. He sipped his drink. "Where are you?"

"Central Park," she said vaguely. "I'm in motion."

"Good. That's the safest way."

Ida's fingers wrapped tightly around the blue gem, and she closed her eyes. "I think it's going to be a long time before I'll be back here again."

After a moment, Paul said kindly, "I will truly miss you, Ida. Please take care of yourself."

"Count on it," she said with force. "And that goes for you too. Watch your back."

"Thanks. I will."

"Goodbye, Paul," she said and hung up.

Paul gazed out across the park for a long moment. Then he got up, went back inside, and closed the door. The sound of the traffic far below faded away. He sat in the middle of the wide living room on a fine antique Turkish carpet. He set his drink aside and lay on his back looking up at the white plaster ceiling.

I'm so sick of this.

He lifted his cell, found a number, and pushed it. After one ring, the call connected and three dull beeps sounded.

"It's me, Mother. Call me. It's urgent." Paul hung up and dropped the cell next to him on the carpet. He laughed, closed his eyes, and whispered, "We are all so fucked."

*   *   *

Artemis and Drew walked north on the sidewalk of Columbus Avenue. At the corner of 76th Street, they stopped to look at the Sunday flea market in the schoolyard across the street. It was crowded with people, most not wearing masks, out enjoying the sunny afternoon searching for bargains in the rows of white canvas-topped stalls selling vintage clothes, furniture, jewelry, musical instruments, and food.

"It's good to know they're still doing this," Drew said. Artemis nodded, and they walked down 76th Street heading east. About halfway down the block, they stopped in front of a five-story brownstone. Artemis looked up at the boxes full of flowers hanging outside the windows.

"It's been painted," he murmured. "Looks nice." He dropped his eyes to the stone steps leading to the sidewalk.

"God bless your parents," Drew said caringly. "Are you okay?"

"Yes," he said. "Let's go." They walked further down the block, checking the numbers on the brownstones.

"This is it," Drew confirmed, and they went up the steps and through a wood door into a small lobby. Drew found the apartment number on the security panel near the inner door and pushed the button.

"Who is it?" a nervous woman's voice asked through the speaker.

"Detective Sweeney," Drew answered loudly. "And Artemis Bookbinder."

After a short pause, they heard her say, "Come up." A buzzer sounded, and the lock on the door snapped open. They pulled up their COVID masks, went into the small vestibule, and started climbing up an old wood staircase that creaked under their weight. They stopped on the third-floor landing. Drew knocked on a door, and it swung open. Anna Canneli looked at them suspiciously. She was dressed in loose-fitting pants and an old work shirt. Her hair was messy, and she seemed exhausted.

"Thank you for agreeing to see us. May we come in?" Drew asked.

"I guess so," Anna said reluctantly as she stepped back, and they walked in. They looked around her small studio. There was an unmade bed with a wrought iron headboard against a red-brick wall. A vase of dried lavender was sitting in the hearth of a small stone fireplace that was surrounded by vintage woodwork. And on the far wall were two large casement windows looking out to the buildings across the street.

"Does the fireplace work?" Drew asked sounding like any curious New Yorker. Anna closed the door and locked it.

"No, it's blocked up," she answered testily. "So, what's so important that you have to come here on a Sunday?"

"Just some questions," Drew answered.

Anna went to the small kitchen counter, sat on a wood stool by a half-eaten donut, and folded her arms across her chest. A framed and signed headshot of Paula DeVong wearing her signature necklace hung on the wall behind her.

"That's nice," Artemis said lightly. "Paula must have loved that necklace. Do you know where she got it?"

"No," Anna said flatly.

"Do you have a necklace like that?" he asked.

"No."

Drew sighed dramatically. Artemis went to the windows and looked down at the peaceful tree-lined street.

"It's still nice on this block," he said. "I grew up here. Did you know that?"

"No," Anna said not bothering to hide the contempt in her voice. "How would I know that?"

"Just a few doors down, actually. I haven't been back for a long time." He turned to her. "Been here long?"

"Um." Her forehead wrinkled as she thought about it. "Since maybe 2003, I think."

"It's nice. How did you find it?" Artemis watched her. She twitched a little.

"Somebody recommended it." She shrugged. "A friend of a friend. I have really liked living here."

There was something wistful in the way she spoke that made Artemis ask, "Are you leaving?"

"Oh." Anna looked surprised. "I don't know. Maybe."

Artemis took this in and caught Drew's eye before he turned to look out the window again. Late-afternoon sunlight was shining down the street, across the leaves of the sidewalk trees and the line of cars parked along the far sidewalk where an old woman was walking a beagle on a leash.

"We've found something," Drew said as she picked up a wood stool, set it six feet away from Anna, and sat. "Do you own a building in Chinatown?"

"What?" Anna said sharply. "What do you mean?"

"It's a simple question," Drew answered. "There's a building on Mott Street that is owned by Iridescent Holdings, Ltd. A company that you are the president of."

Anna's hand trembled a little as she reached for a half-empty cup of tea on the counter. She took a sip. "There's no law that says I can't own property, is there?"

"Nope," Drew said. "As long as nothing criminal goes on there." She looked at Anna and waited.

"My grandfather bought that building on Mott Street, and I got it when he died," she admitted. "The company was set up as a trust for me. I don't have to do anything. There's a professional management company that takes care of renting it out and maintaining it. They're supposed to be replacing all the windows. I think that work is going on now."

"Your grandfather died five years ago," Artemis said as he turned to look at her. "In a fire in Queens." He made it sound like a known fact.

"Yes." She saw the intensity of his eyes above his mask. "He did."

"And he came to America from Italy about the time you found this place," Artemis said as he slowly walked back toward her. "In 2003, you said."

"Yes," Anna seemed puzzled. "He got here maybe the year before that."

"His name was Aldo Canneli, and he moved here from Sarteano, right?" he asked.

"Yes," she said, her eyes growing wider.

"And when he got here, he changed his last name to Mancini." He stopped in the middle of the room.

"Yes. You know a lot. I'm... impressed."

And Drew was too. Anna had just confirmed what they had been guessing.

"We know that he also owned a building on Doyers Street," Artemis continued. "He opened a bar there called the Necropolis in 2003."

"Yes," Anna muttered.

"And twelve years ago, that bar was busted for drugs and never reopened. Since then, a strange sort of school has been run in the basement of that building. They met every Sunday night at midnight. A valuable stolen piece of art was found there a year ago."

Anna blinked a few times. "What does that have to do with me?"

"There is a secret passage that the people in the school used." Drew took over. "It connects the two buildings. So, you must own not just the building on Mott Street but the one on Doyers Street as well."

"I do." Anna sounded upset. "There's another trust company for that one. My grandfather wanted to look out for me, since I'm all alone here. See, my mother and I came over from Italy when I was still a child. She died of a heart attack right after 9/11. So, my grandfather moved here to look after me. When he died, I was shocked to learn that he'd left me those buildings. And I have nothing to do with the running of them." She looked at them both intently. "I swear it. I don't know anything about secret classes or stolen art."

"We'll need the name of the company that manages the buildings," Drew said. Anna got up and went to a small desk in the corner. She opened a cluttered drawer, shuffled some papers, and found a business card. She handed it to Drew. "This is the company and the number. You should ask for Alan. He's in charge there."

"What's his last name?" Drew asked as she scanned the card.

"I don't know," Anna said. "But he's always been very nice on the phone."

"Do you see a lot of income from these places?" Artemis asked.

"Well, I used to get a monthly check for twelve hundred dollars. But a little more than a year ago, the money stopped coming. So, I called Alan, and he said that the buildings were in violation of some code and they had to replace all the windows and do some work. So, the money has been going into that, I guess."

"Aldo Canneli is such a nice name," Artemis said gently. "So, I'm wondering, why did your grandfather change it? Was he hiding from something? Or somebody?"

"I don't know," she said simply. "He never told me why."

"And you never asked," Drew said skeptically.

"No," she turned and glared at her.

"And before Sarteano, he lived in Sicily," Artemis said.

"That's true. How do you know that?"

"The numbers on the photos in your office," Artemis explained as he smiled a little. "You said it was a Sicilian thing that your grandfather taught you."

"Right. He did." She took a breath. "Am I in trouble?" she asked timidly.

"No," Drew said. "But we'll be checking out what you've told us."

Anna looked searchingly from Drew to Artemis.

"What?" Artemis asked. "Is there something else?"

Anna turned back to Drew and changed her mind. "Nope."

"Well, if you think of anything," Drew said as she stood up, pulled a card from her shirt pocket, and gave it to Anna, "call me. Anytime."

"I will," she said.

"Thank you, Anna," Artemis added as he and Drew went to the door, unlocked it, and left. As they started down the stairs, they could hear the sound of Anna relocking her door. As they came outside and down the stone steps to the sidewalk, they both pulled their masks down.

Drew took a deep breath. "That's better. So, do you believe her?"

"That she doesn't know what goes on in the buildings she owns? Oddly enough, I do. But you'll check out the manager, Alan?"

"Count on it." Drew promised.

"Good. And when are you supposed to talk with Jock Willinger?"

"Tomorrow morning," Drew answered as she started down the sidewalk toward Columbus.

"Let's go this way," Artemis said. He turned and walked slowly toward Central Park West. Drew understood and quickly caught up with him.

"You're seeing Roxie tonight?" she asked as they reached the corner and turned south. The street was full of slow-moving traffic, but the sidewalk was empty.

"Yeah, at seven."

"Want me to come with?" Drew asked.

"No, I'm good," Artemis said readily.

"Then I'll get you home and head back to Brooklyn."

"Thanks," Artemis said, and they both fell silent as they walked.

*   *   *

"Cheers," Calvin said as he smiled and lifted his champagne glass above the linen-covered table. Moira touched her glass to his, and they sipped.

"That's nice," she said. "And so is this place. I've never been here before."

Porter House Bar and Grill was on the fourth floor of the Time Warner Building. It was a comfortable open space with modern chandeliers hanging from a wood beam ceiling and tasteful gray walls. Across the vast room, a long modern bar was busy with well-spaced customers. Restaurants had been allowed to reopen for indoor dining in the spring, but COVID protocols were still required. Calvin and Moira sat at one of the tables along the twenty-one foot corner of tall windows that looked out toward Columbus Circle and Central Park. It was just after six, and most of the park was deep in shadow from the tall buildings, but the iconic towers of the Upper East side gleamed in the last golden light of the day.

"Nice to see you again, Mr. Prons," a masked waitress said as she topped off their champagne glasses. "It's been far too long."

"That's so true." Calvin grinned at her.

"I'll be back to check on you in a bit," she said as she put the bottle in a wine bucket and walked away.

Calvin leaned toward Moira and confided. "I haven't a fucking clue what that kid's name is."

Moira smiled. "She seems to like you well enough." She sipped her drink.

"I've been a regular here for a long time. My place is just up there," he said as he pointed to the high ceiling. "Sixty-seventh floor. Looks west and on a clear night, I can see for miles. You should come up sometime."

Moira chose her response carefully. "Maybe so."

"Well." Calvin leaned back in his chair. "Thanks for coming out with me. It's time we get to know each other better."

"You know"—she smiled easily—"I really have missed going out to restaurants."

"Me too. I'm not much of a theater or museum guy. But I missed this. And going to a ball game. I've got an Empire Suite at Citi Field, didn't get there at all last year."

"You're a Mets fan," she said surprised. "Would've pegged you for the Yankees."

He laughed. "You like baseball?"

"To tell the truth, not so much. But my dad loved the Mets. I have lots of fond memories of him yelling at the TV."

"Ah." Calvin nodded, losing interest. "I love champagne. It takes your worries and makes them blurries." He pronounced happily and took a sip.

Moira chuckled. "Okay, that so does not sound like you. Where did that come from?"

"My ex-wife," he confessed with a sigh. "Something she said years ago."

"That was Lucille, right?" Moira asked trying not to sound like a journalist.

Calvin eyed her for a moment. "Yeah," he said quietly. "Fucking psycho. Happy to have all that behind me. And have I mentioned"—he smiled at her—"how great you look tonight. Not that you don't always look good."

Moira murmured self-consciously, "Thanks, Calvin."

"I hope I didn't offend you by saying that," he said earnestly. "It's part of the reason I wanted to have dinner with you tonight."

"Oh, yes?" She waited for him to explain.

"The lawsuit." He looked troubled. "Can we talk about that?"

"Of course." She sat up a little straighter.

"You are the best on-air reporter in the business," Calvin said plainly.

"Hah." She gulped out a small laugh. "Hardly."

"No, I see these things and I know," he assured her. "You're smart and good-looking with those blue eyes and red hair."

She was uncertain where this was going and said nothing.

"You're aggressive, accessible, fair-minded. People seem to root for you."

She smiled. "Nice of you to say so."

"But now, you've been given this shot as anchor. And that's different," he said avuncularly. "You're the face of the program. When the audience looks at you, they need to feel that you're dependable, solid, and always on their side."

Moira slowly ran her fingers through her short curly hair and tipped her head. "That I'm on their side... or yours?"

Calvin grinned displaying his large white teeth. "Is there a difference?"

"Probably not," she answered.

"Good," Calvin said. He took a sip of champagne. "Okay, Moira, it's like this. The network is worried about the lawsuit. They want it to go away."

"I don't think so," Moira said with feeling. "Jock has to answer for what he's done."

"You're right," Calvin said smoothly. "And so you know, I hate what he did. And I swear to you I never knew what was going on until all this legal stuff happened." Calvin sounded sincere. "And Jock has gotten punished. He's fired, all his benefits gone and his reputation ruined. He'll never work in the industry again."

"The lawsuit matters because it's bigger than Jock Willinger," she said. "There has to be consequences, or nothing will ever change."

Calvin shrugged. "This case will drag on in the courts for years. And even if they finally convict him, his lawyers will figure out a way to keep his sorry old ass out of prison. You don't need to go through all that to send a message. Everybody can see what happened to Jock. Right now."

Moira sipped her drink.

"I can't officially tell you this." Calvin lowered his voice. "But Roxie and Deni Diaz have agreed to drop the suit. It's just you now."

"I heard that," Moira acknowledged.

"So, what do you say?" he asked respectfully. "The PR that this will stir up will hurt the network and hurt our show. You're just starting out in this new position. Doesn't it make sense to have everybody on your side right now?"

Moira lifted her glass and looked at the tiny rising bubbles. She took a sip. It tasted dry and light across her tongue. "This does help make the worries go away." She sighed. "All right, Calvin. I'll drop the case."

"Good," Calvin said pleased. "I hoped you'd say that, so I brought this along." He reached into the inside pocket of his suit jacket and pulled out some folded pages. "Would you sign this please?"

"Kinda had that all ready to go?" she said.

"Pays to be prepared," Calvin admitted.

Moira took the pages and started to look them over. Calvin pulled out a gold pen and handed it to her.

"Shouldn't I read this first?" she asked.

"Sure. Or you could just trust me."

She looked at his powerful face. Then she opened the pen, signed the document, and handed it back across the table to him. He checked her signature, folded the pages, and put them back in his pocket.

"Thank you, Moira," he said. "You won't regret this. I promise."

"I'll hold you to that."

Calvin lifted his glass. "To moving on."

They sipped their drinks.

"I hope you're hungry," he said happily. "I'm thinking oysters to start. Sound good?"

"Perfect." She smiled.

*   *   *

Artemis stood staring at the Max Ernst painting. The top of the small but dramatic canvas was a field of dark blue with a series of concentric gold-orange discs in the center—the sun. The bottom was a disturbed stylized pattern of browns, blues, and reds—an earthquake. Roxie came out of the kitchen carrying two glasses of chilled chardonnay and put one down on the built-in bar in front of him.

"It was just before he painted this," Artemis said, sounding faraway, "that he first used *frottage*."

"I thought it was called *grattage*," Roxie said, interested.

Artemis summoned himself back, noticed the glass of wine, lifted it, and took a sip. "Thanks."

She smiled, walked across the living room, and sat on one side of the wide modern sofa.

"In 1925, Ernst was staying at some old hotel in a French seaside town," he said as he looked at her strikingly beautiful face, sensual lips, the casual elegance of her outfit, and the comfortable way she was lounging, slowly sipping her drink. The top few buttons of her white shirt were undone and he could see her silver necklace and the ruby sparkling on her chest.

"Ernst noticed the grain of the wood floorboards in his room," Artemis said. "He got some paper, made some rubbings – *frottage* – and loved all the images he discovered. Because of that he was inspired to create this earthquake by using objects dragged across the wet paint."

"*Grattage*," Roxie purred knowingly and smiled a little.

"The freedom it gave to the work was pivotal to the whole movement of surrealism. Thanks for letting me see it. I think it's amazing," Artemis said warmly as he sat on the far end of the sofa more than six feet away from her.

"My pleasure," she said with a dry smile and added, "I see you're still social distancing."

"Well. It's kind of what I do."

"At least I got you to take that damn mask off."

"Hard to drink wine with it on." He acknowledged and looked around at the contemporary light-colored upholstered furniture, glass and chrome accent tables, and sleek floor lamps. "I like your place."

"Thanks. I love that I can walk to work on a nice day. How many New Yorkers can say that?"

"Not many." Artemis looked at her and said lightly, "You must love that necklace. You've had it on every time I've seen you."

Roxie nodded. "Yes."

"Like Paula DeVong and her necklace. Only hers wasn't a ruby. It was a pink rose quartz."

"Yes," she said, "that sounds right."

"And she never took hers off either. You said that yours was a gift from a friend. I wonder if hers was a gift too. And maybe from that same friend."

Roxie looked at his curious eyes and his lean handsome face. She sipped her wine.

"And Deni Diaz," he continued evenly. "She has one. Hers is pink too. But I think it's a pink sapphire."

"So?" Roxie murmured.

"It's about that sacred school down in Chinatown. Where the stolen chalice from the Gardner Museum was recovered. An eye witness told us that there were five women in that class and all of them wore a different gem necklace. Just like yours."

"Lots of people wear jewelry."

Artemis sipped his wine. "There's a question I've been waiting a long time to ask you. Since we first met sixteen months ago."

"Intriguing," she answered pleasurably. "Game on."

"Do you remember the day you heard about Raphael Sharder's death?"

"Yes," her eyes clouded over. "I was in my office at the studio. I got a call that morning."

"Ah, there it is." He smiled. "He was killed before midnight. The news wasn't released until the afternoon the next day. But you got the news early in the morning. I have an idea who called you, but it would help if you could tell me."

She laughed a little. "No way, Artemis. I always protect my sources. That's what gives a person an edge in the news business."

"I see." He leaned back against the arm of the sofa. "Here's some news: FBI agent Bert Rocca is dead."

Roxie breathed out sharply, then caught herself and sat completely still. After a while she asked, "What did he die of?"

"I don't have complete information yet. But he was found dead three days ago in Sicily. That's where he escaped to after my wife was killed. Did Rocca call to tell you Raphael was dead?" Artemis asked seemingly without judgement. "And before that, did he tell you that Raphael was going to give back the stolen painting?"

She looked at him with open surprise. "What? No. I don't know what you're talking about."

"Okay," Artemis said soothingly. "We know that you were at parties in Southampton at Raphael's mansion with a good-looking man, possibly of Greek descent."

"That maid," Roxie said with contempt, "has no manners."

He pressed on. "That man has a house in the Hamptons. You ate late meals together at the Primrose Restaurant. You said that he bought you this very expensive canvas." Artemis gestured to the Ernst painting. "Raphael picked it out for you at his gallery on 64th Street, but it was a gift from your friend. And so is that fine ruby necklace."

"Yes," Roxie said slowly. "It's true. My necklace and the painting are from the man I'm seeing."

"What is his name?"

She shook her head.

"I'm trying to help you, Roxie," he said with urgency. "Tell me the name of the teacher of the school."

Roxie looked down at her glass.

Artemis got up and went to the bank of windows. The sun was low behind a wall of clouds in the west. Across the Hudson River, the rows of buildings on the cliffs of New Jersey stood efficient and soulless. On the near side of the river, the raised lanes of the West Side Highway were full of relentless-noisy traffic in both directions. He looked to the grassy slope between the highway trestles and Riverside Boulevard far below. There were people out jogging, biking, and walking their dogs.

"Nice view," he said sadly. "If I'm right"—he turned to look at her—"your boyfriend is involved in the death of my wife, Emily. And the death of Raphael Sharder. And the death of Paula DeVong."

Roxie's eyes filled with tears. "I don't believe that," she said forcefully. She got up and went to the corner where the tall windows met. She looked south and could see a large white cruise ship docked many blocks away down the river. She put her drink down on the wide sill, reached up to the latch, and slid open the six-foot square of double-pane glass. The evening breeze washed across her body, and the sound of traffic got louder. "What do you want from me?" she asked.

"Just his name."

"No. I won't do that." She leaned out and looked down thirty floors. Across the street was a small fenced playground. Three mothers with strollers sat on a bench while their toddlers were sitting nearby drawing shapes with colored chalk on the black-matted ground.

"You must be very comfortable with heights," he said.

She faced him, sat on the wide ledge, and smiled. "I am. When I moved in here, the windows would only open a few inches. So, I took off that limiter thing." She indicated a couple of screw holes in the upper part of the window frame. "Really lets the fresh air in."

"Well," Artemis said. "Just don't get dizzy when you're enjoying the view." He put his glass down on the sill. "Thanks for the drink. And for letting me see this." He walked across the room and looked at the painting. "Earthquake, the artist called it. And this"—he pointed to the golden discs—"The Drowning of the Sun." He turned to her. The setting sun glowed across her shoulders and made the ruby on her breast glimmer. "What does he think of this painting, your friend?"

"I really don't know."

He took his mask from his pocket and turned to go. But after a few steps, he turned back. "We got the autopsy report on Paula DeVong," he said. "She died from an overdose of phentermine."

"What is that?" Roxie sounded strained.

"It's for weight loss."

Her shoulders sagged. "Didn't she die of a COVID-related stroke?"

"She did test positive." Artemis watched her. "But she had way too much of the drug in her system. Do you remember her taking anything for weight loss?"

"She might have. She was always worried about her weight."

"Witnesses told us that the man you hung out with in Southampton was a doctor."

"So?" Roxie said impatiently.

"Phentermine has to be prescribed," Artemis said. "Do you know who Paula DeVong's doctor was?"

Roxie lifted her wineglass and took a drink. "Sorry, no," she said with finality. "I just can't help you with this."

"I know," he said pointedly. "I think you're a good person, Roxie. You have my number if you ever want to talk."

"Thank you," she said faintly, and he left.

As she heard the apartment door close, she got up and went into the kitchen. She unplugged her phone from the charger on the marble counter, found a number, and pushed it.

"Is he gone?" Paul said impatiently as he paced in his penthouse apartment.

"Yes, he just left." Roxie opened the fridge, grabbed the bottle of chardonnay, and went back into the living room. "Paul, I'm freaking out. He's asking questions about the school, our gems, and who the teacher is."

"Shit," Paul muttered.

"And he thinks there's a connection between Raphael's death, and Paula's, and his wife's." She refilled her glass on the window sill.

Paul flung open the balcony door and went out. The wind was up and swirled hot air across his face. He looked across the park at the tall buildings of Central Park West where lights were coming on in thousands of windows. "But my name never came up?"

"No, never," she assured him.

"Okay." He took a breath and sat on the edge of a lounge chair. "Did he ask you anything about the box of chocolates?"

"No," she said. "But he said that Paula died of an overdose. A weight-loss drug. They're looking for the doctor that prescribed it."

"Okay, okay," he said slowly, taking this in.

"Paul, what do we do?"

He leaned back into the padded seat of the lounge chair. "I have to think. I'll call you."

"No, wait," she said quickly. "I need to see you. Right now."

Paul smiled. "All right," he said smoothly. "Get here as fast as you can."

"I will," she agreed and hung up. She put her open palms on the sill, leaned far out the window, and looked down to see if there were any cabs waiting in front of the building. She saw the children were still out in the little playground. The colored chalk drawings on the dark ground had multiplied and now there were pink and blue spirals, faces of dragons, and a series of interlocking red boxes.

I think you're a good person, Roxie.

She slowly closed the window, took a sip of wine, and picked up her phone. She carefully punched in a long number. The call connected, and she heard three dull beeps. Keeping her voice calm, she left a message: "It's Roxie. I'm heading to Paul's. I need to talk with you as soon as possible."

She ended the call, finished off her drink, and went to gather her things.

* * *

By eleven, the night air was cooler. Lucille sat on the floor of her studio by the open north-facing window leaning against the wall. She was staring at a crumpled newspaper on the floor beside her. Even though her lights were out, the city-glow was enough to see the headline about Paula DeVong's death.

She slowly got up, sat on the sill, swung her legs out, and looked at her bare feet dangling over the edge of the roof. Nineteen stories down, the sidewalks of 73rd Street were busy with maskless people heading toward Broadway. She looked across the street to the top floor of the Ansonia. Some lights were still on in the Bookbinder apartment, but no one was visible. Just above the windows, the strange terra-cotta faces that decorated the cornice glared at her with their hollow eyes. She turned east, and above the rooftops, she could see the pale moon appearing through the drifting clouds.

"Goddess Moon," Lucille whispered as her eyes filled with tears. "What have I done?"

She heard three knocks at the door. She wiped her eyes dry and soundlessly went across the room. She listened before she asked, "Who is it?"

"It's me."

Lucille opened the door, and Ida quickly came in.

"What's wrong?" Lucille saw the fear in her sister's eyes.

Ida closed the door, locked it, dumped her heavy shoulder bags on the bed, leaned out the open window, and inspected the street below.

"Nice to see you too," Lucille said with gentle sarcasm.

Ida didn't answer.

"What's happened?" Lucille asked as she moved closer.

Ida turned to look at her sister. "How are you?"

"Okay," Lucille said. "Talk to me."

"That's why I'm here." Ida sat on the edge of the bed and took a long breath. "People are looking for us. They mean to kill us."

"Us?" Lucille sat on the floor by her feet. "Not just me?"

"No." Ida smiled a little. "Seems they think I know where you are."

Lucille understood. "Who is after you?"

"Someone I thought was a friend." Ida laughed bitterly. "And lots of his friends."

"You mean Paul," Lucille said with disgust.

"No, he's been helping," Ida said truthfully. "He made me promise that I would take you with me when I go."

Lucille looked at her for a long while, then she asked, "Does Paul know where I am?"

"No, he doesn't."

"Did he know before, when I was living downtown?"

Ida debated for a second and then confessed. "Yes."

"He knew where I was for the past year and a half?"

"Yes, he did."

Lucille closed her eyes. She felt overwhelmed and dizzy. Far away, she could hear the Goddess Moon's high-pitched laughter, mocking her.

You are the Angel of Death and you will be feared.

"I have to make a call in the morning, to finalize everything," Ida explained. "And then we're gone."

Lucille drew her knees up to her chest and wrapped her arms around her legs. "I don't have a passport."

"I know. I won't be using mine either."

Lucille opened her eyes and looked up at her sister. She saw the concern in her face and her eagerness to help. Like always. "Where would we go?" she asked.

"Croatia, apparently," Ida answered. "At least for a while."

"What's there?"

"I don't know." Ida smiled a little. "Hopefully, an infinity pool looking out at the Adriatic where we can sip martinis and take some time to figure things out."

"And what about Paula DeVong?" Lucille gestured to the newspaper on the floor.

"What about her?"

"They said she died from COVID, but that can't be right. She had no symptoms. Nothing was wrong with her."

"How would you know?" Ida asked sharply.

Lucille answered indirectly. "Do you know what I've been doing for the past year and a half?"

"You were supposed to be hiding," Ida said sternly.

"Why? Because I was in such danger from Paul Marin?" Lucille asked scornfully. "The man who knew where I was all the time?"

Ida said resignedly, "All right, you snuck around at night wearing a mask and a cap. Where did you go?"

"I followed the people in Paul Marin's class," Lucille reported. "At first, I'd wait near Paul's building on Fifth. Roxie Lee would pull up in a cab a few times a week, always past midnight." Lucille's eyes grew dark and focused. "Sometimes I'd check out the entrance of TVNews on Columbus. After the show, they'd start coming out. Roxie might go out for a drink with Paula or walk home to Riverside Boulevard. Or take a cab to go see Paul."

"Who else besides Roxie?" Ida asked, keeping her on track.

"I followed Deni Diaz and Greg Schaefer. They liked to go to that diner on 69th and Broadway. It stays open all night. Last summer, when no one could eat inside because of COVID, they would get takeout and wander around as they ate. Sometimes they'd sit by the fountain at Lincoln Center. They'd laugh together a lot. I liked that."

Ida grunted impatiently. "Okay. Tell me about Paula."

"Sometimes she'd walk up Broadway to her apartment on 82nd Street. Sometimes she'd head down to the Time Warner building." Lucille took a long shaky breath. "And... last week, Paula showed up at the place I was staying."

Ida froze. "What happened?"

"It was past two in the morning," Lucille said. "She asked me if I knew the apartment belonged to her. I told her yes. I thanked her for letting me stay there, but she said it was a favor for you."

"It was." Ida leaned forward and asked urgently, "Why was she there?"

"She had an idea for a story." Lucille looked worried. "She said that it was time for Paul Marin to get what he deserved."

"Oh no," Ida said sadly as she began to understand.

"She asked me if I wasn't tired of hiding. And I said I was. She pulled a small camera out of her bag and said that I could finally tell everyone what had happened. And I agreed. She set up the camera, and I told her about the classes, how I had recognized the stolen chalice in Paul's hands and called the cops. And I told her about how he set me up for the murder of Emily Bookbinder."

"Jesus," Ida murmured.

"Paula said it would be on her show. She needed somebody's approval, but she was sure that it would be on by Thursday. This past Thursday."

"And she died on Wednesday, the night before," Ida said.

"And it never aired," Lucille pointed to the newspaper, "or there would have been some kind of news."

"Where is that recording now?" Ida said hoarsely as the events of the past few days came into sharp focus.

"I don't know." Lucille hugged her knees tighter. She looked up at her sister and asked, "Was Paula killed because of my interview?"

"Paula is dead," Ida said forcefully, "because she had no idea who she was dealing with."

Lucille shivered. She slowly got up and looked out the window. There was still no one to be seen in the apartment across the street. "Ida, I need to know something."

"What?"

"Why this place?" Lucille turned to her. "Did you know the Bookbinders would be living there? Is that why I'm here?"

"Yes," Ida admitted and suddenly felt very tired. "Have you seen anything?"

"Not much. They've been unpacking."

Ida took this in and then pushed her heavy bags off the bed. "We should get some sleep. I hope you don't mind sharing the bed."

"Of course not," Lucille said, sounding faraway. "Just like when we were kids."

Ida lay down against the wall and punched the pillow under her head.

"You've always helped me," Lucille said simply. "No matter what. And look what's happened to you. Running for your life."

Ida closed her eyes. "Don't worry about me. I can deal with it."

"I know you can," Lucille said almost to herself. "Ida, I'm not going with you."

Ida rolled on her side and looked at her. "Did you not just hear me say that Paula is dead because she didn't know who the fuck she was dealing with?"

"I did," Lucille said. "But I'm not running from anyone ever again. I still have things to do here."

Ida groaned in noisy exasperation. "I'm too tired to argue with you. You're coming with me and that's all."

"We'll talk about it tomorrow," Lucille said with resolve. "You should sleep."

Ida suddenly felt weary to the bone. She lay back down, closed her eyes, and almost at once her breathing slowed and became softer.

Lucille sat back on the window sill and swung her legs out. She looked up to the east for the reassuring light of the moon, but it was hidden behind dark clouds. "I understand," she whispered to the sky. "This is how it will be from now on. I am on my own."

*   *   *

Artemis stood in the open door of his son's room. It was a little before midnight, and Silas was asleep on his messy unmade bed still dressed in his jeans and a rugby shirt. Artemis frowned as he fought down an almost unbearable impulse to wake Silas, tell him the dangers of contaminating his sheets with the clothes he'd worn outside, make him change, and remake the bed with fresh linens.

Artemis shook his head and remembered a phrase.

You live in here.

He'd say those words in a self-deprecating way to apologize to Emily when the protocols in his mind started to drive her mad. And then she'd laugh, accepting him in spite of his many quirks and oddities. And everything would be all right again. He looked down at Silas and wondered why he was wearing a rugby shirt.

Artemis carefully freed the tangled sheet from under his son's legs and covered him. He gently removed Silas's glasses, put them on the bedside table, moved quietly to the door, stepped out, and closed it. He heard Delia's loud snores coming through her bedroom door down the hall. He smiled and headed for his study.

There, he closed the door, poured himself a single malt, and sat down at his desk. He looked around at the reassuring dark green walls and solid oak built-in bookcases, now filled with his carefully arranged books. Heavy curtains covered the curved bay windows and ensured his privacy from the nearby taller building. He sipped his drink. The outside world was still so uncomfortable. At least here in his study, he had a place where he could breathe and feel safe again.

He looked at the corkboard on the wall where two photos of the stolen pieces they'd recovered were pinned. One was of Rembrandt's masterwork *Storm on the Sea of Galilee*. The art dealer Raphael Sharder had tried to give it back and was killed. The other photo was a dark-bronze ceremonial chalice with Chinese markings. And he wondered again at the seeming randomness of the thirteen pieces stolen from the Gardner Museum that night in March 1990: some paintings, some drawings, and two objects. One, the chalice. It was Shang dynasty, twelfth century BCE. The other was a flagpole finial, a gilded bronze eagle that was once carried into battle by Napoleon's Imperial Guard.

Artemis sipped his scotch. An art dealer had the Rembrandt. It was likely that the teacher of the secret school had the chalice. He wondered about who had the still-missing eagle finial, a symbol of power and a trophy of war.

Artemis thought of the mysterious blue azurite pendant necklace that was found in Lucille's car. And the gems worn by Roxie, Deni, and Paula DeVong. And the break-in at Paula's apartment the night she died. What were they looking for? And did they find it?

He sighed wearily. He pulled off his shoes and put his feet up on his desk, making sure his heels were resting in the middle of a clean legal pad. He put his drink down, leaned back in his chair, folded his hands in his lap, and closed his eyes. And as he drifted off, he worried about tomorrow when he would have to go out once more into the germ-filled world. And if anything would ever really feel normal again.

Chapter Five

Monday, July 19th, 2021

"**A**nything new from Ray?" Mak asked as he steered the car off the Palisades Parkway at the first exit.

"No." Artemis was sitting in the front passenger seat checking his messages. "But I spent a while going over his report last night." In New Jersey, the morning was already getting hot and humid, but Artemis lowered his window halfway to let in the fresh air. He took a long breath.

"How are you?" Mak asked.

"Okay," Artemis murmured. "Thanks."

"So, Bert Rocca," Mak said to distract him. "I wasn't surprised to hear he was dead. You?"

"No," Artemis agreed. "He was a patsy. But I have been wondering about the timing. Rocca was in Italy for more than a year and a half. Why was he killed now?"

Mak turned at a traffic light onto a tree-lined suburban street. Artemis scanned the well-tended houses with their green lawns and manicured gardens. Mak took a quick check and saw that faraway look in his friend's eyes.

"Anything I should know?" Mak asked.

Artemis slowly returned from his mental journey. "Not yet. I have a theory, but... not yet."

The car bumped over a railroad track as they headed through a small town.

"I remember this place," Artemis said wistfully as they passed a vintage-looking diner. "From back when you could still go out to eat. Looks like they're still in business."

Mak knew they weren't far from the house in Halesburgh, but he chose not to say anything. He turned the car into a side street that was marked with a dead-end sign.

"All these expensive houses," Artemis mused as they passed fenced yards and large mansions. "Do you think anyone here knows about this place?"

"I sure hope not," Mak said. At the end of the road, they came to a property entirely hidden by tall hedges. Mak turned the car into the driveway and stopped at a tall iron gate. From a small security box clamped to a metal pole came a sharp voice. "Yes?"

Mak looked at the camera mounted above the speaker. "Good morning," he said. The gate unlocked with a click, swung open, and they drove in. The gate disappeared behind them as they drove along a curved driveway lined with tall evergreen trees. After another turn, the trees were gone, and they could see a Tudor-style mansion. Mak pulled up at the front entrance where a serious-looking woman in a dark suit was waiting for them. As she stepped to the car, Mak rolled down his window and held up his FBI identification. She smiled at him.

"Nice to see you again, Agent Kim."

"You too," Mak said as he pulled a file from the back seat, and they got out. "This is Artemis Bookbinder."

Artemis took out his mask and put it on. As she led them up the steps, the leaded-glass front door was opened from inside by another agent. They stepped into a two-story open gallery with dark wood-paneled walls that were crowded with small landscape paintings. There was a grand double staircase and a heavy cut-glass chandelier. Artemis looked at Mak surprised, but he just smiled.

"This way," the woman agent said efficiently and led them through a large library full of dusty-looking books.

"How is he today?" Mak asked.

"Still confused as to why he's here," she answered as they walked through a wide dining room wallpapered with a countryside mural.

"This would confuse Fragonard," Artemis joked, and they both stopped to look at him. "Oh"—he smiled at himself—"he was a Baroque painter. Did this kind of thing. But... much better."

"Thanks, Professor," Mak said amused. The agent led them through a door and along a corridor past a whitewashed kitchen. They went down a flight of concrete stairs to a fluorescent-lit basement. Here the walls were covered with wood veneer, and on the ceiling, a large metal-grid vent was supplying the room with cool air.

Artemis took a shallow breath through his mask and saw that there were no windows. As he slowly followed, he wondered where the air-conditioner filters were and when they were last cleaned. He felt an impulse to turn around and run. But he commanded his mind to calm down and remember why he was here. They stopped at the end of a long hallway where an agent in a dark suit sat at a small desk in front of a solid-looking metal door. He got up, unlocked, and opened the door.

Mak and the woman agent went in first. Artemis followed, and the door was closed and locked behind him by the man who'd let them in. It was a square utilitarian windowless room with beige-painted cinder block walls. It had some gently used furniture: a yellow-and-black plaid sofa, a round wood dining table, and four simple chairs. Mounted in the upper corners of the room were four cameras with microphones. Against a wall to one side was an unmade bed. On the other side, a man stood leaning against the wall watching them. He was in his mid-thirties with big shoulders and close-cut dark hair. He was dressed in blue work pants and a clean denim shirt. He was handsome enough, but his most notable feature was his strange eyes. His left eye was discernably bigger than the right.

The woman agent stayed by the door as Mak went to the table and sat down. Artemis stayed standing about halfway between them.

"I am FBI agent Makani Kim. What we say here is being recorded. Do you understand that, Mr. Karlovic?"

Ladimir nodded once.

"This is my associate Artemis Bookbinder."

Ladimir looked across the room and inspected Artemis. "I've heard of you. You are very afraid of germs," he said scornfully, his Slavic accent pronounced.

Above his mask, Artemis's eyes woke up. "Who told you that?"

Ladimir turned to Mak. "Why have I been taken to this... lovely place?"

"It was a favor to your grandfather, Andre Karlovic," Mak answered. "He met with us because he was concerned for your safety at the detention center in Connecticut. So, we agreed to keep you here for a while."

Ladimir asked suspiciously, "My grandfather met with you where?"

"Not me," Mak answered factually as he opened his file and read. "He met a senior FBI agent on his yacht, the Trinitas, in the harbor of Dubrovnik, Croatia, this past Saturday, the 17th."

Ladimir considered. "Okay. So, say I believe this. What happens now?"

"That's up to you." Mak gestured to a chair across the table. "Please sit."

Ladimir shrugged, walked over, and sat. Mak pulled a photo from his file and handed it to him.

"This is a picture of the logo of your grandfather's company," Mak said. "A three-headed sea serpent."

"Yes, I know this," Ladimir said disdainfully.

"And this," Mak pulled out a photo of the fresco from the Necropolis Bar and slid it across the table. "Is in a building in Chinatown, New York."

"So?" Ladimir leaned back in his chair, his expression uninterested.

"Tell me about the Necropolis Bar," Mak said.

"Never heard of that place."

"Really?" Mak said as he flipped to a report. "It's on Doyers Street. Some twelve years ago, it was closed after a drug raid. Guess who was arrested there for dealing."

"Oh," Ladimir rolled his odd eyes. "That place. It was a long time ago."

"You were released the next day and mysteriously no charges were ever brought."

"Yes," Ladimir admitted. "I was an innocent victim of circumstance."

"Just like now," Mak said ironically. "Only this time you will stand trial. And be convicted. And sent to prison. Where even your grandfather won't be able to keep you alive."

Ladimir folded his large hands on the table. "They won't let me smoke in here." He scowled at the agent by the door. "Afraid it will be bad for the air-conditioning." He looked to Mak.

Mak pulled out a pack and a lighter and handed it across the table. Ladimir sneered at Artemis as he pulled out a cigarette, placed it between his lips, and lit it. Artemis examined the smoke slowly drifting up to the vent in the ceiling and made a decision. He reached up and pulled the mask from his face. He walked to the table and sat down next to Mak.

"Your grandfather told us," Artemis said sharply, quoting Ray's report from memory, "that there are three heads and one body. Just like that picture and just like his logo. Andre Karlovic, global banker, is one of those heads."

Ladimir sat very still, listening.

"The second is Marta Abruzzo, who lives in Avola, Sicily. Her family has been involved in selling munitions to causes and nations for generations," Artemis reported. "Your grandfather is eighty-nine years old. And he wants you to be extradited back to Croatia. Presumably so you can take over when he's gone."

Ladimir took a slow drag on his cigarette and breathed out the smoke toward the ceiling.

"It will take a lot of convincing for you to qualify for extradition," Mak picked it up. "You would have to be very helpful to us."

"Otherwise, I will be sent to prison and take my chances," Ladimir said, trying to sound bored.

"You will be killed," Artemis said plainly. "The question is, by who?"

"Don't you know, Professor Bookbinder?" Ladimir smirked.

Artemis again registered that Ladimir knew who he was. Then he said, "Who is the third head of the serpent?"

Ladimir frowned.

"One is in Croatia. One in Sicily," Artemis said. "I think the third one is in Greece."

Mak tried not to look surprised as he heard this new theory.

"Because there is a man who comes from Greece," Artemis listed what they knew. "He taught a secret class on Doyers Street, underneath the Necropolis Bar, where the three serpents are painted on the wall. We know that the class met every Sunday night at midnight and there was a tall, strong man who stayed outside and guarded the door."

Mak joined in. "We have a witness who will identify you. There's something about your eyes that makes you... stand out."

"Fuck you," Ladimir murmured as he squinted his overlarge left eye at Mak.

"And sometimes, the witness told us"—Mak continued—"you were joined by a very fat man."

"So, we're wondering," Artemis said, sounding like he was sure, "which guy betrayed you in Connecticut. The fat guy. Or the teacher?"

Ladimir took a second, stubbed out his cigarette under the lip of the table, and sat up. "I cannot talk about this," he said with unexpected sincerity. "And I will not."

"Who is the third head?" Artemis kept on. "Who is the teacher related to in Greece? Is it his grandfather? His grandmother?"

"I will not speak of the Trias," Ladimir said flatly, his upper lip glistening with sweat.

"Trias," Artemis murmured taking in this new piece of information. "That's a Greek word."

Ladimir reached for the pack of cigarettes and lit up another.

"Give us something," Mak said quietly. "Or you will end up in an American prison."

"And dead," Ladimir acknowledged. "The trouble is that you have no idea what you are asking. What these people can do."

"Yes, I do," Artemis said. "They killed my wife. So, I'll ask you again. Who betrayed you?"

Ladimir took a slow drag on his cigarette. "I want to help you. I want to get away from America. But the truth is... I'm not sure."

"It's either the teacher...?" Artemis led him. "Or the fat man?"

"Yes."

"Could it have been anyone else?"

"No." Ladimir wiped his large face with his hand. "Can you promise me that I will be sent home to Croatia?"

"No, we can't," Mak said. "You answer our questions and then we'll see. The more helpful you are, the better your chances."

"That's no guarantee," Ladimir sounded defeated.

"Give us something," Mak urged again.

Ladimir swallowed hard, looked up to the cameras, and then back to them. "All right, but only this much. It is not the teacher's grandmother. Or grandfather. They are both dead."

Artemis and Mak sat still, waiting.

"It is his mother. She is the third head of the serpent." Ladimir folded his arms tightly across his chest. "Do not ask me anymore questions. I have nothing more to say. I'm done."

* * *

"And this is Detective Jerome Clayton Collins," Drew said.

Jock Willinger stood in the open door eyeing the young Black man suspiciously. "That's a lot of names for one man," he said sarcastically and stepped back for them to enter. Clayton shook off the comment as he and Drew walked into Jock's apartment.

"You're from Liverpool, right?" Clayton asked politely.

"Yes," Jock answered in clipped annoyance as he closed the front door.

The two detectives looked around at the glossy white walls and cabinets of his contemporary living room. Drew went to a corner of wide windows and looked out at an impressive open city view to the west. Thirty stories down, she could see Broadway and across the street Lincoln Center where groups of tourists were gathered around the central fountain. The morning was clear, and past the buildings and the wide Hudson River, she could see for miles across New Jersey.

"Nice," Drew said in a friendly tone. "Have you lived here long?"

"Yes," he answered grudgingly. "Since I arrived in New York to work at TVNews, eighteen years ago." Jock went to the kitchen counter where his cigarettes and a full ashtray were.

"It's a block and a half from the studio," Drew observed. "That's convenient."

"It was." Jock's reedy voice was strained, and his hand trembled as he lit a cigarette. He was dressed in dark pants and a wrinkled white button-down shirt. His thin gray hair was messy, and behind his heavy black-rimmed glasses, his long oval face was very pale and his eyes tired. "So, what do you want?"

"What did you think of Paula DeVong?" Drew asked as Clayton took out a pad and pen. Jock took a long pull on his cigarette.

"She was a backstabbing prima donna, and I'm glad she's dead. COVID did some good after all," he said bitterly.

Drew studied him. "Well, that's clear. Was she part of the harassment case against you?"

"You know about that?" Jock reached up and nervously pulled on one of his large earlobes. "No, she wasn't. And the case has been dropped."

"I didn't know that," Drew said.

Clayton turned and looked into the bedroom. Like the living room, it was almost antiseptic with white walls and no decorations of any kind. A half-packed suitcase lay open on the unmade bed. "Are you planning a trip, Mr. Willinger?" he asked.

"What's it to you?" Jock sneered at him.

"Maybe a lot," Clayton said. "Because Paula DeVong didn't die of COVID."

Jock's mouth opened to say something, but no sound came out.

"So, it's really interesting to hear what you thought of her," Drew said as she sat on the window ledge and leaned her powerful shoulders against the glass.

"What did she die of?" Jock asked.

"Overdose," Clayton answered. "Of a weight-loss drug that she didn't have a prescription for. Know anything about that?"

"No, I don't."

"So, where are you heading? Out of the country?" Clayton asked.

"Yes, back to Liverpool."

"I hope your tickets are refundable," Clayton said.

"Why? Am I...?" Jock looked from Clayton to Drew.

"You're a person of interest to our investigation," Drew explained sounding official.

"But why?" he stammered again.

"You hated Paula DeVong," Drew answered, "because she was going to replace you. We know that Paula ingested the drug, but we don't know how. Yet. You had access to her office. How hard would it have been for you to put something in her coffee?"

Jock's eyes opened wide. "Anyone in the studio could have done that. And I'm not the only one who hated that bitch."

"Got a list?" Clayton asked.

"Yes. Everyone!" Jock said emphatically. "Start with Calvin Prons who hated her as much as I did, despite the fact that he was fucking her. And little Moira Weyland, there's a nasty ambitious piece of goods. It's so unfair. If I looked good in a short skirt, I'd rule the world." He waved his hand at Drew. "No offence."

"None taken." Drew shrugged. "I don't wear skirts. But it's kinda scary thinking of you in one."

Jock gaped at her. "Look. I hated Paula DeVong. But I didn't kill her." He stubbed out his cigarette in the overcrowded ashtray. "I swear it."

Drew stood up, stretched her back, and grunted. "You met with Paula after the show, the night she died."

"Yes," Jock answered uncertainly.

"Anna Canneli was there too."

"Yes," Jock said carefully, his Liverpool accent becoming more pronounced. "Paula said something about wanting to have a witness there. More of that harassment *shite*."

"What was said at that meeting?" Drew asked.

"Another of Paula's little ideas," he said dismissively as he pulled out another cigarette and lit it. "She had footage of Calvin's ex-wife, Lucille, saying how innocent she was for something that happened over a year ago. Paula had been trying to get me to okay the piece for a few days. But it wasn't news, and I told her so."

"Paula needed your approval to put it on the air?" Clayton asked as he made notes.

"Yes," Jock answered, annoyed to be interrupted. "And I refused. Which didn't make much difference to her. She knew I was about to be fired."

"Okay," Drew said as she turned to look out the window. "What did Calvin Prons make of that story?"

"I don't know."

She eyed the slow-moving traffic on Broadway far below. "Didn't you tell him? It was his ex-wife."

"Who he had nothing to do with because she was crazy," Jock explained. "No, I didn't bother him with that."

Drew turned back to him. "Do you think that Paula told him?"

"Couldn't say. Calvin hasn't spoken to me much since the harassment thing began."

"Right." Drew pulled out her card and put it down on the counter. "Do not leave town. If you have anything else that'll help our investigation, I expect you to call me right away."

Jock nodded, and Drew and Clayton left.

Outside the building, they caught a cab and headed back across the park to the 19th Precinct.

* * *

"Thanks for seeing me, Calvin," Moira smiled as she closed his office door.

"My pleasure," Calvin said warmly as he pushed aside his work and leaned back in his leather chair. He smiled appreciatively as Moira walked toward him. "That's a nice color on you." His eyes were fixated on her short skirt and the swing of her hips. "Really brings out your blue eyes."

"Thanks." She sat down in one of the chairs in front of his desk and crossed her legs. "And thank you again for dinner last night."

"Sure." Calvin looked interested. "What can I do for you?"

"I floated an idea for a story by Roxie. But she said it was above her pay grade and I had to ask you."

Calvin laughed. "Ask your mother, ask your dad?"

"Something like that." Moira smiled and pushed a wisp of curly red hair away from her eyes.

"Okay, kid," Calvin said and grinned at her. "Whatcha got?"

"The more research I do, the more people I talk to, the more I'm convinced that something is wrong with the way we're reporting COVID and the vaccines. And I don't mean just us. I mean all of the media."

Calvin stopped grinning and pulled on his tie to loosen his collar. "Okay. So, what's the beef?"

"I think we should be presenting more than one opinion. There is a lot of data out there, from credible sources, saying that these vaccines have been rushed and there may be serious consequences."

"No way," Calvin interrupted her. "There's a major fucking illness in the world, and in case you haven't noticed, people are still dying. The vaccines save lives."

"See," Moira said keenly, "that's exactly what I mean. We should have on someone from the CDC who says it exactly like that. And then, I've got a researcher-whistleblower who will tell the problems they've seen. Put them both together, and we'll have a show that will get ratings. It's authentic. And uncomfortable. And if I can run with it, it could be a great ongoing segment."

Calvin looked at her with exaggerated pity. "Sorry, kid. I admire your enthusiasm, I do. But we have to support what the government is doing. This isn't a time for a high school debate. This is war. And losing is not an option."

Moira could hear the echo of Calvin's military past in his words, and she knew that it was pointless. "But people are choosing sides and it's getting ugly. And that's just wrong. Especially in America."

"Forget this," Calvin said with friendly finality. "Any other ideas?"

"I'm working on some things," she said vaguely as she got up to go. "I better get back to work."

"Good," Calvin said dismissively. "Me too."

She walked out of the office and closed the door. Across the wood-paneled reception area, she saw Roxie leaning against her open office door, her arms folded across her chest and a smile on her face that said *I told you so.* As Moira walked past her and down the open-tread stairs to the newsroom, she wondered if she would become like Roxie, a person who would just smile and agree no matter what they told her to do. And Moira remembered how she had agreed to drop the harassment suit, and suddenly, she hated herself for signing that piece of paper.

* * *

The passing clouds above did little to relieve the oppressive heat in the rooftop studio. Ida stood looking out the open window, her arms crossed stubbornly and her face shiny with sweat. Lucille sat on the bed watching her.

"I don't like it, but I guess I have to accept it," Ida said resignedly. She hated losing any argument, but this one was about life and death. She turned to Lucille. "I brought lots of cash." She pointed to her bags on the floor. "I'll leave you half. But I don't know how you'll live when that's gone."

"I'll manage," Lucille said. Ida heard the calm confidence in her words and could see the clear resolve in her sister's eyes.

"Why the fuck don't you at least have a fan in here by now?" Ida asked testily as she started to pace across the small room.

"I hate the noise," Lucille answered. "And I'm getting to like the heat."

"Why?" Ida rasped in exasperation.

"It reminds me that I can't afford to be weak."

Ida stopped pacing and barked out a short ironic laugh. "What, you enjoy sweating to death in the fire of redemption?"

"No," Lucille explained. "More like I'm still alive in a crucible of … opportunity."

Ida stood still and tried to understand but couldn't. Then she announced, "I'm going out. I have to make that call about travel arrangements."

"It's too dangerous out there," Lucille said. "Why can't you do that from here?"

"The less you know about where I'm going, the safer you'll be." Ida explained as she got her cap and pulled out her COVID mask. "Can I get one of your phones? It's probably safer than using my cell."

"Of course," Lucille said as she knelt on the floor, retrieved a paper bag from under the bed, pulled out a burner phone, and handed it to her.

"Thanks," Ida said as she ripped off the packaging and started for the door. "I won't be long. Do we need anything?"

"No," Lucille answered. "Be careful out there."

"I will," Ida said assuredly. "Lock this after me." She went out the door and closed it with a thump. Lucille got up, turned the locks, and went over to the window. She looked across the street to the Bookbinder apartment, but no one was visible. She leaned out and looked down the nineteen stories to the street. In front of the Ansonia, she could see a couple of uniformed cops talking together. The revolving door spun and two people came out—Silas and the young agent who guarded him. They were dressed for running. They talked with the cops, and then Silas, the agent, and one of the cops headed west along the sidewalk toward Riverside Park.

Lucille leaned further out so she could see the street door of her building. After a moment, her sister came out, her hair hidden under her cap and her face covered with her mask. Ida casually walked east on the sidewalk heading toward Broadway. Lucille peered at the cop by the Ansonia and was relieved that he didn't notice Ida, who crossed the busy avenue and disappeared around the corner.

Lucille felt a presence in the top-floor window across the street; she slowly knelt down and looked carefully over the window sill. The older woman who lived with the Bookbinders appeared energetically pulling a vacuum cleaner. Lucille smiled to herself. Life across the street seemed to be so normal, despite the pandemic and all the troubles of the world.

*   *   *

Drew and Clayton walked up three flights of stairs inside the old station house on East 67th Street. They arrived at the unusually quiet open workspace of the Criminal Intelligence Section. Clayton sat at his desk in the middle of the room and checked his messages to see if there had been any word from Beth Schaefer.

"Not yet," he reported, and Drew headed to her glass-walled office at the far end. She sat at her large metal desk, fired up her laptop, and started to log the interview with Jock Willinger. Her desk phone rang, and she answered.

"Detective Sweeney."

"Is this a good time?" Mathew asked respectfully.

"Sure, Dad, what's up?"

"I wanna make us some lasagna tonight, and I need some stuff from the market."

"No problem," she said.

Mathew listed a few things and then asked, "When will you get home?"

"Not too late, I hope. Lots going on here," Drew said. Her father was still so tough in many ways, but she could tell that he was feeling lonely since the Bookbinders moved out of their Brooklyn home. "Before eight anyway."

She finished the call and looked up to a framed picture on the wall by her desk. It was a colorful enlistment poster printed with the slogan: *If you want to fight! Join the Marines.* It was unique because it was from 1917 and the heroic central figure was a woman in a blue-and-gold military uniform. It was a gift from Artemis when Drew made detective.

"I really like that picture," a happy voice said, and Drew turned to see Anne Riley standing by the door smiling. "I think she looks like me."

There was some truth in that. Anne was an attractive fit-looking woman in her late thirties with broad shoulders, short dark brown hair, a healthy complexion, and trusting eyes. She was dressed in jeans and a tight-fitting tee shirt displaying the logo of the nearby health club where she worked.

"This is a surprise," Drew said honestly.

"I was visiting my brother downstairs," Anne said. Her older brother, Austin, was an NYPD sergeant who recently had been reassigned to the 19th Precinct.

"How's he getting along?" Drew asked.

"He's fine," Anne said as she walked over and sat on the edge of the desk. "So, I was wondering if you might be free for lunch?"

Drew took a look through the interior window to see if anyone was watching them and too quickly said, "I'm afraid not. Lots going on right now. Sorry."

Anne sensed her discomfort and moved to the wood chair in front of the desk and sat down. "I haven't seen you around at the gym or the pool. Or at my place." She smiled meaningfully.

"I know," Drew said apologetically. "But things are getting crazy again, the Delta numbers, the case we're working on."

"But you have to eat sometime." Anne laughed a little. "I could get a couple of strip steaks and make us dinner tonight at my place."

"Ah, no." Drew looked uncomfortable. "I just got off the phone with my dad. He's making dinner."

Anne took this in and leaned back in her chair. "Didn't you say he has a place down in Florida?"

"Yeah, but it's too hot there right now. He'll probably go back in the fall." Drew saw the concern in Anne's eyes and added. "I'm sorry."

"It's okay," she said softly.

Drew's desk phone rang, and she grabbed it. "Detective Sweeney," she answered. She listened for a moment before she said, "Hang on." She covered the receiver with her hand. "Sorry, I've got to take this."

"No problem," Anne said as she got up and went to the door. "I miss seeing you. Give me a call if your schedule lightens up."

"I will," Drew said. "As soon as I can." Anne smiled a little and left. Drew watched her walk away through the open workroom before she turned her attention back to the phone. "So, what can I do for you?"

"The last time we met was over a year and a half ago," Barbara Borsa said in a clipped professional tone.

"I remember. You're Raphael Sharder's estate lawyer out in Southampton. You told us the terms of his will."

"Yes," Barbara confirmed.

"But if you're calling to find out about the investigation into his death," Drew said, "I can't tell you much about that. Except that we're still working on it."

"No, Detective, that's not why I'm calling," Barbara said carefully. "I have new information that will be of interest to you."

"In regard to what?"

"The robbery of the Gardner Museum in 1990."

Drew took a quick breath and said sharply, "Where are you right now?"

"I'm here in Manhattan," Barbara answered. "Near Central Park, not far from your station. I'd like to come see you as soon as possible."

"Absolutely," Drew said eagerly. "How soon can you get here?"

* * *

The oval running track in Riverside Park was quiet, as usual. Silas and Flip trotted easily around the worn crushed-stone surface. The uniformed cop that had escorted them stood in the shade of some trees at one end. A gray-haired older woman in a light blue workout suit was sitting on the top stone step watching them as she finished eating a sandwich. She put her trash inside her shopping bag and got up with a groan. She carefully made her way down the uneven stone steps and walked away past the cop and headed south along the wide path of joggers and bikers that ran along the Hudson River.

"Last lap," Flip called out in friendly challenge as he and Silas picked up their pace to a sprint. They finished in front of the stone steps with Flip in the lead by a half dozen strides. He slowed to a walk, and Silas joined him.

"You're getting better," Flip said encouragingly.

"Thanks," Silas said as he caught his breath. "Do me a favor?"

"Sure," Flip said as they continued walking around the track.

"I want to make a call and it's kind of private."

Flip grinned at him. "No problem. What's her name?"

Silas stopped walking and looked up at him puzzled. Flip stopped and saw the confused look on his face.

"Fine," Flip said good-naturedly, "I don't need to know. I'll be over there." He headed toward the cop under the trees, and Silas walked across the grassy middle of the oval track to the stone steps. He sat by his knapsack, pulled out a water bottle, and took a drink. He looked over at Flip and the cop who were watching him as they talked. He was sure that they were far enough away not to hear. Silas pulled out his cell and hit a number.

"Where are you?" he asked.

"I'm with Mak," Artemis answered. "We're more than halfway across the George Washington Bridge, heading back. What's up?"

"We need to talk. There's something that's been bothering me," Silas said, sounding worried.

Artemis looked out his window past the repeating vertical lines of the massive cables supporting the bridge, down to the West Side Highway running along the river. "Traffic's light. We'll be back soon. Can it wait?"

"No," Silas said looking at Flip and the cop. "I need to make sure that no one overhears."

Artemis could hear the urgency in his son's voice. He took a quick look at Mak who was concentrating on navigating the car around the circular four-lane ramp down to the highway.

"Okay," Artemis said. "Talk to me."

*   *   *

Clayton heard the familiar bang of the elevator arriving. He got up from his desk and walked across the open workspace. The metal door slid open, and a handsome young man dressed in summer-weight fashionable business attire got out.

"I'm Detective Collins," Clayton said.

"I'm Greg Schaefer." He put his hand out. Then realizing what he was doing, pulled his hand back. "Sorry. Remember when we could all shake hands?"

"I do." Clayton smiled and led him across the room. "Please," he said as he sat and indicated the chair across his desk. Greg sat down and folded his manicured fingers together. He looked around at the room. "So many desks. Where is everybody?"

"Out working," Clayton answered. "Okay, Mr. Schaefer, you said this is about your sister. Talk to me."

"Beth is here in New York."

"At your place?"

"No, but she's safe," Greg answered. "Beth said to tell you that she will talk with you on the record. On two conditions."

"I'm listening," Clayton said.

"She wants your word that you'll protect her while she's here."

"Protect her from who?" Clayton asked. "Is that why she left town?"

Greg looked worried. "All I'm here for is to set up a meeting. Beth can tell you whatever she thinks best after that."

"Okay." Clayton considered. "I don't know how she plans to get here, but we definitely will protect her. What's the second condition?"

"She wants to make sure that she won't be charged with anything."

"Like what?"

"Can I say something off the record?" Greg asked gently. Clayton nodded.

"Let's just say"—Greg leaned forward and lowered his voice—"and this might not be true, that there once was a person who managed an art gallery here in town..."

"On 64th Street," Clayton interrupted impatiently. "Stop being cute. What happened there?"

"Drugs. Opioids," Greg said guardedly. "Sold to special customers of the gallery."

Clayton held up his hand. "That's all I want to hear off the record. And I can't promise you anything about what consequences your sister will face if she's broken the law."

Greg dropped his head and closed his eyes.

"But she's obviously in danger out there," Clayton said reasonably. "Get her in here, and let us help her. Depending on what she tells us, she can do a lot for herself. And I promise you that I will do everything I can to make sure she's treated fairly."

"Oh shit," Greg muttered. "I guess I can get her here first thing tomorrow morning."

"Good," Clayton said firmly. "Let's say at eight thirty."

Greg looked up at him. "Okay."

* * *

Artemis stood on the sidewalk outside the entrance to an underground parking lot. He was wearing his mask and was staring up at the cloudy bright sky above the tall towers of luxury condos. Mak walked up the ramp and stopped near Artemis, who didn't seem to notice him.

"What did Silas say to you?" Mak asked.

Artemis slowly blinked a few times. "Can you do something for me, Mak?"

"Of course," he answered.

"I need you to talk to Agent Filipowski."

"You can talk with him yourself. Flip's part of your detail."

"I know," Artemis murmured. "But it needs to be official. It would be better coming from you."

"Okay, whatever you need."

"I'll tell you as we walk," Artemis said, and they started off along 66th Street. As they turned south on Columbus, Mak took out his cell and made the call to Agent Filipowski. At 64th Street, Mak pulled on his mask and they entered the glass and stainless-steel lobby of the TVNews building.

Mak and Artemis got out of the elevator on the ninth floor and approached the young receptionist sitting at her large curved desk reading a fashion magazine.

"We're here to see Roxie Lee," Mak told her.

"I'm so sorry, Agent Kim," Barb said apologetically. "But Ms. Lee had to go out on a personal matter."

"But I just made an appointment with her an hour ago." Mak caught Artemis's eye.

"I know." Barb smiled. "She said to tell you that she was sorry and that she could do any time tomorrow."

"I see," Mak said slowly. "Let me think about it. I'll call later."

"Very good," Barb said happily. Mak turned toward the elevator, but Artemis stopped him with a look.

"Let's go out downstairs," he said. Mak understood, and they headed for the open glass staircase.

"Have a nice day," Barb called out as she returned to her magazine.

At the bottom of the stairs, they stopped. Across the busy newsroom, they could see Moira in her glass-walled office working on her laptop. And in the opposite corner, Deni was in her office pacing behind her desk as she talked on the phone.

"I'll talk to Moira, if you want to start with Deni?" Artemis offered.

"Works for me," Mak said, and he started toward Deni's office. Artemis waited until a group of people near the coffee station dispersed and then he made his way across the room, carefully avoiding getting too close to anyone. He knocked on Moira's open door, and she looked up and smiled.

"I didn't expect to see you, Artemis. Please come in."

He went in and sat in a chair in front of her desk. He looked at Moira framed by the large corner windows and the bright cityscape beyond. "It really is impressive here. Congratulations again. How's it going for you?"

Moira looked anxious. She leaned back in her desk chair and spun halfway around to see the view. "I thought I'd like it more than I do," she admitted sadly. "But there's just so much compromise here. I'm not sure what I expected. I was just so excited to have my own show and be heard." She turned back to him. "I'm a reporter. And a good one. I thought that's why they promoted me."

Artemis carefully pulled off his mask and looked at her. Her normally ambitious eyes were clouded with worry. "What kind of compromise?"

"I agreed to drop the harassment case against Jock Willinger," she said, sounding disgusted. "Calvin told me the network would appreciate it."

"And what's happened?"

Moira sighed. "I have a story that needs to be told. I took it to Calvin and he mansplained some reasons and refused."

"What's the story about?" Artemis asked curiously.

"There's a fear-driven war coming between those who get vaccinated and those who refuse," Moira said earnestly. "So, I want to start conversations that will defuse the anger and help us understand more. I think there's room for people to hear from the researchers and doctors who are saying something completely different than what the CDC and our government is telling us."

"I'd be interested in that," Artemis said genuinely. "Silas and I have been looking at lots of data, and every time we find something that questions the effectiveness of the vaccines, it gets taken down."

"I know," she agreed. "To be fair, maybe the government thinks censorship is justified because it will save lives. But what about the problems with the vaccines? There are whistleblowers who are afraid to come forward because they know they will be discredited and silenced."

"You make it sound like a conspiracy," Artemis said.

"Well, maybe it is," she declared. "The entire news media is a corporate-driven machine. Networks might be liberal, conservative, or radical, but they all depend on their advertising income. So, instead of just reporting the news, we sell an opinion. And right now, that means unconditional support for the vaccines. And anyone who questions that is attacked. When did this happen in America? When did we lose the right to ask a question?"

Artemis smiled a little.

"I know, since forever ago. But here's a question I want to ask." She ran her fingers several times through her short hair and leaned forward on the desk. "Have you ever noticed how many of the commercials on our show are for prescription drugs?"

"I have, actually."

"The corporation that owns TVNews has deep ties to the pharmaceutical industry," she said factually. "Have you seen the exponential profits that the vaccine companies have made since COVID began? They're making more money than the GNP of most countries on the planet. Think about that."

"I have been," he acknowledged.

"The news industry doesn't lead, it follows. I knew that. But now I'm starting to think that's wrong. And that I don't belong here." Moira took a breath and leaned back in her chair. "So, what's new with you?" she said and laughed a little. "Sorry to rant. I just feel it's important."

"No, I understand," Artemis said. "And I admire you."

"Thanks." She smiled. "So, while I'm still employed here, what can you tell me about that footage I gave you?"

"I can tell you a few things," Artemis said remembering his promise to keep her informed. "But off the record."

"Agreed," she said professionally.

"We've confirmed that it was Lucille in the footage, kneeling by Paula DeVong's body," he said. "I've been wondering what Lucille was looking for in Paula's bag. She took nothing. Any ideas?"

"No," Moira said. "And what else?"

"The autopsy showed that Paula died of an overdose of phentermine," he confided. "It's a weight-loss drug."

"That is news. Did she have a prescription?"

"Not that we can find."

There was a timid knock at the door, and they turned to see Anna Canneli, dressed as usual in drab brown.

"Sorry to interrupt," she said suspiciously as she eyed Artemis. "But the men are here to take that away." She looked sadly at the large framed picture of Paula DeVong that was still hanging on the wall.

"Fine," Moira said. "Send them in." Anna waved and two men in tan work-clothes came in. Artemis put his mask back on as they started to take down the heavy picture.

"I have to get back to work anyway," Moira said apologetically. "But it was really helpful talking with you. Thanks."

"My pleasure," Artemis said as he got up and went out into the newsroom. He looked to Deni's office and saw that Mak was just leaving too. As the workmen came out with the picture and rolled it away on a cart, Artemis met Mak in an open space in the middle of the room.

"Deni told me that she dropped the suit against Jock," Mak said low.

"Moira did too. Anything else?"

"I pressed her about her necklace, the class, and the teacher. She seemed nervous but didn't give anything up."

"Excuse me," someone said, and they turned to see a distressed-looking Anna Canneli a few feet away. "I need to talk with you." She turned and headed for her little office. Mak shrugged at Artemis, and they followed.

They stepped inside the cramped space, and Artemis could feel the panic rising up in his chest. He stepped to the corner in front of her messy desk and commanded himself to focus. Anna closed the door and sat behind her desk. Mak stayed by the door, giving Artemis as much room as he could.

"How can we help you, Ms. Canneli?" Mak asked.

"I need to know," she said as she looked up at Artemis, "did Paula really die from COVID?"

"No," Artemis answered directly. "She was killed by an overdose of phentermine. Do you know what that is?"

"No," she whispered and her small eyes filled with tears.

"It's for weight loss." Artemis gauged her reaction. "Did Paula take any drug for that?"

"No," Anna said vaguely. "I don't think so." She closed her eyes and tears rolled down her round cheeks. "I need to trust you," she said unhappily. "And I don't trust anyone." She opened her eyes and wiped her face. Then she unlocked a drawer, pulled out a small box, and placed it carefully in the center of her desk.

"I think this might be what killed Paula," she said, her voice trembling with emotion. She carefully tipped open the lid of the box. The inside was divided into four even sections, three of which contained chocolate-covered candies. "She loved these. They were her reward after she'd finish a show. I saw her eat one the night she died."

"What makes you think that killed her?" Mak asked.

"Because everybody in the studio knew that it was my job to buy these and leave them in Paula's desk," Anna answered bitterly. "And they all hate me so much."

"You're saying that someone put poisoned candy in Paula's desk knowing that you'd be blamed," Artemis concluded.

"Yes. That's exactly what I think."

"And when did you take this box from her desk?" Mak asked.

"The morning after she died," Anna answered. "I got to work early, and a few of the writers were here and they'd heard the news on the police scanner. They said Paula had collapsed on the street and died of COVID. But I didn't believe them. How could anyone say so quickly that it was COVID? They have to test for that, right? And Paula was healthy. And so happy the night before. She was about to be promoted. Then I realized how easy it would be for anyone to put something in her coffee or in these." She pointed unhappily at the box of chocolates. "And I remembered something strange. I get these boxes one at a time from a shop a block away from here. Paula wanted them fresh. So, I always left the box the way it came, sealed in that clear plastic stuff. But after the show, the night she died, she took this box out of the drawer and it was already opened. There was no plastic seal on it."

"Are you certain?" Artemis asked sharply.

"Yes," she answered. "And I didn't understand it. I thought maybe she had eaten one before the show. I mean that's possible. But she'd never done that before. And look at them. Only one of the four is missing."

Mak stepped to the desk, got an evidence bag from his back pocket, closed the lid on the box, and put it in the bag. "We'll have these checked out," he said. "What's the name of the shop it came from?"

"Betty's Box," she answered. "A block north on Columbus across the street."

"We'll be in touch," Mak said and turned to go.

"Thank you, Anna," Artemis said. "For trusting us."

"You're welcome," she mumbled, and they left her office.

As they started across the newsroom toward the elevators, Mak asked, "Do you trust her?"

"Strange as it may seem," Artemis answered, "I do."

As they stepped out of the building, Mak pulled off his mask and took a deep breath, but the fumes from a passing bus made him cough.

"Serves me right," he said ironically. They crossed Columbus Avenue and headed north up the busy sidewalk. Artemis focused on keeping as much distance as he could from the fast-moving bodies. After a block, they found Betty's Box. Mak pulled open the heavy glass door, and they went into the little shop where glass-fronted cases displayed pieces of chocolate on white porcelain cake plates and on top of a marble counter were prepackaged boxes of various sizes. Behind the counter, a very thin middle-aged woman with pulled-back gray hair greeted them.

"Welcome, gentlemen," she said happily as she smoothed the front of her white chef's apron, where there were already various splotches of light and dark chocolate.

As Mak fished out his FBI identification and introduced them, the happy expression faded from her face.

"I'm Betty," she volunteered carefully. "The owner. What can I do for you?"

"Can I assume that you've heard about Paula DeVong's death?" Mak asked gently.

"Oh, yes," she said sadly. "May God rest her soul. I saw that report where she lay on the street and nobody would help her, that was so awful."

"So you knew her personally, then?" Artemis asked.

"Sure, I did. She used to come in a lot before the pandemic and everything. Once that started, her assistant Anna would come in to buy these." Betty picked up a small box from the counter display. It was a match to the one Anna had given them, and it was wrapped in plastic. "When things got really rough a year ago and nobody was buying anything, it was Paula who put in a word for me at the studio and then lots of her people started coming in. Really saved my chocolate-covered bacon." She smiled widely, enjoying her own joke.

"Who came in from the studio?" Mak asked.

"Well, let's see. Mr. Willinger. He's the man in charge. He was a big fan of these." She reached into the glass display case and pulled out a dish of chocolate-covered toffee. "Said it reminded him of home," she added as she put the plate back. "And Ms. Lee would come in from time to time. She liked to buy little boxes as gifts for her friends. And let's see. Greg... something. Nice boy. Always so polite and funny. He comes in early for espresso. We only do coffee in the morning," she explained as she indicated the gleaming Italian-made machine on the back counter. "And lots of the staff come in here. I really don't know everyone's name."

"I'm glad you're still in business here," Artemis said. "I've never been in here before, and it's a great shop."

"Thank you," she said proudly. "I really love this place."

"And you make everything here," Artemis said perceptively.

"I do. My only problem is that I can't eat the stuff. I'm diabetic."

"Well, thank you for your time," Mak said, and they left. Outside, the late-afternoon traffic on Columbus had come to a standstill and horns began blowing. Artemis's cell rang, and he saw it was Drew.

"Hey, what's up," Artemis said loudly as he pushed his phone tight against his ear.

"Are you with Mak?" Drew asked.

"What?" Artemis fairly shouted as he and Mak crossed the street and started walking east on 65th Street, trying to get away from the noise.

Drew heard the horns and spoke louder. "Is Mak there?"

"Yes. We just finished at TVNews. Lots to catch you up on."

"Me too. Do you remember Barbara Borsa?" Drew asked.

"Of course," Artemis said as they walked away from the sounds of angry traffic.

"She's here in my office, and she has the most interesting story to tell. About the Gardner Museum robbery. How soon can you and Mak get here?"

"We just have to get across the park," Artemis said excitedly. "We'll be there in fifteen if traffic's not too rough." Artemis hung up as he and Mak reached the corner of Central Park West. Artemis raised his arm to hail a cab.

"Where are we going?" Mak asked.

"To the precinct," Artemis answered loudly.

"But we have a car parked right here," Mak said confused.

"There's no time," Artemis insisted as a cab pulled up and he opened the back door. "I'll explain on the way." He jumped into the back seat, and Mak followed him and closed the door.

"67th between Third and Lex," Artemis told the driver, and they headed back into traffic.

Mak turned to his friend. "You. In a cab. That's new. This really must be important."

"It could be," Artemis confirmed as he rolled down his window and leaned his face into the fresh air.

*   *   *

Roxie stood in her old office looking out the large windows at the streams of tourists moving through shafts of late-afternoon light on the sidewalks of Columbus, eight stories down. She turned to Moira who was sitting in front of the desk reading scripted copy on a laptop. Roxie looked at Deni who was standing, leaning on the closed door with her arms folded across her chest. Roxie sat behind the desk and studied Moira's face.

"That's how the show will end tonight," Roxie said, sounding official. "Are you okay with that?"

Moira closed the laptop and leaned back in her chair. "So, I'm not really a reporter of anything," she said calmly. "I'm just a person who reads approved commentary."

"Tonight, that's true," Roxie answered frankly. "Get established. Build your ratings. Then we can talk about you writing your own material."

"You sound like Calvin," Deni said pointedly as she came across the room and stood by Moira.

"Do I?" Roxie snapped and then stopped herself. "Look. It's about you too, Deni. Everyone is watching to see if you have a future here. Calvin represents the network. That's his job. And in fact, he wants you to fly solo tonight. You'll be the producer in the booth."

"What about you?" Deni asked with concern.

"I'll be upstairs with him watching the show," Roxie reassured her.

Moira shook her head and said softly, "Aren't we all tired of men telling us what we can do and where we should be?"

Roxie smiled wistfully. "Yes, I am. But open revolution will get us fired. And then what will we do?"

"Get unemployment and maybe be happier," Moira said truthfully.

Roxie sighed. "Well, don't do anything you'll regret."

"That I can promise you," Moira said sincerely.

Roxie accepted this and stood up. "Get back to work, you two," she said and left.

Deni closed the door, marched back to the desk, and sat in her chair with an angry thump.

"Thank you," Moira said simply.

"You're welcome," Deni said. "I've gotta tell you, I've only had this job for two days and I'm already not sleeping at night."

"That's not right," Moira said supportively. "You're great at this."

"It's not that," Deni sounded disgusted. "We should never have dropped the lawsuit. It feels like we got promoted to buy us off. And now Calvin is looking for reasons to get us out."

"Maybe," Moira said sensibly. "But I can see why the network wouldn't want to do my story."

"And I don't think there's anything wrong with the vaccines. But I would have supported it," Deni said forcefully. "It would get attention and ratings."

"Well," Moira said lightly. "Maybe we should get out of here and do our own show. A podcast."

"Oh, there's a big money idea." Deni scoffed. "Go from one-point-five million viewers a night to six. Or seven."

"I know," Moira said more seriously, "but we could be our own boss. No corporate backing would mean we'd have freedom to tell the stories we want."

Deni looked at her a moment and then laughed. "We better get back to work. One way or another we'll be on the air in a few hours."

Moira nodded. "One way or another."

*　*　*

By eight thirty, the sky above Brooklyn was glowing in muted red-orange as the last of the daylight faded in the west. Drew walked slowly down a quiet street lost in thought. As she came to her old brownstone, she shifted the weight of the bag of groceries in her arms, pulled out her keys, and jogged up the stone steps.

"Dad?" she called out loudly as she came in.

"Kitchen," he answered.

She walked down the wainscotted hall and found her father pouring a pot of boiling water and lasagna noodles into a strainer in the sink.

"Good timing," Mathew said as he leaned his face away from the hot rising steam.

Drew set the bag on the wood counter and unpacked milk, bread, a box of cereal, and a large garlic bulb.

"That's what we need," Mathew said warmly as he grabbed a knife and took the garlic to a cutting board. "Have to say I missed this stuff." In the year and a half that the Bookbinders were living with them, garlic was never brought into the house out of consideration for Artemis and Silas and their allergy to alliums. Mathew peeled the bulb, dug out two cloves, placed them under the wide flat of his knife, and crushed them with a sharp blow from his large gnarly fist.

Drew put the groceries away as Mathew quickly diced the cloves and scraped them into hot oil in a saucepan. Drew looked up at the sizzling sound.

"I saw you coming," Mathew explained. "Ah, there it is," he added happily as the scent reached his nose. Drew pulled a bottle of beer from the fridge, twisted off the cap, and took a drink. She sat on a stool and leaned her back against the counter.

"How was your day?" Mathew asked as he poured tomato sauce into the pan.

"Interesting," Drew said. "I'll tell you over dinner." Mathew heard the distant tone in her voice and turned. "What's up?"

"I'm just a little tired, I guess." She took a sip.

"Everything all right with Artemis?"

"Oh yes." Drew smiled reassuringly. "He's been pushing himself. Really wants to be back out there."

"Good to hear," Mathew said as he stirred the sauce. "And Silas and Delia? How are they doing in the new place?"

"They seem great," Drew answered.

"Good, good. But I have to admit I miss them. Even bossy old Delia. She was always good to talk to. Though I'm really liking being head chef around here."

Drew watched her father as he set the saucepan and the strainer of pasta on the counter and happily started the layering process in a large casserole dish.

"Dad, ask you something?"

"Yeah?"

"What if I had someone over, from time to time?"

Mathew looked at her, surprised. "That would be great. Drew, this is your home. What the hell are you waiting for?"

Drew considered. "Her name is Anne. Anne Riley."

"Nice name. Sweeney and Riley. Think maybe she's free for dinner? We've got plenty."

Drew smiled. "I guess I could give her a call and find out."

*   *   *

It was a few minutes before 10:00 p.m., and Roxie was sitting in a large leather club chair in Calvin's office. He refilled his drink at the built-in bar and turned to look at her. Roxie was staring out the windows at the dark sky above the buildings. She sipped her gin and tonic, noticed him watching, and smiled guardedly at him.

"We're coming back," Calvin announced as he walked past her and sat down on the leather sofa. Roxie waited until the drug commercial ended, hit the volume-up button on the remote, and the last segment of the night's show came on. Moira was sitting at the news desk looking professional and confident. As the camera slowly moved in, she spoke in support for the need of government mandates for the vaccines. She was reading word for word from the script rolling by on the teleprompter, and she seemed to believe what she was saying.

As the show ended and another commercial came on, Roxie turned off the monitor and looked to Calvin. He caught her eye and reached for the phone on the glass coffee table and hit a button. In the back row of the control room, Deni Diaz saw the red light flashing on her phone and answered.

"Yes, Calvin?" she said cautiously. The staff in the front row turned in their chairs to listen.

"Good show, Deni," Calvin said in a loud patronizing tone. "And good work keeping Moira in line." Deni heard the click as Calvin hung up and felt distinctly like a rewarded pet dog who had pleased her owner with some trick.

Roll over. Play dead.

Deni kept her eyes neutral as she smiled at the staff. "Calvin said good show everybody." The statement was greeted with happy relief, and they started to collect their things and go.

Two floors up, Roxie stood to refill her drink at the bar.

"Hey," Calvin called as he held up his glass. "Can you put some ice in this for me?"

"Of course," she said without hesitation. She took his glass and went to the bar. She added ice to his and refilled hers with gin. She reached for a slice of lime and noticed her reflection in the floor-to-ceiling window. She could see the red gleam of her ruby pendant hanging in her low cleavage. Her left hand touched the gem, and she looked down at it.

"I love that you always wear that," Calvin said as he stretched his legs out across the sofa. "It's perfect on you."

"Thanks," she said easily as she came over and handed him his drink. He looked up at her sensual body appreciatively. "I'm so glad that Jock is gone," he said and laughed. "You're much easier on the eyes."

Roxie kept her face pleasant but passive as she sat down in a chair across the coffee table from him. Calvin grunted disappointedly as he slowly swirled the ice cubes in his glass.

"Seems like Deni and Moira have a future here." Roxie floated the idea and sipped her gin.

"Do they? We'll see." Calvin smirked. "I guess you better have some suggestions ready if they don't."

Roxie's heart sank, but she managed to cover her feelings. "Yes, Calvin." She took a quick sip and set her glass down on the coffee table. "I should head downstairs for the post-meeting."

"Right," Calvin said, and she stood to go. "And I think Deni should be in charge again tomorrow night. Don't you?"

"To tell the truth," Roxie said carefully. "I really missed doing my job tonight."

"I know," Calvin said dismissively. "But in television, everyone is replaceable. Even you. So, let's get Deni up to speed, in case we ever really need her."

Roxie took this in for all that it implied. "I'll see you tomorrow, Calvin." She headed for the door.

"Night, Roxie," he muttered.

Outside his office, Roxie closed the door, went across the empty reception area, and started down the stairs. But after a few steps, she stopped. Moira's words echoed through her mind.

Aren't we all tired of men telling us what we can do?

Roxie took a long breath and walked slowly down the stairs.

* * *

Ida was sitting on the floor by the open window looking out over the sill at the domes of the Ansonia and the thousands of lighted windows in the buildings beyond. She turned to look at Lucille who was finally asleep on the bed. Tomorrow Ida would leave New York, maybe forever, and she worried what would happen to her sister without her being there to help.

Ida reached for her two bags on the floor by the bed and quietly slid them closer. She opened them and divided half of the banded stacks of cash evenly between them. And then something occurred to her. Something that might give Lucille a better chance of survival. Ida dug into her bag and found a pad of paper and a pen. She looked up at her sister's face. She seemed so peaceful and innocent.

Ida thought for a moment and then started to write. When she finished the note, she placed it on top of the cash in one of the bags and zipped it closed. She got up and stretched her back. A movement across the street on the rooftop of the Ansonia caught her eye, and she stepped back to hide. From the shadows, she could see a man slowly walking through the raised garden area. The sky was covered by clouds and the night was too dark to see who it was. It didn't matter. Tomorrow she would need all her strength. She turned from the window and carefully lay down next to her sister. She closed her eyes and tried to sleep.

On the rooftop, Artemis found a clean wood bench under a trellis of wisteria, brushed off the seat with his handkerchief, and sat. He found a number on his cell phone and pushed it.

"Hello, Artemis," a familiar voice said.

"Where are you?" Artemis asked.

"Naxos," Ray said as he walked along the pier heading toward a large blue-and-orange ferry boat. First light was warming the sky revealing the strange blue-green of the vast Aegean Sea. "Karlovic's plane got me this far. I have to go the rest of the way by boat."

"How soon will you get there?"

"We leave in thirty minutes and then it takes five and a half hours. It's like a local on the subway. Makes stops at every damn island before we get to Kimolos." Ray stopped some distance from the other passengers lined up waiting for a half dozen cars and trucks to roll onto the ferry.

Artemis checked the time on his cell. It was almost midnight in New York. "Ray...?" he said and stopped.

"I'm here," the older man said.

"I know you are. You always are," Artemis said. "I want to apologize. For doubting you."

Ray started to say something, but the emotion caught in his throat. He coughed softly, swallowed, and said, "Don't worry. It goes with the job."

"And that too," Artemis said gratefully. "You just keep going. It's been so long."

"I'm like a dog with a bone." Ray chuckled.

"Yes, you are." Artemis smiled.

"I got your secure file about the meeting with the lawyer Barbara Borsa," Ray said as he saw the line of passengers starting to board. "If what she says is true, that the Gardener stuff was taken to the Dalmatian coast, it may be that old man Karlovic really does know something."

"Maybe. But he won't talk to you unless you can get his grandson extradited."

"Right," Ray said as he started walking slowly toward the boat. "And we may be able to do that. Some of our people are working on it. Though it probably won't be me talking to him. I'm done in the fall." The morning sun was just rising, and the sea glistened all around him. "Lately I've been thinking that Greece might be a good place to retire."

"That might work out," Artemis said knowingly. "The FBI has been known to hire expert consultants."

"Well, right now my job is to give some unknown woman a sealed note and see what she says."

"She'll say that the third head of the Trias serpent is a woman."

"You say that like you're certain," Ray said as he walked up the ramp onto the boat.

"I am," Artemis answered. "Her last name is Voskos, and her son is the man who taught the class in Chinatown."

"Anything else?" Ray went up an enclosed metal staircase to the upper deck.

Artemis looked worried. "Call me as soon as you can after your meeting."

"Count on it, son," Ray assured him.

"Good hunting, Ray," Artemis said and hung up. A strange pale light broke through the vines above him, and Artemis turned his face up to see the moon appearing in a break in the clouds. And he shivered.

Chapter Six

Tuesday, July 20th, 2021

Lucille opened the mini fridge under the kitchen counter as quietly as she could so as to not wake her sister. She reached for the quart of milk, shook it, and felt the carton was nearly empty. She saw there was almost nothing left of their food. She carefully shut the fridge, went over to the open window, and looked across the street. There was no one visible in the Bookbinder apartment. The sky above was clear, and the morning air was already hot and humid. She looked down to the street. Two cops were standing, as usual, in front of the entrance to the Ansonia. She turned and looked at Ida lying in a tangle of sheets against the wall. Lucille sighed. She normally would have gotten supplies during the night. But she knew Ida would be going today and she wanted her to have a proper meal before she left. Lucille got her cap and mask and headed for the door. She undid the locks and slipped out.

Ida opened her eyes. She sat up, stretched her shoulders, got out of bed, and went to the window. After a minute, she saw Lucille come out the street door and head west away from the cops.

*   *   *

Artemis and Mak, each carrying a couple of takeout coffees, stepped off the old elevator onto the third floor of the station house. Clayton waved to them from his desk in the middle of the large busy workspace. Mak handed Clayton a coffee and sat in front of his desk, and Artemis continued past toward Drew in her corner office.

"Morning, cousin," Artemis greeted her from the open door.

Drew looked up from her computer and smiled. "Morning."

Artemis came in and set a coffee in front of her.

"Thanks," she said with surprise. "You bought this?"

"Yes," Artemis said as he wandered over to the window and looked down at the jammed traffic on 67th Street.

"From another person?"

"Yes."

"In a coffee shop?"

"Yes." Artemis turned to her, pulled off his mask, and smiled.

"Who are you?" Drew laughed as she pulled the plastic lid off her cup and took a sip.

Artemis took a small pack of 75 percent alcohol wipes from his pocket, pulled one out, and carefully wiped the lid of his cup.

"Ah, that's my boy!" Drew said expressively.

"You're in a good mood today," Artemis noted as he took a tentative sip.

"I guess so," Drew answered.

"Have you had a chance to follow up on that guy who's managing Anna Canneli's buildings?" Artemis asked as he sat on the edge of a table by the window.

"I did," Drew answered. "I called the number on the card for the guy with no last name, Alan. And the number's no longer in service. Hasn't been for over a year. So, I sent some guys to the office address downtown, and guess what? It's bogus. The building doesn't exist."

"Somehow I'm not surprised," Artemis murmured.

"Me too." Drew heard the loud bang of the metal elevator opening across the workspace. "They're here."

Greg Schaefer held his sister Beth by the arm as they came out of the elevator.

"Nice to see you again," Clayton said easily as he and Mak stood up.

From behind the inner window in Drew's office, Artemis observed Beth. She was tall and thin, dressed in new-looking jeans and a button-down shirt. She was smiling nervously.

"Let's hear what she has to say," Artemis said.

Greg saw Drew and Artemis heading over, and he nodded a greeting.

"I'm Detective Sweeney," Drew said sounding formal. "And this is Artemis Bookbinder. We appreciate you coming in." Beth looked curiously at Artemis.

"We'll be doing this upstairs," Clayton explained as he picked up his laptop and a small recording device. "This way, please." He led the group to the corridor and up a flight of stairs to the conference room on the fourth floor. He indicated a couple of chairs in the middle of a long white table and Greg and Beth sat.

"You've cut your hair," Clayton said as he took one of the four seats across from them. "Looks good."

"Thanks." Beth shrugged. "It's been easier having it short."

"Would you like some coffee? Or water?" Drew asked.

"Nothing for me, thanks," Greg said politely.

"Some water would be great," Beth said.

Drew went to a table by the open window set up with a coffeepot and water carafe. "If it's too hot, I can close this and put on the air-conditioning," she said as she poured.

Artemis was just stepping into the room. He stopped and looked worried.

"I like the fresh air, if everybody is okay with that," Beth said.

"Works for me," Drew said with her usual authority as she set down the glass of water in front of Beth.

"Me too," Artemis mumbled. He took a quick steadying breath and closed the door behind him.

"It's all good," Mak said as he sat on one side of Clayton and Drew on the other. Artemis took the last chair next to his cousin.

"Are you ready to do this?" Clayton asked.

"Yes," Beth answered anxiously. Clayton set the small recorder in front of her, checked his watch, pushed a button, and said in a clear voice:

"The time is eight thirty-seven Tuesday morning, July 20, 2021. I am Detective Jerome Clayton Collins. This interview is with Beth Schaefer who is accompanied by her brother Greg Schaefer. Present are Detective First Grade Drew Sweeney, FBI Agent Makani Kim, and Special Consultant Artemis Bookbinder. Note that Ms. Schaefer has declined to have an attorney present." He looked to Beth and smiled. "Please state your name."

"Beth Schaefer," she said, reached for her water, and took a quick sip.

"Tell us why you are here," Clayton instructed gently.

"I've been away a long time, about sixteen months." Her voice sounded strained but calm. "I've been hiding up in Canada. I missed New York and the people here." She touched her brother's arm, and he smiled a little. "But I saw in the news that Paula DeVong had died, so I decided to face the risk and come back." She bit her lip and looked to Clayton. "I'm not sure where to start."

"A time line would be helpful," he answered. "When did you first meet Raphael Sharder?"

"I guess, a little more than seven years ago. He hired me to help out at his gallery on 64th Street. We hit it off from the first. Raphael liked that I was a painter, like he once was. About four years ago, he promoted me to full-time manager because he wanted to spend more time out at his home in Southampton where he had another gallery."

"Right," Clayton confirmed. "Tell us about the gallery on 64th Street. How was business there?"

"It was good. We didn't have to sell many pieces. Everything was of a quality."

"And a price," Clayton said significantly.

"Yes."

"And what else did you sell there?" he asked.

Beth threw a quick look to her brother, who nodded. "Opioids," she said and looked down at her folded hands on the table. "I'm not proud of it. It just sort of evolved through time. Certain clients would come in. There were no names. No records. We'd say a word or two. They always paid with cash."

"How many clients?" Drew asked.

"About a dozen, I guess."

"Would you recognize them if you saw them now?" Clayton added.

"Yes," Beth answered. "Yes, I'm sure I would."

"Did Raphael Sharder know about the drugs?" Artemis asked. She met his eyes.

"Yes, he did. He got a cut, but he never had anything to do with it directly. I handled it." She started to speak more quickly. "Raphael was the kindest man. He was always looking out for me. And he was worried. He warned me."

"About what?" Artemis asked.

"I didn't believe him," Beth said with regret. "But he told me that if he was ever murdered..." She saw their reactions. "I was surprised too. But that's exactly what he said – murdered." She took a shaky breath and went on. "I was to get away as fast as possible. We always kept some cash in the safe in the gallery office. He told me to take the cash and get out of the country as fast as I could. So, I did. I left the morning after he was killed."

"When did he give you this warning?" Artemis asked.

"About a week before he died. Raphael was in New York. We had dinner together. Takeout and wine in the office of the gallery."

"We found your painting," Drew said. "The one you left in your apartment in Brooklyn. You signed it Khloe."

"Yes." She shrugged. "It wasn't much, but I thought Raphael would have wanted me to." She looked at Clayton, and he nodded, inviting her to go on.

"It was that night"—she smiled sadly as she remembered—"we drank wine and talked for a long time. I asked him why he was always so kind to me. He said that I reminded him of his little sister, Khloe, and that he once had a beautiful boat he named after her. Then he said I should leave if he was ever murdered. Like I said, I didn't believe him. We drank some more, talked business, and gossiped. But as we locked up the gallery, he said something else. That everyone thought his sister had died long ago, but Khloe was still alive. And if he was killed, Khloe would be in great danger. I asked where she was but he wouldn't tell me. Then a week later, Raphael was shot. I talked to you that morning." She smiled at Clayton. "After you left, I got the cash, locked the gallery, and outside Ladimir Karlovic was waiting for me. He threatened me and told me to disappear. I assured him I would. I got some things from my place in Brooklyn, and I saw that painting on my easel. It was a seascape I'd done when I was visiting Raphael in Southampton. And then I remembered what he'd said that night—his sister was in danger." She sighed.

"I really liked that painting," Artemis said quietly. "It was a watercolor. And a message. You signed Khloe in blue oil paint."

"I didn't know who would see it," she explained. "But I wanted to do something to honor Raphael. It wasn't much, but I hoped it would help."

"It did," Drew answered. "We learned about his boat." She reached for the recorder and turned it off. "And his sister Khloe is, in fact, still alive. And she's well."

"At least I did a little good, then." Beth folded her arms across her chest. "What else can I tell you about?"

Drew turned the recorder back on.

"Go back to the gallery," Clayton said. "Who supplied the drugs you sold?"

"My doctor," Beth answered carefully.

Clayton looked at his laptop and scrolled through some notes he'd made a year and a half ago. "Your psychiatrist? Has an office on Fifth and 83rd?"

"Yes."

He looked at her. "For the record, what is his name?"

Beth seemed afraid, but then she found her voice. "Marin. Doctor Paul Marin."

"Was he," Artemis asked, "the teacher of the class down on Doyers Street?"

Beth stared at him. Greg reached for her glass of water and took a sip.

"Yes," she admitted quietly.

"Do you have a gem necklace from that class?" Mak asked.

In response, she reached up, undid the top two buttons of her shirt, and pulled out a clear pink gem on a silver necklace. "It's called kunzite," she said sadly as she gazed at it. "It's a spodumene. And very beautiful. I haven't worn it for a long time."

"It is beautiful." Mak agreed. "Paul Marin's class met every Sunday night at midnight. Would you tell us who was in that class?"

"Yes." She looked at him. "Paula DeVong. Roxie Lee. And Deni Diaz. They all knew each other from TVNews. Ida Orsina. She was Paula's dermatologist. And me."

"There were six chairs in front of where the teacher sat." Artemis's eyes had that faraway look. "Was Lucille Orsina Prons the sixth member?"

"Um, no," Beth said carefully. "She replaced me when I left."

Artemis considered. "So, who sat in the sixth chair when you were there?"

"I don't think there was a sixth chair," Beth said vaguely. Greg tapped the side of his foot against hers as a sign of his gratitude.

"And the gems," Artemis continued. "What did they signify?"

"Belonging," Beth almost whispered. "In Paul's class, we used different names. We were each named for our gemstone."

"Which Paul gave to you," Drew said.

"Yes, after you passed an initiation." Beth stopped talking and leaned back in her chair.

"What kind of initiation?" Clayton sounded concerned.

"Sexual," Beth said clearly. "All the women in the class slept with Paul. At least once. Except for Roxie Lee. She and Paul had something going on. At least they did when I was there last."

Artemis breathed out slowly as his mind fit together what Beth had said.

"You have to understand," she clarified. "Paul really helped me when we first met. I was a little bit in trouble with drugs, and he helped me get clean. Then he invited me to join his class, and I was so grateful."

"What happened in those classes?" Drew asked.

"Paul Marin hears sacred voices," Beth said plainly. "And through him, they would speak to us. Give us guidance and support."

"And tell you it was all right to be selling drugs that Paul Marin supplied?" Drew sounded like a cop.

"No," Beth scowled at her. "It was a good thing. The classes helped. That's all."

"Okay," Clayton said soothingly. "Can you tell us how Paul and Raphael Sharder knew each other?"

"I don't know where they met," Beth said. "They were close before I ever knew Raphael."

"Close like family?" Artemis asked.

"Maybe." Beth thought about it. "I really don't know."

"Did Paul Marin drink wine from a bronze chalice during those classes?" Artemis watched her.

"Yes. But I never knew that cup was stolen from a museum until after I was in Canada and I saw the news online. I was shocked."

The group sat in silence for a minute and then Clayton cleared his throat. "You said when you called me two days ago that you were in Maine."

"Yes, at Moosehead Lake."

Artemis looked up sharply. "Why there?"

"There was supposed to be a man there who could help me," she answered. "An old friend of Raphael's. Someone he knew from when he was a student in New York. When I decided to come back, I knew I couldn't use my passport so I made a *very* soft-crossing into Maine and found the address. It was a nice house right on the lake, but it was empty with a real estate sign outside. I called the broker. He said the owner had died six months ago of COVID." Beth looked across the table at Clayton. "So, I called you and just kept heading south."

"What was the man's name?" Clayton asked.

"I didn't have a first name, but his last name was Abruzzo."

The sounds of angry horns from the stuck traffic on the street below came through the open window, and Artemis turned distractedly. He got up, went to the window, and reached out as if to shut it. Then he remembered the value of the fresh, if noisy, air coming into the closed room. He turned back to the group and sat on the edge of the table.

"The men who stood guard outside of the class in Chinatown," Mak asked evenly. "Do you know who they were?"

"Yes." Beth ran her fingers lightly across her throat. "Ladimir Karlovic. And the other, I only ever heard him called Fat Nicky. They both worked with Paul."

"Doing what?" Mak asked.

"I'm not totally sure," Beth said earnestly. "But I think they were selling drugs. Lots of it and far more serious than the stuff I was peddling in the gallery."

"How do you know?"

"From things I overheard. Every once in a while, Paul would meet them at the gallery. I was supposed to leave them alone, but it's not that big a space. Anyway, that's why I left class. I was getting worried about what was going on. And those guys, Ladimir and Fat Nicky, those are very scary people." She turned to Clayton. "That's why I need protection."

"And you'll have it," he affirmed. "We've arranged a place for you to stay for a while."

"For how long?" she asked worriedly.

"Maybe not long at all," Mak answered. "Ladimir Karlovic is in FBI custody."

"And we have an arrest warrant out for Fat Nicky," Drew said, purposely not revealing that Nicky's last name was Abruzzo. "We know he's in New York. We expect to pick him up soon."

Beth took this in.

"And I think it's time we get to work," Drew looked to Clayton. "Put out an APB on Paul Marin."

"And Ida Orsina," Artemis said. "She's a person of interest for sure."

Drew agreed and turned to Beth. "Do you know where Paul Marin lives?"

"Yes," Beth said as she reached for a pad of paper and pen. "It's not far from here, just up on Fifth Avenue." She wrote the address and handed it to Drew. "Top floor. The penthouse."

"Thank you, Ms. Schaefer, you've helped us a great deal," Drew said. "I can't promise you anything in regard to your involvement with selling drugs. But continue to help us and we'll do everything we can to help you."

Clayton turned off the recorder, and Drew went to the door and opened it. She addressed a young patrolwoman who was stationed just outside. "Please escort Beth Schaefer and her brother Greg to my office and stay with them. Greg is free to do as he wishes, but Beth is to stay there."

Beth thanked Clayton as she and Greg stood up. They followed the officer out and down the stairs. Drew closed the door and came back into the room.

"Mak, you and Artemis are with me," she said with authority. "We'll see if we can't find this guy at home. Clayton, you've been to the doctor's office before."

"I'm on it," Clayton said as he got up, grabbed the recorder, and his laptop.

"Get a—" Drew started, but Clayton cut her off.

"I know, a warrant. We'll get everything not nailed down." Clayton hurried out of the room.

Artemis looked to Mak. "The restaurant owner, Maddy Griffin, said that Roxie Lee's boyfriend had a house in the Hamptons."

"That's right." Mak got up and took out his cell phone. "I'll have our guys check it out as we go."

"I just have to use the restroom," Greg said to the patrolwoman just before they stepped into Drew's office. He turned to his sister. "I'll be right back."

Beth nodded thankfully.

Greg headed across the wide workroom. He found the restroom down the corridor, went in, and looked around, making sure the room was empty. He took out his cell phone, stepped into the furthest stall, locked the door, and typed a text comprised of three letters: *RUN.*

* * *

Lucille had been careful outside not to attract any unwanted attention. She shifted her brown bag of groceries to one arm and unlocked the studio door. She slipped quietly in and closed and locked the door. She pulled off her mask and cap and tossed them on the small counter.

"Ida?" she called to the closed bathroom door as she started to unpack. "How do you want your eggs?" And then she felt it. Ida was gone.

She walked to the bathroom door and opened it. She sighed. Ida always hated saying goodbye. Lucille saw the closed bag of money on the floor by the bed. She went to the open window and carefully looked down to the street. The midmorning traffic was getting busy and lots of people were out on the sidewalks. But there was no sign of Ida.

Across the street, someone appeared in the living room window of the Bookbinder apartment. She quickly squatted down behind the sill and watched. It was that young agent who protected Silas. He pulled out a cell and sat with his back to her on the window seat. And Lucille wondered about him. And if they were really safer because they had a guard. She sat on the floor facing into the room. The heat of the day was rising, and she was sweating. She wiped her face with her hands.

And she wondered if she could call Artemis. Just take out one of the burner phones and call him.

And say what?

Tell him about Paul Marin? The last person she talked to about that ended up dead.

There must be something I can do.

*   *   *

Two NYPD patrol cars with lights flashing and an unmarked black sedan turned off of 89th Street onto Fifth Avenue. After a block, they pulled to the curb outside a luxury high-rise building. Drew, Artemis, and Mak got out of the sedan, and four uniformed cops got out of the two patrol cars. Drew gave instructions to the cops and told the doorman to get the manager. She led the group into the lobby and spoke to a startled-looking middle-aged man in a blue suit who said he was the assistant manager.

Artemis stood apart from them and pulled out his cell. He found Ray Gaines's number and pushed it. After a few rings, voice mail picked up.

Mak was close enough to hear Artemis leave a message: "Ray, I expected to hear from you by now. I'm worried about you. Call as soon as you can." Artemis hung up and saw Mak looking at him. "He's at least two hours overdue."

"Maybe the boat was delayed," Mak said reassuringly. "You know he'll check in as soon as he can."

"We're heading up," Drew called from across the lobby, and Artemis, Mak, and three of the cops joined her and the assistant manager in one of the stainless-steel elevators. Drew punched the button for the top floor.

Mak saw the worry in Artemis's eyes as he pulled on his mask. And Mak assumed he was having difficulty with the close quarters of the elevator.

At the top penthouse, the door slid open, and Drew and the assistant manager led them to the only door on the stylish landing. Drew pushed the doorbell a few times, and after a second banged loudly on the door with her fist.

"Doctor Marin," she called out. "I'm Detective Sweeney of the New York Police Department. Please open the door."

When this produced no results, she looked to the assistant manager and commanded, "Open it."

"All right," he answered in a whiny complaining voice. "But I'm not responsible for this. You are." He fumbled through a ring of keys, checking the numbers printed on each one. Finding the right key, he opened the door and stepped back. Drew and the cops went in quickly, followed by Mak and Artemis. Drew headed toward the bedroom as she ordered the cops to search the rest of the apartment.

Mak and Artemis walked slowly around the living room, taking time to examine the bar, the fine furniture, and the view through the glass doors of the tiled balcony and across Central Park.

"Nice place," Mak said as he opened the door and stepped outside. Drew came back in from the bedroom shaking her head.

"It looks like he left in a hurry," she reported. "Have you seen him today?" she asked the assistant manager hovering by the open front door.

"No, but I've been working in the office all morning," he said evasively. "And aren't you supposed to have a search warrant or something?"

"It's coming." Drew fairly snarled at him. "And while we're waiting, you can answer some questions for me."

"Like what," he said as his eyes grew wide.

"Like how often does Roxie Lee visit Doctor Marin. And does she have her own set of keys?"

Artemis went out onto the balcony and stood by Mak at the railing. They looked across the park to the tall buildings of the Upper West Side standing golden yellow in the midmorning sun. Artemis pulled off his mask and took a long breath.

"What do you expect Ray to find on that island in Greece?" Mak asked.

"Proof," Artemis answered. "Of who Paul Marin's mother is. Or was."

Mak turned to look curiously at his friend. "Do you know who it is?"

"Maybe I do."

Mak waited for Artemis to explain, but instead he said, "We should get to TVNews as fast as we can."

* * *

Clayton, with two uniformed cops behind him, stood in the small outer lobby at Paul's office on 83rd Street off Fifth. The intercom buzzed, and the heavy stainless-steel inner door popped open. Clayton went into the sleek reception area, pulled out his badge, and approached the older matronly-looking woman sitting at the large desk in the center of the space. He explained they were looking for Doctor Marin, and she said he was out. Clayton started across the room toward the large mahogany door.

"Then you won't mind if I just have a quick look around," he said as he went into the wood-paneled office and the connecting private bathroom. There was no sign of Paul Marin.

"I really must protest," the receptionist said as she followed him.

"Your protest is noted," Clayton answered politely. "And what is your name?"

She stopped by Paul's desk. "Why? Why do you need to know that?"

"Just routine," he answered. "Is there some reason why I shouldn't know who you are and how long you've been working for Doctor Marin?"

"My name is Flora Stavrakis," she said proudly. "And I have worked for the doctor for over twelve years."

"Stavrakis." He smiled at her. "Is that Greek?"

"Yes," she said. "What of it?"

"Just made me think. Paul Marin is Greek, and I've been wondering about his last name," Clayton said as he wandered back to the reception area. "Is Marin his real name or did he change it, do you know?"

"I'm sure I don't know," she said angrily. "And do you have a search warrant that allows to sashay around like this?"

A low buzz was heard coming from the desk phone. Flora hurried over and pushed a button. "Yes?" she asked impatiently.

"NYPD," a voice said through the phone speaker. Her eyes blazed as she hit the button, the buzzer sounded, the lobby door opened and a uniformed sergeant came in and handed Clayton some papers.

"Thanks, Austin." He turned to the receptionist. "This is a warrant that allows us to take whatever we want from these premises."

Flora opened and closed her mouth.

"Let's get to work," Clayton instructed the cops. "Get the computers."

As they disassembled the equipment on her desk, Flora picked up the phone and announced. "I'm calling our lawyer."

Clayton smiled. "Yes, you should definitely do that."

* * *

Drew, Artemis, and Mak got off the elevator on the eighth floor of TVNews, went through the glass doors, and told the receptionist they were expected. Drew and Artemis headed up the wide open-tread staircase to the executive level. Mak started across the newsroom toward Deni Diaz whom he could see at her desk in her glass-walled corner office. He knocked on her open door, and she looked up from her laptop.

"Agent Kim." She smiled easily at him. "This is an unexpected pleasure. What can I do for you?"

"I have some questions for you," Mak said seriously as he stepped in and closed the door. "There's been a development."

Deni saved her work and closed her laptop. She indicated the chair in front of her desk. "Have a seat." Mak sat and looked at her.

After a moment, Deni grew uncomfortable and said, "Questions about what?"

"Paul Marin," Mak said evenly.

Her eyes froze.

"The man who taught the class you attended every Sunday night at midnight. The man who gave you that pretty necklace." He nodded to the pink gem hanging on the silver chain around her neck. "We have a witness."

"Who?" she asked.

"I'm not at liberty to say."

"So, I was in a class. What's the problem?"

"A stolen chalice from the Gardner Museum," he answered. "The recovery of which TVNews reported. And you said nothing to us."

Deni looked with appeal into his eyes. "I didn't know what it was until after. It was just a cup Paul drank wine from when he was teaching. I didn't want to be in trouble. And I never saw Paul Marin after that."

"Has Roxie Lee seen him since then?" Mak asked pointedly.

"I..." Deni seemed confused. "I really don't know. You'll have to ask her."

"We are."

"Should I get a lawyer?" Deni asked as she lifted her chin defiantly.

"If you like." Mak leaned back in his chair. "Deni, I know you're a good person. Just talk to me."

She gauged the handsome open face of the young man sitting across the desk. "Okay, what do you need to know?"

"I don't understand the appeal. Tell me about Paul Marin."

"He helped me," Deni said candidly. "He's a doctor, a psychiatrist who specializes in people who are having problems with drugs. About four years ago, I knew I was getting in trouble. Paul really cared about me and I got clean."

"And then he invited you to join his class," Mak said perceptively.

"Yes."

"And how did you find him?"

Deni took a breath and said, "Roxie. He was a friend of hers and she told me to go see him."

A flight up, Roxie poured herself a glass of water at the bar in her office. She turned to Artemis and Drew who were sitting in front of her desk.

"All right." Roxie walked to her desk and sat in the big leather chair. "Paul and I are seeing each other and have been for a long time. I have no excuse for not naming him before. God knows you asked me enough times." She smiled at Artemis. "But he's someone I care for and believe in. He told me that he never knew the chalice was stolen. That it was a gift."

"A gift from who?" Drew asked.

"He didn't say," Roxie explained. "I assumed it came from Raphael. I mean, they were great friends and the stolen Rembrandt was found at Raphael's place."

"You really believe that Paul Marin didn't know the chalice came from the Gardner?" Artemis asked. She looked away from his intense eyes, shifted in her seat, took a sip of water, and said nothing.

"And you don't know anything about Paul selling illegal drugs?" Drew asked.

"Nothing," she said trying to sound sincere.

"What about the box of chocolates in Paula DeVong's desk?" Artemis asked.

"What do you mean?" Roxie shrugged unconvincingly.

"Paula died from an overdose of a weight-loss drug"—Drew explained—"that was in a piece of chocolate she ate the night she died."

"We have the box," Artemis added. "The unwrapped box you planted in her desk."

Roxie's eyes flashed. "You can't prove that."

"I think you were just doing what you were told to," Artemis said not unkindly. "By Paul Marin. The only question is whether he meant to kill Paula or just make her sick."

Roxie stared at him.

"Sick long enough to search Paula's apartment and recover a recording of Lucille Orsina telling all she knew about Paul Marin."

Roxie got up and looked out the floor-to-ceiling windows at the wide cityscape. She looked down to Columbus where the sidewalks were full of people heading for lunch, following the endless repeating patterns of daily life. Trying to get ahead. Trying to belong.

"Yes," she said just loud enough to be heard. "Paul said it would only make her sick. But she had COVID and I guess it was too much for her." She turned to Artemis. "Paul Marin is a good man. He would never kill anyone."

"No?" Drew leaned back in her chair. "So you don't think he shot Raphael Sharder?"

"No, I don't," Roxie said emphatically. "Paul loved that old man. And Raphael loved Paul."

"Were they related?" Artemis asked.

"Yes, they were." Roxie took a breath and tried to focus. "Raphael was his great-uncle or something like that." She sat back down and folded her hands on her desk. "What happens now?"

"Depends on you," Drew said distinctly. "We have an arrest warrant out for Paul Marin. Do you know where he is?"

"No." Roxie shook her head. "I haven't heard from him in a day."

"Is that usual?" Artemis asked.

"Sure, he's like that sometimes. I might not hear from him for a few days at a time."

"Would you have any problem taking us to your apartment over by the river?" Drew asked as she pointed west. "So we can make sure Paul Marin isn't hiding there."

"I can do that." She agreed readily. "Let's go." She headed for the door, and Artemis and Drew got up and followed. In the reception area, Roxie told the secretary that she was going out to lunch and would be back by two.

"Yes, Roxie," Barb answered, and she returned to filing her long red nails.

As Roxie stepped to the elevators and pushed the down button, Mak came up the stairs from the newsroom. He was just finishing a call on his cell.

"We found Marin's house in Amagansett," he said. "My guys are hooking up with the local police and are heading there now."

Artemis saw Roxie's shoulders tighten and release. The door opened, and they followed her into the elevator.

*　*　*

At noon, the bars and restaurants of the Upper West Side were full of noisy maskless people doing their best to celebrate the warm summer day and ignore the endless pandemic. A team of plainclothes NYPD officers and FBI agents stood in casual groups on a busy sidewalk outside a closed bar on Amsterdam.

Inside the bar, Fat Nicky was restless and hungry. He had spent the morning trying to find out who was behind moving Ladimir from the detention center, and had failed. He finished his glass of vodka and banged it angrily on the old wood bar. He walked to the shuttered front window, made a space in the blinds with his fleshy finger, and peered out. The street looked busy, as always, and he didn't recognize anyone. Which was a good thing. He knew Paul and Ladimir's guys. He nervously smoothed the sides of his slicked-back hair and went to the front door. He turned the deadbolt and eased the door open. Then as he started to step out, all hell broke loose and he found himself lying facedown on the dirty barroom floor pinned by two FBI agents while a cop loudly read him his rights. And Nicky wondered.

Who betrayed me?

As his hands were being cuffed behind his back, he lifted his face enough to see one of the FBI agents get the small camera with Lucille's interview from the bar and place it in an evidence bag.

*   *   *

Greg stood at the window in Drew's office looking down at the traffic on 67th Street which had finally started moving. He looked at his sister who was sitting in a chair in front of the desk with her arms folded across her chest, her head down, and her eyes closed. Outside the open door, the patrolwoman was talking sports with another uniformed cop. Greg's cell pinged, and he checked the message.

"It's work," Greg said, and Beth looked up at him. "I have to go over there for a while. But I'll be back as soon as I can."

"No worries," she said affectionately. "I really appreciate you being here with me today."

"Happy to," Greg said, leaned down, kissed her cheek, and walked out past the cops.

The woman cop stepped into the office. "We're sending out for some lunch," she said. "Can we get you something?"

"No, thanks," Beth answered quietly. "I'm not really very hungry."

*   *   *

Roxie unlocked her apartment door, stepped in, and held the door for Drew, Mak, and Artemis. Drew headed for the bedroom, and Mak, the kitchen.

Artemis stepped into the living room, and Roxie closed the door and followed him.

"He's not here," Drew announced as she and Mak came into the living room. Mak looked out the large wall of windows at the highway, the Hudson River, and New Jersey beyond.

"Great place," Mak said as he turned to look around the room.

Roxie nodded. "Is there anything else I can do for you?"

"Not leave town," Drew ordered as she handed Roxie her card. "And you will see me at the 19th Precinct tomorrow morning for questioning."

"Can I bring a lawyer?"

"Yes, you can," Drew advised her. "And you should. Ten o'clock. Don't be late. Don't make me come look for you."

"I'll be there," Roxie assured her. Mak's cell rang, and he stepped to the windows to take the call.

"Thanks," he said after a minute. "Let me know if you find anything interesting." Mak hung up. "Paul Marin isn't at his house in Amagansett. They're starting to go through the place now."

Artemis saw the relief in Roxie's eyes. She realized he was looking at her, and she shrugged. "I love him," she said softly.

"What can you tell us," Artemis asked, "about Paul's mother?"

Roxie looked startled. She walked to the built-in bar and poured herself some gin. "Nothing. I never met her."

"What has he told you about her?" Artemis asked as he followed her.

"He never talks about her. Care for a drink?" she asked him impatiently.

"No, it's too early for me."

"For me too. But this is turning into one hell of a day." She took a sip.

"I expect you to call me if you hear from Paul Marin," Drew instructed. "You understand."

"Yes, Detective," Roxie said. "I will."

Drew and Mak started for the door. Artemis felt that there was something else that Roxie wanted to say and stood waiting. She took another sip and looked at him.

"What?" he asked.

"Do you think," she whispered, "that Paul had anything to do with the death of your wife?"

Artemis's eyes focused on her, and he whispered fiercely, "Absolutely, I do."

Her eyes grew wet with tears, but she continued to look at him.

"The ship is sinking, Roxie," he said kindly and looked up at the Ernst painting hanging above the bar. "Earthquake."

"Or the Drowning of the Sun," she murmured sadly.

"You have my number," Artemis said. "Call me anytime."

He turned, left the apartment, and closed the door behind him. Roxie gazed at the painting and remembered how happy she was when Paul had bought it for her. She turned and wandered across the elegant room to the windows and looked at the impressive view. She had gotten everything she had set out to achieve. Position. Power. Money. Respect.

Does any of it really matter?

She sipped her drink, pulled out her cell, and dialed a long number. The line connected, and she heard three dull beeps.

"It's Roxie," she said. "The police are looking for Paul. I don't know what you want me to do." She thought for a moment longer and then hung up.

* * *

Greg had loved living in the West Village. He went up a few steps and unlocked the street door of what had once been a grand home in the 1890s. Through time, the building had seen many changes but now it was divided into four separate rental units, one on each floor. He went up the interior staircase which had been restored a dozen years ago just before he moved in. At the top of the stairs, he unlocked the heavy oak door of his apartment and stepped into a high-ceiling living room with decorative crown moldings, an ornate fireplace, and ten-foot-tall windows looking out over the quiet tree-lined street. He went across the room to the closed bedroom door and gently opened it. Paul was lying across the bed dressed in jeans and a white tee shirt. He looked up at the sound of the door opening, and Greg could see that he'd been crying. Greg sat near him on the bed, and Paul crawled into his lap and tightly wrapped his arms around his waist.

"Oh, Greg," he said miserably. "I don't know what to do."

"Have you heard from your mother?"

"No, she's still not returning my calls," Paul said with disgust. "She's waiting for me to take care of Fat Nicky. And I don't even know where he is."

"I heard the cops, they have an arrest warrant out for him," Greg said, and Paul sat up.

"How did that happen?" Paul sounded worried.

"Maybe your mother gave them information," Greg suggested.

"Or old man Karlovic," Paul said as he got up and walked slowly to the tall windows, leaned his shoulder against the frame, and looked out over the low buildings. In the distance, he could see the top of the Empire State Building shining in the midafternoon sun. "I'm going to miss this place," he said wistfully.

Greg came across the room, stood beside him, and put his arm around his waist. As always, Greg could feel how perfectly they fit together. "Where will we go?"

"No, I'm going alone. I told you it's too risky to be with me."

"Hasn't bothered me so far," Greg answered lightly.

"How do you do that?" Paul asked.

Greg looked uncertain.

"You believe that things will work out and we'll be okay," Paul said sadly. "But you really don't know who I am. And what I have done."

In response, Greg reached up and undid the top buttons of his dress shirt to show Paul the clear light green gem hanging on the silver necklace. "Hiddenite." Greg smiled. "You gave me a spodumene, like my sister's. But this one, no one knows about. Not Beth. Not even Roxie."

"Or my mother," Paul agreed.

"Right," Greg said. "Just us."

Paul sighed and sat on an upholstered armchair by the window. "What did Beth tell them?" he asked.

"Everything," Greg admitted miserably.

"Well"—Paul leaned back and closed his eyes—"It was all going to come out anyway. I hope it helps her."

Greg leaned down and kissed his cheek. "You see, that's why I love you. And I am so fucking going with you no matter what."

Paul smiled. "In that case, you better pack light. We're leaving first thing in the morning."

Greg smiled back. "Perfect. Where?"

"No," Paul said, and he stood up. "The less you know, the better. You'll just have to trust me."

"I do," Greg said simply.

"I have to go out for a while," Paul said.

"But the cops are looking for you everywhere," Greg looked worried.

"Can't be helped. But I'll be careful." Greg saw the intense determination in Paul's lavender eyes and understood.

"You want to say goodbye to Roxie."

"Yes," Paul answered truthfully.

"Will you tell her about me?" Greg asked.

"No, I won't."

Greg felt disappointed but didn't let it show in his face. "Will you spend the night with her?"

Instead of answering, Paul slowly wrapped his arms around Greg and hugged him close. "I love you so much," he whispered. Paul leaned back, held Greg's cheek with his hand, and kissed his lips. "See you soon." He smiled and headed for the door.

Greg heard Paul's footsteps as he walked across the oak floor of the wide living room. Paul got his COVID mask, designer sunglasses, and one of Greg's baseball caps from a table by the front door, put them on, and left the apartment.

Greg went to the closet, pulled a large shoulder bag from an upper shelf, and started to pack.

* * *

It was eight thirty in Greece, and the last glow of the deep-orange sunset was fading over the Aegean Sea. Ray sat on a cushioned deck chair in an open salon of the private yacht he'd chartered to take him to Naxos. One of the crew came down the steps from the wheelhouse and speaking loudly over the noise of the engines running at full throttle, said that they were able to contact the Naxos airport by radio and the Karlovic plane would be ready to fly him to Athens as soon as he arrived. Ray tipped his head in thanks, and the young man returned forward.

Ray checked his cell. He still didn't have a signal, and he was worried. In his pocket was a photograph he'd gotten several hours ago from an old woman who ran a seaside taverna. At first, the woman refused to speak to him. But after she had read the sealed letter from Marta Abruzzo, she sat him down and told him the most amazing story.

* * *

On the Upper East Side of Manhattan, it was just past four and the afternoon rush hour had, as usual, re-snarled the traffic on 67th Street. Clayton stepped out of the station house and looked carefully at the people on the sidewalks and the faces in the slow-moving cars. He held the door open, and Beth came out escorted by three uniformed cops. Clayton took Beth by the arm, and the group quickly made their way down the block, across Third Avenue, and into a small ordinary-looking hotel. Clayton said a couple of words to the desk clerk standing behind a granite counter, who handed him a key.

They got off the elevator on the eleventh floor and went to the last door at the end of a dimly lit hallway wallpapered with a purple floral design. Clayton entered the room, gave it a quick inspection, and waved Beth inside. He thanked the cops and closed the door. Beth looked around the room. It was clean and functional. There was a faded landscape above the bed, a worn desk, a television, and under a counter, a small fridge.

"It's not much," Clayton said apologetically, "but you'll be safe here. There'll be a cop sitting outside the door twenty-four seven if you need anything. I'll bring you some food in a little while." He opened the fridge and saw it was empty. "And some bottles of water. And anything else you like. Maybe a bottle of wine?"

"Actually"—Beth smiled a little—"that would help a lot. Maybe a chardonnay?"

"Done," Clayton said easily. "There's soap and clean towels in the bathroom and there's cable on the TV."

"Okay," Beth said uncertainly as she sat on the edge of the bed.

"I have some news," he said gently. "Maybe it will help."

"You arrested Paul?" Beth looked up interested.

"No, not yet," he answered. "But we got Fat Nicky. They picked him up a couple of hours ago on the Upper West Side."

"Good," she said slowly. "That does help."

"You still have my number?" he asked, and she nodded. "Call if you need. And I'll be back with supplies as soon as I can."

"Thank you, Clayton," she said gratefully, and he left, closing the door securely behind him.

Beth lay down across the bed. The faded white ceiling above her was full of hairline cracks, and she could hear the loud siren of an ambulance going past on the street below. She closed her eyes and breathed out very slowly.

* * *

It was still hot at dusk. The sky was a deep blue, and the moon was low in the east above the building tops. Lucille sat on the floor in her studio leaning out over the window sill. Down on 73rd Street, she saw Delia come out of the revolving door of the Ansonia. One of the uniformed cops spoke to her and together they headed off west down the sidewalk. Lucille wondered if Delia was going to another AA meeting at the little church around the corner.

Lucille restlessly turned into the room and leaned her back against the wall. She saw the bag on the floor that her sister had left. She pulled it close, unzipped it, and examined the contents. The bag was full of stacks of banded cash and on top was a folded piece of white paper. Lucille smiled. Ida hated saying goodbye, but at least she left a note. She opened it and read:

I hope the money helps you survive, but it means nothing if you don't protect yourself. Please don't take risks. Ever.

Lucille shook her head. It was so typically Ida.

I'll be in touch when I can. But it will be a while.

Where did Ida say she was heading? Croatia?

You asked me why I chose this studio for you. I will tell you. It may be dangerous for you to know, but it may give you some leverage when you need it most.

Lucille's body became completely still as she read the next paragraph. The information was confusing, and she slowly read it again. She realized she was holding her breath. She breathed out and forced herself to focus. Then she read the information a third time.

Across the street, Artemis keyed open the front door of apartment 18-18, came in, and relocked it. He looked into Delia's room and saw it was empty, as he'd expected. Further down the hall, he looked into Silas's room. His son was sitting at his desk working on his laptop, and Agent Filipowski was standing by the large window texting on his cell.

"Delia out to her meeting?" Artemis asked.

"Yes," Silas confirmed as he turned.

Flip put his phone away and sat on the wide wood sill.

Artemis came in a couple of steps. "What are you working on?" he asked his son.

"All things Abruzzo," Silas said as he pushed his glasses back up on his nose. "I've been wondering about Anna Canneli. Her father owned the Necropolis. His people came from Sicily where Marta Abruzzo lives. So, I'm trying to find if there's a link between Anna's father, Aldo Canneli, and her. But so far, nothing."

"Well," Artemis said supportively. "Keep after it. I'll be in my study."

"I'll be here," Silas said determinedly as he turned back to his research.

Artemis left the room, went down the hall into his office, and closed the door. He walked over to the bay windows and looked up to the darkening sky. He pulled the curtains closed, went to the bar tray, and poured himself a single malt. He sat at his large oak desk, took a sip, and leaned back in his chair deep in thought. His cell rang. He checked the ID.

"Ray, I've been worried about you."

"Thank you, son," Ray said. "I'm okay. And I'm sorry to be so long getting back. That goddamn ferry boat broke down for a couple of hours. And there's no cell service anywhere."

Artemis took this in. "Where are you?"

"Naxos," Ray said. "Back on Karlovic's private jet. We're about to take off. I'm heading for Athens."

"Why, what's there?"

"A photo, I hope," Ray said louder as the engines of the jet revved up. "Of Demetra Voskos. Her father was a well-known businessman. There has to be a picture of her at a benefit or a wedding somewhere. As soon as we land, I'm heading to the *Ta Nea* newspaper office."

Artemis checked the time. "Ray, it's two o'clock in the morning in Athens."

"Interpol set it up for me," Ray said as the plane picked up speed and the wheels lifted off the tarmac. He looked out the window as they gained altitude, the lights of the island disappeared, and all around was only the vast dark sea.

"Do you have any idea where Demetra Voskos is now?" Artemis asked.

"Supposedly, she's dead," Ray answered. "Drowned in September 2015. I'll be checking on that too."

"Okay."

"And there's more," Ray said quickly as he heard static on the line. "The old woman on the island gave me a picture. And there's no question. Artemis, you were right."

Artemis's eyes grew distant as he assembled the information. The static grew worse.

"Sorry," Ray said loudly. "I'm going to lose you. I'll call as soon as I have something."

"Send me the photos," Artemis added quickly.

"I will," Ray promised and hung up.

Artemis sat very still. He took a sip of his drink, got up, and left the office. He slowly made his way into the living room and over to the large windows. Night had come, and beyond the low rooftops across the street, he could see lights in the windows of hundreds of buildings. He sat down on the padded window seat and looked west down 73rd Street. Between the rows of tall buildings, he could see the wide Hudson River reflecting the lights from the far shore.

Across the street, Lucille was sitting on the floor with her head down and her eyes closed. She felt a strange sensation across her neck. She opened her eyes and sat up. Moonlight was coming through the window and shining across her shoulders. She lifted her hands and studied her fingers lit in the pale white light. She turned and looked out the window. And she saw him, Artemis Bookbinder. He seemed tired. And Lucille suddenly knew what she must do. No matter the risk.

She crawled over and found the paper bag under her bed. She pulled out one of her burner phones, pulled off the packaging, and dialed a number she'd committed to memory. She watched as Artemis pulled out his cell phone and checked the *unknown caller* ID. Her heart was beating fast in her chest as she saw him accept the call.

"Who is this?" he asked.

"It's me," she said clearly.

"Hello, Lucille. I hoped it was you. Are you all right?"

She heard the kindness in his voice. "Yes, I am. And there's something I must tell you."

"Okay," he said.

"Not over the phone."

"I can come to you. Where are you?"

"Near." Lucille took a breath and went on. "I am very near."

Artemis felt a cold chill run up his spine, and he turned to the taller building across the street and a few doors down. He slowly scanned the windows looking up floor by floor.

Lucille stood up, pushed the curtains fully open, reached for the lamp on the bedside table, flicked it on, and stood in the middle of the open window.

As the light came on, Artemis's eyes shot up to the little studio on the top of the building and he saw Lucille. "I'll be right there," he said and hung up.

Lucille watched as he got up and walked away. She wrapped her arms around her chest and looked up at the moon in the clear sky.

Artemis stopped outside of Silas's room. "I'm going out," he announced to Silas and Flip. Flip stopped texting, and Silas turned from his laptop and looked at his father.

"I shouldn't be too long," Artemis said and headed out. He locked the apartment door behind him, pulled on his mask, went down the wide Ansonia hallway, but instead of calling for the elevator, he started quickly down the stairs. There was something about the steady sound of his feet on the well-worn marble steps descending in a repeating rectangular pattern floor after floor that helped him organize his thoughts. At the bottom, he walked through a black metal door into the grand double-height lobby. He came out the 73rd Street revolving door and the two uniformed cops saw him, but he waved them off and walked across the street. He came to the taller building and went into the small foyer. There he scanned the apartment buttons on the security panel mounted by the inner door. He pushed the only one listed for the nineteenth floor, and after a second, he heard a loud buzz and the door unlatched. He went into an unremarkable mid-century lobby, got into the elevator, and pushed the top button. At the eighteenth floor, the door opened on a beige hallway with six apartment doors. He walked to the end of the hall, went through the fire door, and up a thin flight of stairs to a small landing. He knocked, heard the locks turning, and Lucille opened the door.

She gazed at his handsome lean face and deep blue eyes. She could feel his strength and determination in the sure way he stood. She had dreamt of this meeting for so long, it took her a moment before she found her voice. "Please come in, Artemis."

He stepped in, and she closed and locked the door. He walked over to the window and looked down at his apartment across the street. He pulled off his mask.

"How long have you been here?" he asked curiously as he turned to her.

"Not long," she said. "Six nights."

He looked around at the simple furnishings and the open bag of cash on the floor. "Did you rob a bank?" he asked lightly.

"My sister Ida left that for me."

"And where is she?"

"Gone. Out of the country. I don't know where."

"Okay," he said as he sat on the window sill facing her.

"Do you mind if I turn this off?" Lucille asked as she came over to the lamp on the bedside table.

"I don't mind," he said, and she switched off the lamp. He could still see her because of the glow of the city lights below and the bright moonlight coming through the window. "I've been worried about you. Where have you been all this time?"

"Here. In the city," Lucille said as she sat near him on the edge of the bed. "And I promise you, Artemis, I never had anything to do with the death of your wife."

"I know that," he assured her. "You were set up to take the fall. By Paul Marin."

"Yes." She held her breath.

"We know about him. The police are looking for him right now."

"Good," she said. "I've been waiting a long time to hear that." She wrapped her arms around her chest.

"And his associates," he added, "Ladimir Karlovic and Fat Nicky Abruzzo have been arrested."

"That's good too," she whispered. "Thank you."

Her shoulders relaxed and her eyes filled with tears. He could feel her relief and was glad.

"You recorded an interview with Paula DeVong," he said quietly, "about Paul Marin."

"Yes," she confirmed as she wiped her cheeks.

"When did you do that?"

"It would have been eight or nine days ago."

"I see," Artemis said almost to himself. "Was that what you were looking for in Paula's bag the night she died?" She looked puzzled. "There was a security camera near where she fell."

Lucille nodded and explained, "I needed to know why Paula hadn't shown the interview, so I waited outside the TVNews studio and followed her when she came out."

"That was this past Wednesday night?"

"Yes, around eleven thirty. She started walking down Broadway, and she didn't look well. Kept stopping to rest. I saw her fall to the sidewalk and I wanted to help her, but there were so many people around I couldn't. And they all just walked past her. No one cared. After maybe a half hour, it got quiet and I went to check on her. I called 911. I looked for the camera in her bag, but it wasn't there."

"The police have the camera," he reported. "It was in Fat Nicky's possession when they arrested him."

"I see," Lucille said. Then she took a quick breath and picked up a folded piece of paper from the bedside table. "Ida left me this note. It's why I called you." She handed it to him. He turned his body so moonlight fell across the page, opened it, and read it carefully.

"May I keep this for a while?" he asked.

Even in the darkened room, she could see the intensity in his eyes. "Of course."

"All this time..." Artemis sighed. "Everyone's been looking for you. How do you move about unseen?"

"Courtesy of the pandemic." She smiled a little. "I'm just another person in a mask."

"Would you be willing to do something for me, out there?" He waved vaguely toward the street below.

"You have no idea," she said sincerely, "how much I want to help you and your son. Just tell me what I can do."

"It could be dangerous," he said plainly. "So, I'm going to call someone to go with you."

"Who?" she asked.

"A friend"—he smiled—"who I would trust with my life."

Lucille considered and then said, "Okay."

Artemis took out his cell, found a number, and hit it.

"Where are you?" he asked.

"Upper West Side," Mak said as he stepped out of the 20th Precinct on 82nd Street. "I got the camera with Lucille's interview."

"Perfect," said Artemis.

*   *   *

"You know it's not right that I'm drinking alone," Beth said as she refilled her hotel cup with white wine.

273

"Sorry," Clayton said amiably. "But technically, I'm still on call. Besides, I'm not sure chardonnay is perfectly matched with this." He lifted a piece of kung pao chicken from his takeout plastic bowl and looked at it suspiciously.

Beth put down her chopsticks. "Thanks for the food but it's really sort of... disgusting," she said and started laughing.

Clayton leaned back in his chair and smiled widely. "I know. And I'm sorry. That place used to have great food."

"Story of New York," Beth said as she stopped laughing and caught her breath. Clayton watched as she ran her fingers through her short hair a few times. She looked exhausted.

"I'm gonna go," he said as he got up. "I'll bring you breakfast in the morning, say about eight thirty, if that's okay? How do you like your coffee?"

"That's okay. A little milk," she said appreciatively. "And thank you."

"You did good, today," he said. "Doris is the cop outside the door, and she'll be here all night. You have my number if you need." Clayton walked to the door and turned back. "See you tomorrow."

She nodded, and he left. Beth got up from the well-used desk, collected their plates, and tossed them in the trash. She got her cell from her bag, found her brother's number, and pushed it. The call went to voice mail. She sat on the edge of the bed and waited for the beep.

"Greg, where are you?" She tried to keep the worry out of her voice. "Call me. I don't care how late it is." She hung up and looked around the sad little room. She checked the time on her cell. It was a few minutes before eleven, and she wondered if Greg was still at work. She reached for the remote, turned on the television, and found TVNews. An attractive young woman with curly red hair and blue eyes was speaking directly to the camera.

"As we see the Delta variant spreading throughout the nation, it's even more distressing and outrageous that anyone would still selfishly refuse to get with the program and get vaccinated."

Moira stopped reading from the teleprompter and looked over to Deni, who was standing beside the camera. Deni saw the unmistakable look of defiance in Moira's eyes and understood that all of a sudden, the moment had come. Deni smiled a little in support.

"Here the fuck we go," Deni whispered to herself.

Moira checked the show-clock and saw that she had a minute of airtime left. "You know what, I'm done with this." She took a quick breath and went on. "Because there is so much more information available about the vaccines that we're not allowed to tell you. There are opinions that the vaccines are not effective, that our natural immune systems are being compromised by them, and since they are not true vaccines, there is nothing for us but a future of getting shots over and over again. Since the outbreak of COVID, the vaccine companies have seen their profits increase obscenely. At the very least that should make us ask questions. But news networks have sponsors. And I've been told they don't want this kind of discussion." Moira lifted her script off the news desk. "But I think that polarizing our nation into hostile armies of the vaccinated and the unvaccinated is wrong." She tossed the script aside, looked to Deni, and smiled. "And since this is the last time you'll be seeing me on TVNews." She turned back to the camera. "Let me say what a responsibility and privilege this has been for me. I will be creating my own podcast. And if you agree with me that it's time for a balanced discussion of everything that goes on in our world, please find me. We're out of time." She laughed a little. "And so am I. Good night, all."

The studio on-air monitors abruptly cut to black. And then a prescription drug commercial came on. Deni's cell phone vibrated in her back pocket. She pulled it out and saw who was calling.

"This is Deni," she said as she braced herself.

"I know who the fuck you are," Calvin shouted as he paced the floor of his office two flights up. "I've been calling the control room, and no one answered. Where's Roxie?"

"I don't know," Deni said bravely as Moira came and stood by her. "I'm in charge here."

"Are you?" Calvin continued to rant. "Then how could you let that curly-haired ungrateful bitch say that shit on-air? Find Moira and tell her she is so completely fucking fired!"

Moira could easily hear his words, and she winced. Deni's mouth twisted in anger, but she managed to control the tone of her voice. "She heard you. And for the record, I agree with what she said."

"Fine. You're fired too. Get your shit out of my studio tonight," Calvin said savagely and hung up.

Deni put her cell back in her pocket and looked to Moira.

"Thank you," Moira said quietly. "You didn't have to do that."

"Yeah. I did." Deni saw the crew members standing together looking worried. "Go home, everybody," she said firmly. "This show is still on the air and will be tomorrow. Good night." Deni started walking toward the control room to get her things, and Moira walked with her.

"So, Skippy," Deni said wryly. "I hear we're starting a podcast."

"All we need now is the barn," Moira said faintly as what she had done began to sink in.

"And a drink," Deni added.

*   *   *

Artemis was sitting at his desk in his study. Opened in front of him were three documents: a copy of the Boston police report from 1990 describing the robbery at the Gardner Museum, an NYPD report of the death of his parents in 1994, and an FBI report on the death of his wife in 2020.

He heard the front door open and Delia's commanding voice thanking the cop who escorted her home. He heard her close and lock the door. Delia came down the hall and looked in the open door of his study.

"You look tired," she said kindly. "Been a long day?"

"Yes."

"You should get to bed."

"I'm waiting for a call from Ray," he explained.

"Ray? Where is he now?" she asked.

"Athens. Doing some research." Artemis reached for his glass and finished off the last of his drink.

Delia went to the bar tray, got the bottle of single malt, and refilled his glass. "It must be very late there," she said as she put the bottle back. "Or very early."

"Yes." Artemis checked the time on his cell. It was eleven thirty. "It's late here too. That was a long meeting."

"The place was packed," she said as she leaned against the bookcase. "Everybody's worried that the next COVID wave will shut things down again and there won't be any more meetings."

"That makes sense." Artemis lifted his glass, leaned back in his chair, and took a sip. "Thanks for the fresh pour, Big Dee."

She barked out a short laugh. "You haven't called me that for a long time. Now quit it."

"Okay," he agreed.

"Well, I hate to admit it." She stretched her shoulders and groaned. "But I'm pretty tired myself. Did Silas have dinner?"

"Yes."

"Good." She gave him an approving nod and headed for the door. "I'm off to bed. See you in the morning."

"Good night," he said. He heard the sharp strike of her shoes as she marched to the far end of the hall, went into her bedroom, and closed the door with a thump. Artemis slowly sat up, pushed his drink away, and laid his hands across the three neatly arranged documents on his desk.

⋆　⋆　⋆

The Press Lounge was on the rooftop of a hotel at Eleventh and 48th Street. Deni and Moira sat together on an outdoor sofa looking out at the view of the Hudson River. A few blocks to the south, they could see the World War II aircraft carrier *Intrepid*, which was now a tourist attraction. And to the north, a large docked cruise ship was garishly lit up. Around the outdoor space, people were standing in chatty groups, taking selfies, and enjoying the warm night.

The waitress arrived and put down a champagne for Moira and a rum-herb concoction for Deni that was a house specialty. "Enjoy, ladies," she said pleasantly through her mask.

"No ladies here," Deni joked. The waitress laughed and walked away.

Deni held up her glass. "So, here's a toast: may Calvin Prons go directly to hell."

Moira chuckled as she touched her glass to Deni's. "They'll probably put him in charge."

Deni took a sip and swirled the ice around in her tall glass. "I have to talk to the police tomorrow morning," she said worriedly. "Over on the East Side."

"Want me to come with you?" Moira asked.

"Yes." Deni smiled relieved. "And thanks."

Moira nodded, and they both took a drink.

"Oh, that's going to help," Deni said. "Though we really should've gone to some hole-in-the-wall. We're both officially unemployed."

"I know." Moira smiled. "But tonight, we should be celebrating. We stood up against the network. And tomorrow, you and I start working on doing things better."

Deni took a moment and then laughed. She lifted her glass. "To the death of television."

"At least as we know it," Moira agreed and took a sip of champagne.

Chapter Seven

Wednesday, July 21st, 2021

Roxie walked along 64th Street heading to work. She wondered why it was so quiet and no one was around. She came to the corner of Columbus and stopped in amazement. The avenue was empty: no cars, buses, taxis, bikers—no people anywhere. She crossed the street to the TVNews building but stopped when she saw her reflection in the lobby windows. She was naked except for her ruby pendant necklace. As she moved closer to the glass, the ruby glowed to life casting a soft red light across her sensual body. From above, she heard overlapping voices whispering. She looked up past the tall modern structures to the searingly hot white sun that made her eyes water. The voices grew more insistent, but she couldn't understand what they were saying. She felt a nervous tremor deep in her chest, looked back at her reflection, and saw that the ruby was beginning to melt under the heat of the sun. She felt a visceral thrill in her pelvis and up the length of her spine as the surprisingly cold liquid slowly ran across her breasts, over her hips, and down her legs until her beautiful body was entirely encased. Then something felt wrong. The ruby-red liquid started to freeze solid, squeezing her body with more and more pressure. She tried to run but could not move her legs. She tried to call out, but the pain was strangling her. She could not escape. Finally, she willed her mouth open and shouted hoarsely, "Help me please!"

And the sound of her own voice woke her, and she opened her eyes. Roxie was in her own bed, in her own apartment. It was still night. Her naked body was wet with sweat. She wiped her face dry with her hands and sat up. Through the sheer curtains, she could see the familiar lights of the buildings outside. She took a long breath. She looked to the side of the bed where Paul had been and wondered if he was still in the apartment. She felt the weight of the ruby gem hanging above her breasts. She carefully reached up and undid the clasp at the back of her neck. She wrapped her fingers around the red gem and held it tightly in her fist. She slowly got her feet on the floor, stood up, wrapped herself in a silk robe, and headed for the living room.

"I heard you cry out," Paul said as he saw her. He was sitting across the room on the window sill, backlit in pale white moonlight. He was dressed in his white tee shirt and jeans, had a drink in his hand, and his cell phone beside him. The wide window was fully open behind him, and even at 4:00 a.m., the sound of the constant traffic on the highway thirty stories down was loud. "Are you okay?"

"Not really," she said as she went to the bar and looked up at the Ernst painting. "Earthquake," she said loud enough for him to hear. "The Drowning of the Sun." She turned to look at him. "I loved you so much when you bought this for me. But I never asked you. What do you think of it?"

Paul looked at the painting. Even in the shadows, the golden yellow of the sun was easy to see. "Never understood it," he admitted. "I was just happy you liked it."

She walked across the room and felt the warm air coming in around him. "I thought you'd be gone by now."

He reached up and tenderly ran his fingers across her cheek, leaned to her, and kissed her lips.

"Tomorrow, I have to talk to the police," Roxie said as she backed away a couple of steps. "What do you think I should tell them?"

Paul shrugged. "I'll be gone. Say whatever you think best."

"They know it was me that put the box of chocolates in Paula's desk," she said gravely.

"So tell them I asked you to."

"I did already."

Paul's eyes flashed dangerously. "All you had to do was retrieve that box the morning after Paula died. And you failed."

"It wasn't there," Roxie said heatedly. "I think Anna Canneli got there before me."

"Why?" he asked.

"Who the fuck cares?" she shouted. "The point is you set me up."

Paul shouted back. "I never meant for that to happen."

She glared at him.

"It doesn't matter anymore," he said exasperated. "Tell them everything."

"Even the things you don't know about?" she asked more quietly.

He looked at her curiously. "Like what?"

"About your mother," she answered. "Who she is."

"How do you know about her?"

Roxie could see the uncertainty and fear in his eyes. "*Because* I work for your mother, Demetra Voskos. My job is to report to her. About you."

"Your job?" Paul stared at her, unable to understand. "Your job for how long?" he asked in a choked whisper.

"From the beginning," Roxie said. "Ten years ago. I had just gotten promoted at TVNews, and Raphael introduced me to his niece, your mother, Demetra. We became friends, and after a while, she asked me if I could do her a favor. She was worried about her son. He wasn't living up to his potential. He needed contacts like me to find his way. And she was willing to pay. A lot."

"I loved you," Paul said in quiet shock.

"I can't do this anymore," she said simply. "Not any of it." She lifted her right hand, which was still in a fist around the ruby necklace. She opened her fingers so he could see it. "Take it," she commanded. "I don't want it."

Paul hung his head in defeat for a long time before he found his voice. "I understand." He took the necklace from her hand and studied the stone. "This was the best of all of them," he said sadly. He lifted his head and focused on her. "Did you ever love me?"

"Yes," she said honestly. "From the moment I met you. And I still do. But Paula's death changed everything for me."

Tears filled his eyes. "I know. Me too."

"I'm going to take a shower. I don't want to see you here when I come out."

"You won't." Paul tried to smile. "Goodbye, Roxie. And thank you for telling me the truth."

"Goodbye, Paul." She turned away, walked across the room, and closed the bedroom door behind her.

Through the open window at his back Paul could hear a siren far below moving off. He looked around and saw Roxie's cell phone on the glass end table beside the sofa. He heard the shower start in the master bath. He picked up his cell from the window sill and punched a number. Roxie's phone rang two times and then it went to voice mail. Paul breathed in and smiled.

"Roxie," he said. "I want you to have this when you talk with the police." He thought for a second and then began. "This is Paul Marin. I confess that I killed Paula DeVong to keep her from doing a damaging story about me. I added phentermine to some chocolates and told Roxie to put them in Paula's desk. They were supposed to make her sick, that's all. But her death is entirely my fault." He swallowed hard and went on. "I know there'll be lots of questions about my involvement in things. So, for the record: I did not kill Emily Bookbinder, but I did send Lucille Orsina so she would be blamed. I did not kill Raphael Sharder. I loved that old man, and he was always so good to me.

My mother killed Raphael. My mother killed Emily. Find my mother, if you can. Her name is Demetra Voskos."

Paul hung up. He set his phone down, lifted his drink, and toasted. "For you, Mother." He drank it off and put his glass down.

He breathed in.

He could sense the pull of the vortex of darkness behind him. He slowly leaned back over the sill, and he could feel the hot strong air coming up the sheer facade of the tall building. He slowly leaned forward, and his eyes went to the painting above the bar. He coughed out a soft, ironic laugh.

"The Drowning of the *Son*," he whispered. "That is funny."

He spread his arms out left and right, and his consciousness slowly walked back away from the painting, away from the room, outside into the warm air. He leaned back. And as he fell, he saw the moon in the black sky growing smaller and smaller and smaller.

* * *

Artemis was asleep leaning back in his chair, his feet up on his desk. His cell rang. He sat up quickly, checked the ID, and answered it.

"Ray," he said as he got up and closed his office door. "Did you find it?"

"Yes, I did," Ray said sounding weary. It was past ten in the morning in Athens, and Ray was sitting on a stone planter in front of the modern three-story offices of the *Ta Nea* newspaper. He took a deep breath and went on. "I just sent two files."

Artemis hurried back to his desk and hit a button to wake up his laptop. "Yes," he confirmed. "I have them." He sat and opened one of the files. There were four press photos of Demetra Voskos from different periods of her life. Artemis examined them carefully.

"You still there?" Ray asked with concern.

"Yes, I'm here." Artemis assured him. "Thank you, Ray. You must be tired."

"That's for certain," Ray admitted.

"Get some sleep and we'll talk later," Artemis said as his cell beeped with an incoming call. It was from Drew. "I'm going to sign off quick," he explained. "Drew's calling."

"I understand," Ray answered. "Bye, son."

Artemis switched to the incoming call as he checked the clock on the bookcase. It was four twenty-one in the morning. "Drew, what's up?"

"I'm heading your way as fast as I can," she answered loudly. She was driving a police cruiser speeding across the Brooklyn Bridge with lights flashing and the siren blaring. Traffic was light, and cars were pulling over to let her pass. "I got a call from cops on the scene. Paul Marin is dead. Fell out of a window."

"Where?" Artemis asked.

"Roxie Lee's building on Riverside Boulevard," she answered pointedly.

"Suicide?"

"No idea yet," Drew said. "But I called Clayton. He lives on the Upper West. He's heading to Roxie's place now. I'll call you when I get there." She hung up.

Artemis put his phone down and rubbed his face with his hands. After a moment, he got up, went to the door, and quietly opened it. He walked into the living room and saw Flip asleep on the sofa. Artemis walked down the hallway to outside of Delia's room. As usual, he could hear her snoring loudly through the heavy door. He went back down the hall to his son's room, knocked on the door, and went in. Silas was asleep across the bed. His shoes were off, but he was still dressed in his jeans and an orange-green rugby shirt.

Artemis closed the door, walked over to the desk, and flipped on the light. Silas stirred and opened his eyes. He saw the serious look on his father's face.

"What's happened?" Silas said as he sat up and got his glasses from the bedside table.

Artemis sat down on the desk chair. "We were right."

* * *

Roxie, wrapped in a large bath towel, was sitting on the floor of her living room in the corner below the large open window. Tears were running down her face, and she was breathing in short panicked gasps. A strong warm breeze was coming in, and she could hear more sirens arriving thirty floors below. She forced her mind to focus. She lifted her phone and started to dial a number. Her fingers were trembling, and it took her some time to hit all ten digits.

"Demetra," she said, her voice strained and choked. "I know I'm not supposed to call this number, but something terrible has happened."

* * *

It was just past dawn, and pale yellow light filled the sky above the Upper West Side promising another hot, dry day. Delia opened her bedroom door and started down the hall. She was wrapped in a robe, her hair not brushed, and her eyes red. She stepped into the kitchen and stopped in surprise. Sitting around the kitchen table were Artemis, Silas, and Drew. Agent Filipowski was sitting by the window. Silas got up, went to the counter, poured some coffee in a mug, and set it down at one end of the table. Delia smiled at him. She sat down and sipped the coffee.

"You're here early," Delia said to Drew, who was sitting to her right. Across the table, in front of her, Artemis sat watching her. Silas sat back down to her left. "Thanks for the coffee." She looked over her shoulder to Flip. "So, is this an intervention?" she asked lightly.

Drew reached into her pocket, pulled out a small recorder, turned it on, and placed it in the center of the table. Flip got up, walked past Delia, and stood in the arch that led back to the hallway.

"Demetra Voskos, also known as Delia Twist Kouris," Drew said very clearly. "You are under arrest for the murder of Raphael Sharder and of Emily Bookbinder." As Drew continued, Delia slowly sipped her coffee.

"You have the right to remain silent. Anything you say can and will be used against you in a court of law. You have the right to an attorney. If you cannot afford an attorney, one will be provided for you. Do you understand these rights as I've explained them to you?" Drew asked.

"I do," she said quietly.

"I'm recording what we say," Drew said officially. "Is that okay?"

"Yes," Delia answered.

"I heard your phone ring around four thirty," Artemis said. "So, I assume you know about the death of Paul Marin." Delia stared at him.

"His birth name was Paul Voskos. And he was your son."

She considered and then said, "Yes. How long have you known about me?"

"Not long, Demetra," Artemis said plainly, trying out her real name. "It was a few days ago when I was saying goodbye to our home in New Jersey, something odd happened. I was standing at the sink in the bathroom at the top of the stairs, where you were standing, cleaning that mirror, when you were struck from behind by someone you said you never saw. Then Leah came up the steps behind me. And I saw her and realized how unlikely it was that you never saw your attacker."

Demetra took another sip of coffee.

"And the green box," Silas said, and she turned to look at him. "I was going through some of my mother's stuff in that old shoebox. I looked through some photographs from when she was just a kid. And I noticed there weren't enough of them, the count was wrong. So, I went through the negatives. They're in numbered strips of five shots each. And three strips of negatives were missing. Fifteen shots. And the matiasma bracelet was in there, the bracelet you supposedly gave my mother when she was little. And then I remembered something strange. My mother was wearing it and she showed it to you, and it was like you'd never seen it before. And she saw you. And she was dead the next day."

Demetra looked at him. "I regret what happened to Emily. I liked her. And a boy needs his mother."

"You used a burner phone when you called Emily," Artemis said forcefully. "And when she got home, you shot her from behind. You and your pawn, Bert Rocca, went upstairs and he hit you with the gun and tied you with tape. You just had to lie on the floor and wait to be discovered. As you'd planned, Bert Rocca waited across the street for Lucille Orsina to arrive. Then he planted the gun in her car. When Lucille saw the dead body of my wife, she ran back to her car and drove away, followed by Rocca who was supposed to kill her. Lucille would have been blamed. But she escaped from him."

"He was too old," Demetra said with contempt.

"So, you had him killed in Sicily," Drew said.

"What does it matter now?" Demetra said angrily. "My son is dead."

"You fooled us all for over five years," Artemis said loudly. "Why did you come to live with us?"

"Because of you," Demetra said fiercely. "Just as clever as your father. You were getting to be a famous police detective, just like him. And in the newspapers, you were quoted saying you had a passion to solve the Gardner Museum robbery. So, I needed to know more about you. I needed to be close enough to watch what you were doing."

"And you showed up pretending to be the real Delia Kouris," Drew said. "What happened to her?"

"She was a friend of mine," Demetra said dismissively. "She drowned swimming in the ocean some years ago."

"That's partly true," Artemis said evenly. "But she drowned because you struck her from behind with a rock as she stood in the shallow water not far from the taverna she and her husband ran on Kimolos Island. She must have trusted you enough to turn her back. And then you had the body you needed. Demetra Voskos was declared dead. And you became Delia." Artemis shook his head. "Did you know her a long time before you killed her?"

"Her husband, Stavi, worked for my uncle," she said vaguely.

"And when Stavi died, you showed up to comfort your friend Delia"— Artemis kept on—"You learned that she hadn't been back to the States for a long time. That her only living relative was her niece, Emily. And that Emily was married to me, the detective who was obsessed with finding out about the Gardner robbery." His eyes focused on her as he remembered. "You were always so supportive when I gave up police work and started teaching again."

Her lips twisted into a wry smile.

"How can your son have the last name of Voskos?" Silas genuinely asked.

"I never married Paul's father," she explained freely. "I've never done what people expect of me."

"Your uncle was Philip Voskos." Silas listed what they'd learned. "He was one of three heads of the Trias. Along with Andre Karlovic in Croatia and Marta Abruzzo in Sicily. Where Bert Rocca turned up dead."

Her eyes opened wide in surprise. "You have been busy, little genius, haven't you?"

"Yes," Silas answered factually. "When Philip was killed, leadership of the Voskos shipping empire was offered first to his brother, your uncle, Raphael Voskos. Known in this country as Raphael Sharder."

"Raphael was always too sensitive," Demetra said with disgust. "He refused. The next in line would have been my father. But he was killed by the same car bomb that killed Philip. So, the responsibility came to me, and I accepted."

"And what about his sister, Khloe?" Artemis asked sounding curious.

"She's gone a long time now. She died a few months after Philip."

Artemis filed her response in his memory and was pleased that Khloe's deception had worked and the old woman was still safe. "So, why did you kill your uncle Raphael?" he asked.

"Raphael was a nice old man," she said casually. "Old men get sentimental and want to make amends."

"Like giving back a stolen painting," Drew said.

"Yes, like that." Demetra crossed her arms and looked around the table challenging each of them. "You really don't have very much on me. Except your theories and that I hurt your pride by fooling you for so long."

"Mak," Artemis called out, and Mak and Lucille walked in from the adjoining living room.

"I know you," Demetra said. "You were at the AA meeting last night."

"Yes. And my name is Lucille Orsina."

Demetra gulped, and her eyes looked worried. Then she recovered herself. "Nice to meet you. I've heard so much about you."

"We wanted to know how you were communicating with Paul and the outside world," Mak said. "Lucille witnessed you getting a burner phone from the man you sat next to at the meeting last night."

"You took it with you when you left the room for over forty minutes," Lucille reported. "And returned it to him when you came back."

"Proves nothing." Demetra scoffed.

"We've arrested the man," Mak said patiently. "And traced the calls you made on the burner. Those people are being picked up right now."

"So, I made some calls."

"Lucille got this note from her sister, Ida Orsina," Artemis said as he took the folded paper from his shirt pocket and handed it to Lucille.

She opened it and read: "The Bookbinders think that the woman who takes care of them is Emily's aunt Delia Kouris. But her real name is Demetra Voskos, a very clever and dangerous woman. She is Paul Marin's mother. And she killed Raphael Sharder because he was going to give back his stolen painting." Lucille handed the note back to Artemis and turned to stare at Demetra.

"Ida is another of my son's jealous girlfriends," she said disdainfully.

"Speaking of girlfriends," Drew said, "Roxie Lee is in custody, and she's being very helpful. She told us how you hired her to spy on your son. For more than ten years. Maybe that's why Paul recorded a confession before he tossed himself out the window."

Her head snapped toward Drew, and she grunted angrily. "Show some respect."

Drew continued calmly. "His testimony will hold up in court."

"Paul would never betray me," she said firmly. "You're a liar."

"I thought you might say that," Drew said as she took out her cell. "This is a copy of what he sent to Roxie Lee's phone. I hope you can recognize your own son's voice." She pushed a button:

I did not kill Raphael Sharder. I loved that old man and he was always so good to me. My mother killed Raphael. My mother killed Emily. Find my mother, if you can. Her name is Demetra Voskos.

Demetra's eyes filled with tears, but she wiped them dry immediately.

"We're convinced," Drew said quietly as she put her phone away, "that these were your son's last words."

"Everything I've done," Demetra said faintly, "I did for Paul. So he could one day become the head of the Voskos family."

"Like you," Drew acknowledged.

"Yes," she answered proudly.

"I doubt he wanted that," Lucille said. "Paul was sometimes lovely and sometimes scary. But he was never a happy man. That's what you did to him. And now he's dead."

Demetra regarded her strangely. "I think you may be right. Paul was more like Raphael, too sensitive. He was never really born to lead." She looked fondly to Silas. "But I do believe in you. Like your father, you have an amazing mind."

Silas didn't answer.

But Artemis did. "Did you kill my parents?"

"No," she said easily. "But I know about them. Your father was getting too close to knowing certain things about the Gardner robbery. People in Boston asked a favor from friends here in New York, and the job was done. Your mother just happened to be in the wrong place at the wrong time."

Artemis swallowed a few times and then found his voice. "Thank you," he said bitterly. "And the Gardner robbery?"

Demetra's proud shoulders slowly rounded forward. "No, I will say nothing about that. Ever." She looked to Drew. "I'm very tired, all of a sudden. Don't you have some nice place where I can sleep for a while?"

"I do," Drew said firmly, and she turned off the recorder.

*   *   *

At midday, passing clouds and a light breeze were keeping the temperature bearable. Deni and Moira walked out of the 19th Precinct and headed east on 67th Street.

"How was it?" Moira asked as they turned south on Third.

"Actually, not so bad," Deni said loudly over the sound of the heavy traffic. "That cute FBI agent Mak Kim asked most of the questions."

"I see," Moira said knowingly and laughed.

"I wouldn't mind," Deni grinned as they went into a busy coffee shop and ordered two iced coffees to-go. As they stood waiting, Deni noticed that the television on the wall was set to TVNews and the noon broadcast was just starting.

"What the fuck is that?" Deni murmured astonished, and Moira turned. Behind the news desk was Calvin's pretty blonde secretary.

"Hello. I'm Barb Hamilton," she said carefully and then remembered to smile. "And this is TVNews."

"I wonder what she did to deserve this," Moira said drolly.

"We start with a developing story here in New York," Barb read cautiously as she squinted at the teleprompter. "Involving the death of a prominent psychiatrist who was under investigation for his involvement in the robbery of the Gardner Museum. Doctor Paul Marin died early this morning in Manhattan, apparently by suicide."

Moira heard a soft gasp and turned to look at Deni. She looked stunned, and tears were running down her cheeks.

"I knew him," Deni managed to say. Moira was uncertain what to do. She gently put her arms around her, and Deni quietly cried.

Anna Canneli stood behind her desk in her little cubicle resolutely packing her things into a large cloth bag she'd brought from home. She looked up annoyed at Barb's pretty face on the small TV on her bookshelf.

"As you may remember," Barb said nervously. "TVNews was first on the scene last year when the GU chalice was found in a deserted building in Chinatown."

Anna rolled her eyes and continued packing.

Two floors up, Calvin leaned back in his large leather chair, put his feet up on his desk, and swirled the ice in his glass of vodka. He looked at the eager, nervous face of Barb Hamilton on his monitor and smiled greedily. "I fucking love television," he said loudly to the empty room and took a long drink.

Outside of Beth Schaefer's hotel room, the uniformed patrolwoman looked up from her cell. Through the door, she could hear Beth crying and wondered if she should check on her. She returned to her texting.

Inside the room, Beth turned off the TV. She went into the bathroom and splashed cold water on her face. She dried herself with a washcloth and looked at her red, exhausted eyes in the mirror. She went back into the room, got her phone, and sat on the bed. She found a number and pushed it. After a couple of rings, it went to voice mail. She waited for the tone and then said:

"Greg, it's all over the news. So you must know about Paul." She swallowed. "I don't know where you are. But I love you. Call me when you need to." She hung up and put the phone down. She went over to the window and pushed the curtains aside. Through the dirty glass, she could see across an alley to the back of a much taller, newer building. She craned her neck and looked up the rows of shaded windows trying to see the sky. But could not.

Greg tossed the TV remote as hard as he could at the black screen of the monitor in his living room, and the glass front fractured like a spider web. He walked slowly into his bedroom and saw his packed bag on the bed. He pushed it fiercely to the floor and sat down next to the overturned bag. Greg hugged his knees to his chest and hung his head.

"Paul," he whispered as he wrapped his fingers tightly around the green hiddenite gem hanging on his chest. "Paul," he said again, his voice broke and he began sobbing.

*   *   *

At dusk, Artemis was sitting on the window bench in the living room looking south. He looked up to Lucille's apartment across the street. The window was open, but he knew she wasn't there. Drew had asked her to come to the 19th Precinct to make a statement. He heard the doorbell ring and after a moment, Silas greeting Leah. Artemis got up and walked into the kitchen just as they arrived. Leah was carrying two brown bags of takeout food.

"I figure you two haven't eaten much today," she said as she put the bags down on the stainless-steel counter and started unpacking. "So I went to that little Italian place up by me on Amsterdam." She turned and smiled.

"Chicken piccata, plain pasta, and enough caprese for three. Guaranteed to have no garlic, onions, or any other allium."

"That's very good of you, Leah," Artemis said as he opened a cabinet and got some plates.

"And you're right," Silas said as he got flatware from a drawer. "Food was the last thing we thought of today."

"I understand," Leah said as she started putting food on the plates. Artemis got three glasses, a pitcher of filtered water and set them on the kitchen table.

"Some wine?" he asked Leah as he pulled a bottle of chardonnay from the fridge.

"Don't mind if I do," she answered as she brought the plates over to the table. Silas and Leah sat as Artemis uncorked the bottle, poured two glasses, and joined them. He looked distractedly at the meal in front of him.

"Eat something," Leah said. "Both of you, please."

"Okay," Silas agreed and picked up his fork. Artemis smiled at her and dutifully took a bite. He put down his fork and took a sip of wine.

"I feel bad," he said. "Demetra fooled me, fooled us all for so long."

"Like a sleeper agent," Silas said as he carefully cut his chicken. "She pretended to be Delia for five and a half years. There was a KGB agent that was undercover here in New York for more than fourteen years."

Artemis looked at his son and smiled sadly. "But she wasn't some agent from Russia. She came here specifically to watch me. And I was too blind to know it. And that's cost us so much."

"Emily would be so proud of you both," Leah said strongly. "Because you never gave up."

Artemis started to say something, but she went on. "And we know that you had some trouble when COVID was first starting and Emily had died."

"Some trouble?" he said ashamed. "I couldn't leave my room."

"I remember. I was there," Leah assured him. "But the point is that you did. And you and Silas are here today, this moment, having a meal in your lovely home because you didn't let your fears conquer you."

Artemis nodded and sipped his wine.

"What do you think Lucille will do now?" Silas asked curiously.

"I don't know," Artemis answered. "But I'm sure she'll be okay."

"Because she's a survivor," Leah said. "Like you two."

"Thank you, Leah," Artemis said gratefully. "For everything."

"My pleasure." She smiled.

Coda

Thursday, October 21st, 2021

"It's so nice being back here again, even if it's for the last time," Patty Figgins's voice was thick with emotion.

"Me too," Maddy Griff said as she looked out at the group gathered on the back terrace of the Arethusa. Ownership of the mansion was surely going to be tied up in the courts for years to come, but Barbara Borsa had managed to cut a deal and get Taki Fukuda a portion of his inheritance from Raphael Sharder's estate. In gratitude, Taki got permission and decided to throw one last party at the mansion.

"Here," Maddy Griff handed Patty a plate of hors d'oeuvres. "Take this around. I'm right behind you with a tray of drinks."

Patty popped one of the tiny baked rolls into her mouth. "That's incredible. I love shrimp," she said happily, though her Irish accent and full mouth made it hard to understand her.

"Thank you very much," Maddy Griff said as she turned Patty toward the terrace doors. "Now stop eating everything and get out there."

"Everybody, a toast," Taki said loudly, and they all turned to him. The pool was covered, the gardens were growing wild, and the wood-plank path leading to the shore was edged with very tall grass. But it was a beautiful fall afternoon in Southampton, seventy-three degrees and sunny with a mild breeze coming in off the ocean. Taki was dressed in a bright madras plaid jacket, pink button-down shirt, powder blue linen pants, and leather sandals. He smiled at his guests. Khloe, in a long light blue dress, was sitting with Barbara Borsa. Artemis and Silas were standing near them lifting glasses of champagne from Maddy Griff's tray.

"That's champagne, you know," Maddy Griff said softly to Silas and threw a questioning look to Artemis.

"He knows," Artemis said with quiet approval. Maddy Griff smiled and walked away to serve the other guests. "But go easy," Artemis said privately to his son. "There's a lot of cops here." Silas laughed and took a small sip.

"I like it," he pronounced happily.

Drew was standing by the tall grass border with Anne Riley. They moved closer to Taki.

"I won't be too long," Taki said apologetically. "But I want to say something about Raphael." He looked to Ray Gaines who was wearing uncharacteristic light colors. Mak and Lucille were standing beside him.

"I know that Raphael must have done some bad things," Taki said lightly. "After all, you did recover that beautiful painting here."

"Which will keep me employed in probate court for years to come," Barbara added happily, and the group laughed.

"But for me," Taki continued cordially as he looked to Khloe. "And for the people who knew him best." He turned to include Patty Figgins, who hastily swallowed another shrimp puff and smiled at him. Behind her, Maddy Griff tipped her head appreciatively to Taki.

"Raphael was a kind and caring man," Taki said wistfully. "He always loved a good party. And there were so many here at the Arethusa. So I know he would have liked you all being here today at his home where it all started. So much has happened since that painting was found. I only hope that we can put to rest all the unpleasant things. So, with your indulgence." Taki solemnly lifted his champagne glass. "To Raphael. May he be at peace." They all lifted their glasses and silently sipped.

"Thank you." Taki smiled at them, went over to Khloe, and sat down.

"Very nicely done," the old woman said approvingly. "Raphael would have liked that."

"Thank you. Have you given much thought to what you'll do now?"

"Of course," she said gravely. "I give everything a lot of thought."

"I was wondering..." Taki started timidly, stopped, and sipped his drink.

"What?" she asked as she eyed him.

"Raphael left me the gallery here in Southampton," he said quickly. "And I was wondering if you'd like to work there? With me."

Khloe chuckled. Though she was smiling, the sound was throaty and dark.

"Still really creepy," he said. "You can't do that around customers or they'll run away."

She leaned back in her chair and laughed. "Thank you for your offer," she said happily. "It's the most interesting idea I've heard in a long time. But I have lots of money and absolutely don't want to work anymore."

"I understand." Taki bowed his head graciously.

"But I am thinking of living here in Southampton," she said with a mischievous glint in her eyes. "So, I expect you are going to see a lot of me."

"I would really love that," Taki said genuinely, and Khloe chuckled again.

"So, Mathew's back in Florida?" Ray asked as he came over to Drew and Anne.

"Yes," Anne said. "He kept saying that he didn't want to get in our way"—she grinned—"which he could never be."

Drew laughed a little. "The fact is he's really glad to be back with all his retired buddies down there."

"Hell, I'm retired," Ray said. "Maybe I'll head down and visit."

"He'd love that." Drew smiled.

"Gotta travel while we can," Anne said sensibly. "I'm glad the Delta thing is quieting down. But they're saying we'll be dealing with the next variant soon enough."

"Omicron"—Drew reported—"I hear this one spreads faster but isn't as serious."

"We'll see." Ray sipped his drink.

"So," Mak said as he joined them. "I heard a rumor that you're planning to move to Greece."

"It's beautiful there," Ray mused. "So, why not?"

"Or maybe to Croatia," Mak said. "To be near to Andre Karlovic. The man who said he knew where the rest of the Gardner pieces were hidden."

"We'll see." The wrinkles around Ray's eyes multiplied as he smiled. "A man should have a hobby when he retires, you know."

"No, you're like a bloodhound," Artemis said, joining the group. "It'll never be a hobby. You love the hunt too much."

"That's true, son." Ray ran his thick fingers a few times through his short gray hair. "But I have to admit, this last sprint through Europe really made me feel my age. But still—"

"But still, you're wondering," Artemis picked it up. "What old man Karlovic knows."

"Yes, I am," Ray said truthfully.

"What about his grandson, Ladimir?" Mak asked. "Do you think he'll be extradited back to Croatia?"

"I don't know," Ray said. "They won't let him go until his grandfather talks."

"Which he won't do." Mak lifted his champagne. "Because he's not stupid."

"Right," Ray agreed. "But I'm working on it."

Artemis laughed. "Of course you are." He lifted his glass in a toast. "To Ray Gaines on his pretended retirement."

Ray grinned at Artemis.

"We heard that your sister might be in Croatia," Silas said as he and Lucille stood away from the group at the edge of the tall grass.

"That's probably true," Lucille confirmed as they started walking side by side on the wood-plank path heading toward the sea. "But I haven't heard from her since she left. She could be anywhere by now."

* * *

Ida looked out the screened windows of the loggia. It was night in Avola, and down the wide grassy hill, she could see the lit torches of the workers walking along the rows of the vast vineyard.

"This is incredible," Marta said enthusiastically. Ida looked at the old woman lying under a white sheet on a padded table, her head on a linen-covered pillow. Marta's face was covered with a pale green mud mask and slices of cucumber rested on her eyes. Ida stood near Marta's head and gently started massaging her shoulders and neck.

"No, really." Marta moaned in pleasure. "I'm having a religious experience."

Ida chuckled. "How is it possible that you've never had a facial before?" For years, Ida had heard about the amazing wealth and cunning of the woman they called the Crow.

"I never had the time," Marta admitted.

"Well, I'm glad you're enjoying it," Ida said.

Marta reached up, took the slices of cucumber off her eyes, and gazed at Ida. "I have been looking for someone clever like you for a long time," she announced. "I think we will be friends."

Ida smiled at her. "Yes, Marta. I believe you're right. We will be."

*　　*　　*

In Southampton, the warm sun was low on the horizon. Silas opened the gate at the top of the seawall, and he and Lucille carefully made their way down the steps to the edge of the rocky beach. Lucille sat on a large weathered boulder, and Silas sat beside her. She looked up to a passing cloud hanging low over the water to the west.

"A swan," she said, and Silas studied it.

"I used to do that with my mother," he said softly. "When I was little."

"Me too," she said and turned to him. "Now that it's all over I'm not sure what I'm supposed to do."

"Life is like riding a bicycle," he answered. "To keep your balance, you must keep moving."

"Where did that come from?" she asked surprised. "A fortune cookie?"

"Albert Einstein," he said, and she laughed.

"He wrote that in a letter to his son. And I think"—Silas smiled at her—"that you can do anything you want."

Lucille looked at him for a moment. Then she stood up and opened her arms wide to embrace the beautiful setting sun glistening like a golden road across the wide dark blue sea.

The story continues in Book Three of The Bookbinder Mysteries:
What Ever Happened to Anna Canneli?

Author's Note

I would like to express my appreciation to the editing team at BookBaby, and to Linda Hall and Kevin Coogan for their precise proofreading and notes. And most of all, thank you Gwen Ellison, for your clear insight, steady guidance, and constant support.

It's important to note that the robbery of the Isabella Stewart Gardner Museum on March 18th, 1990, is a real event. Around one thirty in the morning, two men disguised as Boston police officers, tied up a couple of guards, and stole thirteen pieces of art. But beyond that, the story told in this book of what might have happened is entirely fictional. None of the stolen art pieces, including Rembrandt's *Storm on the Sea of Galilee*, have ever been recovered. However, a vast amount of material is available about the robbery, investigations, and history of the truly wonderful Gardner Museum. I hope you explore further, and enjoy the journey as much as I have.

Conal O'Brien

The Characters in
Death of Television

Bookbinder Household:

Artemis Bookbinder – a former professor of art history, former NYPD detective, lifelong germophobe, and driven investigator.

Silas Bookbinder – his fourteen-year-old, introverted, genius son.

Delia Twist Kouris – their live-in housekeeper, and Silas's great aunt.

Leah Carras – therapist who came out of retirement to help Artemis.

NYPD:

Drew Sweeney – she is Artemis's cousin, and lead detective in the Criminal Intelligence Section.

Mathew Sweeney – her father, a retired captain, staying with Drew in Brooklyn.

Jerome Clayton Collins – a young Black detective and innovative researcher.

FBI:

Ray Gaines – a senior agent, has been on the Gardner Museum case since the beginning.

Makani Kim – known as Mak, a young capable agent of Hawaiian and Korean lineage.

Bert Rocca – an agent and longtime partner of Ray Gaines.

Steve F. Filipowski – known as Flip, has been assigned to protect Silas.

New York City:

Ida Orsina – a forceful woman, owns and runs a successful Madison Avenue dermatology practice.

Lucille Orsina – Ida's younger sister, and a survivor.

Paul Marin – a charismatic psychiatrist, specializing in drug treatment recovery.

Ladimir Karlovic – Paul's business partner and friend.

Fat Nicky Abruzzo – another business partner of Paul's.

Beth Schaefer – former manager of the 64th Street Gallery.

Sammi Lau – a feisty-looking young woman, a barber in Chinatown.

TV NEWS:

Paula DeVong – popular anchor of her own nightly show.

Jock Willinger – her Executive Producer, an older gaunt man from Liverpool.

Anna Canneli – Paula's devoted, frumpy assistant.

Roxie Lee – Supervising Producer, is involved with Paul Marin.

Moira Weyland – an ambitious reporter.

Greg Schaefer – a handsome openly gay man, and Beth Schaefer's brother.

Deni Diaz – an up-and-coming writer, and close friend of Greg's.

Calvin Prons – Head of Network, an aggressive misogynist, and Lucille's ex-husband.

In Southampton:

Raphael Sharder – a wealthy art dealer, deceased.

Taki Fukuda – former manager of Raphael's gallery on Main Street.

Patty Figgins – Raphael's former housekeeper of many years.

Barbara Borsa – lawyer of Raphael's estate.

Maddy Griffin – owner of the Primrose restaurant, and good friend to all who come there.

Toby Brown – a tough old sailor, owner of a yacht for hire in Sag Harbor.

Sheila Brown – Toby's granddaughter, runs the marina in Southampton.

Elsewhere:

Andre Karlovic – Head of a multinational banking corporation centered in Croatia, and Ladimir's grandfather.

Marta Abruzzo – Fat Nicky's grandmother, runs her empire from her villa in Sicily.

Rosa Abruzzo – Her loyal niece and companion.

Go to *conalobrien.com* to learn more about
this book and other Bookbinder Mysteries.